I0824644

BETWEEN SUN AND SHADOW

BETWEEN SUN AND SHADOW

LAURA GENN

PEACHTREE
Teen

Peachtree Teen
An imprint of Peachtree Publishing Company Inc.

Text copyright © 2026 by Laura Genn
Jacket illustration copyright © 2026 by cherriielle
All rights reserved. No part of this book may be reproduced, transmitted, or stored in an information retrieval system in any form or by any means, graphic, electronic, or mechanical, including photocopying, taping, and recording, without prior written permission from the publisher. Additionally, no part of this book may be used or reproduced in any manner for the purpose of training artificial intelligence technologies or systems, nor for text and data mining.
Printed and bound in January 2026 at C&C Offset, Shenzhen, China.
Edited by Jonah Heller
Book design by Lily Steele
PeachtreeBooks.com
First Edition
1 3 5 7 9 10 8 6 4 2
ISBN: 978-1-68263-818-7 (hardcover)

Library of Congress Cataloging-in-Publication Data is available.

EU Authorized Representative: HackettFlynn Ltd, 36 Cloch Choirneal, Balrothery, Co. Dublin, K32 C942, Ireland. EU@walkerpublishinggroup.com

To Leigh Bardugo, who believed in
fourteen-year-old me before I did.
And to my mother, who believed in me
before I could hold a pen.

—L.G.

PROLOGUE

Once upon a time, the planet Pagomènos stopped spinning.

An asteroid—massive, merciless, over a mile in all directions, gleaming with a distant galaxy's heretofore unknown power—lurched free of its belt. Whether by idle fate or by the thoughtless hand of a cruel god, the rogue rock struck Pagomènos, rapidly pursued by the tongues of its sun. All at once and forevermore, the planet's spin lurched to a near halt.

Tidally locked, Pagomènos's rotation synced with its solar orbit, and the planet was split into light and unrelenting dark. Days, nights, seasons, and a lifetime tracked in seconds and minutes and hours became confined to a distant past.

This cosmic change bore natural disasters: vicious wind storms at the intersection of night and day, and unwavering pressure from either extreme heat or cold on the the planet's far sides. In time—though it would become impossible to track how long—the people would find that the meteorite, which had embedded itself in the planet's surface, bled power and poison. Their world had been irrevocably changed, and with it, their bodies.

Preternatural energy warped every living thing it touched, transforming it to be as fierce as the increasingly hostile planet.

Even before the physical changes revealed themselves, the Pagonians were terrified. While core memories—identity, recent events, simple tasks like food and sleep—remained untouched, the people found their broader understanding slipping through their fingers like so much sunbaked sand. Where had they come from, before they settled Pagomènos? How had the technology that enabled such interstellar travel been built? History crumbled to ash in their minds with every passing moment. They feared their very senses of self would soon dissolve alongside it.

In the daylight, the people fled belowground. They gathered their wisest inventors, their most advanced technological prodigies, and constructed a memory-storage device for every survivor: a simple microchip, surgically installed as a ward against eventually forgetting all they had ever been. Aboveground, where the remaining animals achieved ever more alarming new forms—evolving at an impossible rate, fueled by the asteroid's unimaginable power—the daylight people never dared to tread without armor. Apocalypse be damned, they would not join the ranks of Pagonian mutations. And they would not forget what it was to be merely human.

In the darkness, the people scraped and clawed for purchase, but they simply could not prioritize invention when utter sightlessness loomed supreme as a challenge. Cut off from Pagomènos's sun, they sought the gleaming asteroid itself, and their exposure to it accelerated their mutation beyond even the planet's animals. Soon there were people who could move objects with a thought, others bearing wings to carry them through the frigid wind currents. There were even those who could produce azure energy, like the asteroid's own, from their hands—with which they would build a looming torch for their shadowed home.

The people of the light had worried that, absent microchip installations, they would forget even their own names, deteriorated by the asteroid's energy, becoming ever less and less. But the people of the night, embracing their invader as one might a godlike visitation, found instead that in fully giving themselves to its power, they became much more. Their knowledge of extended history, former technology, and the like were laid like sacrifices before their intergalactic interloper. Of events yet to unfold, they would keep meticulous records. And unlike what the daylight people had feared, they never forgot themselves entirely.

After the cataclysmic impact, Pagomènos should have been a graveyard for human life, sentience erased from its surface as surely as if an Earthside starship had never landed. Instead, as the asteroid's energies permeated everything, the dead planet became undead, its people walking monuments to purgatory. In the daylight, there were armored, sheltered beings, still clinging to technology, constructing ever more advanced methods of living somewhat as they always had; but in the nighttime, wings and claws and teeth overtook the land, lit by impossible fire conjured by hulking, powerful creatures who hardly recalled what their bodies had once been.

Once upon a time, half of Pagomènos descended into eternal night. Once upon a time, half of Pagomènos ascended into eternal day.

Once upon a time, a whole world slipped and fell out of time as they had known it.

CHAPTER 1

KORI

I came to the Morpheus Market to buy a memory, but instead, it seems I'll be making one I'd rather forget.

I'm only partway through my transaction, trading a pilfered memory of a starship crash for a useful nugget of firsthand mech-repair knowledge, when everything goes sideways.

Every joint in my right hand stings from 45P3C7—better known as Aspect, my own personal mech—anxiously gripping my fingers, a stark reminder that I've instilled an alarming amount of humanity in what was once a hollow machine. Memories are meant for human experience, not installation into a synthetic. But making friends is next to impossible when your mother rules your entire society—which, unfortunately, also includes every detail of your life. So I took friendship matters into my own hands. And nuts. And bolts.

Hopefully, buying this new memory will only broaden my (mildly to severely illegal) modification possibilities. One step closer to sentience. One step closer to Aspect truly seeing me.

In my left hand, my comms tablet buzzes, insistent. I glance toward its message from my mother, sliding across the screen in electric-blue text.

CHLOE: KORI, WHERE ARE YOU?

Licenses to trade in the clandestine Morpheus Market aren't as simple to acquire as standard settlement rations or a freshly printed set of clothes. Chloe didn't grant me market access so I could trade for whatever memories I liked. She definitely didn't do it so I could build simulated neural pathways in a government-issue mining mech. Usually I would hurry through a personal transaction like this, do my best not to raise any inkling of suspicion, but the seller won't stop haggling.

The mechanical hand in my own squeezes hard. Twin optical processors meet my eyes. No eyelids—just twin bulbs, like headlights on a starship, flashing on and off as the gears and servos whirring behind them process my undoubtedly frustrated expression. "Message—for Aspect?"

"No, message for Kori," I mumble under my breath, trying to focus on the transaction. I give their hand a reassuring squeeze back. A standard mining mech has limited touch sensors, primarily to identify either extreme heat or a total system malfunction. I took the liberty of enhancing Aspect's hardware long ago, to the point of practical pain sensors—so while a hand squeeze may not be enough to calm them, at least I know they can feel it.

I can't see the seller's face through the full-body anti-radiation gear that all dayfolk, myself included, wear outside our settlement, but I have a very vivid imagination. In my head, he has beady black eyes, with hardly any whites to speak of, and a profound, judgmental outcropping of jaw, like a cliff's edge about to collapse into an avalanche.

"You can't provide more than a single flight memory in exchange?" the seller drawls. The sign above his crooked booth displays MECHANIC MEMORIES, the neon light on the second *M* rapidly blinking.

Dayfolk masks flatten emotion and tone, but even so, I can tell he's not annoyed with me. He's amused. Haggling is a hobby for this man. He's not arguing with me; he's toying with me.

I suffer enough of that from my mother.

But I school my voice into unmistakable neutrality, even as the message from Chloe buzzes again. "Two-for-one trades are commonplace only for rare or classified memories."

"Message—for Kori—important?" Aspect chimes, gesturing to my comms tablet with one elbow.

"Not now," I whisper. This time I grip their hand less as a comfort, more as a plea. *Please do not decide to develop full-blown anxiety before I've even installed a proper personality, okay?*

The seller scratches his head. I doubt he can actually feel his nails through his helmet, which means he's stalling for time I don't have. "This is very high-level mechanical insight you're buying."

It's one I could easily learn from Hyrra if my stomach didn't do somersaults every time she and I made eye contact at the repair station, but I swallow my frustration. "I showed you what I'm offering. Take it or leave it."

The seller releases a deliberately dramatic groan.

"Or I could report you to the Coalition," I press, "if you make a habit of raising prices after receiving an offer."

It's a low blow. We both know it. The entire Morpheus Market functions always and only at the whim of the Coalition. When you break the Coalition's rules, your Morpheus Market license goes bye-bye. Sometimes your known whereabouts along with it. Maybe a few fingers and/or toes. Your average citizen isn't even supposed to know the Morpheus Market exists, unless an insider recommended them for a license. Getting kicked out of the market often means getting kicked off this plane of existence, too.

Memories also can't be stored on a remotely accessible network. Early in Morpheus tech's development, settlement records report attempts, but the memories went sour like forgotten rations; they turned strange, wrong, like waking nightmares when accessed. So, even if you escape a ban from the Morpheus Market with your life, getting kicked doesn't just make it *harder* to obtain new memories for sale. It makes it *impossible*.

Aspect's head bobs. "Kori is mean—when Kori has—maybe important messages—not for Aspect."

Aspect's insistence on always calling me by name—even here in the Morpheus Market, where everyone only uses codenames—is also a security risk if anyone connects that name with the monarch's daughter. If Chloe ever realized this was happening, she'd probably have Aspect reduced to scrap metal. I try not to think about it too often, or else I can't breathe. If Aspect ruins this trade, I'll have only myself to blame. I'm the one who couldn't settle for a mining and general maintenance mech like every other dayfolk citizen. I'm the one who tried building a friend out of wires and metal.

The seller releases the longest, fakest sigh I've ever heard in my admittedly short life. Finally, blessedly, he says, "You have a deal." He presses a shiny Morpheus sphere into my palm.

Somehow, even though we're both wearing gloves, it feels slick and sweaty. I wince a little as I tuck the sphere into my belt pouch, before handing over my own in exchange. Thankfully, the armor we all wear includes an extensive array of pockets and pouches, primarily concentrated at the waistline, for carrying items. I've been told that at one point, the men's armor had more pockets than the women's, but the public complained so much, the government officials eventually standardized everything regardless of body type.

The comms tablet buzzes a fourth time.

Aspect raises their free hand to get my attention, but I quickly nudge it back down to their side. Multiple messages shimmer across my tablet.

CHLOE: KORI, WHERE ARE YOU?

CHLOE: I SENT YOU ON ASSIGNMENT, NOT VACATION.

CHLOE: I NEED THAT MEMORY ASAP.

I huff out an exasperated breath. Once again, just like every previous trip to the Morpheus Market, my actual assignment is cutting the visit short before I find a memory I'm confident can begin prying Aspect's possible self-awareness open. I suppose it doesn't help any that I don't know what I'm looking for. A sentient mech has never been—*should never be*, if you ask the government's engineers—created. Nor are human memories supposed to be installed in a machine. I haven't the slightest idea what sort of memory could jar Aspect into being more person than science project, kicking their servos into something more akin to neurological synapses, but I'm determined to keep looking. I will always keep looking. Somewhere in this bundle of bolts, I know there's potential for the truest friend I have to feel what I feel, to choose me back.

But every visit to the market, without fail, ends with a flat, unfeeling reminder that I'm on a schedule, my mother impatiently awaiting my return with her merchandise—without any knowledge of why I *really* want to be here.

CHLOE: I MIGHT JUST FIND EXTRA HOMEWORK FOR YOU IF THIS MEMORY ISN'T ON MY DESK WITHIN MY CURRENT SLEEP CYCLE.

Briefly, I tab over on my comms tablet from the messaging module to the hourglass. There's hardly any sand left in the upper half on my display, and Chloe tracks her sleep cycles more religiously than most, always turning in when the hourglass turns over. My margin for error is rapidly shrinking if I'm going to make it home before she wants to sleep, and I haven't even picked up my assigned memory yet. In my defense (not that my mother would care), Aspect's detour became a full-blown digi-game side quest.

I want to ask why Chloe needs her own memory delivery so urgently, or what the memory even is, but I've learned the hard way not to pester my mother with questions. It never leads to answers. And it usually leads to an even more watchful parental eye monitoring my every move. Not to mention extra homework.

I stifle a groan. If I see one more math sheet in my next ten sleep cycles, it'll be too soon.

Another squeeze of cold metal fingers on mine. "Aspect is—"

"Leaving," I interrupt, tugging them away from the Mechanic Memories booth. "Kori is leaving, and so are you." The second *M* on the seller's sign sparks and dies entirely as we depart.

We're immediately sucked back into foot traffic.

The Morpheus Market is a hub of constant motion, but it's confined to a limited space. To evade notice by unauthorized dayfolk (or too-curious nightfolk), it's miles beneath the planet's surface, with a singular elevator entrance connecting to four narrow, stacked floors.

Each floor is piled with vendors in a very literal sense. It's a strange, metal vegetation gone wild, booths overlapping like shoddily stacked teacups. Every wall blossoms with merchants, each of their spaces encroaching on one another's territory. Walking at all means asserting yourself through an ever-shifting horde of bodies, everyone here for their own glimpse of someone else's life.

No two vendors are the same. Some stalls offer secondhand tastes of rare cuisine, others a recollection of advanced education few can access, and so on—the embrace of a lover like you've never had; the thrill of victory in a contest you'd never dare to enter; an understanding of depression's bleakest depths.

Neon signs hum at varying frequencies. Voices chatter, mumble, and curse all around. Aspect locks one cold, metal hand around my wrist and doesn't let go.

I check my tablet again for Chloe's specific instructions. Per usual, she's provided coordinates for a certain booth and the salesperson's code name, but nothing else. Because the universe hates me, the person I'm looking for resides on the fourth and bottom floor, while I'm currently on the first. I break into a sprint, Aspect in tow, spiraling back toward the central elevator units, various vendors' setups passing rapidly through my peripheral vision in jagged sweeps of color and light. An elevator is bound to be faster than running multiple flights of stairs down to the fourth floor, and I don't want to risk losing my hold of Aspect in the dash—or gamble the integrity of my finger joints from how tightly Aspect grips back.

It's impossible to really memorize a route through the Morpheus Market; the ecosystem of buying and selling is practically a living organism. Every time we visit, vendors have shifted, maybe merged, maybe swallowed up smaller ones in a power grab, maybe begun actively fighting over a particular corner of shop space. But despite the ever-changing layout, I travel like a heatshot rifle bolt, straight and true, to the elevators—undeterred by the haphazard pressing, pushing, pulling of so many bodies.

Eventually, we reach the booth where Chloe's vendor is waiting.

"Echo," I say, by way of greeting.

It's a clever code name. What is a memory, really, but an echo of a person?

"Monarch." Echo inclines their head, having obviously been expecting me.

I can't help but grin at the moniker, which is why I chose it in the first place. Even black markets have unspoken rules. If you want to sell, trade, or buy a memory, you need a licensed alias. Mine is Monarch, ostensibly like one of the orange-winged creatures native to the former Earthside world; it's also a pun for obvious reasons, me being the heiress of the Daylands and all.

I'd love to blame Aspect for my terrible sense of humor, but the nickname precedes them. I'm just like this.

I have only the most basic details for my first impression of this seller: a narrow set of pinched, birdlike shoulders; arms akimbo as if in a confused first flight; a voice high and clipped, even through the mask's filtering.

I slide Chloe's provided memory from my waist pocket. I could've snooped on this sphere, too, I suppose, but I haven't bothered investigating Chloe's trade materials in ages. They're always the same self-referential snippets: The architecture of Chloe's quarters when she first assumed the throne. The settlement's meeting chamber, as seen from the dais from which she gives her speeches. An agonizingly slow, panning shot of her jewelry, or her library, or her damn crown, which she only ever wears for the most painfully dramatic formal appearances.

Everyone wants to know how the queen of the Daylands—the last celebrity on our far-flung, interstellar settlement—lives. *Might as well monetize it*, Chloe says. But I gag when I think about it, recoiling as if from curdled soup. She's nothing special, really. It's all gilded trappings for an ordinary woman.

And her ordinary daughter, who will be expected to uphold the illusory legacy.

Echo climbs onto an overturned crate, rifling through another container somewhere above us. Spare Morpheus spheres clatter and roll across the floor. Aspect winces, repeating, "Mess, mess, mess," in a low whisper.

Great. The mech 100 percent has anxiety, courtesy of yours truly.

With a self-satisfied snort, Echo careens off the crate, sphere in hand. We authorize each other's code names as users via voice commands, so that the respective spheres can now be verbally opened by their new owners, and exchange the goods wordlessly, barely a nod passing between us.

Aspect tugs at my elbow. "MESSAGES—FOR KORI—"

I swallow a scream. "I know, Aspect. I know."

Chloe's memory in hand, we slide back into the crowd. Aspect's unwieldy tension always spikes in a throng, hence the death grip on my hand, the low hum they emit like a radio tuned to a dead channel.

But I love the untamed collision of people that is the Morpheus Market's open floor. I wish I could slow down and enjoy it, rather than feel my heart climb into my throat as I slip between buyers and sellers, struggling to maintain speed. Here, body to body, sharing subterranean air, legs tangling together like so many rogue vines, voices fighting for territory like so many wild beasts . . . Here, I am simply part of the everyone. A code name, a passing breeze of a girl, unburdened, unnamed, all expectation revoked.

Here in the Morpheus Market, I could be anyone.

But if I don't get back to my starship now, what I'm going to be is royally screwed. And swamped with unnecessary math homework.

Aspect and I all but sprint to the exit lift. It's a compact cylindrical chamber, barely large enough for both of us, almost akin to an escape pod—but instead of ejecting us into the world below, it projects us rapidly toward the realm above. We rise, lightning fast, to the surface from which we came. If there's a memory in the market that could activate self-awareness in my metal bestie, it's farther away with every passing instant, and my stomach churns, nearly sick, at the nagging thought.

My ears clog from the lift's rapid ascent; I force a yawn to clear the eardrums. "Goodbye, Monarch," the lift's automated voice intones as the lift doors slide open, reintroducing us to Pagomènos proper.

Despite the planet's light being much gentler in the Passage than in the Daylands, it's always a jarring transition from the artificial underground illumination of the Morpheus Market to the actual sun that defines our world. Tears wet my vision, and even Aspect, with their entirely mechanical visual processors, raises one hand to shield said processors from the brightness.

When my vision clears, the vastness of the Passage once again sprawls before me: Dunes rolling into still more dunes, viciously blown to and fro by the Passage's wild winds. Assorted outcroppings of heavily worn sandstone. Chunks of wrecked starships from the Territory Wars, when the nightfolk attacked the dayfolk and were driven back across the Passage and into the shadows for good. Now-lost weaponry and tech blasted some kind of massive explosive that tore through everything in range and formed the wasteland: uneven rock formations, pieces of starships, and odd hills and dips throughout the landscape, amidst the unending sand.

The Morpheus Market is basically right on the planet's terminator line, directly between the Daylands and Shadowlands. It's a striking visual contrast depending on where I look. To the west, there's even more blinding brightness where the Passage becomes the Daylands, the sky going from semi-twilight obscured by sand to a brutal, nearly cloudless crimson. To the east, after the beautiful miasma of reds, yellows, and purples that is the eternal sunset, the Shadowlands loom—a line of dark, jagged peaks, partially cloaked by cloud cover, their accumulated snow and ice chaotically lit by an unnatural blue glow. What animal life persists in the Passage is either heavily armored and hunkered down or simply underground like the Morpheus Market to escape the wind and sandstorms. I'm the only living creature I can perceive, as far as my eyes can see. Aspect's hand in mine, though chilly and robotic, helps steady my breathing as the inescapable eeriness of the Passage again sets in.

A field of parked starships would quickly expose the Morpheus Market's existence in the Passage, so visitors usually let their transports fly free until it's time to depart. I tap the summoning signal on my helmet, just above my left ear, and my starship's autopilot voice chirps just beside it: "COMMENCING RETRIEVAL."

Charon waits for me. It may have more scuffs and scratches than most, given my frequent Morpheus Market runs across the Passage, but thanks to my mother's insistence that I focus on bettering myself instead of bonding with my peers, I have plenty of time alone with the ship to keep it spick-and-span. Its surface, battered as it is, gleams like a mirror. I'm sure it would reflect my mounting panic over my pending lateness if I weren't wearing my mask.

Few dayfolk have access to one of the remaining Earthside starships. Most are collectively owned by branches of the settlement's government, used for ferrying mechs out to do mining aboveground, offering classes of schoolchildren brief opportunities to see natural sunlight, or checking tech functionality like the sonic-wave deployments around the settlement that keep predators at bay. As the Daylands heiress,

I'm one of the privileged few to have my own. And having this ship, my beloved *Charon*, may be one of the only "perks" inherent in being Chloe's daughter that doesn't feel more like a bedazzled set of shackles.

Charon could be a standard-issue starship from when humans first settled this planet. It could be a military vehicle. It might have originally been intended for something as dramatic as ferrying diplomats or something as simple as delivering mail. Nobody actually knows what any of our remaining Earthside starships were first meant for. But to me, *Charon* is more like home than anything else in the actual dayfolk settlement. *Charon* is one place where, even if only for a brief moment, I'm out of my mother's reach.

She tries to track me, of course. She hired a security detail at one point—five grizzled soldiers of varying genders, all very "cut to the chase" and "don't make this harder than it has to be." I tormented them with all manner of pranks until, one by one, they all abandoned their posts with such passionate exasperation that my mother decided hiring another security detail would be a total waste. My personal favorite prank remains when Aspect feigned a software glitch, in which they were forced to sing the same obnoxious song over and over and over, for multiple sleep cycles in a row. I nearly lost my own mind by the end of it, but I laughed so hard, I nearly peed myself at the increasingly pained expressions of my unwanted supervisors, all desperately trying to pretend they weren't bothered.

The security detail having proven pointless, my mother decided instead to install a tracker in the one thing I would always, always have with me—Aspect. But my mother failed to consider two things: One, Aspect would happily let me tinker with that newly installed tracker. And two, I would inevitably find a way to hack it. That tracker is now spoofed with semi-randomized, totally believable routines that can override my actual location as needed. Like when I need to make unrequested stops in the Morpheus Market. (Or if I don't particularly care for my mother to know how long a bad serving of rations kept me confined to my quarters one morning. Curse you, artificial chicken!)

My mother never really sees fit to enter *Charon*. If she needs me, she sends a message to my comms tablet or, if she *really* wants to grind my gears, sends another person to retrieve me under her orders. But she can't really be bothered to trek all the way from her luxury quarters to the private hangar where I dock *Charon* in the settlement. She has the ship periodically inspected to ensure my safety, but I don't think she's ever actually been in it. And that makes it feel more like home than anywhere else.

Charon descends from orbit, its silhouette primarily an X with two additional vertical bars reinforcing the shape near the center on either side. In the center sits a long horizontal space where its occupants actually enter. While I may call *Charon* homey, that doesn't mean it offers extensive room.

The boarding ramp drops from its center and brings me and Aspect through a closet-sized decontamination chamber, where we're blasted with a chilly surge of dense white smoke and rapid scan of neon-green laser sensors, confirming the outside radiation has in fact been purged from us before we move to the inside.

It's a single space that I collectively call the cockpit, even though the pilot's chair, passenger chair, and assorted controls occupy only about the front quarter of the area. The rest of the room is a cramped dome, with assorted storage units on basically every wall to make the most of it. There's a rectangular table and accompanying bench (both a little rickety but still securely attached to the floor) where I've eaten meals, done homework, or simply tinkered with Aspect. Since we're in the Passage, basically the entire viewport dome above us is transparent, allowing the sun to naturally illuminate the cockpit. In the Daylands, where the sun rapidly becomes too much, I can close an outer shell and switch to the same harsh, fake white light as the Morpheus Market's secret halls.

Now that we've been through the decontamination chamber, it's finally safe to collapse the various segments of my armor. Aspect absently whistles to themself while they wait. My helmet peels back like a cocoon from my face, the rush of fresh oxygen intoxicating.

The bunched, stretchy compression rings around my gloves and boots loosen, no longer needing to protect every joint from potential radiation poisoning, and allow the armor plates to roll back to my shoulders and hips respectively. I'm wearing a full standard outfit beneath, but at least now it isn't clinging to my body.

Ripping off my gloves for a better grip on the controls, I collapse into *Charon*'s pilot seat. "One memory delivery, coming up."

Aspect pokes one finger into the small of my back. "Memory—for Aspect?"

"Not this time. I just picked up some more info about how your memory core works, so I might be able to do a more intensive installation next time."

"Extensive—how?" I can hear an eyebrow raise in Aspect's voice, even though they don't have any eyebrows.

My shoulders slump. "I . . . don't know." There's no template for any of this. I'm hoping that a deeper understanding of mechs' deepest mechanisms will enable me to install a memory that takes . . . a deeper hold, I suppose? Has a more potent, noticeable impact on Aspect's potential ability to self-determine, inspired and empowered by directly understanding how humans do it every day? But I don't actually know if the memory I just acquired will accomplish any of that, or anything at all. "But I can promise you we'll come back for more memories, Aspect. For you next time."

Aspect doesn't have facial expressions. They have bright-to-dim optical processors, a visibly obscured vocalization box, and a crudely carved mouth that I scraped into existence with a spare screwdriver. Aspect is perpetually attempting a smile regardless of the circumstances. But I swear to the stars, right now, they look sincerely . . . disappointed. I would feel bad if I weren't currently in a panic about making this delivery to my mother ASAP.

I pull *Charon* into takeoff, hard. We launch with such force that I won't be surprised if my shoulders bruise from jamming back into the pilot's chair. Aspect staggers, sliding on their heels. The earliest mech designs for mining the newly hostile Daylands had wheels, but it became quickly apparent that as the world turned to sand, wheels would only get stuck and wear down far faster than artificial feet, which are what Aspect has. They're a prime example of (modified) Mech Model V5.30, per settlement records.

Aspect's feet squeak across the cockpit floor, and I sigh to myself. "Literally why are you not strapped into the copilot's chair right now?"

Aspect half shrugs as they rise from the floor. "Surprise—for Kori."

"Is the surprise you losing a limb? Because this is going to be a bumpy ride. Strap in, now." I sigh, hating the Chloe-like edge to my voice. "Please?"

Aspect rapidly shakes their head. "SURPRISE—FOR KORI."

"Aspect, this is not the time," I fire back, tapping away at *Charon*'s controls. Normally I'd use the autopilot to get back to the settlement's singular aboveground entrance, but *Charon* likes to beep at me when it judges my flying as too high, too low, too fast, or too close to me having any measure of fun. So, instead, I engage *Charon*'s secondary thrusters (without disabling the primary) via a small lever on the side of the square steering wheel.

I need all the firepower I can get if we're going to reach home while Chloe is still awake. The woman barely rests. She's too busy running the entire settlement (and micromanaging my entire life). We have precious little time to make it back within her sleep cycle. Having changed Aspect's tracker to feed fake location info won't do me any good if my mother expects me at a specific location personally.

A harsh buffet of wind and sand hits the side of my ship. *Charon* lurches, threatening a nosedive. I pull it back into a smooth flight path, simultaneously reaching for an overhead switch to activate its full shell. We're getting closer to the Daylands—something that the onboard positioning system indicates, but the increased sunlight makes very obvious regardless. The intensity is rapidly becoming difficult to bear without my helmet to reduce it. Segmented armor plates slide into place around *Charon*, cylinders of artificial light activating all around me. An additional layer of glare protection descends over the remaining transparent viewport.

Out of the corner of my eye, I notice Aspect remains on the move, banging and bouncing their way to the tiny storage closet. My knuckles go white around the steering lever as I spin in my chair to face the mech. "Aspect, what are you—?"

That's when the dessert platter slides up the floor, catapulted by my metal friend. It comes to a stop right beside my pilot's chair, wetly squelching. I blink once, twice.

Back when Pagonians used the old ways of tracking time, we held gatherings called birthdays to mark a child's age, but I've never wondered how many times a set number of "days" and "nights" have passed since I entered the world. Now all we have is the massive hourglass in the settlement's center, ever flipping to indicate approximately when it's a good idea to take a sleep cycle and start anew. The hourglass is also digitally linked to a universal application on dayfolk comms tablets, so anyone can check how close the hourglass is to emptying at any time. By this measure, I'm older than a child, but not quite an adult. We simply accept life as it comes, cycle by cycle.

But I must've programmed one of those historical remnant memories of a proper birthday into Aspect and then forgotten, because I don't know how else to explain the goopy nightmare concoction resting on my floor, crudely labeled *CAKE* in swirly purple icing. A single wax candle sticks crookedly out of the center.

How long has it been since I cleaned *Charon*'s cabinets? How long has Aspect's monstrosity been festering and melting together in there?

Why does it smell like gasoline and old shoes?

It's becoming increasingly difficult to pivot my attention between my navigation and diagnostic stats at my fingertips, and the slow-motion culinary disaster happening behind me. My neck is already cramping from the rapid swinging back and forth. Nothing prepared me for this when I decided to turn a robot into a friend. Probably because, by any logical law of nature, I'm not supposed to be turning a robot into a friend.

"Your watch shows—it has been—5,840—hourglass cycles—since you first began—sleeping and waking—Kori," Aspect announces. They toddle back up to the front of *Charon*, lean one arm on their copilot's seat (while still refusing to strap in), and elaborate upon the specifics of how long I've been alive.

Of all the things for Aspect to seize upon and obsess over in an installed memory . . . Apparently, 365 "days" was a "year" which was a "birthday," so by that logic, my watch—which has been tracking sleep cycles since my birth—does mathematically indicate that this sleep cycle is my existence anniversary. When Aspect checked that digital total, I have no idea. Were they looming over me while I slept, ever-so-gingerly tapping my watch to check when a long-abandoned method of time tracking dictated that they take up baking immediately (and badly)?

I want to vanish into the floor. "I'm . . . touched," I say, with as much sincerity as I can muster.

That's when the full-blown, pay-attention-to-me-right-now alarm goes off, scarlet lights reeling in panicked pinwheels all around the cockpit, bouncing off the domed ceiling and Aspect's metallic surface alike. It could be for anything from a mechanical failure to a detected incoming sandstorm to a fuel leak to a landing gear weakness, but whatever it is, the ship has deemed it high enough priority to scream at me from every angle that now is the time to check my text display, with full attention, rather than be distracted by the so-called dessert's menacing approach.

Gritting my teeth, I spin back around in my chair to view the specific diagnostics. Blocky fluorescent-green text scrolls rapidly across the central panel: *GROUND FLUCTUATIONS DETECTED. HIGHER FLIGHT PATH IS ADVISED.*

I swear under my breath. Ground fluctuations while in flight across the Passage can only mean one thing—predators just beneath the sandy surface, ready to spring from the ground and swallow *Charon* whole.

"Aspect, love of my life," I say, not turning my head, my every syllable deliberate, "for the sake of my sanity, please put your seat belt on."

Aspect wiggles their head in refusal, which I know even without turning around from the distinct creak of their neck movement. Their voice arches, grates, and I realize they're attempting to sing. Aspect doing a mechanical whistle is endearing; Aspect singing is enough to make me question every single life choice that led me to this moment. I don't know the song, and based on Aspect's unbearable keening, I sincerely wish I'd never learned it. "Happpppy—biiiiiirthdaaay—to Koriiiiiiii—"

This should, put simply, not be a thing that ever happens to anyone. Mechs are made, not born, and they have no concept of existence preceding them. They have no concept of anything, really, but what their programming dictates—except, in Aspect's case, also whatever scraps of humanity I've illegally installed into their mainframe. Morpheus spheres can instill only so much sentience. But they sure can create problems that nobody in their right mind would be prepared to handle.

My ears burn almost as severely as my face.

"HAPPY—BIIIIIIRTHDAAAAY—TO KOOOOORIIIIII—"

At the edge of *Charon*'s front window, where I can still see out across the landscape, a flash of color—a massive serpentine head lunges out of the sand. Twin fangs slash from its reptilian mouth, framing a forked, thrashing tongue. I scream, tugging the steering lever back. *Charon* jerks into a near-vertical ascent, its rear end bonking the serpent's face on the way up.

Sun serpents are blind, directed entirely by scent and sound. That's why sonic signals successfully deter them from our underground settlement. Hopefully the hard smack against its head causes some disorientation.

"HAAAAAPPY SIXTEEEEEEEEEEENTH—FROM ASPEEEEEECT—"

Per the navigational instruments at my fingertips—which represent *Charon* as a tiny, blinking green dot on a massive green grid—we're already at least halfway back to the dayfolk settlement. Pagomènos's sun, directly above us, now shines directly in my face. I squint, tears springing to my eyes, and try to realign the ship by feel without sending us back into a jerky descent where the serpent lurks, fanged and hungry.

When the burn behind my closed eyelids becomes mostly neutral again, I finally force my eyes back open. *Charon* has returned to a stable, albeit bumpy, flight path. I lean toward the left side window to see that the serpent, despite its massive size, is now far too low to possibly reach us.

That doesn't mean it isn't going to try.

Aspect's voice keens on a dramatic finale. "HAAAAAAAAAPPY BIIIIIIRTH—DAAAAAAY—TO—KORIIIIIIII!"

Curling into a knot of muscle and scales, the sun serpent launches its entire body into the air. It's at least three times *Charon*'s length, the head alone long enough to swallow me in one greedy bite. Lidless black eyes soar closer and closer to the window. I flinch despite myself, even as the wyrm eventually collapses to the ground, thanks to gravity's inexorable pull.

We're alive. And in one piece.

The stench of smoke fills my nostrils. I turn, eyebrows arched, to see that Aspect apparently also commandeered a lighter from the closet. The cake's single candle burns in defiant, irresponsible celebration of a holiday that no longer exists.

"Happy birth!" Aspect proclaims, clapping. Little puffs of smoke blow into my face from the motion. "Happy sixteenth!"

It was almost an unhappy death. I groan, rubbing my temples. "How are you still not wearing a seat belt? How is the cake not plastered on the wall? Where did you even—? You know what? I don't want to know."

Laughter, absurd and violent, bubbles up and bursts from me, hard enough to blow out the candle. The important thing is we're still alive, we're almost home—and I may not have a birthday, but if I did, Aspect cares enough to celebrate it. To celebrate *me*.

"Happy birth!" I cackle, clutching my ribs from the force of my laughter.

Aspect lifts the platter with both hands. "Would Kori—like—a slice of cake?"

It smells like a melting trash chute. Nose wrinkled, lips pressed tightly together, I shake my head. "It's so . . . it's just beautiful, Aspect. It's too beautiful to eat." It looks like if a dessert could hate you, and absolutely wanted you to know about it. But I'm not about to tell Aspect that. "Why don't you sit down, put your seat belt on, and hold it? So I can get a better look at it for the rest of the flight home."

Maybe it's silly to feel guilty, given that Aspect can't even eat, but I swear those visual processors widen into pleading saucers when they look at me. "FORK!" they shriek at an unholy volume, opening one mechanical hand.

Aspect, being a mech, is understandably disallowed from the settlement's dining hall. Part of the reason I so frequently eat meals in *Charon*, instead—Aspect is better company than most anyone else. Apparently, their solution sans dining hall access was to pry a piece of armor from their own shoulder and fashion it into what I suppose could be mistaken for a fork, if I had a concussion at the time and had also never seen a fork.

"FORK! FOR! KORI!"

I don't think Aspect is programmed to understand mockery, but I'd rather err on the side of caution. I bite my lip on a laugh. "Oh, what a wonderful fork! Why don't you put it by the candle and have a seat?"

That finally seems to satisfy Aspect, who finally buckles into the copilot's chair. It's a good thing that mechs have a basically humanoid design, or traveling with Aspect would be a much more complicated affair that likely involved stowing them in one of the storage compartments like so much luggage. I admire the cake for a prolonged moment to satisfy their apparent pride. Then we both turn to *Charon*'s windows and watch the last of the Passage travel by far below. I've seen more than enough action for one sleep cycle, so I switch to autopilot, letting my thoughts drift and swirl alongside the sprawling sands.

There's nothing quite so strange and intoxicating as interim stretches spent in the Passage, the only place where the Daylands' light collides with the Shadowlands' abyssal dark. It would be a far better place to live than either of the strictly divided sides of Pagomènos, if not for the Territory Wars that ravaged what habitable land remained.

The Cataclysm took much from us—our technology, our history, even priceless fragments of memory—but it didn't take the entire planet. We did that ourselves. We finished the asteroid's work with our own weapons, our own overzealous repulsion of the nightfolk assault. As surely as the Morpheus Market is a gallery of alternate lives, the Passage is a graveyard of all that might have been.

A human friend might see the flicker of grief on my face, but Aspect isn't human. Instead, they search their archives for whatever applicable mortal memory applies. I can practically see the gears turning behind my clumsily drawn attempt at a smile. At length, Aspect stands again, leaving the cake on their chair, and lays a mechanical hand on my shoulder. Scavenged visual processors hold my gaze. "There," Aspect says, monotone. "There."

"I'm fine, Aspect."

"Kori is—prettier—when Kori—smiles."

I groan. I don't remember programming an obnoxious man's memories into Aspect, but I suppose any of the memories I've scavenged and integrated could be from an unpleasantly biased source. I push a stray lock of brown hair out of my face, tucking it back into the tightly coiled braids I always wear. "I'm not trying to be pretty."

"Under—stood." Aspect nods, then turns back to the squishy, half-melted "cake" that clearly isn't very concerned with looking pretty either. "Kori—eat cake now?"

I swallow a surge of bile. "Sure." At least I'm not wearing my gloves, so I won't stain them with purple goo. Aspect plucks the fork from the "cake" and extends its crooked tongs to me, hopeful.

Clearly waiting for me to start eating.

"Oh, Aspect, can you do me a favor? Go run a diagnostic on the helical engine. I want to make sure it's still dysfunctional, just in case there's a shot at getting this delivery done even faster."

Helical engines, once a method of hyperspace travel between planets and galaxies, haven't worked since the Cataclysm. The radiation subsequently permeating the planet caused some kind of decay in the mechanisms, and any memory of how to repair it was lost before Morpheus chips came into play, grounding Pagonians to this tidally locked planet forever. *Charon*'s engine is no exception to the rule, but Aspect doesn't question my instructions. Mechs are designed to obey.

"Under—stood." Aspect waddles around the cake, out of the cockpit, and into the polished silver main bay. I should really fix Aspect's slightly lopsided gait eventually, but honestly, the perpetual wiggle is so endearing that unless the mech requests it, I might just leave them be. Frankly, I should've considered the consequences more before entertaining Aspect by reading a record of an Earthside "fashion show" a while back. Their permanent poorly mimed runway walk is 200 percent my fault. "Aspect will return—in three hundred clicks."

"You don't have to be *quite* so specific," I say, but Aspect has already begun tracking the time, their beeping diminishing as they wobble farther into *Charon*.

Aspect has been hyperfixated on tracking elapsed time ever since I installed a particularly old memory relic into their mainframe. Now I'm afraid that if I remove it, they'll start smoking at the joints. Apparently, the memory belonged to someone whose career had relied on highly specified arrivals and departures, back when that sort of thing mattered. Immediately upon installation, it became Aspect's favorite memory for whatever reason—probably just good old-fashioned bad luck—and now, unless I remember to specify that timing is irrelevant, Aspect stubbornly clings to the old way of things, before the Cataclysm.

Earthside units of agonizingly specific time tracking have no meaning on this planet anymore, and Aspect's insistence upon it is damn annoying. But beyond their base programming—harvesting runs, identifying low-charge symptoms, simple greetings for interacting with sentients—everything Aspect knows is pilfered from an illegally installed memory.

For a mech to truly have being, to become a person instead of an increasingly complex algorithm, they'd require an entire human's worth of consistent, unified memories squished into their mainframe. I'd have better luck trying to grow a third arm than I would finding a willing volunteer for a proposition like that. It's so incomprehensible on the face of it, I don't think the government has thought to make it illegal. And even if I could do it, the mech person—or person mech?—would surely blow every gasket at once from the stress of such a transition.

Until I can get my grubby little gloves on a memory that counteracts the presently installed one's love for Earthside time management, this is who—or what—Aspect is. And I really have no one to blame but myself, so I try to lay off the complaining. I'm a good robot parent that way.

The beeping eventually becomes distant enough that it stops ringing inside my skull. I take the fork from the cake, lick an icing glob from the too-sharp tongs, and immediately wince. It tastes like the baker's foundation was oil, which it probably was. It's Aspect, after all. I toss the cake and fork alike down *Charon*'s disposal chute, to be later dumped and consumed by the lava below Pagomènos's surface. This planet has been messed up on every layer since the Cataclysm. Miles beneath the Daylands surface, there are pockets of roiling magma; above that, a thick layer of rock only sparingly mined to gain access to the magma pockets without creating a volcanic situation; above that, the sunbaked sand within which the dayfolk settlement is nestled; and aboveground, depending on where you are, either the savage sunlight of the Daylands or the deadly storms of the Passage. At least the magma's existence, while alarming, makes object disposal a lot simpler. I toss the so-called fork down the chute only when I'm certain Aspect isn't looking.

Somehow, some way, I'm going to raise Aspect to proper sentience. I'm going to bring this little haphazard mech just a little bit closer to being, well, more person than science project.

At the edge of my awareness, just loud enough to be heard over Aspect's enthused counting, my tablet dings again. A message in electric-blue text slides across the screen.

CHLOE: ALMOST HOME, KORI?

I bite my tongue on a curse before politely texting back, *ALMOST HOME.* I can nearly feel shackles click back around my wrists and ankles, holding me fast at my mother's command. I wish I could tell her about evading the sun serpent, about tinkering with Aspect, about anything but what she wants to hear.

When I'm flying far above the planet, the sprawling cluster of stubborn sub-settlements spread below like a paper Earthside map, I feel infinite. But every message from my mother (or one of her enforcers) is a reminder that I am finite, and so are my choices. When your mother is Chloe, monarch of the Daylands and leader of the last proper Pagonian colony, constant poking and prodding from fellow Important People comes with the territory.

The tablet flashes again.

CHLOE: EDNIT WOULD ALSO LIKE TO RUN A DIAGNOSTIC CHECK-UP. HE'S WAITING.

I groan. She thinks she's slick, blaming Ednit, but per usual, I know the checkup was my mother's idea. If she were here right now, she'd tell me to be grateful for dayfolk doctors, but that doesn't make the constant appointments any less unbearable. I feel more like a rare species of pet, too valuable to lose, than a daughter sometimes. But I could never hate Ednit. He's known me since . . . before I can recall. Even more so than my mother, he's someone I couldn't bear to disappoint. He may not be family, but I don't remember my father, who passed during my infancy, and Ednit has always cared for me. Sometimes in a more tangible way than my mother ever could.

I blow out a breath through my nose. "Aspect?"

The mech spins on their heel. "Kori has—interrupted—my—counting."

"I'm sorry. But I forgot I need to do something. When we get back to the settlement, I need you to stay on *Charon* for a bit."

"Aspect—go—with Kori."

"No, Aspect finishes checking the helical engine."

Aspect's optical sensors gleam. "And Aspect—will watch—the cake."

"Actually, I—I already ate it," I stammer, grateful that Aspect probably can't detect the shiver in my voice. I haven't obtained any Morpheus spheres that introduce the concept of lying yet. Even memory smugglers are often loath to admit untruths in their pasts, via business transactions or otherwise. "It was delicious. Thank you, Aspect."

"Kori is—welcome. Back soon?"

"Back soon," I promise, flashing a quick smile at the mech before steeling myself, shoulders squared.

Once we get back to the settlement, it's just one appointment with Ednit. One brief stretch of smiling at my mother, dutifully present, perfectly happy, as the Daylands heiress should be. I lift my jaw, tighten the brown braids at my back, poise the arch of my spine. I can do this.

Reaching down to my hip, I retrieve the latest Morpheus sphere, tracing its seamless edges with a fingertip. "What are you?" I mutter to myself, curiosity sparking.

I'm not supposed to view the memories that Chloe requests from the market. I'm the delivery service, not privy to such things. But whether it's my apparently chronic lack of sleep or my fresh annoyance at another medical appointment, my wonder overwhelms my good sense. Looking left and right as though I might get caught, despite such a thing being impossible, I roll the Morpheus sphere in the palm of my hand.

"Test," I whisper.

A red light shifts to green on the sphere's surface.

"*IDENTIFICATION*," the device chirps.

Since I was the smuggler assigned to retrieve it, it's set up to permit access to my code name, triggered by my registered voice sample on the marketplace. "Monarch," I say, as clearly and crisply as possible, though my voice shivers with anticipation.

"ACCESS GRANTED."

The entire sphere exudes a faintly blue light. Eyes shut, I press an open palm to the surface, knowing what to expect, but the initial lurch of entering a stored memory never ceases to be jarring. And amazing. White light overtakes the darkness behind my eyelids as my eyes fly open of their own accord, wide and unseeing, doubtless more pupil than white.

I plummet like a wounded butterfly into someone else's memory.

CHAPTER 2

ADRIA

The Shadowlands are ensconced in absolute, unrelenting night, pockmarked by winking stars to which we can no longer travel. In the center of my family's fortress, on the highest of its towers, elevated like a fallen celestial body to light our world, a massive torch burns brilliant azure. Visible from any of the smaller surrounding structures, and reignited by the torchbearers every time its fuel dwindles, it is the only way we nightfolk deign to track time's march. The only fixed, final indicator of when one ought to lie down and when one ought to rise.

It's completely invisible from the Depths.

When the asteroid Diakópsei first collided with Pagomènos, it seemed like a thoughtless force of nature. But it was, in fact, a borderline sentient thing—a stone that exerted will, whose sediment shimmered with intent. The twisting, underground labyrinth whose entrance looms just ahead of me was built not by nightfolk hands, but by the explosion of energy from the impact site.

The Cataclysm site should've become a crater. Instead, by the sheer force of its far-flung, interstellar power, the Diakópsei fashioned itself a home. A cathedral, if you ask the Elysian cultists who live here.

The Elysium cult, dedicated gatekeepers of the Depths for generations now, are the only ones who are supposed to come down here—the only ones who abandoned a system of time tracking altogether, their labyrinthian abode perpetually lit by the pulsing indigo light of the asteroid itself. It's the same blue as our blood, the same blue as the undercurrents of our people's skin, the same blue as the Diakópsei's unique gifts to its people. If I could see the sky as it once was, set afire by Pagomènos's sun as the Daylands are, I imagine it would be this blue. This impossible, endless, unflinching blue.

Yet the color feels purer here, undiluted, when it emanates directly from the asteroid. The light is to my eyes what swallowing a spoonful of raw spice powder would be to my tongue. Even at the Depths' entrance, still a while away from the Diakópsei itself, my vision stings and waters. My throat twists as if on a withheld cough.

The Diakópsei raised us nightfolk from our merely human origins and imbued us with alien magic.

Uplifted. Empowered. Transformed.

Monstrous, the dayfolk say, but their minds are rotted by the endless sun. Or so I've been told.

The subterranean Elysium cult worships the Diakópsei for obvious reasons. So why, at the threshold of beholding it firsthand for the first time, do I feel cold all over when I should be thrilled?

"Beautiful, isn't it?" Father says, laying one of his four clawed hands on my shoulder. "Soon, my child, with our own eyes, we will behold that which made us what we are."

It doesn't escape my notice that, per usual, he calls me *child* and not *daughter.* For all my parents' attempts to evade any mention of the truth, it's been glaringly obvious since my earliest memories: They wanted a son. But asked to choose between a childless future, absent of heirs, and accepting the miracle (or perhaps cruel joke) that was their daughter's birth, they chose the latter.

And dedicated their lives to hardening every soft edge, leashing every threatening emotion, and training every cell of my being into an heir worthy of the Shadowlands.

I incline my head toward the waiting Depths, its alien light glinting off my horns. It shines faintly through my wings as well, making their bulk shimmer like gossamer. Said entrance is a straight vertical drop—no ladder, no visible indents for climbing down. The presumption is either wings or telekinesis. "Why have you brought me here?" I ask.

"Not only you," says someone behind me.

I pivot almost instantly, my wings lifting my feet just above the stone ground, to lock eyes with Mother. Her mutations are more akin to the ones I inherited. She has only two arms and two legs, but altered enough by Pagomènos's radiation to enable natural travel on all fours, as she approaches me now. Unlike Father, who was graced with a second pair of arms, Mother's spine twirls into wings like my own, and the horns crowning her head curl and arch away from the skull, whereas Father's are smaller, smooth cones. My horns are somewhere in between the two, arching through the short dark curls of my unkempt hair.

Trailing Mother, the new arrival is closer to a standard humanoid height than her seven feet or my own eight; she has a foot and a half on the stranger, at least. It's possible the stranger will hit a dramatic growth spurt later in life—the radiation affects every nightfolk in a unique way—but he looks to be more boy than man, more child than soldier.

And the stranger has neither wings nor arms; in fact, he has no arms at all, only legs, and stands straight as a metal rod, head in the clouds above despite being dramatically below everyone else's eye level. I would wonder what gift the Diakópsei bestowed upon him, but the absence of arms makes it obvious. He evolved beyond the need for nature's former designs; he's a telekinetic.

I incline my head to the stranger. A steep incline, given his profound lack of height for a nightfolk boy. "Adria," I say, by way of greeting. It's not really an introduction, as we're both well aware.

"I know who you are," the stranger says. A high voice, ringing with youth. Definitely a child, then. I may not quite be an adult myself, but I've been on this planet far longer than he.

I shift my eyes to Mother. "You told me one of your soldiers had volunteered for today."

Her answering smile doesn't reach her eyes, the corners struggling to lift as if under unseen weight. "Isek's father is one of our lead generals," she explains, laying both hands on the stranger's shoulders from behind. "He entered training for the service early."

"I'm s-so very grateful to be here," Isek stammers, "P-Princess Adria, inheritor of the Shadowlands. My lord." Unlike my father defaulting to *child* over *daughter*, there's no hidden jab in Isek calling me *lord*; to the nightfolk, any ruling party, queen or king, prince or princess, can bear the title. Without hands to wipe sweat from his brow, Isek gives his head a little shake. "My liege. My—"

I raise a clawed hand for silence, and he trails off before the next title. I'm tempted to take a knee so that we're eye to eye, so he can see there's no threat behind my gaze, but there are standards for leaders, even with youths. I swallow, throat tight. "*Adria* is fine."

Normally, I'd feel a thrill in my stomach at Isek's deference, knowing I'll someday take my parents' mantle. But this stranger, this Isek . . . this is a *child*. He shouldn't be so afraid of anything, least of all me. Fear is a tool like any other to keep the powerful in line before their rightful master. It shouldn't be at all needed with this small, shrill boy, even if he is a telekinetic and a respected soldier's son.

My father points toward the entrance before us with both left arms. "Shall we proceed?"

Mother whispers something to Isek. Isek's amber eyes shut tightly, his forehead crinkling with concentration. Simultaneously, my wingless father ascends above the ground and surges forward, hovering above the waiting chasm. A moment later, eyes still shut, Isek rises to meet him.

So I was right. I know a telekinetic when I see one.

Mother and I spread our own wings, keeping pace with Father and Isek's slow supernatural descent.

The drop is a seemingly interminable blur of jagged rock and azure light. A ways down, I glance to Mother. "Is this the part where you tell me what's happening?"

She laughs. A slick noise, like spilled oil. "Are you suddenly so eager to understand the intricacies of rule? You could pay better attention in your studies, you know."

"You're deflecting. You always brief me on my mission. Usually it's so the nightfolk can see their next leader's face, but the only subject here is a child."

"Some things are better seen for yourself than foretold."

Heavy cold always blankets the Shadowlands, but pure ice shoots down my spine now. I don't like not knowing. And I especially don't like being kept deliberately ignorant. "What sort of bargain did you strike with Elysium, that we haven't already been attacked? Why would they—?" But my mother's stern gaze and upraised palm are enough to silence the rest of my sentence. No one will respect me as queen one day if I cement myself as a thickheaded princess who never listened to counsel.

Eventually, after a nearly unbearable stretch of silence broken only by wingbeats and pluming white breath, my feet touch the ground. Isek opens his eyes and sags from the effort of having sustained such prolonged telekinesis, nearly bent double, forehead close to his knees, breaths rasping and uneven.

"Well done, Isek," Mother says, but does not reach to steady him.

If they're going to treat him like a soldier, I'm expected to do the same. "On your feet." I force the command too much, injecting it with undue harshness.

Isek straightens, panting. Still almost-imperceptibly shaking.

"Come," Father says, motioning forward with two of his four arms again.

Isek's fiery eyes meet mine, seeking understanding. I can almost hear him say, *Why are we here?*

I wish to the Beyond that I had an answer.

Like all nightfolk, I know the events of the Cataclysm as surely as I know my own name. Once, when time yet mattered and the planet yet spun, the asteroid Diakópsei struck the planet Pagomènos. Its surreal power, beyond human understanding, rewrote the very nature of the planet and its inhabitants.

The dayfolk fled from it, fled even from the light of their own sun, burrowing like vermin to live beneath the surface. But the nightfolk embraced this present from the Beyond, their bodies reformed into something new—wings, multiplied limbs, height once uncommon. They and their children were also graced with gifts. Telekinesis. Telepathy. Summoning and manipulation of the planet's own energy. Superhuman healing.

Within a generation, they were hardly human anymore. They were better.

The Diakópsei is our maker and remaker, our greatest strength and heaviest burden as a people. Every nightfolk knows it. But none have seen it in generations, save for the Elysians who worship it.

And yet an Elysian in the flesh greets us around the next bend. "Er," he says, by way of greeting, offering no more than his name. He's a telekinetic like Isek, without arms, and where the aboveground nightfolk wear loose, flowing robes that somewhat portray the architecture of the bodies beneath, the cultists wear thick, heavy, draping things, with raised hoods. So it is a nearly faceless, subsequently silent Er who leads myself, my parents, and Isek through the labyrinth and toward the Diakópsei's central chamber.

Stalactites and stalagmites sprout, toothy and jagged, above and below us, as though we are walking, like so much foolish prey, into a massive beast's waiting maw.

It isn't as though the aboveground nightfolk have never cooperated with Elysium. Beyond those who are born Elysians, nightfolk occasionally join from aboveground, including my father's little brother, my uncle Azarii. But Azarii went rapidly from newfound believer to religious fanatic, convinced that proximity to the Diakópsei had elevated him beyond his brother, bequeathing to him a right to rule the Shadowlands aboveground, too. The Elysians collaborated with my father to stop the subsequent coup, and Azarii has been imprisoned somewhere in this labyrinth ever since.

Preventing (and punishing) Azarii's coup is the last time my parents and the aboveground nightfolk's government willingly worked with Elysium, and I was a small child at the time. So I can hardly fathom what may be unfolding now. Ever since Azarii's betrayal, it's not as though my father is overly fond of Elysians. For him to partner with them . . . there must be larger stakes here than I can fathom.

The Diakópsei's blue light gleams brighter and brighter as we near its central chamber. I watch in barely leashed awe as Mother confidently proceeds, clearly feeling none of my lingering trepidation. The chill in this chasm is crisp, pure, welding my feet to the floor like twin blocks of ice, despite the powerful wings at my back. I flap them hard to force myself forward.

Isek, duty bound, is already several steps ahead of me, my father at his back, urging him forward with all four hands. Briefly, the brightness is too much. My eyes sting, racked with tears, desperate to close. I force them open. My vision shifts.

We enter the Diakópsei's chamber, and I can see everything.

The asteroid itself is here before us, in all its rumored glory. When it first collided with Pagomènos, our records indicate it was miles wide. But it broke apart on impact, leaving this core piece as the Diakópsei we know: a jagged oval perhaps twenty feet long, large enough that even if a massive nightfolk lay upon it, their arms would reach not even halfway around. It resembles an immense slab of obsidian at first, but upon further examination, it pulses and shifts like an organ, veins of deeper azure flickering through it like savage lightning. The beating heart at the center of my world.

My own heart races at a strange rhythm, like music brought to heel in a foreign key, harmonizing with the asteroid's resonant power.

This chamber holds the Diakópsei's surviving smaller shards, too—those that didn't simply shatter into so much dust on impact, that is. Twin sconces, only accessible by a cultist's Elysian key, bookend the asteroid—each filled to the brim with palm-sized spherical gems like fruit in a bowl.

I'm so caught up in staring that I don't notice Isek until I hear the crunch of his knees meeting the ground. If he had hands, they would doubtless be uplifted, palms open and pleading. "My lords, my lieges, my king and my queen, twin scythes of the Shadowlands—"

"Spit it out," Father snarls, not even deigning to use the child's name.

I flinch, somewhere else for a moment. A girl much younger, chastised not only by her father but by her king, taught a lesson not only by words but by wounds.

Isek shakes his head rapidly, as if forcing some cerebral sediment to settle. His voice rattling on every word, he asks, "Will I ever see my mother again?"

"Perhaps, if you honor his calling and our summons," Mother says, wings spread so wide that they actually cast a shadow amidst the surrounding blue glow. "But certainly never again if you fail upon the threshold."

My own voice bursts out of me like an animal cry, against my own will. "What in the Beyond is this?" I wheel upon my father, both pairs of his arms defiantly crossed; I turn to my mother, whose visage betrays no emotion. Er, the Elysian, hovers behind us at the door, wordless. "You tell me nothing of what to expect. You greet me with a stranger's son, more boy than man. And you ask me to watch as you threaten him ever closer to the planet's forbidden heart?"

My chest aches. I look at them, the people who raised me, the leaders whose legacy I will someday be asked to preserve, and I'm not even surprised by the lack of compassion. I've seen that stony apathy before, in moments I've tried and failed to forget. Claws against my face. Cruel words scraping at my ears, burrowing in forever.

I never stood up for the girl I once was. But I can speak for this shuddering boy who pleads to see his own mother.

Mother glares. "Adria." It's not an admonition; it's a command. It means, *Sit and watch, my child. Remember who you are. Do not force me to mold you into a leader with my own hands. I take no pleasure in it.*

"Answer me." My chest heaves, breaths coming too fast. "Why bring him here? Why bring me here? What have you done?"

"It's not what we've done," Mother says, "but what we've come here to do." Before I can react, she drives one powerful foot between Isek's shoulder blades.

I hear a scream, tortured, faraway. I don't recognize it as my own, but my throat burns from the force.

Isek staggers forward, sobbing now—without arms to catch his fall, and too startled to telekinetically break it. He lurches headlong toward the asteroid. The impact of his forehead on the rock is a wet, fleshy sound, followed by a heavier booming one from the rock itself, like a primordial response to the contact.

The light down here was already ferocious, but now it flares beyond belief. Even the inside of my eyelids is blue, blue, blue. I hear Father's and Mother's exultant shouts, Isek's faint weeping, my own uneven gasps for air. When the rush of light recedes to the Diakópsei, Isek is still there, curled into a ball, like a child in the womb. But that ball is much larger than it would've been mere moments ago. He's taller, thicker, corded with muscle that threatens to swallow his frail, developing bones. His mouth is a grimace, graced with fangs. His face looks generations old.

"Isek," Father snaps, a call to attention. "Look at me."

Shaking, Isek does. When his eyes slide open, they're the same electric blue as the asteroid itself. He opens his mouth on a scream, and the very ground beneath us shudders, splits. Cracking open. Telekinesis is supposed to demand a specific target, visible and defined, but Isek seems to be molding the planet's very surface to his will like pottery clay.

Mother is wordless, her gaze wide with wonder.

"What have you done to me?" Isek howls, earsplitting, as the ground threatens to devour us all whole at his command.

Only now does Er, the Elysian, peel himself away from the entrance, sauntering toward us, his bootsteps heavy on the stone floor. "So we see, it is as the Elysian scholars always predicted," he half snarls through his teeth. "The Diakópsei graced us with visitation, but its divinity is beyond us. It is to be beheld, not crudely *held*. Not violated with mortal flesh." Telekinetically, he pulls his hood back, at last revealing his face. Yellowed, sulfuric eyes. Wrinkled black-blue flesh. Long, dutifully polished horns. He is an old man, set in his ways, those ways now as validated for him as ever by the horror that deviating from them has produced. He wheels upon my father. "You will fix this." It's neither a question nor a request.

The splintering ground worsens. I stagger as a new crack opens between my feet, nearly knocking me down to one knee. Isek keens and cries and howls. Understanding eludes me. Why go through all the trouble of convincing the cultists to run this experiment? Why sacrifice a child, of all people, to science? How will they possibly soothe his torture now?

He's suffering, I try to say, but my tongue sticks to the roof of my mouth, no sound forming at all.

"You've done well, Isek." Father smiles at the child, the way I've always wished he would smile at me. "You've honored your people, honored your father."

I am the inheritor of the Shadowlands, a warrior in my own right, the only inhabitant of Pagomènos who could possibly hope to stand against my father. But when I see that smile I've craved for years, that explosive joy spread across his face, I resent every bit of the longing in my body. Whatever I do, whoever I become, I hope to the Beyond that I never, ever make him proud.

I fear I'm making him proud now, my strength brought low in his wake, very nearly the deadly, deferent daughter he always wanted—my feet stuck to the rumbling floor, my jaw slack, my voice caged like a domesticated beast. I can't find the will to move. I can hardly breathe.

Isek recovers himself for the briefest instant. The ground stops splitting, though it does not reform. The surrounding dome of the chamber rattles but doesn't threaten to entirely collapse and bury us. Not yet, anyway.

Isek straightens, teeth gritted, shoulders drawn back, and pleads in the steadiest voice he can manage, "I want . . . to see . . . my mother." Flames flicker in his newly blue eyes. "She . . . will be . . . so proud."

"Indeed she will," my father says.

Two of his four hands seize either side of Isek's head. The child stares at him, irises blazing with indigo power but watery, shimmering, a baleful plea beyond language. Father doesn't break their locked eyes, doesn't so much as blink, as he twists, and *twists*, like tearing a weed out at the root. The first twist isn't enough. The sound, forever seared into my memory, is one of breaking, but not ending. A life dangling by a frayed thread, swinging loose from the tapestry, still fighting stubbornly against a merciful release.

"*Finish it*," says the Elysian.

My mouth tastes like sick. Father adds his two other hands, all four on the child's head now, and twists, twists, *twists*, until Isek's skull snaps clean off the shoulders.

CHAPTER 3

KORI

A mirror's surface, clear as crystal. I observe my own reflection: pitch-black hair in an unhindered cloud of curls, framing my deep-brown eyes and deeper brown skin, my teeth absently worrying at my lower lip. "I am Jelza." My breath fogs the glass. I say it again, willing steel into my veins, calling courage into my knocking knees. "I was chosen for a reason. I was deemed worthy. I am Jelza, and I can do this." I turn on my heel, away from the mirror. The monarch of the Daylands is waiting. I refuse to disappoint her.

I jerk, nearly losing my footing as I boomerang back into myself, but I've entered foreign memories enough times that I recover my balance. Thankfully *Charon* has been on autopilot during this entire memory dive. I've never seen that woman before, but clearly, she knows my mother. She was selected for an honorable role that elevated her own sense of self. But what sort of role? Why remove this memory of her initial hesitation? And why, after the removal, buy it back from the Morpheus Market?

The questions gnaw at me, but deep down, what settles in my stomach is disappointment. I was hoping for an entertaining dive, at least, as a reward for daring to break the rules. This memory couldn't possibly have been more innocuous. At least now, if I'm asked whether I interacted with the merchandise, it won't be difficult to lie. This memory . . . it's hardly worth remembering at all.

My tablet blinks and vibrates again. I curse under my breath. I don't even want to look at the digitized hourglass and see how little sand remains in its upper half.

The dayfolk settlement's surface entrance is coming into view—a single elevator, not unlike the Morpheus Market, but broader and more prominent, even from a distance. I switch *Charon* to a landing sequence, already feeling Aspect's impending absence at my side.

"I'm coming, Mother." I sigh, slipping the Morpheus sphere into my waist pocket.

Like an Earthside dog on a leash, at its master's beck and call. *Coming, Mother. Always. Wouldn't dream of anything else.*

Here's hoping, sun serpent be damned, that I'm not too late.

The walk from the docking bay to my waiting mother is long, but I know every step by heart.

The Daylands colony is a complex network of underground tunnels and sub-settlements, but it's also the only location most dayfolk see in their lifetimes, so we memorize the layout in early childhood. When the Diakópsei struck, the Cataclysm forever altering our planet, most aspects of Pagomènos were infected. Altered.

When the planet stopped spinning, radiation spread, and every surviving animal or human who was left unprotected mutated into something new, something strange and unfathomable.

Our surviving society retains only scribbled snippets of what our ancestors wrote—the ones who predated Morpheus tech's invention—and lost an unknown breadth of broader knowledge that will never be recovered. The records we have are . . . sparse, but not without value. Enough to know that we came from Earth, powered by helical engines, and that we settled unpopulated Pagomènos as the first interstellar human colony. We also have simple knowledge of Earth's inhabitants, both human and animal.

But communication with Earth was severed when the Cataclysm stalled the planet, destroyed the helical engines' functionality beyond repair, and began the creeping process of irreversible mutation. Countless pieces of Earth-linked technology exploded when the asteroid hit, torn apart by the first wave of radiation even before it affected organic life. And when memory slipped away, so did knowledge of how to ever restore or rebuild the helical engines.

Earth is a thing of the past; we're all purely Pagonians now.

If, on the other side of the infinite unknown, Earth retains galaxy-spanning travel capabilities, Earth's citizens seem to be in no rush to use them. Nobody ever came for us. We are a world to ourselves now, severed from history, slowly shifting beyond recognition.

After the Cataclysm, our ancestors sought a threefold solution. For the sun's brutal heat, the dayfolk escaped to a colony beneath the earth, deliberately far enough from the magma pockets to draw on them as needed without simply being flambéed alive. But a few layers of sand and stone weren't enough to protect us from the radiation, and it took the most precious thing we had: the extended reach of memory. In response, we developed a new metal, uniquely equipped to resist radiation. And for our rapidly fading memories, we created a neurological implant to serve as extended storage: the Morpheus chip, now mandatory for all dayfolk.

It's the only reason any of us know who we are.

It takes careful application of both the Daylands' heat and lingering radiation to craft Pagonian plate, the new metal that forms the exoskeleton of our colony, interweaves with the armor we wear to venture out, and more. The layer on mechs is the thinnest, since every mech—including Aspect—is powered by the radiation itself.

Since only mechs can craft Pagonian plate at a reasonable speed, it's a painstaking process, the mechs risking damage by the environment or its predators whenever they venture beyond the colony. So our underground home grows, but slowly. I've never been surprised by a new hallway or additional room. I know this place's layout as surely as if it were programmed.

Ednit waits for me after six halls, two left turns, a right, a U-turn, and a ride down one of our reliably chugging escalators. My mother, Chloe, stands beside him, comically tall and pale beside the squat brown doctor. I hear her talking before she notices my approach.

"She needs to focus on her studies, Ednit, and her health. I'm tired of her endlessly tinkering with that mech. A hobby is one thing, but not at the expense of her well-being—"

I see the moment Chloe spots me. Her lips press into a tight pale line, her jaw setting firmly, locked. Meanwhile, Ednit's expression betrays no emotion.

"Kori." Quiet and dutiful as ever, Ednit doesn't even tell me off for arriving inefficiently late, the last specks of sand in the upper hourglass reduced to flickering pixels on my comms tablet display. "Good to see you well."

"Ednit." I incline my head in greeting. Despite my resentment for these overly frequent medical appointments, a smile stubbornly spreads across my face.

It's impossible to dislike Ednit. He's only doing his job, and he's beneath my mother's sway as surely as I am—as surely as everyone in the colony is. And frankly, with the rest of my spare moments occupied by either fiddling with Aspect or attending to my academic studies (for fear of parental retribution), I don't have many people close to me. Certainly nobody who has known me even half as long as Ednit. Certainly not *boys*.

Chloe has always been adamant about keeping boys away from me, since she "knows what they think about" and I "deserve so much better."

I've been getting lectures about denying "the pull" (usually stated with her fingers curled into actual quotation marks) to boys for as long as I can remember.

The joke's on Chloe, really—I feel *the pull* all the time anyway. My heart skipped when bulky gym rat Brett slid his thigh close to mine and asked if I'd ever attend "real school" and sit with him, as surely as my breath caught when Hyrra from the mechanics division demonstrated how to oil a malfunctioning mech and I couldn't take my gaze off the deft movements of her hands. But in both instances, I promptly tripped over something (a fallen homework sheet with Brett and a discarded wire with Hyrra) and spat out a distinctly unladylike four-letter word through the pain.

No *pull* has a stronger hold on me than gravity. Chloe has nothing to worry about.

Chloe nudges her shoulder into mine, almost playful. The unexpected tenderness brings me back to the moment, but deep down, I know she's all business. Passionless isn't just her default—it's her only setting. "You have the merchandise?"

Normally, given the sensitive nature of my assignments, she wouldn't dare mention them in front of anyone else, but Ednit is practically her left hand, far more pliable and obedient than her right (which would be me). I'm not surprised he knows everything. Probably knows more than I do.

"Of course." I slide the Morpheus sphere out of its compartment at my waist, before pressing it firmly into Chloe's waiting hands. "One memory, fresh from the Morpheus Market. That'll be thirty-five credits."

I'm joking (mostly), and she knows it (probably), but Chloe sighs, "I raised you, Kori," and slides the sphere into her own hip pouch.

I've never been paid for these monarchy-sanctioned memory-smuggling runs, unless, of course, you ask her. My mother will gladly list everything she's ever done for me, presumably starting with my conception and including every moment of parental obligation since then, from clean bedsheets to healthy meals to a monarchical inheritance I never asked for.

With the Morpheus sphere handled, Chloe turns her attention back to Ednit. "I know I don't have to tell you to take good care of my daughter."

"You don't," Ednit says, "and yet you do."

She laughs at that; it's a high, thin noise, fragile from disuse. There are so few people who can easily joke with my mother. Most of the time, I'm not one of them.

"Come," Ednit says, waving me forward with one white-gloved hand, and I follow, leaving my mother blessedly behind.

There's a pregnant pause. My boots click on the synthetic floor, while Ednit's surgical booties squeak and shuffle.

"She worries," Ednit says.

"She does."

We walk to the examination room in silence, for which I'm grateful. It's a compact cubicle of a room, made even more claustrophobic by Ednit's tendency to collect more medical posters than he has actual wall space. They overlap all over the wall—a diagram of a human knee here, an analysis of how mech anatomy was inspired by evolution's work on our own kind there—interspersed with punny science cartoons that only a middle-aged doctor would find funny. *That'll only cost you an arm and a leg*, one doodled doctor says, holding up prototype replacements for both after an apparent amputation surgery.

The cool-white countertops feature assorted medical devices, both for human bodies (a stethoscope, a blood pressure cuff, a thermometer) and our mechanical alterations (namely, assorted probes and prods for installed Morpheus chips).

I leap up to the familiar exam table in a single deft movement; as a little girl, I once needed a stool or a helpful lift. At least, I think so. When I think about my childhood for too long, it starts to get fuzzy, like static on a comms tablet, like staring out into the Daylands without a helmet's visor to dull the glare.

Chloe says most people forget their childhoods to make more room in their Morpheus chips for important adult things. I wonder what else I'll be expected to discard someday, when I take over the monarchy—when my mother is long gone but her ghost's lingering weight drives me to accept the title.

"Lie down." Ednit gently eases me back on the table with soft, careful hands. He's so good at being a paragon of health that it's almost infuriating. Only the best for the Daylands heiress, I suppose. I can smell fresh, minty toothpaste on his breath. He straightens the collar of his white coat. "Do you still experience unpleasant subconscious Morpheus chip malfunction?"

My face burns. That's one way to say *whack-ass dreams*, I suppose. I've been having nightmares whenever I close my eyes for . . . well, a long time. But I don't talk about it anymore, not unless I have to. Not even to Aspect, whose simulated concern nevertheless makes me feel guilty for sharing the imaginary horrors in the first place. The nightmares worry Chloe. She worries enough, and when she worries, my life's options narrow to a medical needlepoint. "Yeah, I am."

Ednit clicks restraints around my wrists, ankles, and throat. "For your safety, Kori."

"Of course." I'm quite used to my mother and her lackeys enforcing unwanted restrictions for my safety. What's a cuff while I'll be asleep anyway? I don't have it in me to protest. But my heart gallops in my chest.

"The exam will be quick. I only need to confirm the functionality of your Morpheus chip. As always, it will be performed remotely, but it is best done while you are thoroughly unconscious." Ednit reaches for a long, thin needle. "I am going to give the injection now."

I laugh dryly. I haven't slept in ages; I avoid it like Chloe tells me to avoid distracting relationships, and idle time, and most everything that makes me happy to be a person. I should really consult the Dreamgiver Devotees or the Old Seekers eventually, consider the wisdom of both spirit and science regarding my troubling dreams, but thinking about them for too long gives me a headache.

I'd rather stay conscious for as long as I can. It's easy in a world without nightfall, which means that when I can get away with ignoring the digitally omnipresent hourglass, I get more done than anyone else in the commune. And no one notices if I conduct another Morpheus Market smuggling run when I'm presumed to be asleep.

I regard the syringe. It hovers over my wrist. "Go ahead, Ednit." I close my eyes.

Exhausted to my bones, I'm gone before the needle pierces skin.

I fight sleep like a grappler in the ring, condemned to death in a public spectacle, but there's no one to observe my subconscious struggling. So my mind, detached, floats like a corpse abandoned to deep space. Unreachable. Undone.

Visions split like fractals against the back of my eyelids.

Faces don't form correctly in my sleeping state, but I think the shimmering outline of a person, hovering nearby, is my mother. I know that militantly shaved curve of blond hair, the relentless gaze of those deep-brown eyes, even when I fail to truly see them.

I'm lying supine, stomach up, staring into nothing. I can't feel the bed beneath my back. I can't feel my lungs; it's like I'm not breathing at all. I smell antiseptic, cloying, choking.

Where am I? My voice seems to come from someone else. My tongue tastes like salt, swollen against the roof of my mouth.

My name is Chloe, my mother says, her warm fingers brushing my forehead. *Do you remember me, Kori?*

A rogue shard of certainty pierces my consciousness. I try to jerk upright, but metal restraints pin me to the bed at my wrists, my ankles, my throat that's closing up, swallowing my voice.

I wake, sweat-soaked, on Ednit's examination table, jerking as much as my restraints will allow, my head slamming back into a pillow I don't even recall Ednit placing on the exam table. I boomerang back into my body. My neck aches, despite the restraint below my chin. Numbly, I try to reach back to tighten one of my braids, which slipped loose from its pins with the sudden motion—but my hands remain locked.

"Welcome back, Kori." Ednit's minty breath shakes me fully awake.

"Hello," I mumble through the sleep haze.

"Your Morpheus chip is as functional as it has ever been. I made some minor quality-of-life adjustments to ensure ongoing positive results, but you needn't worry about your capacity for memory." Ednit flashes a smile nearly whiter than his coat. "You will be a well-educated, fully optimal leader of the Daylands when your time comes."

"Lovely." I meant to inject some semblance of enthusiasm into my voice, but it sounds more like I accidentally stepped in something squishy while speaking. "Can I go?"

"I'll walk you out. Where to?"

"Charon."

Ednit arches a disapproving eyebrow. "I hope you don't plan on launching it anytime soon. You ought to take it easy for a while, recover from the sedative."

"Oh, I will." I lurch to my feet, ignoring the delicate spinning of my vision. "I like to sleep aboard my ship. More privacy that way."

"Really." Ednit sounds utterly unconvinced.

"If more dayfolk had starships, I think it would be a common practice. I'm very blessed to be the monarch's daughter. I have so many things that the laypeople do not."

Ugh, I hate the sound of my own voice, donning this pompous air of superiority, but I have to convince Ednit so that he convinces my mother

I'm still a rule follower to the letter. Not the sort of girl who buys unassigned memories in the market, let alone installs them into a mech.

In reality, I need to get back to the Morpheus Market ASAP, this time with more focus on my own mission: a new sphere for Aspect. If I can convince Ednit and Chloe that I'm asleep, all that's needed is to set Aspect's tracker to stationary mode, reporting that I am in fact unconscious on *Charon*, and I'll be home free. Worst-case scenario, if someone in the records department notices that *Charon* and Aspect were logged as leaving the settlement, I can weave some story about wanting natural sunlight when I woke, having put the ship into autopilot on a safe loop.

I've kept Aspect waiting long enough. I can't afford to accidentally sleep even more. Not now.

I watch the discomfort slide off Ednit's face like sand from a window. "Very well."

He leads me from the office by the hand, as he has since my childhood. I'm older now, but I think it's more for him than for me. It's not his fault that Chloe would rather I spend my days studying fractured Pagonian history than making literally any friends. It's not his fault that my political destiny squashes my interpersonal aspirations like gravel beneath a boot.

I squeeze his hand back, and together we leave the examination room. In my eagerness to get away from here and back to Aspect, I stumble directly into the line of Ednit's other waiting patients. A woman collides with me forehead to forehead with a near-comical crack. I stumble away, catching my balance against the wall.

"Stars above, I'm so sorry," I sputter, but whatever the woman says back is drowned out by the sudden rush of white noise in my ears when I meet her eyes.

Rich brown eyes, their hue like the old Earthside foundation, set like gemstones in a round face. Deep copper skin, older than my own but nevertheless smooth and well cared for. A dark, tightly coiled afro blooming naturally around it, lightly frizzing at the edges. It's not just that she's beautiful, though that would've caused my lungs to malfunction anyway before I recovered myself. It's the woman from the memory. Jelza.

It feels obscene to have been inside Jelza's head, to have seen through her eyes and known firsthand her racing heart, when she has no clue who I am. Like running into a one-night stand in a formal context, trying to pretend you haven't seen them without their clothes.

I fade back in. Jelza is apologizing to me, too, talking with her hands, so I catch the gist even over my roaring pulse in my eardrums.

"Please watch your step, Kori," Ednit admonishes without missing a beat.

"I know, I know, I'm so sorry," I stammer, giving the woman her space bubble back.

What is she doing here? She was chosen for something significant in the memory, something her insecurities told her she didn't deserve—was it access to Ednit, the Daylands' best doctor, reserved for only the highest of government officials? I've brushed shoulders with countless stuck-up compatriots of my mother, and Jelza was never among them. Have we just coincidentally never interacted before? But why conceal the memory I so recklessly pried into? Is she government or not, and if she isn't, then what the hell is happening here?

I shake my head just to clear the thickening smog within it, then sigh, "Be well, Jelza."

I only realize what I've just done after the words leave my mouth.

Jelza arches an eyebrow. "I'm sorry, have we met?"

No. No, no, no, no, no.

"I—I saw Ednit's patient list on the way in. I have a really good memory. The patient after you was, uh . . ." I glance at the acne-flecked redheaded boy behind her. I'm fairly certain he's the grandson of a government advisor I met, but both the advisor's and grandson's names are completely escaping me right now. "You know what? I should definitely get going. Come on, Ednit, you have other patients waiting!" I force a fake laugh. It may be the most annoying sound I've ever heard, and it came out of *me*. I resent that.

Ednit leads me away from the line of patients and back toward the reception area. Only when we're out of earshot does he catch me by the wrist, more forcefully than ever before. I don't know how his lean arms, half a lifetime older than my own, carry such strength.

"Kori, Kori. There are things you cannot know, for your own good. Listen to me, and more importantly, listen to your mother." His grip makes the bones of my wrist sting. I feel itchy all over, desperate to pull away. "There are consequences that even the heiress of the Daylands cannot be protected from."

I'm under no illusions that he believes me about the patient list. I've exposed my illicit dive into the delivered memory. That's what we're talking about, even if he won't dare to voice it directly.

"Just . . . don't tell Chloe. Please." I force my eyes wide, hoping for a sign of tears. I think about everything sad I can muster. Aspect's present absence of sentience. My inability to maintain eye contact with remotely attractive peers of any gender. The bizarre dreams that torment my patches of fitful sleep. These constant, inescapable medical appointments at Chloe's insistence. Come to think of it, my life is actually quite sad all on its own. "I'll be good. I swear, Ednit."

He waits just long enough for my stomach to drop into my shoes. Then he releases my wrist. "Then be good," he says, and continues leading me to the reception area.

Chloe briefly interrupts us, flinging her long, lithe arms around me in an embrace.

I would return it, but my arms feel pinned to my sides. I grin awkwardly. "Healthy as ever, Mom. Nothing to worry about."

She looks to Ednit for reassurance because of course she does.

He nods. "Your daughter is in peak condition, my lady. She assures me she'll be lying down for a while in the examination's aftermath."

"And then studying, I hope." Chloe clicks her tongue. An innocuous sound, to be sure, but one that drives me absolutely nuts. I'm half convinced she does it on purpose.

"Studying," I parrot.

Thank whatever gods are out there, Ednit isn't going to rat me out.

"Any subject is all right," Ednit offers, deliberately keeping my secret. I could crush him in a hug right now. "Whatever you think you can handle so soon after a Morpheus chip exam. I would stay away from heatshot target practice for a bit."

"I will."

"Be good." Chloe presses a fleeting kiss to my forehead. My heart stumbles. I want so badly to feel something other than nagging resentment, but I feel more like a mech than a dutiful daughter. My heart of stone slows, wearily, against my ribs of steel. "Be safe."

"I'm always safe."

"And when you're rested, Kori . . ." Her voice drops to a conspiratorial whisper. "There's another package I need you to retrieve from the market. Sorry to send you back so soon, but I wasn't aware of the second when I gave you the first assignment. Monarchical duties have been . . . hectic. I'll send the details to your comms tablet. Whenever you're ready."

I nod, this time with real instead of feigned enthusiasm. Doing her dirty work is the same burden as always, but a formally sanctioned visit to the market means another opportunity to buy memories for Aspect. I remain ignorant of what exactly I'm looking for—something that will finally raise Aspect from a consumer of thoughts to a creator of their own—but I'm consumed with the countless possibilities, all the angles of human experience I have yet to offer them. I can hardly wait to get back to the market. And if I'm brave (or foolish) enough, I can also investigate what other memories Chloe wants me to retrieve, and why.

I follow Ednit to the hangar and dismiss him at the threshold. Then I run, full sprint, casting exhaustion aside like a too-heavy jacket, all the way to *Charon*'s boarding ramp. Whatever else happens here in the colony, far below Pagomènos's surface, I still have the skies.

I still have a world's worth of memories to explore.

CHAPTER 4

ADRIA

Overcharge. That's what Father calls it after Isek's body has gone cold, after the severed head rolls abandoned across the stones and comes to a lifeless, wide-eyed rest. Father carries the dead child with two of his four arms like a sack of supplies, like a *thing* and not a vessel for *being*—shattered far too soon. Er uses his own telekinesis to levitate Father out of the Depths and back to the surface, while Mother and I use our wings. Mine feel impossibly heavy at my back, almost too much to move them at all.

The Elysian and my parents exchange reassurances that I hardly hear over my mounting headache, my heartbeat roaring through my entire skull. Only when Er is long gone, completely swallowed back into the Elysian labyrinth, does Father turn to me, his gaze wide with wonder where it should be deathly serious. "For so long, my child, we've approached the Diakópsei with open hands, waiting to receive. But we've grown stronger since the Cataclysm." He seizes either side of my face with his free pair of hands, the ones that aren't carrying the murdered child. Forces me to look at him, and I glare, unblinking, back. "Now we can take that power for ourselves, seize it in a closed fist. Become more."

I don't know how to tell him that I can't imagine anything worse than being more of what he is, of what I'm expected—maybe biologically destined—to become. Forget *more*. I would settle for *other*, for being anything or anyone but the sort of leader who prods a child into the Depths, knowing full well that they'll never see the surface again.

"That isn't what you told the cultist," I say, in a terribly steady voice that seems to come from someone else. "You said this was a mistake. That this would never be repeated."

"A child could not be trusted with such power. Even a soldier's son."

"Why use a child at all?" My throat cracks, splintering the edges of my words. "You have how many loyal soldiers? You could've sent any one of them. Hell, even the boy's father would've been a willing volunteer—"

"What if the experiment had failed?" Mother interrupts, brow furrowed gravely. "A grown soldier is not so easily replaceable."

I turn away in a rush of wind and wings, my pulse pounding. "Do you think his father considered him replaceable?"

"His father knows his betters," Father snarls at my back, "unlike certain children." My stomach roils. "There will be a ceremony," he goes on, "that both yourself and our most revered soldiers shall attend. And together, they will witness their lords' ascension to a higher state." I barely hear him through the pulse in my eardrums.

"We won't be confined to the shadows anymore," Mother breathes, voice rich with awe, devoid of regret. "With this sort of power at our command, perhaps also gifted to our most trusted warriors, we can seize the Daylands, too. At long last, after generations of lost history, we can take their archived memories for ourselves—and so honor where we came from, even as we grow far beyond those origins."

I swallow a thousand curses, instead saying only, "Elysium will never allow it."

"Elysium," my father says, even as he slams Isek's corpse to the ground with a horrible, wet, fleshy sound, "will have no choice in the matter."

"You mean to go to war."

"Not a war," Mother says, arms and wings both folded, poised. "It will be a *purge*. The Elysians provide nothing to the Shadowlands. They cower below ground like accursed dayfolk, grovel before a power that would elevate us all if they only had the boldness to claim it. They will concede before our proper nightfolk army, or they will be consigned to the annals of history, where they belong."

Father takes one knee to retrieve Isek's body, now even more mangled just so he could make a point. I don't know where they intend to dispose of it, but surely the boy's family will never know what happened here. They'll be fed a false story of some fashion, then made to march into the Depths and execute a merciless genocide, goaded by promises of the Diakópsei's power—which was clearly never meant to directly touch mortal flesh.

How many will lose their minds upon overcharge? Will their fellow soldiers snap their necks, too, leaving only the most resilient to return to the surface and rule less evolved nightfolk with unholy strength? How many lives are my parents willing to trample underfoot to secure leadership beyond challenge, to prevent someone like Uncle Azarii from ever daring to raise claw or freezeshot rifle against our dynasty ever again?

Words claw their way from me without my consent. "And then what?"

"Then what?" From Mother, the echoed words are a laugh. "Anything we want, Adria. At long last, as it always ought to have been, the planet will truly belong to the strong—to the ones who fully embrace what the Diakópsei gifted."

I tense against a full-body chill as the realization dawns. "You mean to invade the Daylands."

Father nods as though I were merely commenting on the weather. "Yes."

"With an overcharged army."

"Yes."

"To do what?" I'm fighting a scream so fiercely, my voice is barely audible at all. "Assert absolute planetary authority? Enslave them? Slaughter them all?"

"That will depend on how well they concede defeat," Father says mildly, as though he were merely commenting on wind patterns or the current strength of the timekeeping torch. "Adria, the opportunity here cannot be understated. Surely you understand that."

I shake my head, which does nothing to lessen my pounding skull, but he keeps talking.

"The dayfolk have further-reaching historical records than the nightfolk. Locked away to rot, useless, in their bunkers underground. We have a right to that knowledge, to fully understand where we came from—that we may fully embrace all we can now become. If they turn it over without heatshot-blazing resistance, then perhaps we can arrange something of a truce." Two of Father's hands curl into defiant fists. "But they will finally, fully, know their betters."

My blood could freeze solid in my veins right now. Dayfolk haven't interfered with nightfolk business in generations. They may be disgusted by our mutations, even terrified of us, but nobody could say they've aimed for armed conflict. Invading the Daylands would be an unprovoked act of war. If the dayfolk are unprepared, invading them will be an extinction-level event, wiping them out entirely. All in the name of asserting our superiority—and seizing the Daylands' historical records for ourselves.

My tongue feels like a lump of sand in my mouth. I choke out a single dry word. "When?"

Father's voice is venom. "When what?"

"When do we return to the Depths? Blaze a path through Elysium? Overcharge the army?"

"Soon" is all Mother says, through a smile that makes me want to keel over and be sick upon the stone underfoot.

"You'll know." Father's voice, but I don't look at him. Refuse to see what Isek's body looks like now. So small held against my father's bulk. Mangled, wasted. Tortured in his final moments, only to be tossed aside. "We will summon you, Adria. It would be a terrible shame," he says, "to miss the final stage of our evolution."

Father leaves us to dispose of Isek's body—where and how, I am too horrified to ask. Mother and I leave him behind and complete our flight back to the fortress together, the distance between me and her nevertheless cavernous. When we arrive home, the torch has burned nearly to azure cinders, signaling the cycle's end. Mother and I part ways to our respective chambers.

The fortress consists of layered rectangles, shrinking in size as the levels increase in height, with the torch burning at our home's highest point, giving light to both the fortress and the civilian areas beneath it. My room is on the fourth highest of seven levels, so it would necessitate ascending multiple stairways, were it not for my wings.

The fortress also features towering cubic parapets at its four corners, with one additional parapet along each of the walls. As the current shift of guards knows my face and questions me not at all, I alight on the southmost parapet, the one directly above the building's looming entrance gate. Then it's only around three levels down and a turn west to reach my chambers; not too much of a difference, I suppose, but at least it's downhill instead of uphill. My legs feel like lead, impossibly heavy to haul up and down, even with the help of my wings. I could roll like a stone down these stairways, if I allowed myself. Crash through the wall into my chamber, propelled by gravity alone, and simply lie there, waiting to disappear.

Eventually, I do reach my chambers, though not by careening into them like an avalanche. Where most nightfolk have just enough space to call a home, I could lay four or five of myself lengthwise in any direction around this jagged, unevenly circular room that houses my relentlessly racing thoughts. I hardly even register my surroundings, opulent as they are for the overlords' only heir. Glimmering, ever-polished mirrors on the walls, perfectly reflecting how the blood has entirely drained from my face. Metal shelves installed cleanly, embedded in the otherwise-stone walls, but not strong enough to hold the weight I now carry.

I collapse onto a vast double bed and stare, eyes heavy, up at the domed ceiling, painted like a brilliant twilight where the Shadowlands meets the Passage: swaths of hand-brushed purples, blues, and emeralds, hues befitting honored royalty soon to violently subjugate their own people.

When she lays her head down, I suppose Mother dreams of victory this cycle—of blue light flooding her veins and her eyes. I see only Isek's severed head, eyes wide and blind, spirit flayed clean of the flesh; but its mouth still moves, blue lips working, awful groans shuddering out.

It asks me why I did nothing.

I wake drenched from horns to toes in sweat, burdened with hideous knowledge: As the sole heir of my family's dynasty, I am the only one who can stop this. The only nightfolk strong enough to resist my parents' cruel rule. Likely the only one who even fully knows what's coming.

The last person to resist my parents was my uncle Azarii. Somewhere in the Depths, behind a wall of freezeshot, in a solitary hovel of the larger, labyrinthine Elysian structure, he's shriveling into nothing, imprisoned forever. Abandoned to the dauntless passage of time, which endures even beyond the old cycles of night and day. That could be my fate, too. A cell would be a mercy, really.

For Father's brother to betray his authority was one thing—first by defecting to Elysium, then by staging an armed rebellion—but Father's daughter? His only offspring, bearer of both his legacy and his shame that I was not born a son? I could face public execution. I wouldn't put it past him to tie me to the timekeeping torch and let all the Shadowlands hear my tormented screams as I burned down to memory and ash.

But if no one resists my parents, they'll lead us headlong into senseless slaughter. Destroy the planet we all call home in a cursed quest to fully claim it. If I don't act soon, it will be altogether too late. And the nightfolk will paint new borders for our kingdom with the blood of innocents.

I'm still struggling to breathe without escalating into a full-blown panic when there's a knock at my electronic door.

"My lord," says someone from the other side. "Your king has summoned you."

You mean my father, I could say, but more than that, first and foremost, Father has always been my king.

I press the heels of my hands into my eyes, groggy. "And who bears this message?"

"Isek."

All the breath rushes out of me in a single gust.

General Isek. The murdered child's father, not the child risen from the grave to confront my inaction. His voice drips apathy, colder even than the ice and stone that comprises the Shadowlands. I wonder if, beneath it, he yet grieves. Where is Isek now? Did Father honor his sacrifice at all, or is the mangled body in a ditch somewhere, abandoned to the creep of ice, the decay of time?

I promise myself it will not be for nothing.

"I'm on my way."

I throw on a fresh outfit, a traditional cloak of the nightfolk, allowing for ease of movement with varying limbs and wing structures. The Shadowlands leadership has no need for a fashionable signifier of status or power. The blood dried beneath my father's claws is enough; the quiet, razor-sharp threat on my mother's tongue is enough.

General Isek is shorter for a nightfolk, not even seven feet, but carries himself with poise that could never leave his dignity in doubt. His wings are folded neatly at his back like a fresh set of clean clothes. Everything about him in this moment portrays carefully constructed serenity. Beneath, I know in my heart that he must be screaming and screaming for his son until his voice, too, lies in an early grave.

I follow General Isek through the labyrinthine fortress's halls, despite knowing every path by heart. Where I imagine the dayfolk's underground hovels must be narrow and cramped, our obsidian halls are broad to accommodate nightfolk height and breadth. Banners of the same twilight shades that adorn my ceiling hang vertically at intervals, occasionally interrupted by braziers of blue flame conjured by our own gifts, tended periodically by the lowest-ranked soldiers.

Windows, though they would let starlight pervade the fortress, would simply be too great a security risk. To leave this place, one must either take flight from a parapet or exit through the main gate, to which we proceed now. The higher-ranked soldiers patrol on rotating cycles; we pass several on our way outside, though I don't make eye contact with any of them. I feel like my body is proceeding of its own accord.

I don't fully process what's happening until we're completely outside, bathed in refracted starlight from ice and stone, and Isek unfurls his wings, taking to the sky, nodding in the direction of Elysium.

The invasion is now. The execution of the cultists, the overcharge of our army. *Now.* No time to prepare, no stretch to consider the most effective way to stall or interfere, no readily available opportunity to plead with my father to reconsider. Rather than being gifted by the light, he is determined to consume it, to become it, alongside my mother. Together, they will inflict the full breadth of its barely contained wrath upon the dayfolk, for the sake of their own insatiable appetite for conquest.

"It's happening, isn't it?" I look to General Isek. I don't even have to say what.

Isek's eyes slide almost imperceptibly away from meeting mine. "I only wish my son could've seen it."

My throat constricts. "Did my father tell you what happened?"

"He died a hero," Isek says, onyx eyes faraway. "Pushed himself to the absolute limit of his youthful strength. Proved it was possible, but the Diakópsei overcame him."

I could tell him of the severed head, the squishy noise of its bounce, the strange angle at which it finally came to rest. But I won't take a hero's death from little Isek. It's what should've been; it's the only comfort his father has.

"I've planned a moment of honor for your son. If I'd known how soon the rest of the army was to be elevated, it would've been well prepared, but alas, this all happened too quickly. Would you forgive me if I flew on ahead, to make final preparations before the over-charge takes place?"

Isek's eyes flick sharply back to mine, pooling with what I can only read as barely repressed hope. Surely, even being ignorant of his son's true fate, Isek can't fully support this heinous escalation. Surely he wouldn't be the only soldier to stand against my parents' decision, if he knew others were willing to fight.

Isek finds his voice. "Does the king know?"

"Actually, it's to surprise him as well. I know he loved your son, too." The lie tastes like filth, but I swallow the revulsion just long enough for General Isek to bid me farewell.

I fly so fast that my wings sting with every beat, stretched thin as old parchment. Desperate to beat my parents to their intended prize, I plunge like a stone at the first sight of the pit. I land with such force, wings and arms splayed, that the chamber's walls rumble. Aboveground nightfolk were not expected here again. At once, hooded cultists materialize from the shadows, some bearing stone daggers, others armed with more advanced freezeshot pistols and freezeblades—all with shadowed eyes locked on me, wordlessly demanding an explanation.

"They're coming," I say.

"Who?" says a cultist, fingers hovering over their pistol's trigger.

I raise open palms toward the ceiling, a signal of peace. "My parents. The army. They were never going to be satisfied with one evolution, with one body. They intend to empower the entire army. Wipe out any of you who resist. Take that army to the Daylands, exert absolute authority over the planet. Please, you must understand—"

"So you came to warn us?"

My teeth worry at my lower lip. "A warning wouldn't be enough."

I hear the clicks of countless triggers ready to snap and unload freezeshot into my body, dropping me like a batbeast for this ill-advised intrusion. One Elysian lifts her voice. "Then what are you proposing?"

Briefly, I pause, considering what I'm about to do. There's no turning back from this. If I go through with my plan, I'm seizing my parents' title—and these Shadowlands—for myself. For little Isek, for the innocent dayfolk, and for every nightfolk soldier who would otherwise throw themselves into a useless war for endless conquest.

I don't want to hurt the people who made me. But I can't let them recklessly hurt everyone else. Molding our people into killing machines. Slaughtering a society that has left us in peace.

I suck in a deep, cold breath. Fill my lungs to bursting before I let it go. Then I summon every ounce of azure energy I can muster, a starburst of gifted power exploding out of me, blinding every cultist—and myself, too. I lunge sightlessly forward, barreling through shouting Elysians, hoping to the Beyond that my memory of the path to the Diakópsei is correct. More Elysians materialize out of corners and angles as I sprint, full throttle, but no one here was prepared for visitors. If my parents and the army had gotten here first, they would've made quick work of everyone. But I merely crash through every obstacle, slamming every cultist to the floor so that they might not pursue me. Some of them shriek when they land. I hope I haven't broken any innocents' bones, but I can't afford to be gentle right now if I'm going to reach my goal without being restrained.

No, what gentleness I have left in me, that which even my parents' harsh hands could never kill, has come here to die.

At long last, following the radiant asteroid's light, I stagger into the Diakópsei's host chamber. I stride forward as if confident, my gait unbroken, palms open, wings folded in resignation against my back, heart pounding through every inch of me. Only one thing can overpower a monstrous king.

A monster all the worse.

A scream in my throat, my own blood salty on my tongue, I throw my entire body upon the Diakópsei, embracing it with both hands, calling its power into myself. Blue light floods my vision. I collapse, and sharp rocks bite into my knees, but I barely register the pain. Impossible, supernatural strength courses like poison through my veins, the kind of cold that brings with it a vicious, cleansing burn. It burrows into the marrow of my bones, pumps my muscles to absurd proportions. I think there are Elysians behind me, terrified, shouting, but all I can clearly hear is my own voice, unmoored, screaming and screaming and screaming. The Diakópsei hears me, extends to me the purest gift, one my body can no longer refuse.

To save my planet, I will become even more inhuman than any nightfolk ever were.

Once upon a time,
the princess of shadow
became darkness itself.

CHAPTER 5

KORI

"Ready to—progress into—the Passage?" Aspect shrieks, as soon as I return to *Charon*. "The cake—gives strength. The cake—fuels—ADVENTURE!" Aspect waves their arms, violently enthused, before apparently recalling a contradictory memory from someone else. Their whole body freezes mid-flailing. "The Passage—dangerous—must exercise—precaution—"

I remember installing the memory in question. During a smuggling run, *Charon* flew above what I thought was a stranded Daylands traveler whose starship had malfunctioned. Instead, it was a recently deceased body.

Even through my anti-radiation gear, I felt waning warmth where blood had recently pulsed. It was an old man, pale, grizzled, with white-gray stubble scattered across a face that looked stern even in death. Quickly, and only with my hands, so as not to draw undue attention from sun serpents, I buried him in the sand, offered a moment of silence. But I also took his Morpheus sphere, where he'd deliberately stored his final memories.

I'd hoped to determine the man's cause of death via his last recollections, but what I found was that he'd done the unthinkable, even to a memory smuggler. He'd deliberately fled the Daylands, fixated on a supposed better life in the Shadowlands, where dayfolk are forbidden to tread. Above all other rules, licensed members of the Morpheus Market never fraternize with the denizens of the Shadowlands. Children of the light do not deign to dip even a toe into the dark.

Honestly, though, there are moments when I've wondered what it would feel like to be cast into boundless blackness and left to define yourself—absent your heritage, your settlement, even your former name, if you so willed.

This man died in the Passage as an enemy of the state, a potential shatter point for a fragile peace that has remained for generations. My mother, by necessity, would have branded him a traitor and seen the body incinerated, tossed into a trash chute and served to the magma like so many half-eaten ration sandwiches. Better for him to have gone missing. Better for his family to mourn whatever idea of his passing gave them the most peace.

But I kept the Morpheus sphere, if only for the flicker of purest fear that the man felt in its final recording. Aspect had leapt from an impossible height the day before, nearly snapping both their legs like ancient driftwood. I needed to teach them some degree of hesitance.

Apparently, all I'd taught Aspect of humanity was anxiety. I suppose that makes two of us.

"Hey," I say softly, the way Ednit speaks to me when I wake from frightening dreams on his examination table. I do a one-eighty with my spinning chair, before taking Aspect's metal hands in my own. "When I found that man in the Passage, when I scavenged his last moments for building you up, I did it to teach you caution. Not to make you afraid. You have nothing to be afraid of, Aspect. Not when I'm with you."

Aspect's visual processors flicker now, accompanied by a low whirring—another memory slotting into place.

"Kori will be—with Aspect—forever, correct?"

My flesh will decay. Aspect's mech body is quite literally fueled by Pagomènos's radioactivity, built to withstand the Daylands' savage heat waves and the inexorable passage of time alike. But I give their hand a squeeze. Their visual receptors hold my gaze without the slightest flicker. "Forever," I say.

"Affirmative?"

"Affirmative."

Briefly, I expect a human thank-you from my mechanical companion, but Aspect remains only a hodgepodge of pilfered human experiences. They straighten, whirring and beeping, and return to duty, at once a machine again. "Is Kori ready—to depart—into the Passage?"

I grin despite myself. Aspect isn't wrong about the dangers of the Passage, but I live for those moments between the two worlds of our divided planet. They're my only chances to make memories of my own.

"Lock in," I say, snapping my pilot's harness into place over my head. "I have a few new flight maneuvers I'd like to try today."

Another memory flickers across Aspect's body, indicated by a disconcerting collision of creaks and whirs. "If *Charon* spins—upside down—again, Kori—Aspect may—vomit—all over the shiny—cockpit."

Mechs don't vomit, and I installed that memory to excite Aspect about the thrills of aerial tricks, not the discomfort of stomach trouble. That's one memory I should definitely uninstall. But I don't tell Aspect that.

Instead, I imagine oil all over *Charon*'s viewport and laugh. "If you do, you're cleaning it up."

Then I reach forward to the main control panel, pulling the launch lever tight to my chest. In response, *Charon* seizes beneath me like a fossil drawing breath, twin engines bursting light against my mirrors, even brighter than the never-ending sun.

Aspect screams like a disconcerted microwave, frantically locking into the copilot restraints. A fraction of an instant later, the ship blasts into the stratosphere.

Storing my journey through the Passage as an autopilot path is risky, I know, and has the potential to expose my Morpheus Market membership to those other than Chloe and Ednit if ever my ship were investigated. That could create a whole convoluted mess for my mother to clean up, both burying knowledge of the Morpheus Market from the general public and concealing my own involvement in it. But no one looks twice at me. They look at my mother, resplendent in her governance gear, her outstretched arm like a promise to the dayfolk that we'll continue to survive.

So I leave the Passage route programmed, because at the halfway point, when my starship nearly breaches the planet's atmosphere, I can't resist the urge to look down at the graveyard of half-understood history.

The Passage isn't like the Daylands or the Shadowlands. The temperature is neither searing nor freezing; the light isn't blinding, but darkness's cloak doesn't reach this far. Really, in a better world, the Passage would be the ideal place for dayfolk and nightfolk to live, or at least to convene, in harmony. But that's the thing about limited resources. The nightfolk demanded it all for themselves, and now everyone has nothing.

Starships from before the Cataclysm lie beached, half buried in the Passage's endless sand, their paint slowly fading in the admittedly temperate sun. A wing juts free from the ground here; a stray control panel abandoned there; a shattered cockpit, its remaining transparent viewport like a monster's jagged teeth.

I gaze out the viewport and marvel at the skeletal remains of our once-mighty civilization. Thanks to the Territory Wars over the Passage, instigated by the nightfolk, Pagonians collectively wrecked our hopes of peacefully living in the only fertile land left. And our tech, whether lost in the war or destroyed at the Cataclysm's impact, will never be recovered, the recollection of its construction also subsequently lost.

Helical engines for hyperspace travel. Interstellar, galaxy-spanning comms for signaling Earth. Laser cannons, rifles, and pistols. Maybe even sentient AI. All sacrificed to our pride, our vanity, our insistence on being better than the other. Now we're trapped on a far-flung world in an unknown galaxy, unreachable by the planet our ancestors left, unable to venture beyond our atmosphere, left to struggle and squabble over what fragments of tech remain.

What I wouldn't give to go back in time, even for an instant. What I wouldn't offer to whatever distant deity watches over us, all for a chance at a world where possibilities still bloomed. I would leave this divided planet. I would leave my ever-watchful mother.

I don't know where I'd go, but I'd never come back.

In the copilot's seat, Aspect beeps cheerily. "Almost in—the dark place—Kori. Where the monsters—live."

"Don't say that," I say, my hands tightening around *Charon*'s controls, even though autopilot is engaged.

Aspect's optical processors blink. "Kori doesn't—fear—the shadow people."

"I have a purely scientific interest in them, alongside appropriate caution. I don't *feel* anything. Not even fear."

"Scientific—interest—in Aspect, too—Kori?"

I shake my head. "I care quite a bit about you."

"Who else—does Kori—care for?"

I take a sharp breath. This is why programming sentient AI is so strictly forbidden. Mechs exist to mine resources, traveling where humans fear to tread, serving as passionless emissaries between light and dark. A mech questioning my interpersonal relationships is unthinkable. I don't know if Aspect even knows what they're saying. But the question smacks me upside the head all the same.

"My mother." It tastes like a lie, sour, sticky sliding off my tongue. "I care for my mother."

"Why?"

I sigh. This will be the first of many questions. Grasping at human memories for the first time, Aspect is sometimes more like a toddler than anything else.

"Because she's my mother."

"Why?"

"Because she made me."

"Why?"

"I don't know." I stare out at the waves upon waves of abandoned sand. "Maybe because she was lonely."

"Like Kori—made Aspect?"

"Yes."

"Was Kori—lonely—before Aspect's making?"

I press my shoulders squarely into the back of my seat. "You ask too many questions."

Aspect leans back in their own chair. Their laser-like gaze flicks about the cockpit. "Aspect does not—compute—this caring. But Aspect thinks—if Aspect did—have caring—for Kori—it would not—be—because Kori—made Aspect."

I swallow a sudden lump in my throat. Maybe Aspect is closer to human intelligence than I've dared to hope. Either that, or their ability to mimic the remembered emotions I've implanted is becoming terrifyingly on point. "You don't know what you're talking about. Clearly I need to reboot your vocal box."

Aspect vigorously shakes their head. As if I hadn't spoken at all, they continue, "If Aspect—had caring—it would be—because—Kori had caring—for Aspect first."

"My mother cares for me."

"How?"

"In her own way."

"How?"

Words bubble up, unbidden, clogging my throat. My mother loves me by keeping me close to her chest, like an heirloom piece of jewelry.

My mother loves me by welding my feet to the floor. My mother loves me by ensuring that no one, least of all a dayfolk commoner, toys with the monarch's daughter's heart, even with platonic affection. My mother loves me by teaching me to love her back.

"Enough with the damn questions!" My own volume rattles me, quivering against my ribs. I smash my fist on the control panel, grateful that autopilot already disengaged the manual buttons. "She cares. She does."

Aspect holds my gaze with their visual receptors for a long moment. Then they spin the copilot's chair away from me. "Affirmative," they say to the wall. Their voice is always an inescapable monotone, but I swear it sounds more drained of feeling than ever.

I let out a long breath, shaking the sting out of my fisted hand. "I'm sorry."

The words feel utterly ridiculous as soon as they leave my mouth. This is what my life has come to, apparently. I've built a mech, originally meant for mining minerals or delivering packages, that instead wants to know about feelings and families and birthday cake recipes. And now I'm apologizing to it.

"What is—sorry?"

"Depends on who you ask." My mother, it would seem, believes that *sorry* is the salve that heals all wounds, no matter how many times the scab is torn back open. "I'd say it means I won't do it again."

"Raise—the volume—of vocalizations?"

"Yes."

"At Aspect?"

"Yes."

"For no—fault—of Aspect."

Now it's my turn to spin my chair away from the mech. "Rub it in, why don't you."

"Affirmative."

"When did I install a sarcastic memory into your mainframe?"

Aspect attempts a mechanical laugh. "Ha. Ha. Ha." They spin their chair back around, leaning forward to force eye contact. "Aspect learned—that—from Kori."

"Lovely."

"Affirmative."

A bright blue text message scrolls across *Charon*'s viewport. *NOW APPROACHING DESTINATION.*

I've missed my chance to lose myself in the ruins below, wondering what everyone's old lives were like. But it's probably for the best. I switch *Charon* back to manual control.

In the distance, beyond the deserted expanse we've just traveled, loom the stark black mountains and towers of the Shadowlands, their edges gleaming an eerie azure. Here, the radiation that drove the dayfolk underground thrives, unchecked. There, what my people call the kiss of death has imparted an unnatural, new sort of life.

But directly below us, well concealed by the ever-shifting sands, visible only to the well-trained eye, is the entrance to the Morpheus Market.

Easing onto the landing pedal, I simultaneously tap out the code for a dispersal signal and pull the release lever down from above my head. The dispersal signal is a sonic wave, beyond the pitch of human hearing, enough to at least briefly repel any nearby mutated predators of the Passage.

The ground rumbles as nearby sand serpents scatter, their bodies even longer than *Charon*'s wingspan. I hear howls, snarls, and snuffling as various misshapen beasts flee, their heads like Earthside dogs, their bodies mostly limbs like overgrown insects. The viewport briefly darkens as winged creatures also take flight, their guttural cries rumbling through the ship. Their open beaks are packed with teeth, and though they lack seeing eyes, I swear their milky-white pupils lock with mine before they vanish along the horizon.

Charon settles soundlessly, set to autopilot a simple orbit as soon as we disembark. I cut the engines and nod to Aspect, who knows the drill.

"Armor, Kori," they say, reminding me to activate the collapsed pieces around my body, from the heavy filtration helmet to the ribbed boots.

This armor protects me from so much more than the surface's high temperatures. If the atmosphere ever touched me, through even the slightest fissure in my gear, I'd be infected with Pagomènos's radiation, never to be the same. With exposure that direct, I would be doomed to die, possibly mutating along the way into something not unlike the toothy birds or oversized snakes of the Passage. An animal, without thought or conscience.

Unlike the colony we call home, the Morpheus Market doesn't purge all radiation despite being so deep underground. No one is entirely certain if it's because the expense would be too great or because requiring protective gear further ensures anonymity of buyers and sellers.

Absently, I feel for the heatshot pistol at my waist. Once initial laser weaponry was lost to the Cataclysm, the Pagonians had to improvise. Dayfolk designed heatshot weapons to be continually powered by the Daylands' brutally hot atmosphere, rather than relying on bullets. More advanced than Earthside weapons, but weaker than what ought to have been. Quite the metaphor for life on this forsaken planet, honestly.

Charon slows its movement, the exit ramp extending to release us before the starship enters patient orbit around the lift. Aspect follows me to the ground and toward the faint circular outline of an entrance. I slip one hand into my pocket, retrieving my coveted individual-access card, and wave it over the silhouette. The ground shudders and bucks. Aspect stumbles, but I stand tall, smiling behind my helmet, never so alive anywhere else.

If this were any other rote assignment, I would chafe against the concept of returning so soon after my last visit, but this is the Morpheus Market. My memory runs may be sanctioned by Chloe, but this is one place where she has no control over what else I do. What I learn. Who I meet. What I allow myself to imagine I become.

Somewhere amidst these competing vendors, hidden innocuously amidst forgettable wares, there must be a memory that can awaken Aspect's sentience. I may officially be here on government business, but that boring chore isn't what accelerates my heartbeat to a gallop as the door in the floor hisses open, unveiling the market's entrance lift. I take Aspect by the hand and step onto the panel, squaring my shoulders, taking and holding a deep, deliberate breath. *This time.* Surely this time, I'll take one step closer to achieving my real goal: finding the right shard of human experience to imbue a robot with a soul.

If only I knew what to look for.

For an instant, as the lift lowers us into the elevator shaft, we're coated in complete darkness. Then circles of lights illuminate all around us, blinking from top to bottom of the elevator chamber.

"Welcome, Monarch," the security voice intones. The elevator drops into an immediate descent so fast that my stomach threatens to hop into my throat.

The elevator then stops almost as sharply. "Welcome to the Morpheus Market." The door slides open, and Aspect toddles after me as the hustle and bustle of memories bought and sold absorbs us once again.

I never know what memories for Aspect might catch my eye. Or Aspect's simulated eyes, for that matter. On one memorable journey, I had to practically drag Aspect by one leg away from a booth dedicated to, shall we say, *adult* memories, as Aspect riddled me with unwanted questions about intimacy and bondage.

This robot has more than enough idiosyncrasies without introducing queries like, "Kori, what is *horny*?" The question very nearly made me trip and fall on my face at the time. I very nearly said something about Hyrra's careful hands tinkering with the mechs. But I caught myself.

On this visit, on the second floor, Aspect fixates on something else entirely. A shimmering pink sign that says, SEA MEAT. Being a mech,

Aspect can't taste or smell, so the prospect of recalled food carries much more significance for them. The memory carries a low credit cost, too; the dayfolk colony breeds fish in an artificial environment without much difficulty.

I can't imagine who, besides Aspect, would consider this memory valuable or notable. Seafood definitely won't be a human experience that rattles Aspect's artificial brain into realizing they are a person having an independent, autonomous, meaningful experience of being alive. But I can't say no to those pleading optical processors, so I scan my card and make the purchase with standard credits, hushing Aspect all the while.

Bringing a modified mech for security or assistance purposes is normal in the Morpheus Market. The mech personally requesting a simulated experience with seafood is . . . not. Better not to draw undue attention to ourselves, and better to entertain Aspect while I keep my eyes open for the truly right memory.

Like bribing a toddler with sugar, I promise Aspect they can access the sea meat memory when we return to *Charon*, but only if they behave. That means no more loud questions about human mating rituals in public, not gripping my hand tightly enough to threaten the integrity of my fingers, and staying close at all times, ridiculous runway gait be damned.

Aspect nods eagerly as we turn away from the booth. I can't help but sigh and shake my head, even though my frustration isn't with them. "Always the same," I mutter to myself, under my breath. "Food. Fistfights. Songs. Sex." I pinch the bridge of my nose. "I need something *else*." But I have no idea what, not in the slightest idea.

For all I know, the barrier to Aspect's awakening could be not the absence of something, but the *presence* of a memory I've already installed. And what would I do then? Uninstall it? Deprive them of an experience I already offered as a gift, which has become their own? That would make me no better than the planet's radiation.

And I've tried—oh, how I've tried, on every ill-fated visit here—asking vendors for something weird, something different, something positively *odd*. But it always results in obvious discomfort and confusion from the vendor, who often stares at me like I tried to order a sandwich at a memory store. Sometimes they believe that I'm seeking rightfully illegal, exploitative, or heinously violent material, which I most definitely do *not* want (and have reported to the Coalition when necessary). Once the hopelessly awkward conversation is over, I have to run along, before I raise so much suspicion about my true motives that I get *myself* reported.

"Something *else*." I grunt, my footsteps unnecessarily heavy as we trudge away from this useless, useless Sea Meat booth.

At the corner of my eye, at the very edge of my peripheral vision, I think I see . . . a smudge? A splatter of ink, forming and re-forming. But as soon as I look, the shape is gone. My exasperation is veering into hallucination at this point. Is that what it will take to awaken Aspect? A final step over the edge, into a proper evil scientist?

Our path to the elevators and down to the third floor is a blur, my mind elsewhere. Eventually, we reach my mother's memory vendor. Aspect tugs pleadingly at my elbow throughout the entire transaction. If their optical processors could widen, they'd be round wheels of hope right now. "Sea meat soon, Kori?"

"Soon." I pat them on the head briefly.

My attention is painfully split. After the odd recollection of Jelza I experienced, I can't help but wonder what this new Morpheus sphere contains that my mother could want. I'm also half-feral with the desire to find a properly unique, mechanically significant memory to install in Aspect. And mild annoyance at this entire sea meat diversion still simmers underneath my skin.

I pocket the Morpheus sphere for my mother, waving Aspect away from the vendor's booth.

That's when another shadow moves.

It's distinct this time, far from an imaginary ink splatter. My peripheral vision distinguishes something akin to limbs. With my pulse pounding in my temples, my hand flies automatically to the heatshot pistol at my waist. "Who's there?"

A voice like oil speaks from everywhere and nowhere at once. "Not here."

A whirl of . . . fabric? The wave of a hand? Something directs me toward an accidental alleyway, wedged between two memory booths—just barely wide enough to allow two or three bodies to squish in and have a less-than-public conversation.

"Kori . . . ?" Aspect's voice is an uncommon squeak.

Against my better judgment, I take one of their hands between both of mine, lean close to their auditory processor, and command, in the firmest voice I can muster, "Stay close."

Together, we step backward into the alleyway. One step from the crowd, two, three. The miasma of conflicting voices from the crowd steadily shrinks. Even the light from the competing booths dims, distancing. Everything tunnels. I keep my eyes firmly on the main market, ready to bolt back toward public view the instant it's necessary, but even so, almost of their own accord, my legs keep carrying me farther back into this accidental wedge of space, farther and farther from the sales floor.

A secret place within a secret market. Only I could get myself into a jam this absurd.

"Further in," the oil-slick voice says, somewhere close. "Further up, and further in."

Back and back, farther and farther, my legs lead us. My heartbeat is an emergency siren, nearly splitting my rib cage wide open. I should have a hand on my heatshot pistol, but I can't bear to let go of where Aspect's metal fingers are squished securely between all of mine. Back and back and back. The market is a faraway smear of color. I know we've reached the complex's wall only because it's terribly cold when it presses against my back.

"Here," hisses the voice, and if I squint, I can just barely make out the spidery outline of a person.

Hunched, slightly shivering, cowering even in the near darkness of this clandestine alleyway. Layers of mismatched clothes—deep greens, faded maroons, patches of yellow, and threadbare blue—conceal whatever anti-radiation gear they must be wearing underneath. It all grants them the appearance of a secondhand clothing shop come to life, bumbling about on its first day of improbable sentience.

"Your hand, darling."

Aspect, ever courageous in the face of absurdity, pipes up, "The market—does not—sell hands."

For an instant, I think my limb is indeed the price for whatever ware this stranger is about to offer. Then a shuddering gloved hand extends toward me, fingers pinching something tightly between them. "Open your hand."

Barely breathing, I extend one open palm, the other still gripping Aspect's so tightly that every metal joint digs painfully into my skin. A tiny rectangle drops into my gloved hand, somewhere between the size of a fingernail-sized Morpheus chip and a handheld credit card.

"You seek a memory, of another kind." The voice is thick. It sticks to the inside of my skull, makes me want to gag. I swallow a surge of sick. "If you mean what you said, and I think most people mean the things they say, when they think no one else is listening, then that"—one gnarled finger taps the rectangle in my palm—"is my card."

"You have nothing to sell?" My voice is a sudden, stubborn half snarl.

This feels, as strange as it all is, like the closest I've ever gotten to a special, specific, impossible memory—the kind that could bring Aspect into full awakening—and now all I have is a dusty gremlin's business card?

"You, a stranger, haul me into an alley. I follow, against my better judgment. And the best you can do, for my taking this risk with my mech in tow, and with only a simple pistol to protect myself, is your *card*?" I close my fist around the meager offering, my voice rising despite myself. "Who are you? What's your code name? Where is your license—?"

But all at once, there's an explosion of thick white smoke. My knees sting; I've collapsed, coughing, retching. Actual sickness threatens at the cloying chemical smell that ensconces me—a terrible experience to have while wearing a sealed anti-radiation helmet. Darkness flickers across my gaze.

The next thing I register, Aspect is shaking me with all the force their mechanical arms can muster. Then straight-up kicking one knee into my gut. "Kori. Kori. *Kori.* KORI. *KORI.*"

Choking on a mouthful of spit, I come fully back to myself. With effort, I pull my body back up to standing. "How long . . . ?"

But Aspect has already retrieved my comms tablet from my utility belt, wildly tabbing through its various applications with both hands until the digital hourglass appears. The sand is far emptier than it was when I arrived at the Morpheus Market. But if we hurry, we can still make it home before suspicions are raised.

"Home," Aspect pleads. "Aspect takes Kori—home to the sands—before Kori's maker—wants to unmake."

Numbly, I feel for the Morpheus sphere at my belt, the one my mother requested. It remains nestled comfortably in my pocket. So, too, my heatshot pistol remains sheathed at my side. My credit card is where I left it. My armor is unbroken in any way, protecting me from Pagonian radiation. What did this gremlin want, if they didn't even take anything? Their tiny business card lies discarded, just barely visible in the half-light, at Aspect's feet. I must have dropped it after the smoke bomb. Gritting my teeth, I snatch the card up and pocket it before I can think better of the decision.

This strange, undeniably risky encounter can't have been for nothing. If this card can open a path to Aspect's awakening . . . that's worth any risk. Scientific breakthroughs have never been made by playing it safe. No matter what happens next, I need to know that, given the opportunity, I was willing to try. I was willing to fight my good sense for a shot at something greater.

"Come on," I say, nudging Aspect back toward the distant light of the still-teeming, never-sleeping market. "*Charon*'s waiting."

Sure enough, Aspect and I are soon safely ensconced in *Charon* once again, my anti-radiation gear collapsing to smaller pieces at once. Somehow, despite Aspect's eager bouncing on their metal toes, I manage to buckle them into the copilot's seat. "And here you go," I say, pulling their new sphere from my pocket. "One sea meat memory for the best mech I know."

Aspect squeals. "Install now, Kori?"

A human can access a Morpheus memory and at least vaguely recall it later, despite the cognitive distance. Installation to their own internal Morpheus chip—a process that requires sedation and hands-on tinkering by a professional like Ednit—is only necessary to be able to access the fully detailed, lifelike memory at a moment's notice, anytime, anywhere. But for Aspect, short-term memory is a precarious region in constant development. Another's memory, experienced at a distance, dissipates almost immediately, like a wisp of fading smoke.

"I'll install it back home," I offer.

"Why not now?"

Because I am too tired to hold a conversation, and letting you watch this thing over and over instead of retaining it should keep you from pestering me with existential questions. "Because I said so," I mutter, sounding like my mother and immediately hating myself. Nobody ever said that parenting an illegally semi-sentient mech would be easy, I suppose.

I can only imagine the conniption Chloe would have if she knew what I'd really been plotting in the Morpheus Market. Imbuing metal with being . . . it's unthinkable. I already feel like I'm reporting to a parole officer anytime my homework is late. If Chloe found out I'd been dropping pieces of personhood into glorified mining equipment? I might find myself tied to a rusty chair with nothing but an algebra notebook to keep me company until I died of sheer boredom.

I set the sea meat Morpheus sphere to test mode, accessible at anyone's touch, and leave Aspect to access it repeatedly. Which I know is happening not only from the tiny flashing light on the sphere each time it's activated, but from Aspect's renewed shriek of delight at every go-around.

Exhausted from the entire gremlin-merchant ordeal in the alleyway, I set *Charon* to autopilot us back to the settlement. My eyes remain heavy, my wrist sore from Aspect's perpetual nervous hold, my lungs uneasy from the smoke bomb. I could sleep on the trip instead of just waiting to return home. But my mind races even behind closed eyes, scattered thoughts darting through my consciousness. What did that mysterious merchant really want? Could they eventually provide me with a memory capable of awakening Aspect's sentience? And what sort of memory did my mother send me to retrieve this time around, anyway?

I should've known that snooping on Chloe's memory sphere would never be an isolated incident. Now my whole body craves knowledge, if only because it's forbidden. Huffing out a breath, I seize Chloe's new sphere from its pouch at my waist and press an open palm to its surface.

"Test," I blurt before I can think better of it.

And I dive, the memory closing over and around me.

Nothing hurts.

Everything *hurts.*

I curl one finger inward at a time, until my right hand (not my hand) is firmly balled into a trembling fist, attached to a trembling arm that feels like it belongs to someone else. I clench harder to still the shaking, and my nails bite into my palm. It bleeds; why does it bleed?

"Is it not brilliant?" the doctor says, from somewhere behind me, from another world entirely.

I uncurl the fist. I reach up and thread my fingers instead through perfectly woven braids, not a hair out of place, as gorgeous a crown as I've ever had. A crown from someone else's kingdom. An obligation I am only now beginning to fully comprehend.

My queen chose me for this, the highest of honors. I should be proud beyond words. I should be leaping, dancing, alight with the fervor of youth, but I feel numb all over.

"Jelza?" the doctor says, and my name might as well be a foreign language.

I don't look at him. Instead I cast my gaze down, at the handheld mirror on the rolling table. I lift it, and I look, and the reflection is me, and not me. Will I ever not lurch, as if sighting a poltergeist, when this woman blinks slowly back at me from beyond the glass? Will Dawn—

"I want to see my daughter." My voice; not my voice.

"I'm afraid that is unadvisable, so soon."

Again my hand becomes a fist. I press it against the wall—no, I launch *it like a killing blow, and the wall crumbles in on itself, the indentation of my knuckles pressed unflinchingly into the metal.*

"Appropriate limitations, to prevent rapid wear and tear, take time to become active, I'm afraid," the doctor says. "And the pain receptors—"

Pain. Oh, the pain. It seizes upon me all at once. I'm on one knee, clutching my hand, tears in my eyes. It isn't broken; it should be.

If I'm unbreakable now, why do I feel so broken anyway?

"—take time to recognize those limitations," the doctor finishes, matter-of-fact, like he's talking about filing financials.

I clutch my gorgeously, hideously unbroken hand to my chest, over the place where my heart roars and roars its too-late warning. I stare, wordless, again at the mirror. Alert brown eyes, rimmed with thick lashes. My braids, my deep brown skin, the strong curves of my cheeks and jaw and lips.

I don't know her.

Will my daughter know this face? Can I wipe her tears away with this hand? Dawn, Dawn, I named you for beginnings in a world long dead, for light breaking golden and unstoppable across a velvet black sky. Is this a beginning? Do I even want to see it through to the end? Do I have a choice?

Somehow, my voice still emerges clear as crystal. "What have I become?"

"Only what you volunteered to become, Jelza."

"I want to see my daughter." The room shimmers and blurs. Everything tastes like salt. I hurt and I hurt and it isn't pain, and it's never ever going to stop. Eternal midnight, thick as the Shadowlands could ever be, opens in my chest like a sinkhole pit, ready to swallow me alive, bones and all. "Please, please," I'm pleading, tears streaking this other Jelza's cheeks, her lips quivering, her composure unwoven entirely, "I want to see my daughter."

I jerk back into myself so abruptly that my head smarts where it smacked the seat. *Jelza.* The same woman, again. And with Ednit. He knows more about this than he ever let on. I don't understand anything about what I just saw. What sort of procedure did Jelza undergo? Some sort of experimental limb replacement? Had her arm been in an accident? Been suffering from a progressive disease? Prosthetics would hardly be new tech in the Daylands, but one so visually convincing at first glance would be a breakthrough, right down to still drawing blood at the prick of her nails. But then, why was she so distressed? Does the body reject this advanced prosthetic like a stranger's mismatched organ?

And why remove the memory? Was this new limb tech so advanced, so wildly experimental, that even the recollection of it had to be hidden as scientific research toward perfecting it continued? Then perhaps Chloe lost track of it in a mishap, and it found its way to the open market, from which I needed to retrieve it. Or was Jelza's haunting distress so intense that she removed this memory independently and sold it to get it as far away from herself as possible? Chloe has eyes everywhere; she could easily have found out about such a thing, ordering me to retrieve the memory. Regardless of how it ended up in the Morpheus Market, why was ending its circulation so critical? I don't know what I expected to unearth in Chloe's Morpheus sphere, but it most definitely wasn't this.

"This makes no damn sense," I mutter.

Unconsciously, I look to Aspect, uselessly hoping for an expression of understanding. It's a pointless exercise given that A) Aspect's face is locked in a singular expression, complete with a slightly crooked mouth, courtesy of my negligible art skills, and B) Aspect is presently experiencing their new fishy memory for at least the eleventh time.

I sigh, throwing my head back against the padded pilot's seat, eyes sliding shut. Not knowing things makes me itchy all over. Sleep creeps at the edges of my mind, pressing in like a soft blanket, and briefly, despite myself, I almost drift. Then a persistent beeping startles me fully awake. In a pocket of my utility belt, something is vibrating so violently that it hurts my hip bone. Is my comms tablet having a digital seizure? Am I losing my grip on reality from all these recent dives into other people's memories? I fumble in the pocket, but it's not the one that contains my comms tablet at all.

It's the pocket where I stashed the gremlin's business card.

The card, incessantly shuddering, continues to freak out once I have it back in my hands, but it doesn't appear to have any sort of interactable interface. Unless . . .

I tear off my gloves, safe from the planet's radiation within *Charon*, and press one warm, open palm directly to the card's surface. It unfolds like an alien origami flower, the pistil emanating a pulsing emerald glow.

For an instant of purest terror, I fear I've been foolish enough to willingly accept a bizarre bomb. I contemplate crushing the false business card in my fist and lobbing it out the nearest trash chute to rot in the Passage below. Then the emerald sheen intensifies, thin lines like pollen rising from the pistil until they coalesce into a creature's cloaked shape.

Not a human. At least, not anymore. While it's impossible to identify colors from a purely green hologram, the depicted stranger's skin is drawn tightly across thick, punchy muscles. They have horns, but small ones, barely visible through the sheet of long wavy hair that descends past their shoulders—and by shoulders, I very much mean the plural. Six arms, with no sign of any legs. A tail, too, extends past the spine, laced all around with spikes. A single eye in the center of the face looks out at me.

A voice, filtered so severely as to be unidentifiable, hisses through the device's static. The only clear distinction I can make is that by the pitch and intonation, it's likely a woman. "Hello, Monarch."

Pagonians don't have holographic one-to-one communications, which means this must be pre-recorded. But even so, hearing my code name directly from this increasingly weird gizmo sends a chill down my spine. I almost drop the device entirely, steadying one of my wrists with the other.

"Who are you—?" I start, despite myself, as the recording continues to speak over me, unbothered.

"Your people use code names for transactions such as this," says the hologram, the image hissing and spitting between syllables, brightness flickering in and out like a market sign with a dying battery. Even so, I can tell it's not the same voice as the gremlin I encountered in the Morpheus Market. No, they were only my entry point into something far more complicated. "So you may call me *Alpha*."

Most code names are more memorable, based upon former Earthside animals, bits of barely remembered geography, or what few historical figures we've preserved on Pagomènos. But I suppose the first of an ancient alphabet is suitable enough.

"I seek a memory," the stranger—Alpha—says, "of the Daylands sun. And I suspect you seek a memory of another kind, another perspective. One that you will never find in the Morpheus Market. A moment as the *other*, that your people barely dare to fathom. A memory of the nightfolk."

My heart leaps, my stomach dropping at the same time, dizziness overtaking me. Alpha might as well have offered me a compass that doesn't point north, a smell I could hear, a word in a language spoken only between constellations. *A memory of the nightfolk.* Such a thing has never been done, *should* never be done, to a degree so much more severe than my experiments with Aspect, it threatens to make me nauseous. How would a nightfolk even remove and encapsulate a memory, without a dayfolk Morpheus chip in their head? How is this even happening?

And why, despite the floor seemingly spinning beneath my feet, do I know for certain that my stubborn hope is about to pummel my fear in a fight?

"When you are ready"—the confidence of *when*, not *if*, is staggering, but I suppose I've already fallen interminably far from the Coalition's grace—"meet me by the Triple Crown, at the base of the Second Spire."

Swearing, I bring a closed fist down on my knee. If this Alpha wanted to blackmail me, they already have everything they need to present me as untrustworthy to the Coalition and revoke my Morpheus Market license . . . or worse.

"I give you my word, all will be secret, and all will be as promised," Alpha's recording says. "I swear it on all I still hold sacred—on my brother's blood, on my own beating heart."

Two of the six arms pause over the creature's heart, and my own skips a beat. Nothing could've properly prepared me for sincerity, family bonds, and emotional assurances from those I've always been told are little more than animals, their humanity swallowed up by the Diakópsei entirely.

A one-way communication with the Shadowlands is marginally better than if I could talk back right now. Conducting memory trades over private channels risks exposing the Morpheus Market's existence to the general (largely unlicensed) populace, drawing attention (and swift retribution) from the Coalition. Communicating with the Shadowlands at *all* is just straight-up illegal. That's how you end up like the body I found in the Passage, abandoned to unknowable time and endless, endless sand.

And if my fraternization with a nightfolk were discovered by my mother, and the settlement's government at large . . . math homework for eternity. And, well, possibly calling the legitimacy of Chloe's entire ruling dynasty into question, which wouldn't be fun either.

But I still accepted this card from the gremlin. I'm still listening, intently, to Alpha's recording. This unexpected contact from the planet's night side only deepens my hunger to know more.

I can't deny the desire to experience the planet's forbidden side through equally forbidden eyes. And what if this is *it*? The answer I've been desperately searching for? It may be an unholy thought, twisting my stomach into knots, but dayfolk memories alone haven't been enough to awaken Aspect into sentience. A piece of the alternate experience, the counterpart mindset, could unlock a whole new branch of perspective. Maybe enough to authentically *be*, rather than merely mimic. Enough for Aspect to begin to *become* of their own volition.

I glance at my mechanical friend. They've grown bored of the sea meat memory, but now they clutch the Morpheus sphere against the metal plating of their chest, rocking it protectively back and forth, guarded against any potential bumps and jolts in *Charon*'s flight path. It looks almost like a mother cradling her child, but I know better. It's the echo of an installed memory from me, when I nearly broke my data tablet by tripping on a floor panel. Nothing organic yet. Nothing original.

But this could change that.

"I will greet you by code name," Alpha says. "The exchange will be done in a breath. And you can return to your sun, one shadow memory richer."

I huff out a long breath, pushing the mounting anxiety out of my lungs. This is a once-in-a-lifetime chance to turn my mechanical project into a living, thinking friend. The first, longest, and best friend I've ever had.

I know it's a one-way recording; I know Alpha can't hear me. But even so, leaning so close to the hologram that my breath fogs the jittery display, I say, with my heart in my throat, "Yes."

And just like that, the flower, wilting, its purpose complete, curls back into a tiny flat rectangle that lies lifeless in my open palm. I close my fingers around it and hold it close, not unlike Aspect and their sphere. For the first time in so long, awakening Aspect to proper awareness feels wildly possible. A friend, with fears and dreams and needs of their own making. A friend, beyond my mother's oversight.

"Aspect?" I chirp.

Their head pivots, ever-so-briefly distracted from the Morpheus sphere. Optical processors blink and whir. "Yes, Kori?"

A wicked smile curls my lips. "We're going on another adventure."

CHAPTER 6

ADRIA

I don't know how many sleeps it's been since the burial, but I still feel the blood on my hands, sticky and viscous, whenever I dream. My claws at Father's throat, my voice an animal bellow. *I won't let you make monsters of us all.* If I must become a monster to stop a legion . . . so be it.

But I only ever meant to undercut their twisted dreams, not snuff out their very lives.

The strength granted by the Diakópsei was more than I could've ever fathomed, more than my merely mortal frame could contain. I tried to silence my father's voice, and beneath my tremulous grip, I felt the last breath shudder out of him. Raised a hand to stop my mother from also charging the asteroid, pushed her back with the barest reserve of my newfound might, only to feel her skull splinter in my palm like a boiled eggshell.

I set out to stop my parents from committing mass murder. In the process, I murdered them both.

Every time I dare to sleep, I replay the fractured, terrible moment. I wake sweat soaked, wings rigid, spine coiled to spring, like a child who imagined a spirit lurking in the shadows. My radiation-mutated dog, Russ, is the only one who dares to stay close, never once recoiling from the awful sounds my mouth has learned to create.

The Elysians demanded Isek's execution immediately upon his overcharge. But Isek was a child, unable to bear the breadth of his newfound power, a plausible threat to everyone around him. Perhaps he could've been calmed, trained, his impulses contained—but as the Elysians saw it, that would never have outweighed the risk.

Meanwhile, my first act upon overcharge—even with my vision overtaken by azure, even overcome by power clearly never meant for mortal flesh—was to fight off the soldiers my parents sent marching on Elysium. Without me, the place would have been ash by the time the timekeeping torch burned low once again. Without me, the nightfolk army would've collectively seized the asteroid's power and immediately wrought needless warfare in the Daylands, too.

So I may be an apostate to Elysium—an aberration, an abomination, who dared to look upon a stony god with an unveiled face. But it was my hands that guarded the Depths' mouth, my jagged teeth that tore through what soldiers were unwilling to fall back, my blasts of gifted energy that blinded anyone else who dared make a run for the Diakópsei's chamber. So Elysium is content to call me a dark disciple. A redeemed sort of demon.

I should not exist, but if I didn't, neither would they.

It was not a clean battle. The blood lingered under my clawed nails for too many washings, the dust and rubble in my lashes and eyebrows and the wild, increasingly overgrown curls of my hair. The soldiers fell back. Some, stubbornly loyal to my parents even after witnessing their last stand, fled to recoup, needing a new leader. Others, seeing that I had stopped a needless march on the sunlit lands, laid down their weapons and pledged allegiance at my feet.

Somehow, as my world descends into chaos, my first ally is the cloistered cult that my parents, and their parents, for generations back, made every effort to avoid. It is, in fact, Er, who witnessed Isek's execution, who tells me with tremulous breaths that after sifting through the carnage, clearing collapsed tunnels, and honoring the dead as best they could, they found one body unaccounted for.

My uncle Azarii, his cell unlocked from the outside. By whom, nobody seems to know.

In the following sleep cycles, my scouts report scattered outposts appearing beyond our fortress proper, taking full advantage of the near-total darkness beyond the torch's reach to scurry away and regroup. When will the remaining rebels attack? Where? In what numbers? The details elude my regiment, but one name appears with terrifying certainty in messages from the front: Azarii, their proud leader.

Ever the fanatic, Azarii reportedly cares little that by overcharging myself, I singlehandedly saved Elysium (and likely the Daylands, too). By drawing the Diakópsei's unfiltered glory into myself, I committed a mortal sin in his eyes. And I slayed my own parents in the process—something Azarii once attempted himself, but still finds is excellent propaganda to rally a rebellion.

Despite my stated goals of peace, despite sending soldiers to aid Elysium in locking down the Diakópsei, despite my desperation to never allow another overcharge . . . according to Azarii, I cannot be trusted to lead the Shadowlands. So, in a cruel twist of fate, my parents' loyalists side with the man who once sought to personally usurp them. He promises them that only by overthrowing me—the ultimate symbol of violence and slaughter—can the Shadowlands see peace.

No one calls to invade the Daylands anymore. Nevertheless, in the name of peace, we are killing one another.

There is no coronation for me. There is no need of it. I returned to the fortress, caked in crimson, gleaming azure, battered and bruised and gasping for air through my own horror—even more powerfully built than I already had been, my body screaming, visibly racked with spasms of heretofore unfathomable power—and with soldiers carrying my parents' mangled bodies in tow. My word was immediately law, written in spilled blood.

The soldiers who didn't defect to Azarii swore their loyalty to me, on their knees before their new lord, heads bowed low in deference. Among them, General Isek, whose son I utterly failed, whose trust I will never deserve.

Accessing the Diakópsei is again forbidden, as it always ought to have been, with a constant rotating guard of both Elysians and my own allied soldiers placed over it. Isek leads the guard himself. I do not tell him of the sounds, the blood. Out of shame, and to my shame, I don't even tell him that I was present as a witness, that I could've stopped everything before a child paid the price. But when I finish explaining, Isek knows enough of what became of his son. He vows that never again will anyone recklessly touch the Diakópsei on his watch.

My army sees my suffering with every breath I take. They believe, wholeheartedly, that I would only ever have become this—only ever have done what I've done to the very people who made me—as a desperate act to prevent further atrocities.

My scouts report that somewhere beyond the fortress, in his speckled rebel camps, Azarii tells his rebels, by the light of their little campfires, in furtive but furious whispers, that I have merely become that which I swore to destroy.

I bury Father and Mother without ceremony or fanfare, maybe a quarter mile from my fortress, surrounded by an overgrowth of charred, leafless trees. The torch's cyclical light casts strange, ever-shifting, spidering shadows through the dead branches. To cement my rule, my parents are formally branded as traitors to our people, reckless warmongers rather than wise guides. No one else is allowed to see the grave site. I visit alone, too enraged to cry, too grief-stricken to slash the titles from the headstones.

Why was a child's life not enough? Why was my body, mutilated by raw, boundless strength, not enough? Why was it not enough when Father fell and ceased to breathe? Why Mother, too? Why by my hand?

Why was this the price of preventing a planetary war between light and dark?

I barely close my eyes anymore. When I do, it's beside the graves: twin metal tablets, severe in their simplicity, utterly identical save for the engraved designations of *Father* and *Mother*. Time passes, uncertain, in eternal nights unbroken by day. I lose track of the torch's lighting, burning, and relighting. My own heart burns within me without relent. When I eat, it's often followed by sickness. When I sleep, it's always followed by nightmares.

I am a queen in name, but it's really the Shadow Court who delivers my orders: a circle of our wisest politicians and fiercest generals, deferent only to me, enacting my will upon my people. And my will is absolute, in the eyes of those people. Yet I fear I have become an animated corpse. I fear Azarii and his rebels are right—that a creature such as I should never have been allowed to exist. But what was the alternative? A religion wholesale slaughtered? A sunlit society invaded? A planet overtaken by unfeeling strength above all else?

I carry impossible amounts of muscle in every limb now, but I feel like a clattering collection of confused bones, staggering from moment to moment, eye sockets hollow, jaw working without language, wondering why I'm still alive at all. The first time I see my own reflection in my chamber's many mirrors, I howl like an animal and shatter them all.

One of Russ's heads bites at my cheeks, the second ruffling my hair, the third licking at my eyes and mouth to bring me back to myself, but I hardly even know who that is. My attendants feed him, bathe him, fill his water dishes, brush his thick obsidian fur. I don't even care for myself. My hair is greasy, longer than I've allowed in ages, brushing the tops of my ears; my skin is caked in sweat and what dried blood has refused to fully fade. All my words become sobs become screams become strangled shudders of air. Only to eat and drink does the dog leave me. I kiss every single one of his heads and hold them close to my chest when the night terrors always, always come back.

What arrives when I wake is all the worse.

I'm kneeling beside my father's grave, my horns pressed to the cold metal tablet, when the shooting starts.

It's a low rumble at first, standard Earthside weapons, just common bullets rattling against my fortress's impenetrable stone walls. Then the noise becomes punctuated with punches of hissing power—the advanced freezeshot blasters of the nightfolk—and I know I can't stay.

I trace each letter of my parents' engraved names with a single claw. *Father. Mother.* The words are trapped in my throat. Every open wound on my body pulses like a heartbeat. My rolling rage is so fierce that if I could find my voice, it would only rise into a roar.

Another freezeshot sounds, ricocheting off the fortress's stone gate.

I will bring honor back to our line, I silently swear, standing, eyes steady on the graves. I spread my wings, their span even greater than my eight feet of height. They block the blue torch that blazes behind me, casting my immediate path into absolute dark. It's all right; my eyes are used to it. I blink hard, and the fortress's harsh lines come back into view.

The flight back to my fortress is brief. After leaping into the black sky, wings and claws splayed, I alight on the central parapet, just above the entry gate, and look down to behold the madness below. This band of rebels is surprisingly well equipped. Freezeshot blasters. Radiation-forged armor plating. Only one thing is consistent among the clambering chaos of bodies: These resistance fighters don't display a single set of wings, a rogue claw, or even a scale-plated section of flesh. They've molded armor around themselves like the shells of sun serpents' eggs, hiding any evidence of nightfolk mutations. Not one of them calls upon the planet's gifts to our people. They might as well be dayfolk.

They might as well throw their bodies upon a pyre now and beg the Daylands' forgiveness for having evolved into nightfolk at all.

Already, my loyal soldiers are locked in combat with the assailants. Shouts of "For Azarii!" fly between blows and shots, in case there was any doubt of his involvement. Freezeshot and Earthside-style bullets ricochet off the fortress's walls, punctuated by radioactive blasts. As my observation draws me closer, I weave and dodge, varying my flight path, lest I find holes blown clean through my flapping wings. Eventually I reach a strong vantage point, directly above the fortress's main gate. The battle unfolds before me like a general's map of miniatures.

Every nightfolk citizen has their own gift from the Diakópsei—or curse, I suppose, if you ask the insurgents—and here, they are on full display. Blasts of energy, among the most common abilities. Violent spikes that lurch from the earth to impale opponents. Wounds knitting back into whole, unbroken flesh almost as soon as bleeding starts. Telekinetic redirection of shots, either toward their enemies or simply away from their own.

I briefly glimpse a lanky, long-armed youth, with his perpetually furrowed brow, storm cloud–gray eyes ever alert. It's Thaane—my friend since childhood, now among the most promising young leaders of my new militia—and he is, as always, seven steps ahead of all the others.

Aloft on his twin pairs of wings, Thaane waves a three-clawed hand, turning the stone floor beneath his opponent to perfect glass. The opponent staggers, the ground too slippery for her to stand, and as she flails, a shot from another of our own soldiers strikes her dead between the eyes, where even her makeshift armor failed to cover. She collapses, as if weightless, her being severed clean from her body, in a bedlam of shattered glass and blood.

Furious power floods my body all at once, like a void when a lantern goes out. I raise one hand, energy sparking into being like rogue flame between my claws, and launch it toward the scrambling militia at the gate.

Black light explodes, atomic. Bodies scatter, but their armor hasn't fractured. That's the strength of metal and stone forged together by nightfolk power. The same power these rebels deny with their attire. The same power they fear.

"It's the usurper!" one of them shouts, blue eyes glinting with terror as they meet mine from below.

"No," I say, even knowing they can't hear me from the ground. "It's your queen."

I raise both hands this time, bring them together with a crash like a thunderclap, and energy spears from my open hands to the screaming rebel's chest. This time his armor shatters like glass of the Earthside era, shards of it digging into his now-exposed chest. It's ringed with scales like my own, alternating with stripes of clotted blood where he clearly tried to peel them away.

Azarii has convinced these people that they're monsters, through and through. But what makes them think they're the only ones, that their horror is special, that their grief is worthy of anything more than a passing note? I swoop down and finish this rebel with my teeth, his blood slick and salty in my mouth, because I am a monster, too. The worst of them all. At least I admit it.

Monsters are needed when the alternatives are nightmares.

The other insurgents go stock-still at the sight of me. I know what they see; I know what I've become, transformed more dramatically now than any other nightfolk ever has been. Eight feet of bulging muscle, growing so thickly out of me that it looks more like fungus. Arms more like legs, or perhaps legs more like arms, all equipped with ruthlessly sharp claws. Broad wings, thick enough to be used as insulation by a smaller creature, if ever they dared to sever them from my spine. Skin bluish white as a bruise, pockmarked as a moon, like any nightfolk, but drawn impossibly tight over tired bones. Eyes that gleam purple in the half-light of the eternal night. The proud arc of obsidian horns that crowns my head.

I'm in my element in combat, raised to new heights of destructive potential by the Diakópsei that I've embraced, so my lips lift into a bloodstained smile. It probably looks more like a snarl to the insurgents.

Chaos. Now that they've seen their so-called usurper, they know better than to fight me. They try to run. Of course they do. But one woman hesitates, scaly knuckles tense around her freezeshot rifle. Target locked right between my eyes.

"My lord." Thaane is at my back now, just behind my shoulder. One hand raised to summon more glass from stone.

I raise my own hand for silence, keeping my gaze fixed on the insurgent. "A bold one." I spit blood on the ice-coated stone. "Go ahead. Pull the trigger. I'm more tired than you know, and a little blast of proper cold might just wake me up."

The woman's arms rattle like dead tree branches in a gale. One finger shivers, twitches, against the trigger. Pulls hard and fast.

When I open my mouth again, it's not to fling another retort. More radiation blasts from my throat, swallows the freezeshot in midair. Slivers of ice rain down between me and the insurgent. A few pierce my feet, stinging. I'm more than awake now. I'm an open flame. All else is merely tinder.

Thaane laughs. A harsh, cold noise. "Well done, little princess."

"Thank you," I say, and then I lunge for the insurgent before she can scream.

Zalel doesn't deign to announce his arrival in my chambers. He's still a young boy, otherwise easy to miss, but his own mutations are far from tame, his breath pluming as bright blue flame before him. I see the flicker beneath my closed door before he speaks at all. It's neither his only nor his most notable gift—that would be his healing abilities—but it's certainly the most distinctive.

I clear my throat. "What does she know, Zalel?"

"Maybe nothing," he says from the threshold. "Maybe more than anyone should. She hasn't broken yet."

The insurgent from the previous battle, the one who dared to send a freezeshot blast between my eyes, has been in our custody since. She's a bold one, fire-struck, bursting with the planet's power that she denies. The kind of person her lot would trust. The kind with secrets that could end their rebellion.

I rise from my bed, sleep now far out of reach, wings uncurling from my aching body. "I don't want her broken. I want her lucid so she can tell us everything she knows—not tortured fragments between pleas for her life." A thought niggles at the back of my mind. "Who has been interrogating her?"

Suddenly, Zalel is barely audible, but I can feel the tremble in his voice, even from behind a closed door. "Thaane, my liege."

A growl rises in my throat. Thaane may be my friend and among my greatest soldiers, but he's doing what he does best: leaping to the next stage of a plan he never bothered explaining to anyone else. He could've pinged my comms tablet. He could've sent a live messenger, if typing a message himself was too much work. Even before I took over leading my late parents' army, Thaane was known for his little insubordinations. Breaking a door in the process of opening it. Injuring a combatant in a friendly sparring match. Pointed criticisms of his legion commander under his breath, despite the elder soldier's established seniority.

"Open the damned door, Zalel."

He does. Zalel's skin has gone sickly pale with worry, so white it nearly blots out the bluish undertones of all nightfolk flesh; stress lines his forehead, indents the angles of his face. The Shadow Court judged me in need of a personal attendant since my parricide, and I was in no state to resist. He's been flitting around the edges of my awareness for countless sleep cycles now, feeding my dog, sweeping up the shattered glass in my chambers, delivering meals I have no desire to eat. By now, I expected he'd have adjusted to my temper. But it seems not. Fair enough.

Sometimes the stubborn, wriggling rage in my chest catches even me by surprise. I don't remember a time before it crouched there, like a dragon in its lair, always in wait.

"Thaane," I say, before Zalel can interrupt me, "was not assigned to the task."

Zalel swallows the lump in his throat. "He volunteered, my liege."

Another curse slips, unbidden, from my mouth. I want to throw something, and I'm at once both grateful and furious with past Adria for breaking nearly everything in sight and having Zalel remove the fragile remainder from my sleeping quarters. "This will not stand."

"I will file a report with his legion commander. He will be swiftly—"

"Take me to them."

Zalel nods stiffly. I follow him into the hall. Still terribly young, he has to think harder than most about the fortress's layout, visibly second-guessing each turn the instant before he takes it, but I leash my frustration. Better to save it for Thaane. God help him if he's broken my best lead on the rebellion beyond repair.

By the time we enter the interrogation chamber, I've assembled a short list of things to possibly expect. The prisoner, battered by Thaane's own claws or torn to shreds by his four wings. Burned, perhaps, by a blast of demanding radioactive power. Having her own life threatened, or even hearing a bluff regarding the lives of those she loves. But what I see is none of those things.

The rebel cowers, like a lost child, in the chamber's center. The table and restraints for questioning are empty, abandoned, but she remains caked with dirt, dust, and gravel. Blood has dried along the arch of her throat, which I threatened with my teeth before taking her prisoner last night. But otherwise, she shows no signs of injury. Not by weapons. Not by energy. Not even by Thaane's own three-fingered clawed hands.

She rattles like ice beginning to splinter, teeth chattering. Outside of her obstinate armor, her own mutations are now visible. A sweep of scales along her spine. Spikes tearing through her skin all over, clearly designed to protect, but they've all been bent back, many broken, by the force of wearing armor over them.

I wonder why she seems to cringe into the floor, rather than away from me. Then I realize she's covered her eyes with her hands, nails digging into the skin of her own face.

Thaane looms behind and above her, not one of his four arms raised, but jagged teeth glinting in a bestial smile.

"What in the hell—?" I start.

Thaane raises a singular claw and points up.

The breath whooshes out of my lungs. Thaane's gift from the Diakópsei is displayed in glittering, horrible glory before me. Thaane's energy manipulation turns stone into glass. Something he can bend. Something he can shatter.

The entire domed ceiling has become a hectic clash of mirrors, all angled toward the captured rebel. Even the walls are glass now. As I step over the threshold and into the room, I realize the floor, too, is now reflective. Bile rises in my throat; I swallow it down. "What's the meaning of this?"

"She thinks she's better than us," Thaane says, smirking. "She thinks she can bury what she is, what we all are, under some cheap armor and platitudes." He gestures broadly to the spiked, scaled, shuddering woman at his feet. "Before she leaves this place to whatever punishment you decree, little princess, I'll ensure she knows herself to be wrong."

My tongue feels too swollen for my mouth. "This isn't what I ordered," I breathe, glancing sidelong at Zalel. "This isn't procedure for interrogations. What have we even *learned*—?"

"You're asking the wrong question. Think what *she* has learned." Thaane drops to one knee, tilting the prisoner's chin up with a freshly sharpened claw. "Look at me, girl," he says, his stormy-gray eyes holding hers fast. "Are we so different, you and I? Is it worth all this trouble, to dethrone a leader who acknowledges what we are?"

My voice spears from my throat, so fierce I half expect a blast of energy to involuntarily follow it. "I'm nothing like you. *We're* nothing like you. What are you accomplishing here? What has been gained but your own sick pleasure at watching someone else *suffer*—?"

"You seemed rather pleased with yourself in the last battle," Thaane says, "when you tore out her fellow combatant's throat with your teeth. Or when you put an end to your father, your mother, not so long ago. Remember that, Adria? The thrill of unleashed potential?"

Zalel reaches to catch my arm, to hold me back. Too late. I'm already between Thaane and his charge, who's become a quivering mass of spikes and skin behind me. My wingspan is broad enough to swallow her up; it casts her into total shadow.

"Why yes, Thaane," I say, his name falling like a curse from my tongue. "I am a monster." I plunge one clawed hand into his chest. His mouth hangs open with surprise, blood and foam bubbling on his lips. "I revel in my strength," I say, twisting my claws for good measure as he gasps, writhes. "I exult in the power bestowed upon us."

The light flickers, threatening to leave Thaane's eyes entirely. I lean close. I ensure he is looking at me.

"But I—am not—an animal." I yank my hand back, coated with blood. Thaane collapses to the ground, both hands clawing at his ruined chest, the whites of his eyes wide as moons. "Zalel." I nod in the healer's direction. "Attend to him, please. He will stand trial for war crimes, as the law dictates."

"War crimes?" Thaane spits on Zalel as the latter kneels, one healing hand extended. Where I am built to break, Zalel is built to mend. "This chamber you authorized is rife with implements of pain."

Thaane isn't wrong. I quickly scan the wall of blades and manacles, some showing signs of dried blood. "Bodies are always broken in war. A soldier's spirit is sacred, even in captivity. This thing you've done—" I don't understand why phantom tears, unshed, threaten to swallow my voice. "You think she doesn't know that she's exactly what she fears, what she's fighting? You think it doesn't haunt her every day?"

Of all the things I've broken in my quarters, overcome by rage since my unspeakable parricide, so many of them have been mirrors.

Behind me, barely audible, the prisoner sobs.

"Blood dries. Scars fade. Flesh knits itself back together. What you've done to this prisoner will follow her as far as she could ever run." I turn to the shuddering girl, lift her by the shoulders so that we're both on our feet. "You threatened my fortress. You fired upon your queen. There are punishments for that sort of insubordination, but this—this is not one of them."

She blinks at me, rapidly, eyes open and shut, open and shut. Her quivering mouth cuts off her words.

I ask, "What is your name?"

At that, her rapid blinking slows into a wide, haunted stare that holds my own. Her eyes are watery, red-rimmed, the pupils broad black discs in her pallid face. "Eridian," she says.

"Zalel," I say without turning around. My voice is nearly a growl. "Release her back into the Shadowlands."

Zalel, bless him, doesn't choose this moment to question my authority. He simply nods and takes the prisoner by the hand, wincing when one of her rogue spines digs into his shoulder. She glances rapidly between Zalel and the door, tense as a bowstring, before turning to meet my gaze one final time.

"Now heed my words, Eridian. This is no small mercy after your defiance of the crown. Follow my servant. Keep your eyes fixed ahead. If you look back even once, my soldiers will strike you down for good where you stand."

She nods stiffly, her mouth forming words but no sounds coming out, and Zalel leads her into the maze. Out of the fortress.

Thaane's wound is healed. Yet he clutches at it, grimacing from phantom pain. He spits on the ground. "Your father would be ashamed of you."

"Then it's a blessing he isn't here. Now get on your feet, you bastard." I seize a pair of handcuffs from the wall, originally intended for Eridian. "We owe the Shadow Court an explanation for this—and if we stay here much longer, Thaane, I'm afraid I'll be delivering you in pieces."

CHAPTER 7

KORI

My sleep is brief, not troubled but vivid. In my dream, *Charon*'s wingspan barely fits between the sheer verticality of the obsidian mountains, their jagged edges visible only by faintly twinkling starlight. I bring *Charon* down slowly, carefully, to rest beneath a vast outcropping of stone. It casts my entire cockpit into chilling darkness. I close my eyes, just for an instant, to gather my thoughts—

And open them, awake in the cockpit, back in the settlement, where everything began. My hand remains on the Morpheus sphere in my pocket, where I stored a new memory. Not a stranger's from the market, this time, but one of my own. Presented with the possibility of a forbidden nightfolk memory, I had no time to find a suitable trade from one of my clients, so I resorted to pilfering my own mind's cluttered storage.

I can feel an outline of where the memory once resided, like the imprint of a hand in sand, but it's already distant, slipping. A strong enough wind could blow it away entirely, tossing the sand back into chaos.

It's of the first time I stepped aboveground again after a long, icky flu as a child. The sun flooded my gaze, even through my necessarily masked face. The heat was cleansing, renewing, boiling the clinging remnants of sickness away. Beautifully blue sky swept like a paintbrush in every direction, shimmering from the intensity of the Daylands' heat, blue and blue and blue into infinity, puffs of cloud adorning its breadth. There, aboveground, everything was sunlight. Anything felt possible again.

Aspect nudges my hip with a metallic foot. "Kori makes—loud unpleasant—exhalations—when recharging—sometimes."

I blink, clearing the lingering sheen of sleep from my eyes. "Are you saying I snore?"

"Aspect is programmed—to mimic—human behavior. Aspect can—provide example—if Kori wants."

"That won't be necessary, Aspect, though I appreciate the—"

Aspect has already launched into the most enthusiastic rendition of a "snore" I could possibly imagine. It sounds more like the dying gasp of a mech being slowly squashed into a dinner plate. And it's *loud*.

"Th-that's enough," I stammer, then shout it again to be heard over the truly awful (and please, please not accurate, for the love of all things good in the world) snoring.

Aspect lets up and leans back in their chair, evidently pleased. "Kori is—welcome."

I laugh despite my annoyance. For all Aspect's quirks and foibles, they continually succeed at their primary purpose: making me feel less alone. The laughter ripples through me like a cleansing wave, brings energy back to my stiff limbs. All at once I feel ready to *do this*, to really dare to enter the Shadowlands and return with a personal fragment of the nightfolk.

But Chloe will be expecting my memory delivery, and I've already been asleep for . . . only Aspect knows how long.

I take a deep breath, in through the nose, out through the mouth. One last delivery. One last performance of the dutiful daughter, eager to serve. Then I can take my first step into the other side of the world, where even my mother can't pierce the darkness to contain me, where perhaps the secret to Aspect's latent sentience finally lies.

I stand, stretch my arms, roll my shoulders. Tap the pocket at my hip, just to check that the Morpheus sphere is still there. "Aspect, I'll be right back."

Aspect does a little hop, their feet clanking. I really need to oil their joints again. "And then—adventure—with Kori?"

I smile so big, it feels comedic, but I can't help it. "An adventure even you won't be able to forget," I say, ducking out of the cockpit.

I deliver the requested memory with a remarkably straight face, but Chloe's every micro-expression prickles the back of my neck with paranoia. The barest lift of her lips here. A casually raised eyebrow there. "Now don't fall behind on that math homework," she says as I leave, and I can't help but suspect a sarcastic undercurrent, even though she can't possibly know what I'm up to.

I hightail it back to *Charon* and to Aspect, proceeding to shove a sandwich into my mouth with both hands while the ship autopilots to the center of the Passage. The tracker embedded in Aspect is set to indicate a casual loop, *Charon* never straying too far from home, as though I simply wanted some natural light while wrestling with algebraic amalgamations of letters and numbers. Chloe won't suspect a thing. At least, that's what I keep telling myself. I'm too close to a true breakthrough to falter now.

Between my chewing and my being lost in thought, the trip through the Passage should be silent. Should be, but most definitely isn't, thanks to Aspect's creaking, squeaking, excitedly twitching joints. I can't even think of a specific installed Morpheus sphere to blame for that—it's just Aspect, in all their wacky, wonderful glory. Sometimes I think I'd deck somebody for this mech. Occasionally, I daydream about somehow repairing the irreparable helical engine and leaving Pagomènos altogether, but even in my wildest fantasies, where I settle in a new galaxy beyond my mother's grasp, Aspect is always there. Wreaking havoc, of course. But lovingly.

Charon's AI breaks me out of my reverie as the accompanying message scrolls across the viewport. *NOW APPROACHING [REDACTED]*—that being the Morpheus Market's entrance. Tapping several buttons on the control panel above, I return *Charon* to manual control.

"Sorry, buddy." I sigh aloud, reaching for the steering lever. "We're going somewhere new today."

NEW PATH DETECTED, the ship reports. *WOULD YOU LIKE TO RECORD THIS NAVIGATION FOR THE RETURN TRIP?*

"Absolutely not."

There needs to be no record of this trip ever having taken place, save for my memories of the event and (hopefully) Aspect's increased awareness.

If only to conserve charge, Aspect's rattling eventually quiets down. We fly in near silence for a while, the only sound being *Charon*'s determined engines, faithful across so many trips to the market and back. Given the temperature differential, the wind currents generally travel from the Daylands toward the Shadowlands, so the planet itself bears *Charon* forward, audibly smacking against the ship's rear, propelling us.

After a prolonged quiet, Aspect presses an open hand to the passenger side of the transparent dome. "It's so—very—beautiful—Kori."

"Aspect, we've flown through the Passage a thousand times. What's so special about this trip?" Curious, I look away from the navigation controls.

And all the breath whooshes out of my lungs.

This close to the Shadowlands, where the light bleeds away and the dark slithers to meet it, night and day just barely graze each other, a stolen kiss, an impossible embrace, shadows entwined with sun. The Cataclysm's radiation runs rampant in the Shadowlands, constantly replenished and magnified by the nearby asteroid buried somewhere in the night. The lingering light of the Daylands doesn't merely fade or ebb; it collides with the wall of invisible power, splinters into every color my eyes can perceive.

Waves of undulating iridescence paint the horizon, beginning at the planet's surface far below and continuing straight up into the atmosphere, beyond where any Pagonian creature dares to tread.

Unlike the Dreamgiver Devotees, I lack the critical spark of belief that this was all crafted by a benevolent god; and unlike the Old Seekers, I can't bring myself to dismiss it as mere scientific phenomena. Without knowing who or what, without daring to voice the wonder or diminish it with a name, I feel close to something here, or someone—the great Beyond of a galaxy greater than me or my mother or Aspect or Pagomènos itself.

I'm not sure I've ever sincerely believed in a purpose for it all like the Devotees. But as the lights dance along *Charon*'s wings, painting vanishing masterpieces on the surrounding dome, I feel bigger than blood and bones. Call it faith; call it delusion. Trying to describe it would only weaken it. I press an open palm to the dome, just like my mechanical friend, and we both watch the lights, without a need for words, until the darkness opens its gaping maw and gulps us down.

It's not as though I've never experienced dark. All light in the underground settlement the dayfolk call home is either funneled from the surface or artificial; either way, its presence can be limited as needed. *Charon* can reduce the transparent sections of the dome for a comfortable napping environment. Most sleeping quarters in the settlement, whether private or communal, are perpetually lightless to allow visitors to sleep as they see fit.

The Shadowlands are not *dark*, the descriptor—*dark*, the opposite of *bright*. They're *darkness* the noun, darkness as a presence, a massive, fanged, primeval beast that swallows everything within reach and never, ever lets it go. I knew dayfolk weren't meant to visit the Shadowlands. But now I wonder, in an instant of raw terror, whether a trespasser will ever be permitted to leave.

The only light source is a massive blue pyre burning in the distance, clearly something built by the people here to prevent them from living entirely without sight. But its light is alien, otherworldly. Instead of putting me at ease, the shimmering blue on *Charon*'s dome makes me shiver all over.

Or maybe that's not the only reason I'm shivering.

"So—cold," Aspect mutters. Their temperature sensors, intended to avoid combustion amidst a boundless desert, were never meant for this opposite extreme.

"We aren't even outside yet," I counter, but I feel it, too, creeping through my bones.

Charon was modified to withstand the Daylands' extreme heat by absorbing as much cooler air as possible. In the Shadowlands, that means my ship eagerly offers itself to the lashing, icy winds. Already, ice forms around the dome in jagged lines like wintery webbing. I grip the control stick so tightly that my bone-white knuckles ache.

"*TEMPERATURE FLUCTUATION DETECTED*," the ship says brightly, before adding less hopefully, "*AT ALTITUDE 2,500 FEET.*"

"I know—I *know*," I stammer, uselessly hitting the air jets as a reflexive response to low visibility. It does nothing to clear the rapidly forming mosaic of ice along the window.

Aspect unleashes a string of four-letter words that they undoubtedly learned from me. I shush them, face burning, and lean closer to the main window, desperate to maintain some view of what lies ahead. I can't fly like this, but switching back to autopilot will launch us out of the Shadowlands, back into the Passage from which we came.

"No. *No.*" I blink hard to clear tears, which nearly freeze as they roll down my cheeks. "We've come too far to turn back now."

"Kori."

"Not now, Aspect."

The mech waves their arms wildly. "*Kori*." When I ignore them, again, they screech, "KORI!"

"What?" I snap through my chattering teeth.

"Aspect—is"—their voice rattles from the cold, but it's a convincing facsimile of human terror—"afraid."

There's no time for comforting words, not that I have any to offer. The entire ship whirls sideways, weighted down by gathering ice on the right wing that I can barely see through the iced-over passenger side of the dome.

"*Shit*." Now I'm the one cursing (terrible robot parenting, but also entirely reasonable given the circumstances).

I tug the control stick with both hands, as hard as I possibly can, but the ship doesn't budge. Instead, it pivots into an uncontrolled spin. My harness holds me fast to the pilot's chair, as does Aspect's, but the sudden jerk knocks all the air from my lungs—or maybe that's the scream I can't restrain. Panic-stricken, suddenly more concerned with survival than success, I smash the autopilot button that should be above my head and is now, I think, dangling below it. My center is gone, everything careening off its proper axis. It's a blessing my tiny table and associated bench have always been secured to *Charon*'s floor, because they might have caved in my skull by now otherwise.

"*ALTITUDE 2,400 FEET*," the ship chimes. "*SIGNAL NOT AVAILABLE.*"

"Yes it is," I gasp, punching the button again. "Yes the hell it is, come on, come on . . ."

SYSTEMS EXPERIENCING TEMPERATURE FLUCTUATION. This message is written, not spoken, and it shimmers, cracking apart just like the ice on the windows before vanishing altogether. *SYSTEMS MUST REB—OOT—REB—OOTI—NG—*

Charon continues spinning, careening through the air like a discarded toy.

"Dizzy!" Aspect shrieks. "Aspect—is—dizzy!"

We can't keep hurtling like this, completely out of control. With a final choked scream, I let go of the stick altogether. Instead, teeth gritted, I put both hands on the emergency brake pulleys, yanking them toward my chest with all the strength I can muster, trying to hard stop *Charon*'s forward momentum.

Three things happen in rapid succession.

One: Some two thousand or so feet above the planet's surface, *Charon* does, in fact, stop spinning. We're still upside down, and my neck stings something fierce from the whiplash, but we're stationary again, the ship hovering silently in the sky's black expanse.

Two: Like a cruel joke, every light in the cockpit blinks out.

Three: Before I can even exhale, before Aspect can release a poorly timed victory shriek, before *Charon* can possibly complete a system reboot, it falls like a dislodged star.

A distant, eerie blue light—the strange fire? the asteroid?—is just enough to illuminate the rocky ground as it lurches to meet us. I'm screaming, Aspect is screaming, and the alarms would be, too, if *Charon* had any power.

If we don't eject now, this crash will almost certainly kill me. And if I eject without my anti-radiation gear, which I never don until landing, Pagomènos itself will poison me the moment its atmosphere makes contact with my skin. I'll lose my mind, maybe even my body, most definitely everything that makes me human and not merely a mutant monstrosity. And if somehow, against all odds, I survive both this crash and the Shadowlands' unrestricted radiation, I won't really be me anymore. And there will be no going back.

An awful groan of metal on stone. *Charon* bounces off a nearby mountain spire, one I can only hope is close to our destination. In my disorientation from all the spinning, what I thought was the ground just ahead was, in fact, the side of a peak.

High, sharp cracking noises fill my ears. The dome above (below?) us looks to be a light breeze away from shattering entirely, then spitting us out into the Shadowlands raw.

I choke on a gasp. "Aspect, my gear—"

Since first activating their too-curious eyes, Aspect has caused me no small share of trouble: Inedible birthday cakes. Existential crises. Commentary on my sleeping habits. But this time, the universe takes pity on me. Aspect's optical processors blink, their head bobs, and I know that somehow, they understand how dire our situation is.

Retracting their harness, Aspect launches themself across the cockpit, by which I mean they fall out of their upside-down chair and then lunge desperately sideways, crashing into one of *Charon*'s walls with a heavy thud. Seizing hold of the appropriate storage closet, they proceed to toss sections of armor my way as fast as they can.

Whether by sheer adrenaline or the terrifying closeness of death, I have a peculiar bodily awareness as we plummet from the sky. Following Aspect's lead, I drop from the inverted pilot's seat and armor myself faster than I ever have, even when wildly excited to enter the Morpheus Market. Each armor piece snaps into place and expands to meet the others in rapid succession—the helmet blooms across my neck, the chest panel across the rest of my torso, gauntlets linking into my gloves, leg armor latching into my boots.

Charon isn't big enough to have come equipped with an escape pod. In outer space, the likely intended environment for this ship's design, a parachute wouldn't have stopped suffocation, so we don't have those either. Dayfolk armor has small propulsors at the back—not enough to qualify as a jetpack, but activated by a sudden fall, designed to prevent severe injuries from surface-world work accidents. Aspect's feet have similar standard-issue mini-rockets. But will either be enough?

In a breath, I'm equipped to meet the planet's uncompromising atmosphere. I just have to avoid being crushed to death when *Charon* hits the ground. Terror tears at my stomach. I could survive the impact just to break a dozen bones, just to lie writhing and gasping in the gathering dark, wishing someone, anyone, even the damned Coalition, knew where I'd been left to die.

I could survive the impact just to look to my left and find Aspect an empty shell, unseeing optical processors forever staring up, up, up into the night.

"Aspect." I meet their gaze, clinging to the nearest useless control lever for balance. "The dome is already compromised. I'm going to kick as hard as I can, right here. I'm going to jump. And I need you to follow me."

"The probability—of surviving—such an—endeavor—is approximately—"

"We're losing altitude. This is our only chance. On the count of three."

"Koriiiii—"

"One."

I brace the heels of my boots against the side of the dome.

"Two."

I suck in as much air as possible and hold it, insurance against another building scream.

"Three."

Swinging back, pushing all the strength of my body into the kick, I shatter the last barrier between us and the darkness.

The dome splinters in every direction, a glittering shower of destruction lit by the Shadowlands' faintly blue glow. Jagged shards rattle and bounce off my armor; otherwise, I'd be tearing pieces from my arms, legs, maybe even my face, for countless sleep cycles to come.

Aspect follows an instant later, lurching through the carnage, arms spread in a defiant T pose as they, too, begin to fall. It's a dreamlike descent, the ground so far below and so poorly illuminated as to be invisible. We're spinning and spinning, dislodged from standard perceptions of up and down. I'm plummeting forever, nothing to catch my fall but a pair of thrusters meant to reduce the impact of slipping from a scaffold or tripping on a dune.

The thrusters at my back activate automatically. I barely hear them burst to life over the cacophony of the ship's crash. *Charon*'s core form, somehow mostly intact, sails beyond me and Aspect entirely. I'm so disoriented that the ship almost appears to be falling upward.

If I hit the ground wrong, I may never wake up.

My directional perception is only reoriented because just above me, *Charon* collides headlong with another rocky spire. Smoke and fire surge, the reinforced X of *Charon*'s core frame screeching and warping; the smoke makes me cough even through my mask's filtration, but the flames' violent glow reorients my body. Hunks of plating rain down around us. One nearly knocks into my skull, no doubt heavy enough to knock me out cold, but I roll aside, just barely, its uneven edge scraping my armor as it veers past. The jets at my back barely feel like they're slowing my fall. Aspect whips in and out of my peripheral vision, the speed of their own descent similarly impossible to track.

Has a two-thousand-foot fall ever been survived by any Pagonian? Let alone their illegally modified robot companion? I curl my head to my chest, arms around my knees, and aim to land on them rather than risk snapping my spine. Fully expecting the breath to be knocked from my lungs, I inhale as much as I can.

Then impact.

My armor takes the brunt of it, but the fall's height and momentum send me careening across the rocky ground on my side, jostling on the uneven stone, one arm viciously pinned between my torso and the ground, my skin splitting and stinging and blood no doubt spilling behind my protective gear. I taste rust and salt in my mouth, too, and only then do I realize I've bitten my tongue between my gritted teeth.

At last my sliding comes to a stop. I roll onto my back, chest heaving for air, every limb thoroughly hating me. My vision swims, swirls. I can't tell if the darkness all around me is the Shadowlands or unconsciousness threatening to steal me away.

"Kori."

A warm metal hand tests the pulse at my wrist. I groan, confused, expecting Aspect's chilly touch, but by comparison to the frozen wastes about us, their hand is practically heated.

"You're"—I cough, hard—"okay?"

Okay is a stretch. Aspect's head lolls at a corpse-like angle, locked into looking at me askance. Both their feet are smoking, the metal blackened, where their propulsion rockets fought so desperately to slow their fall. When they move to kneel beside me, they practically collapse to their knees.

I finally manage a full breath; it shudders through my entire frame. "I'm okay," I say, mostly to myself. "I'm okay."

Aspect tries to shake their head, but the servos just sort of scream. It's stuck in that terrible hanged-man twist. "Kori's arm—is not—okay."

"What?" I say, not understanding. My voice shakes like the surface of a water glass. Or is it my whole body that's shaking, harder and harder, even though every shake brings with it a jolt of stabbing, vicious pain in my—

Oh, stars above, my left arm.

Aspect's head is cosmetic compared to this. I look like a discarded marionette. A shoulder should never, ever twist at that angle, almost inverted on itself from instinctually attempting to break my fall. I want to scream and scream, but all that comes out is a child's terrified whimper. "No, no, no, it hurts, it *hurts* . . ."

"Aspect will find—help."

"Aspect will stay right here until I can stand up."

"Aspect—is not sure"—they move to rise, pushing up with their hands, but their feet are wobbly, ringed with smoke—"that Kori—or Aspect—should stand. But Aspect would rather—it were Aspect."

A second heartbeat throbs in my shoulder. Only continuing to quicken, my breaths rattle my whole body, intensifying the anguish. Logically, an arm injury shouldn't prevent standing on my own two feet, but even shifting my weight on the ground makes the shoulder pain surge so severely that I see stars, and not the twinkling ones above us. I stare, woozy, into the vast dark landscape. I'm still alive, but it feels like the shroud has come for me already.

"We have to find Alpha. They're the only one who can help us."

"Others must—live here?"

"*Others*," I echo, my throat constricting. "Not like us."

And here we are, guarded only by the mountains spearing into the darkness behind us. On every other side, we're completely exposed. Worse predators than the Passage's sand serpents likely live here, and I don't even know what to watch for. If random nightfolk stumble upon us, they could do anything they want to me, torture us both for sport instead of simply letting me die.

I feel through my pockets with a shivering hand; miraculously, my Morpheus sphere for trade remains intact, but my ruined comms tablet meets my flesh as pricks of broken glass. Likewise, I can feel two unevenly broken halves of the "business card" given to me by the Morpheus Market gremlin.

There's no way to signal for help. Nobody who knows we're here. Even if I reset Aspect's installed tracker to be accurate—presuming it even survived our crash landing—I strongly doubt it can transmit across the entire planet. It was never meant to mark travel further than the Passage's midpoint. For all her desperate attempts to control and micromanage my movements, Chloe has really, truly lost track of us, and at possibly the only time when I don't want that. Even my mother, incandescent with rage at what I've done, would bring grateful tears to my eyes right now.

The truest dark I've ever known watches and says nothing.

Aspect moves their hands to my good arm, just under the armpit, poised to lift. "Aspect—helps—Kori stand?"

"That won't be necessary," I start, but the mech is already heaving me to my feet with all the force I've managed to install into their spindly, squeaky frame.

It *hurts*, oh, how it hurts, and I'm shrieking just to prevent biting clean through my own lower lip, but I find my footing.

"Kori stands!" Aspect proclaims, hands brought together in celebration, even as their own footing on their smoking feet remains uncertain. "Now—where?"

I look up to where *Charon*—or what's left of it—remains wedged in the mountains. Absent the covering dome, the cockpit caved in on itself. One side of the wings seems gone entirely, the other bent at assorted strange angles, a proud bird brought low and humbled, reduced to a smoking, burning husk. Tears sting my eyes. But as my gaze wanders farther up, hope bursts anew.

Like a primitive Earthside spear, *Charon* impaled itself in the second of five consecutive stone spires. *Meet me at the Second Spire.* We've reached the agreed-upon meeting place after all. And Alpha is nearby, bearing the memory that may finally awaken Aspect's potential—and hopefully a method of exiting the Shadowlands before the other nightfolk realize we're trespassing (or Chloe realizes I'm gone).

Despite everything, a smile overtakes me. "I think we're exactly where we need to be."

CHAPTER 8

ADRIA

The Shadowlands prison has occasionally housed dayfolk trespassers—defects from their arrogant, isolated society, foolishly convinced the dark would be more welcoming—but not since long before my birth. This is a cage not for rebellious dayfolk but for criminals of the night.

Like our freezeshot weapons, all four walls of each stone cell have integrated wiring to channel a thin layer of deadly cold energy, continually sourced from the Shadowlands' freezing climate. Rather than metal bars, a wall of freezeshot shimmers a holographic blue. Only the floor remains mere stone beneath a prisoner's feet, and if they move too suddenly, a sheet of agonizing cold slides into place there, too.

Upon seeing me, Thaane lurches to his feet, triggering the floor's freezing wall. The energy spears straight through his ankles, and he collapses, knees pulled close to his chest, rage giving way to immediate regret. "My lord," he gasps.

"Don't patronize me," I say, standing just outside his cell. "You're lucky your gift doesn't involve your voice, or you wouldn't be talking at all."

The hallway is lined with additional imprisonment gear, depending on the unique talents of each nightfolk resident. Muzzles for those who, like me, can call the Diakópsei's power from their throats. Manacles for those who rely upon their hands. Adjustable restraints for wings, tails, and the like.

Thaane's wrists are bound securely together to prevent his morphing any stone floors into breakable glass, but I saw no need to bind his mouth. He spits on his cell's floor, the saliva turning almost immediately to ice.

"I also advise," I say, venom on my tongue, "against condescending to me."

"Adria." Veins pulse and writhe, blue and bloated, in the tension of Thaane's forehead. "Everything I've ever done in the line of duty, I've done for our people. If my methods were wrong—"

"They were."

"Forgive me."

Thaane shifts his weight, wrists still locked at his back, and falls to his knees before me. I have a solid foot of height on him under normal circumstances. Now I loom like a gravestone over his pitifully crouched form.

"I am not who you ought to ask for forgiveness," I breathe. "The Shadow Court will decide your fate."

"Must they? Can you not pardon me?"

"As your queen?"

"As my friend."

I try to ignore the twist in my gut. "That only worsens the crime. You ignored procedure and defied my leadership, in wartime, no less. In service of a petty grudge against a convenient victim." I shake my head. "We will not win this war by torturing its fallen."

Pain, all too poignant, flashes across Thaane's face. Quivers through his jaw. "The dayfolk already despise us. But to have one of our own deny what we are, cloak her gifts in shame, wear our people's nature like manacles—"

"And you think she's proud now?" I roar, despite myself. "Who wouldn't want to be like you—so enthralled by your power, you simply must demonstrate by drawing blood?"

"I never touched her."

"You tortured her. You didn't make her believe we're more than animals. You fulfilled her every fear. You became what our enemies say we are."

Thaane lowers his head, eyes gone glassy as the interrogation room. "Adria." His voice breaks. "We've fought together, haven't we? Siblings-in-arms. Together amidst the insurgency, freezeshot all around us, rebels falling in our wake. I was proud to call you my princess." A razor-sharp intake of breath. "Even more so to call you my queen."

Countless battles shimmer in his gaze, and for an instant, I'm back on the battlefield, eyes frantically scanning the horizon, not bothering to watch my back, knowing that my allies—knowing that *Thaane* is there, prepared to fight.

Words build up in my throat, too many to break free. Everything tastes sour.

Softly, Thaane says, "I didn't do it to torture her."

"Thaane." My trusted advisor. My loyal brother-in-arms. Thaane, who sided with me when I overthrew my parents. Thaane, the first to volunteer for my new militia. Thaane, whose gift is for breaking and shattering, but who has stood solid as stone through all this upheaval, trying to weld the nightfolk back together. Now all I can see when I look at him is that cruel curve of mouth, that shudder of laughter at the prisoner's shame, forced to behold her own likeness reflected a thousand times. "Then why?" I snarl.

"I only made her look." Thaane wrings his hands, not looking at me. "I didn't tell her what to see."

"You knew what she would see."

"When you look into a mirror, Adria, do you tremble? Do you curl into yourself like a corpse in the Passage and hope to die?" Thaane says through his teeth. He's still kneeling before me, but his shoulders arch, body pulled taut. "I gave her a chance to behold her own strength, her own true nature, and claim it. She chose to cower. She chose to drive every shard of glass back into her own heart."

I swallow. I can't meet his eyes any more than he can meet mine. The captured rebel saw a monster in the mirror. That's the crux of Azarii's renewed rebellion: a total rejection of our gifts, my existence as an overcharged overlord serving as the ultimate evidence that the Diakópsei turns ordinary people into animals. I've told my people otherwise, raised a new empire against that very belief, but nevertheless, my chamber is devoid of reflections, littered with shattered glass.

"It takes time," I growl, "to be proud you are a monster."

"A princess of monsters, even."

"A queen."

Radiation spears through me from my forehead to my feet. It rings in my horns and claws, gleams electric behind my eyes as they drift shut. I offered myself to the Diakópsei like a living sacrifice to an unfeeling god. I am the greatest monster the nightfolk have ever birthed. My body exults in the thing I become in battle, feeds on the rage that yet pulses at my temples. But my heart aches, stone-cold, in my chest.

What would Father and Mother think of me now, stronger than they ever were? Still too weak to take pride in it?

Unsteady, Thaane rises to his feet. "Forgive me, Adria." The freeze wall between us makes him flicker. Shimmer. An ice sculpture of a man. A mutant that a single punch could shatter. "It is no small thing, to look upon a face I've known since birth, and comprehend that now she holds our entire world in her hands."

"It was no easier," I say, throat raw, "to watch my childhood companion drive a prisoner to the brink."

Thaane opens and closes his mouth several times, gnawing on the right words, before answering, "I am your friend, Adria. Through Azarii's first uprising, through your claiming of the throne, and now through his pathetic second stand. Please. I know you don't want me at the mercy of the Shadow Court." His skin is more white than blue, more veins than flesh. "Let me redeem myself. Put me on the front lines. Pelt me with freezeshot. Paint the darkness with my blood. I don't care. But don't let me waste away in this cage. Don't let those sniveling cowards on the Shadow Court, who know nothing of what a soldier sees, decide what to make of me."

My wings flap idly at my back, twitching with anxious energy. Thaane isn't wrong. This thing he's done, it wedges like a splinter beneath my skin, but I am no better. I can still taste rebel blood on my tongue. I can still feel the sick exultation in my belly, beholding the prisoner's fear before I took her down.

I pin Thaane with my gaze. "The next time we take prisoners, you deliver them to a qualified questioner. Understood?"

"Yes, my lord."

I tap the control panel with a singular claw. The freezing wall between myself and my friend flickers, then drops away into nothing.

"My first order?" Thaane says, all eagerness. But hesitance underpins his voice, as it should.

"Go back to your quarters. You stink of blood and Earthside bullets."

"And then?"

"Wait until I call you." I gesture down the hall, toward the prison exit. "I've been awake for too long, and unlike you, I didn't have the pleasure of a private nap. I want to be alone."

"As you wish," Thaane says, and scurries out of sight.

Exhaustion gnaws at my mind, but I'm wound far too tightly to sleep now. After all the ugliness I've seen this sleep cycle, even the dark behind my eyelids encroaches like a looming predator, suffocating, threatening to swallow me whole. I suppose that sleep, even in irregular and forced spurts, is a luxury that princesses can rarely afford. Let alone queens. Let alone in wartime.

So in a world devoid of sun, a distant twinkle of stars will have to do.

The fortress's balcony is a collection of eight parapets, linked together with narrow bridges. The bridges are ideal for a crouched sniper, just barely peeking over the wall, poised to pierce a bolt of freezeshot directly into an enemy's skull. The parapets are broader, open, perfect for winged nightfolk to launch themselves headlong into battle or otherwise.

I've used these parapets for takeoff more times than I can count, simply needing to feel the wind beneath my wings, the gratifying snap when they prevent me from meeting the ground, my body arching upward, set loose into the sky, unbound by anything. But tonight, all I want is an unmarred view of the stars above.

I stare off into the inky dark to which my mutated eyes have long ago adjusted. The loneliness comforts me, even though there's almost nothing to see. A smattering of stars like fragments of bone. The familiar, reliable hulk of the Shadowlands' mountains, most noticeably the Crown—a quintuplet of similarly sized spires just beyond what could rightfully be called the fortress's outskirts. And behind me, ever steady, the torch that lights our world illuminates the corners and edges of my chosen parapet like an unnatural sun. For an unnatural people, as Azarii would certainly say.

A streak across the sky, silver-bright, like a sliver of foreign moon. I whirl and lean forward on my elbows against the parapet's edge, eyes gone wide, wings reflexively unfurling as if to jump. A starship? It could be nothing else. A dayfolk starship, just beyond the mountain range that contains my fortress, too close to be an accident.

What's a dayfolk pilot doing in the Shadowlands?

A terrifying thought darts across my brain—perhaps the insurgents from the recent attack have allies beyond the Passage. Perhaps my uncle, damn him, determined that any opponent of mine ought to become his army's friend. Perhaps, after the tenuous peace and strict division brought about by the Territory Wars, my own subjects have allied with the dayfolk to overthrow my empire.

I don't know what the dayfolk could possibly promise that would make nightfolk trust them not to eliminate us. But no one ever said insurgents were smart. I remember that girl at Thaane's mercy, knees curled to her chest, mutant spikes ripping through her flesh, eyes shut tight against the shame of what she was. Maybe the insurgents hate themselves enough to throw their own bodies on a pyre, if it means my rule burns. I don't know. But I can't afford to take any risks.

Up here on the parapet, overlooking my vast obsidian kingdom, I don't have easy access to a comms tablet. I left it in my chambers, not wanting to be disturbed, knowing I ought to be sleeping. But if I return to my chambers to call for backup now, I'll lose sight of the rogue starship. May never find it again. May let a spy or interloper simply slip, unhindered, into the Shadowlands.

The starship begins arching away, and only now do I register that the crude engine coughs a trail of smoke and flame, a shower of glass sparkling like glitter all around it. I've never been to the Daylands or seen their ships, but nothing about that seems intended. Shock and awe alike spear through me as the dayfolk ship collides, nose first, with the Second Spire on the horizon.

The pilot should be dead.

Then again, after committing regicide to cement my own claim to the shadow throne, I should be dead, too. For better or for worse, things are not always as they should be on Pagomènos.

If the pilot is dead, their technology may be salvageable and provide some indication of why a dayfolk pilot veered into my kingdom. If the pilot is alive . . . I can hardly fathom the thought. A Pagonian nursed by sun, rather than clawing for scraps of the Diakópsei's glow; crowned by light, not shadow; heedless of what lurks in the dark, boldly venturing into the endlessly visible, endlessly possible bright world before them.

I should be infuriated that a dayfolk pilot trespassed into my kingdom, but despite myself, I know the clench in my gut is hope, not hatred.

They should be dead; I should want it to be so. If they're alive, I should send a soldier to put an end to that. Thaane wouldn't hesitate before slitting their throat, ensuring no rogue factors threaten my already-tenuous newfound rule. And I know that would be the wise course of action. I know full well. That's why Thaane is one of my lead soldiers and why I proudly count him among my closest confidants—he sets his personal feelings aside and does what must be done, a straight arrow launched by logic alone, absent any distractions from his purpose.

But so help me, I want the pilot alive. I want to pull them from the wreckage with my own hands, see their strange heat-born body with my own eyes. Before I cut out their tongue for their insolent invasion, I want to hear with my own ears what it's like to live in the day. For that, perhaps I'll even send them home to the Daylands with their heart still beating.

My father would see the pilot executed publicly, brutally. Thank the Beyond, in this at least, I am not my father. Perhaps I remain more rebel princess than honored queen. Perhaps I will always be more monster than leader, ravenous with my own plans and eager for order. I spread my wings and leap into the black sky.

They may have crashed into the Crown, but I will show this trespasser why I am the one the shadows call queen.

Once upon a time,
the princess of sunlight tumbled into the dark,
and it swallowed her whole.

CHAPTER 9

KORI

I don't know how I walk, my good arm trying to hold the ruined one as still as possible. Every step is excruciating for me, and Aspect's feet cough smoke like a robotic sneeze. Blessedly, we reach Alpha before long. Even in the Shadowlands, where the entire landscape is an inky assembly of bleak silhouettes, Alpha's form is immediately noticeable from an impressive distance. They're at least seven feet tall, outlined by shimmering, preternatural blue power. Alpha waits beneath what was likely a tree before the Cataclysm. It's charred black now, empty branches reaching for me like a blackened skeleton's outstretched hand. Unlike the dayfolk, Alpha doesn't need to protect their body from the planet's ever-present radiation infection. Nightfolk have become one with Pagomènos's curse, born and bred by it, infused with its power.

I recognize their form from our previous communication, though it's far more striking in person, in full color. Blue-white skin stretches across the thick muscles, small horns poking through cascading white hair that descends past the shoulders of six separate arms, two of which they walk upon like legs. Despite the wildness of their mutations, if I had to guess their age, it would be close to my own, perhaps a tiny bit older.

My voice is filtered, mechanical, through my protective mask, but remains evidently choked in pain. "Alpha." I incline my head in greeting. I want to be formal, professional, but all I am is desperate and afraid. My whole body rattles like a malfunctioning machine, shock slowly overtaking me from my injury. "Please, my ship crash-landed. My arm . . ." I gesture to its horrible angle. "I have no way home, no way to call for help. If you could—"

"Did you bring the memory?" Alpha's voice is smooth and syrupy, designed to put me at ease, which only sets me more on edge.

"Y-yes," I stammer. "Yes, of course I did."

"Then first, Monarch, our trade," Alpha says, with a little nod. "Then I will see what I can do to help you." Their single gray eye darts about warily, then settles on Aspect. "What in the Beyond is that?"

"My mech."

"You said we were meeting alone."

A chill darts down my spine. "A mech isn't a person." I want to cover Aspect's auditory processors even as I say it. Maybe they aren't a person in a traditional sense—at least, not yet. That may very well change after today, once I've expanded Aspect's consciousness with their first nightfolk memory. "We—the dayfolk—use them for all kinds of tasks. But they aren't recording. They aren't transmitting. See for yourself."

Alpha slowly blinks their singular, centered gray eye. They saunter over to Aspect, feeling around the mech's angles and joints with all four free hands. Anyone being so close to Aspect makes me tense from neck to toes, but despite their powerful, faintly glowing frame, Alpha tests Aspect's joints with poised curiosity, bending each of the fingers in wordless awe. When Alpha gets to Aspect's neck—still twisted and stuck at that terrible sideways angle—it doesn't budge at all. Aspect giggles, somehow finding morbid amusement in our compounding peril, but I shoot them a glare that keeps them still. Eventually Alpha completes their assessment, steps away, and declares, "Fair enough."

I smile in relief, even though Alpha can't see it through my mask. "Your Morpheus sphere?"

"Yours first."

With my good arm, I gingerly roll my sphere from my pocket into my gloved hand.

Alpha nods in acknowledgment. Then their tail whips abruptly around, and for an instant, I think I'm about to be attacked. My left hand instinctively wanders to the heatshot pistol at my hip, despite knowing it has no way to recharge in the frozen Shadowlands, meaning my ammo is strictly limited to stored charges. Thankfully, I don't need it. Alpha's tail ends, absurdly, in a seventh hand. Said hand is holding their Morpheus sphere.

A thought abruptly occurs to me: How did a nightfolk, absent an installed Morpheus chip, even transfer their memory into a sphere? They could have acquired the sphere from a rogue wanderer, like the dead man I found in the Passage, but without a Morpheus chip, implanting their own nightfolk memory should be impossible.

Then again, haven't I already shed what I formerly thought possible like a childhood coat, reality grown far too broad to fit? I'm transforming a mining machine into a sentient friend. My fate is in the (seven) hands of a mutant. Does it matter how they installed a nightfolk memory into a Morpheus sphere, if it's what finally raises Aspect to independent personhood?

I swallow my questions down alongside the roaring pain in my arm. We exchange spheres, dropping them into each other's outstretched hands—not daring to touch, even through my protective gear.

"Temp access," I say, as Alpha's hand taps their new Morpheus sphere.

Normally, a person's unique handprint is permanently linked to the Morpheus sphere, its only key. But I won't officially transfer permissions until we're both satisfied with the merchandise; this access will work only once. Following my verbal directions, Alpha does the same for the sphere in my hand.

My new Morpheus sphere spins, like our planet once did, a little whirlwind in my palm. It glows faintly, beeps, and my eyes go wide and blank inside my helmet. Then, all at once, I'm gone.

My name is Lail, and I am full to bursting with hope.

This is the first time I've looked at myself in at least a dozen sleep cycles. I stare firmly at my reflection, and I'm not afraid of it. Not of my seven hands, my singular eye, my rows of muscled shoulders. None of it. My name is Lail, and I am nightfolk.

I may be a monster, but I will put an end to glorifying this twisted form we have embraced. And that is beautiful. I am beautiful.

I clench one hand's fingers tightly around the freezeshot sniper rifle at my back. It's time to end the brief but all-too-lengthy reign of the rebel princess. Once we take the fortress, once we return the empire's iron fist to the people, we can begin seriously considering how to contain the Diakópsei's radiation. Under Azarii's leadership, we can begin anew. Maybe, just maybe, we can slowly return to the proud human species we once were, more flesh than unnatural power, more skeleton than shuddering strength.

My name is Lail, and I feel hope. I believe things can get better.

I will make them better, or I will die trying.

My whole body shudders, triggering a fresh wave of pain from my dislocation that brings me fully back to myself. I blink, and I'm inside my body again.

So Alpha—Lail, apparently—is trading me a glimpse of utter belief. Could this be the missing piece of Aspect's synthetic brain? A firsthand understanding of what it is to face down the future and *feel*, burning in your heart of hearts, that the best is yet to come?

I didn't know there was any kind of political conflict in the Shadowlands, least of all a full-blown rebellion against their current leader, but I'm not here to meddle in the nightfolk's internal war. I'm here to trade memories.

I look at Alpha. The hand that holds her Morpheus sphere tremors, and her single eye is slick with tears. I didn't know nightfolk could cry. The droplets freeze like snowflakes as they slide down Alpha's face.

I'm grateful that my mask somewhat conceals the shocked shudder in my voice. "Satisfied?"

"Yes," Alpha chokes out. "I only wish I could install it, as your people do. Make it my own, to be brought to mind whenever I desire. But alas, this sphere tech of your people—it can interact with our physiology, but we are not equipped with those implants of yours. There is no way for myself and this memory, this *light*, to become one."

The obvious question pokes me again. This time, for better or for worse, I allow it to become words. "If you don't have a Morpheus chip . . . how did you remove one of your memories? How did you even find a sphere for the transfer?"

"I don't think you want to know." It might've been a threat if not for the padded softness in Alpha's voice, like an apology.

"Let's say I do."

"I was in the Passage, hunting." I arch an eyebrow at that, before Alpha frantically clarifies, "Hunting the wildlife, not your people. The tastier beasts are those with access to some warmth. Something winged, ideally. Anything the sun serpents haven't already swallowed whole. But I digress. I was in the Passage, well within my rights, far from the Daylands, and I saw the sands swirled strangely, and when I landed to investigate, there was . . . there was a body. One of your kind. Already mostly bones, but one decaying hand still clutching this sphere."

Alpha waits, singular eye slowly blinking, observing my reaction.

"It's not like the skeleton needed it," I say, in what I hope is reassurance. "So you took it. Fair enough." I'm not about to judge her scavenging while I'm trespassing in the Shadowlands.

And I have a broken arm to show for it, plus I'm depending on this mutant stranger to find me a way home. But I don't say that part out loud.

"Fair enough," Alpha echoes, the tone wavering, quivering, in something that is almost—but not quite—an answering laugh. "The Diakópsei gifted me with strength," she goes on, flexing four of her six arms for good measure, "but it blessed my younger brother's mind, not his body. He can move things with a thought. When the usurper sought to evolve beyond reason, to become the most monstrous of us all, my brother did not yet understand the horror of what she'd done. In the chaos of the conflict, he reached out to the Diakópsei himself—was himself corrupted, overcome with power never meant for us."

Alpha pauses again, braced as if for a blow. But I'm not here to judge the nightfolk and their wars. I ask, "What happened next?"

"The Diakópsei's power twisted all of us, to some degree. But to touch it with an open mind, to see its surface with your own eyes . . . It was overwhelming. He could not maintain contact for long. But for long enough. The usurper's powers were always strength and concentrated energy, so it is those that were enhanced. But my brother moves things with his mind. So now . . . now he moves other minds."

My head spins so badly, I wonder how hard I knocked it against my helmet during the crash. "You're telling me your brother manually transferred a specific, targeted memory from your head to that sphere . . . by *thinking about it*?"

"I am."

"I can't believe that."

"Truth persists, regardless of what your kind, deluded by the light, choose to believe," Alpha says, arms defiantly crossed, but then she seems to soften. "They say your people trust their eyes too much, when they see so very little. But I'm grateful, child, that you saw me. That you came here and granted me a glimpse of your glorious sun." Alpha shakes her head again, overcome, her singular gray eye again glassy with tears. "I can only hope it helps to balance my brother's troubled mind. It is no gentle thing, to be suddenly beset by the inner thoughts of anyone you touch. He is overcome, writhing deep within . . . This may draw him back toward himself." Her lips lift into a little smile. "Thank you . . . Kori."

At that, my whole body goes rigid, ice-cold. I nearly cry out from a fresh, unbearable wave of anguish in my shoulder.

It's bad enough that a handful of my dayfolk trading partners learned my real name from talkative Aspect's running commentary. But a *nightfolk* trading partner? This is so, *so* bad. I've broken so many rules this sleep cycle, I could write a dissertation of apologies and still have sins left unaddressed. A nightfolk knows my *name*, has record of my agreement to this illicit transaction, and could turn me over to the Coalition at any time.

I swallow hard and steady my voice, despite knowing that the mask would flatten its tone regardless. "I haven't used your real name, Alpha. There are rules to the Morpheus Market." Rules I've flouted today with reckless abandon, but this is a valuable opportunity for leverage. "I can forgive this violation, if you can only find a way to get us home."

Aspect toddles closer to my side. "Home," they echo in a whisper. "Aspect—will take—Kori home."

Alpha clutches her sphere with three hands, holding it close to her chest. "Forgive me, Monarch. You have done as you promised." But she casts her eye to the ground. "I want to help you, truly. But our people have no need of starships. Your only way back through the Passage is on the back of a winged nightfolk."

My stomach sinks, nearly nauseous.

"I know your presence here is already a risk," Alpha continues. "I know showing yourself to yet another of our kind may be deeply unsettling. But if you let me take you to our resistance, surely one of

Azarii's soldiers would be willing to carry you and your . . . machine . . . home. Uncorrupted as you are by this planet's sickness. You could be an emblem to them, a glimpse of that to which we hope we may return." She gestures to my mangled limb. "And one with a healing gift could attend to your injury."

Morpheus Market transactions are supposed to be quick and clandestine, not uncomfortably personal. Despite desperately needing Alpha's help, I feel sweaty all over inside my suit. "Alpha—"

"When you return to the Daylands," Alpha says, heedless of my discomfort, "I see your mother holds sway there . . . I will not speak of this again. I swear it. But, please, if you can, tell her . . . tell her we are certainly people of the night. But we are not beasts. We can be better."

My mouth has gone dry, my tongue stuck to its roof.

I don't know what to say. Actually, I do. I should say, *Just take me to my ride home*, pass the Morpheus sphere to its proud new owner, and get the hell out of the Shadowlands. I never expected such a show of emotion from any of the nightfolk. I meant it when I told Aspect they aren't monsters, but only in a clinical sense—they're sentient, after all.

But if you'd asked me yesterday whether nightfolk were *people*, well . . . I don't know what I would've said. I certainly wouldn't have said that they could cry, or that they care what we think of them, or that they care for much of anything at all.

Aspect looks at me, visual processors blinking. Almost hopeful. They can learn hope now, in its proper form. Maybe it'll be enough to bring my mechanical friend to life. I'm on the verge of tears at this point, and not just from my dislocated arm. I take a deep breath, trying to calm the whirlwind of emotions.

That's when the ground beneath me blasts apart.

CHAPTER 10

ADRIA

Among the Shadowlands' many creatures, empowered by the Diakópsei's radiation, is the batbeast. Half the size of the average full-grown nightfolk, they use one pair of limbs as both spindly arms and legs, but there's power behind their seeming fragility. They've been known to lift a child clean from their mother's arms and carry them off into the dark, never to be seen again.

Somehow that's the first thought that comes to mind when I see the crashed starship's survivor. She's small, like all dayfolk, though perhaps tall enough among her people, not quite six feet. Narrow shoulders and hips, a long, taut neck, lanky limbs that overshadow the rest of her body. One of her two arms hangs at an odd, sickening angle, clearly an injury of some sort. I'm larger, bulkier, stronger than her, but despite being visibly wounded, she has undeniable strength of poise. Even though I can't see her eyes, I somehow know they could pin me to the floor.

This is a creature built and trained for taking what she wants and then vanishing, unhindered, back into the Pagonian wilds. It will not do to underestimate her.

The survivor also has just enough muscle definition that it shows through her protective gear, which adheres closely to its wearer. Foolish dayfolk, fearing Pagomènos's power, the Diakópsei's gift. I embody everything that suit is meant to keep at bay. And it won't be enough to hold me back.

My new and too-often-unwarranted rage, first seeded during my overcharge, pulses in my chest again like a brutal secondary heartbeat. I tamp it down with all the force I can muster. This girl is useless to me dead (or close to it if her suit leaks). I must play this carefully.

I perch above on the Second Spire's nearest ledge, just below where the crashed starship remains wedged in the mountain, overlooking the scene. The survivor isn't alone. She's accompanied by one of the dayfolk's mechs, though it waves its arms and interrupts with uncharacteristic enthusiasm for a machine. Its head is cocked at an absurd angle that can't possibly be practical.

And right across from girl and robot, flouting my kingdom's laws with impunity, is one of my own people.

Regardless of the context, I certainly don't allow my citizens to fraternize with trespassers. Yet here stands a nightfolk girl, likely close to my own age, undaunted, reaching for a Daylands-forged Morpheus sphere.

Since the nightfolk embraced the Diakópsei, we have no need of dayfolk Morpheus chips to "protect" our minds. Their standard usage (and rumored black market) exists well beyond my jurisdiction or interest. Most of what I've heard of its inner workings is likely mythology rather than firsthand reports. Many nightfolk are inclined to dismiss the market's reality altogether; I very nearly did. I was wrong. The knowledge stings, like needles under my mottled skin.

I lean forward on my wrists to listen more closely. And that's when I catch the specifics of their dialogue.

"Thank you, Kori."

Kori.

The spire, despite being solid stone and ice, seems to waver beneath me. I grip it tightly with my claws. Head spinning, I struggle to process. *Kori.* I know better than to trespass in Daylands territory, but I know full well who this girl is. Daughter of the Daylands' monarch. Heiress to their nation. And a willful criminal, apparently, judging by her presence in the Shadowlands and the smooth silver sphere of contraband memories in her open palm. Dayfolk don't meet with nightfolk, and they definitely don't offer an inner glimpse of their minds.

I mean to be careful, tactical. But the anticipation of a clash with dayfolk royalty overwhelms my good sense. A blast of radioactive power builds in my throat. I struggle to bite it back, teeth gritted, thoughts rushing through me so quickly that they stumble over one another, a tangle of conflicting possibilities.

Kori.

On this side of Pagomènos, Kori's presence alone could acceptably be answered with death. But in her own kingdom, she remains the heir to the throne, despite boldly flouting her people's laws by venturing into the dark and fraternizing with its denizens. The dayfolk would do anything to bring their heiress home.

Would *pay* anything.

Enough to solidify my rule in the Shadowlands, perhaps? Enough to crush Azarii's futile rebellion in one fell swoop?

My jaw practically pries itself open to let the furious blast of energy out.

The ground at Kori's feet explodes. Fragments of ice and rock scatter like freezeshot shrapnel. The girl stumbles, her mask-filtered scream swallowed by the roar of my power, her body reduced to a frail silhouette behind the blue-black haze of the blast's aftermath. The ground beneath her has become a gaping chasm. She falls.

The nightfolk woman scrambles back from the abyss on six of her seven hands, her last one frantically searching for a handhold in the confusion. She's a criminal, too, daring to trade for dayfolk tech, even if she never entered the Daylands. But she isn't my priority. This entire affair just became much, much bigger than her.

And, thankfully, in her terror at the sight of me, she loses her grip on the Morpheus sphere, which rolls. Bounces along the rocks. Plummets into the newly formed chasm with the Daylands girl.

Swooping down into the crevice, claws splayed, I pin Kori before she can run. Claws clamping around her wrists. Wings alone nearly twice her height. She likely couldn't flee anyway, her twisted arm surely even more agonizing after her fall, but I need to be sure.

She goes stock-still beneath me, not daring to resist with my claws so close to where her gloves meet the rest of her armor. One leak in her protective gear, and the planet's radiation will slip into her very being, impossible to revoke. One slash across her armor is a death sentence, even if I never draw blood.

"KORIIIIIII!"

I turn my head, not loosening my grip on the girl. The shriek came from her mech, whose optical processors whirl with light and . . . panic? Last I checked, humans—even mutated nightfolk—were the only fully sentient Pagonian beings. I don't know how to process what looks awfully akin to fear in the simulated eyes. The mech draws its arms back, little hands curling into tiny, metal balls, and runs full force directly at me.

"ASPECT! PROTECT! KORI!" The shriek makes my ears ache, but the mech is doing a painfully weak impression of protection. It rails against me, fists beating against the thick leather of my wings, feet kicking uselessly at my ankles.

My breath plumes, stark white, in the Shadowlands' cold. "Call off the mech," I breathe into Kori's throat. I wonder if she can feel the heat of my breath through her protective gear. Her eyes, the pupils just barely visible through her mask, are pools of wonder and terror.

"Or what?" The words have such venom, I imagine if she weren't wearing a mask, she would spit defiantly on the ice.

A laugh rattles through me. "Do I really have to tell you?" I hover one claw, barely, above where Kori's right glove meets the rest of her gear.

"If you were going to kill me," Kori says, body limp but voice pulled taut, "you would've done it already."

"You're clever." I slam one open hand down, claws spread, pinning the girl to the ground by her throat. With the other, I whirl and catch the mech, seizing its uneven left leg. "But I might not be so merciful to your friend."

"Friend? They're—it's a mech," Kori stammers. Her filtered voice is mechanically flattened, but the slip of phrasing betrays her fear. "It's property. Not personal."

"Liar." I pull, as hard as I can. There's a satisfying pop, a grating of metal, as the mech's left leg lurches free of its main body. The mech collapses with a disoriented *beep*.

Kori screams, the sound shaking against the press of my claws at her neck. Suddenly, she seems to remember herself. She wraps one hand around a weapon at her belt before I can process. I hadn't noticed it before. All at once, the muzzle of a heatshot blaster presses, coldly, against my neck, even as I loom over the girl.

Even with one ruined arm, the Daylands' princess fights back.

"Let me make myself very clear," Kori says, every syllable deliberate. Measured. "I charged this blaster before I left the Daylands. I've got a full clip ready to fire, enough to leave you with burns even this frozen hellscape won't easily cure. You can release me now, let me gather up what's left of my mech, and we'll be sprinting out of the Shadowlands in a blink of your nightfolk friend's singular eye. Or I can pull this trigger."

"And I'll slit your armor."

"Then I guess neither of us is leaving this place."

A heatshot blast at my throat is no bluff. I've yet to take a direct hit even from a freezeshot weapon, but a blast to my shoulder in a previous combat left me reeling and staggered, one wing rigidly useless, for far too long. And my body has evolved to defend against cold. Nightfolk know nothing of sun, heat, burning. My rule is fresh and tenuous enough that a visible wound, a physical limitation, might be enough to dangerously bolster Azarii's rebels.

"Does your mother know you're here?" I ask.

"Does it matter?"

"It would be a shame if the heiress of the Daylands never even received a funeral. If the body were lost in the dark."

"You wouldn't dare."

"You have no idea who I am."

"Usurper."

For an instant, I'm caught by genuine surprise. Then I remember she's traded memories with my now-escaped subject, who must be one of Azarii's rebels. How a nightfolk managed to sync her memory with dayfolk technology, I have no idea, but this is undeniable proof that it happened.

"Your own people hate you," Kori growls. "Do you want to validate their fears by murdering me in cold blood?"

"I wonder what your people would think, if they knew their heiress spent her private time slithering through the shadows."

"We all have our secrets."

I crack a smile despite myself. "And now you'll be mine," I snarl, twisting to clamp my teeth around the heatshot pistol's muzzle.

I feel the surge of awful distilled heat, like a brand against my lungs, but a fresh breath of radioactive power is already in my throat and swallows the shot. I hurl the pistol aside. It clatters to the stone ground, out of reach, and lands alongside the fallen sphere. I spit blood and ice and bits of charred flesh, retching. Both hands now around the trespasser's throat.

"Oh, but I've forgotten my manners." I leash my fury, press only its barest edge into my clenched hands. "Welcome to the Shadowlands, heiress. It's been a long time since we've had a dayfolk tourist." Her thin breaths go murky, distant. "Enjoy your stay."

Kori, heiress of the Daylands, goes limp beneath me. I press two fingers to where her glove meets armor at her wrist, though, and a pulse faintly ticks beneath my touch.

So she's alive. Good. Now would've been a terrible time to lose all control. I step away from her limp body, reaching to retrieve her fallen Morpheus spheres from where they lie. A single light blinks on the surface of each sphere. Bright red. Access denied, and brute force will hardly be enough to change that.

"Kori." The mech drags itself toward me by its hands, busted leg abandoned. I almost forgot about the strange amalgam of metal and apparent emotion. "Kori. Kori."

"Don't worry," I say, turning my attention back to the mech. "We'll prepare accommodations for two."

"I revoke—my request—for adventure," the mech says, before I crush its vocal box with my foot.

Once upon a time,
the princess of sunlight slipped into shadow,
and fell, and fell,
and fell . . .

CHAPTER 11

KORI

The moment I'm conscious, my hands fly to my throat, grasping at restraints that aren't there. I come to, coughing and rasping, still feeling the press of a monster's claws at my neck, cutting off my oxygen. Only then, with both hands fully mobile, do I realize my left shoulder's been restored to its proper angle. I feel around the joint with my right hand, testing; I give the arm a full rotation; even then, nothing hesitates, and nothing hurts. A dayfolk doctor resetting the joint would've advised physical therapy and medication for what was certain to be prolonged pain in the aftermath. But however the nightfolk healed me, it was with something beyond science.

My fingers trace the grooves of my full-body protective gear. From helmet down, the suit is unbroken, my flesh fully guarded from Pagomènos's deadly energies. A monster she may be, but the nightfolk warrior who attacked me didn't want me dead.

Whatever she does want, I need to get out of here, wherever here is. I blink rapidly, waiting for my surroundings to come back into focus, but I'm swallowed up by total dark. Abruptly, it hits me like a smack—I'm inside a fully enclosed structure. Before *Charon* crashed, I saw a massive azure pyre in the distance, serving as an alternative light source. But even that light can't reach me here. And my helmet/mask is designed to reduce extreme sunlight, not illuminate the unseen.

Cold snakes down my spine, settles in the pit of my stomach. The suit's heat resistance doubles well enough as cold resistance, since it's internally self-regulating, but I've never tested it over long periods before. I could die here. I could freeze to death, and it would be so very slow.

"Aspect." My voice is raw, strangled. I cough again. "Aspect, are you there?"

Silence.

I swallow a sob, or maybe a scream; if I don't let it out, I won't have to know. I would give anything for that stammering mechanized voice right now. I'd renounce my title as heiress of the Daylands (I may want to do that anyway). I'd part with another childhood memory. I'd shove that entire failed birthday cake down my throat and like it.

"No, no, no, no . . ." My voice is terribly steady, filtered by my mask, but my panic rises anyway. I stuff it down.

A plan. I need a plan.

Step one: Figure out where the hell I am. Slowly, gloved fingers splayed, I crawl backward (or is it forward?) until I meet a wall. It's chilly stone, smoothed to perfection, more solid even than bone. I'm definitely inside a nightfolk building. I worry at my lip with my teeth. There must be a door somewhere in this chamber.

I pivot what feels like 45 degrees, crawling until I meet an identical stone wall. Pivot again. This time, my fingertip brushes something strange and cold, and I make the mistake of plunging my entire hand forward. A sensation like arctic lightning spears through my blood-stream, my veins turned to ice. I scream and lurch away, knees pulled to my chest, teeth chattering something fierce. I might as well have turned my single clip of heatshot ammo on myself.

The heatshot pistol.

When I've gathered my composure, I reach for where the weapon ought to be sheathed at my hip, but just like my faithful mech, it's lost in the endless blackness.

Suddenly, it's all too much. Tears well in my eyes and my throat, and I swear, even though I can't see anything, the darkness shimmers. "No. *No.*"

I'm defenseless in forbidden territory, captured by a monster with unknown intentions, unable to contact my mother or even my mech, the only one who knew where I was going. My comms tablet was destroyed in the crash, which also left *Charon* badly damaged and embedded in the Second Spire. My only functioning Daylands weapon is gone. So is my sight. And this wall of sheer freezing power is impassable.

"Stars above. This can't be happening." I grasp the sides of my mask so hard, it's a wonder it doesn't snap in half. "This can't be happening."

In the distance, beyond my chamber, wind rushes suddenly. Swallowing, I pull myself up to my feet, prepared to meet whatever's approaching. An interrogator, maybe. Or an executioner. I've broken both dayfolk and nightfolk laws, crossing into forbidden territory to make an equally forbidden trade. A quick death is more mercy than I legally deserve.

A crackle, a hiss of sparks, and illumination bursts into being before my eyes. I blink, not believing what I'm seeing. It's a torch's flame, to be certain. It shivers and dances and burns. But it's blue fire, like the massive one that broadly lit the Shadowlands on my approach, blue as veins pulled taut in an arm, and it's suspended in the air, hanging on nothing. It shouldn't be possible.

"How . . . ?" The question escapes of its own accord.

"We nightfolk," the monster says out of the dark, "have many abilities your people would decry as unnatural."

"That's not fire at all, is it?"

"No." The blue light is just enough to illuminate the open palm above which it hovers, and the face of its carrier, but only in indistinct lines. A cruel sweep of jawbone. The barest twitch of a smile. "No, we have no use for such primitive things."

I square my shoulders. They crack and groan with the motion, but my healed shoulder holds fast. I think I already know the answer, but I ask anyway, "Are you the one who captured me?"

"Yes," she answers, her mouth's movement barely visible in the dim unnatural light.

"Then I've already seen your monstrous form," I say, with more boldness than I feel. "You have nothing to hide. Step into the light."

The monster chuckles. "There's nothing here worth seeing."

"Concealing yourself won't be enough to make me afraid. If you want to intimidate me, or make me tell you of the Daylands, or bring me pitifully to my knees, begging for mercy—you'll have to do more than hide."

There's an awful beat of silence. Then the monster blows out a breath, and the false torch greedily absorbs it, whirling violently, intensifying. Soon it engulfs the monster's entire hand, which remains outstretched and unburned. Its brightness brings the rest of my captor into view.

Her skin is moon-luster white, but with undercurrents of blue, like an entire network of split, broken veins. It stretches like old parchment over the amalgam of enlarged muscles that she presumably calls arms or legs; the bulk is such that I can't tell if she has only arms and no legs, or vice versa. If she wanted to, she could easily pursue an enemy on all fours, or else wield a freezeshot weapon in every one of her clawed hands. Or feet. My brain spins from trying to process. Wings, too, arch powerfully from her shoulder blades, their span broader than my height. They look like aged leather. I have the strangest urge to, if I were closer, run my fingers across the membrane, see if it feels as strong and solid as it looks.

"Better?" the monster says, sardonic.

She draws her arm back, the ball of false flame now illuminating her face. My breath catches in my throat. She looms above me, even as I rise up on my toes, her height terminating at perhaps eight feet. That arch of jawline could've been carved from glass, and likewise the curves of her cheeks, the solid line of her brow—her face is more bones than skin, a skeleton animated, a corpse confused at its own continued breath.

Beginning on her face, descending past her throat and all across her body, persistent half-healed wounds spot the overstretched canvas of her skin, as though her very blood cannot bear to be contained in such a form. Her hair looks as though it was closely cut, but the unruly ink-black curls have grown longer, with two proud horns poking through. Twin flashes of violet hold my gaze with unrelenting intensity.

"Better." My voice would certainly tremble if not for the mask's filtering.

"I could ask you to do the same and show yourself," the monster says, torchlight flickering in her irises, "but your kind would wither outside those accursed suits."

"Sorry to disappoint." I cross my arms, again keenly aware that while this monster queen imprisoned me and separated me from Aspect, she's also the only reason my left arm is a functional limb. Deep down, beneath the layers of obvious threat, she may harbor a remnant of mercy that could get me out of this nightmare alive. "You already know my name," I venture. "It's only fair that you tell me yours."

The claws encircling the torchlight shudder. The monster's mouth lifts, almost imperceptibly—a sham of a smile, but a smile all the same. "Adria," she says, in a clear, ringing baritone, and then she waits.

I fidget with my gloves. "Is that supposed to mean something to me?"

"I suppose not. Your people know little of what transpires in the shadows. I prefer it that way."

"And here I thought you had nothing to hide."

The monster—Adria—laughs sharply. If sound had a shape, the shards of this amusement would scrape her throat on the way out. "The Shadowlands is not to conceal us from you. It is to spare us the sight of your pitiful civilization."

"Lovely."

"Do you make a habit of back talking people who've imprisoned you?"

This time, I'm the one who laughs. "I have lots of practice with my mother." Something shifts in Adria's face, but it's gone in an instant, drawn back into unreadable tension. I press on, emboldened. "What do you want from me?"

Adria starts to pace, every lumbering step vibrating through the stone floor. The indigo torchlight dances wildly against her skin as she moves. "You're a valuable asset to your people, Kori of the Daylands."

Caught somewhere between exhaustion and fear, I almost laugh again. Sometimes I think I could disappear into the relentless sun and never return, and no one would notice. Sometimes I think about vanishing with nothing but Aspect, a pack of supplies, and a cache of Morpheus spheres. How long could I make it in the Passage, selling memories, making memories, being my own person until I fell victim to the elements? *A valuable asset.*

I close my eyes. "Depends on who you ask."

"You committed a crime against the Daylands by leaving, but also against the Shadowlands by coming here. Your people might like to see you suffer. But your mother . . ."

"Oh, she'll punish me, all right."

"She needs an heir to her monarchy."

"And who's to say it has to be me?" I say, almost yelling now. "Maybe I'm not the perfect daughter her position demands. Maybe I'm not the heiress the Daylands deserve." I shake my head. "Maybe they should pick someone else."

"But she won't," Adria says, resolute. "If there's one thing your people resent above all else, it's change. It has to be you." Her purple irises bolt me in place. "And she'll pay to see it be so."

All the oxygen whooshes out of me. "So you aren't trying to kill me."

"As a matter of fact," Adria says, stepping close to the freezing wall between us, "I'm dedicated to keeping you alive."

"What payment from the Daylands could you possibly want?"

"Why do you need to know?"

"Why shouldn't you tell me?"

Adria snorts. The flame in her open palm wavers. "Because you're set to inherit the only opposing power on our shared planet?"

"Right now, I'm caged like an animal, without my pistol or my mech," I say, every syllable deliberate. "If I ever get out of this place, Adria, rest assured that no matter what I know of the Shadowlands, I'll be terribly eager to forget it."

"And profit off the memory? Return to my territory with a fresh Morpheus sphere, when my eyes are cast away?"

I should say, *No, if you let me go, I'll never come back.* But spite is a hell of a thing, so instead I snarl, "Maybe."

Adria laughs again. The freezing wall between us shimmers in the firelight, making her form flicker in bursts and starts, lending her whole body the unsteady half presence of a flame. "Frankly, Kori, I have no idea just what you're worth yet."

My throat clenches. "I don't believe you."

"Why would I lie? I could simply withhold information altogether. I still need to consult with my advisors, then communicate with your people."

If only I could get out of this damned cell, surely I could shake free of nightfolk chains. "You could send me back," I venture, forcing confidence into my voice despite knowing that the mask will filter it regardless. "Send me bound, broken, to kneel before my mother. Beg her to take me back. She'd give you whatever you wanted."

My stomach twists. My mother values me because of what I represent, because I hold the Daylands' future in my hands, because I alone can rule when she passes on. But the Daylands would never accept a criminal for a queen. If I returned home in chains, I would be disgraced. The people would riot. I doubt I'd be worth a ransom. I doubt I'd be worth remembering at all. Maybe my mother would simply force all recollections of me into a Morpheus sphere, see it buried deep in the scorched earth, and try to move forward with another heir, chosen based on skill instead of blood.

But Adria doesn't know that. Her forehead creases as she considers my words. "You're a bold one, heiress." Her voice drips with contempt. "No doubt planning an escape. I will have you know, in no uncertain terms, that your mechanical friend will not survive if you evade my grasp."

Despite being nearly pitch-black, the room nevertheless seems to spin on its axis. My voice bursts out of me, so loud that it emerges from the mask laced with static. "Aspect. No, they didn't do anything, they're only here because of me, they're practically property—"

"Property," Adria says. "And yet you gave it a name."

"For ease of pronunciation. Aspect's code is 45P3C7. It doesn't exactly roll off the tongue."

"You're a practiced liar. I'll give you that. But a lifetime spent in the Shadowlands teaches a woman to look more closely at what true intentions lurk in the dark." Adria crosses her arms. "You won't leave without your mech, and I won't let you see it unless you comply."

My gloved hands curl into fists. "Everything I've read about your people . . . that you were cruel, heartless, hardly human at all anymore . . . it wasn't true." I glare without blinking. "You're *worse*. Embracing mutation made you a thousand times worse. Is there no compassion left beneath your wounds and wings?"

Adria wheels, her back turned to me, her wings flaring wide as her false torch collapses into darkness. Her voice hisses down my spine in the dark. "I could scrap your friend for parts, but I haven't. I could deliver you to your mother minus your rebellious tongue, but I won't. Tell me what's more monstrous, heiress: Giving a trespasser a second chance at returning to the light? Or creeping like a spirit through the shadows, confusing my people with memories never meant for them?" Her snarl shudders through the floor. "I could've slit your armor and watched the planet take you, turn you, make you like me. You'd see there's not so much difference between us, once you peel away your armor."

My mouth tastes like salt. "I'm nothing like you."

"If you want to return to the Daylands in one piece," Adria says, "I sincerely hope you're wrong."

I blink hard, half against tears, half in a vain attempt to adjust my eyesight to the darkness. But the blackness is total, this place like the planet's stomach, soon to digest me down to bones.

Somehow, I find my voice. "I'll prove it."

Adria says nothing, but wind rushes as her wings clench, coiling like fists against her shoulder blades.

"My Morpheus spheres," I say. "The one I brought, and the one I traded for. You took them both, didn't you?"

"What of it?"

"You can't open them. No matter what sick energies you unleash, no matter how you scrape and scrabble, they won't open for you." I lift my chin, squaring my jaw, hoping my posture can communicate even beyond my mask. "You intercepted the transfer of permissions. So, the one I brought, only I can open. The one I traded for, only my trading partner can open."

"Who's to say I didn't capture her, as well?"

"Maybe you did. Maybe you didn't. I don't care. At the very least, the sphere I brought? I'm the only one who can open it. And you'll have to tear my shoulder out of socket all over again before I do *anything* for you."

Adria laughs in the dark. "And why should I care what contraband you were carrying?"

This is my only opportunity for real leverage. My legs tremble, threatening to give out from under me, but I press my minimal advantage and take a careful step forward, closer to the freezing wall between us.

"You don't wonder what it's like?" I ask.

"A pocketed memory?" Adria huffs a heavy breath through half-bared teeth. "I have greater concerns."

"No, I mean the sun."

Blue flame ignites like spikes along Adria's spine, an unnatural luminescence. The planes of her face are stark, that sweep of perfect jaw quivering, her powerful posture undone. At last she turns to face me. Her eyes, a violent shade of violet, pin me where I stand. She lifts one hand, fingers splayed, palm open, and for an instant, I think she's going to slash my armor open, let the planet make me a monster, too. Instead, she extends an open hand like an invitation, her long, slender fingers just barely avoiding the freezing wall between us.

Her voice emerges, hoarse. "And what do you want in return?"

"That's the difference between you and me," I say.

I lift one hand, palm open, fingertips hovering a hair's breadth from my cell's freezing gate. Her hand is so much bigger than mine. She could crush my face like a melon if she wanted to; she could break me with an idle shove.

"The sun doesn't ask what the planet offers in return," I breathe. "It simply shines, time after time after time, until time doesn't mean anything at all. It's the way of things. It's the way of my people."

I force myself to stare into the fathomless purple eyes.

Adria blows out another frustrated breath, a burst of white in the Shadowlands' cold. I feel its heat even through the wall of freezeshot between us. She lowers her hand. "You do realize I cut off oxygen to your brain?"

"I'm in my right mind. I know what I said. You think I'm a monster like you. I may be a disaster of an heiress, but I'm still a daughter of the sun," I say, pleading. "So let me show you."

Adria's mouth lifts at the corners. A sun serpent's warning before a strike? An involuntary shudder of power? No, it's a smirk if ever I've seen one. I don't know what to make of her laugh, which rattles the floor with its ferocity.

"Get some rest, Kori of the Daylands. When I visit you again, we'll see what some time in the shadows has done to your promises."

The flames licking at her spine go out. I'm blown back into darkness. I jerk despite myself from the suddenness of it, involuntarily colliding with the freezeshot wall again. Its sheer ice spears through the marrow of my bones. I stagger, too pained even to scream, my body trying to shrink into itself. My mouth tastes like rust, my teeth stinging from the force of clamping them together.

"Adria?" I gasp, when I've recovered myself.

But there's only the silent stone beneath my feet.

CHAPTER 12

ADRIA

I'm supposed to head directly to a meeting with the Shadow Court, Thaane in tow. From him, they'll demand updates on how our troops are fighting back Azarii's uprising; and from me, they'll need a suitable asking price for Kori, delivered intact to the dayfolk. Instead, I wind like a stubborn river back to my chambers.

In the corner, all three of Russ's heads blissfully doze, his subconscious canine snores echoing off the walls. I envy sleep intensely right now. I want to curl up against him again, bury my face in his deep-black fur, and hope to the Beyond for a dreamless rest. But I find myself returning to the locked metal box beneath my bed. One claw pries it open with a hiss.

Inside, the two Morpheus spheres that I confiscated from Kori and the nightfolk girl glow steadily red. I know they won't open for me, but some reckless impulse makes me scratch at one sphere's seams anyway, poking its blinking light with one claw. Anger rears up in my throat, and I nearly try to tear into the sphere with my teeth before I come to my senses.

You don't wonder what it's like? The sun?

Everything inside me clamps shut like the sphere in my palm. Ribs locking together. Overgrown muscles drawing back against my joints. My wings ache—a persistent, tired tug at my shoulder blades. The Diakópsei granted me many gifts, flooded my veins with power, birthed me all over again as a new, vicious creature from its poisonous womb. But my power only holds sway here, in the Shadowlands. I've never dared to venture beyond the dark.

I've never even glimpsed the fabled sun, save for faint traces in the Passage.

If I did, would I even be able to behold it? Or would my eyes melt in their sockets, my skin dripping off my bones, like so many living things that failed to survive the Cataclysm?

My claws have nearly dented the Morpheus sphere. If I shatter it, there will be no recovering the memories within. A moment as seen by the dayfolk. An instant bathed in ceaseless heat and light.

The sphere wavers and blurs. I brace one arm against the floor, practically on all fours now, to stop from pitching forward. I hunger for sleep. I should have been unconscious when I first spotted Kori's ship, and I haven't slept a wink since capturing her.

"My lord." The voice from my doorway hits me like an electric jolt.

"Thaane. I would have met you at the Shadow Court."

"The court is three floors up. Zalel saw you pivot away from the stairwell, back toward your chambers."

"Then why isn't he here?"

"He hesitated to confront you alone," Thaane says, measured. "I volunteered."

A hollowness settles in my stomach. Zalel is still more boy than man, more servant than soldier, and he's seen far too many of my private rages. Swept up far too many of my shattered mirrors since my overcharge, and all the bodies left in the wake of it. Part of me pities him for being assigned to me at all. No doubt, I looked ashen and haunted when I left Kori's cell. It's no wonder Zalel didn't want to confront me. The boy is doubtlessly tired as well; it was he who used his gift to heal the prisoner's mangled arm before her awakening.

I blow out a breath, its tendrils curling stark white from the constant cold. "Fair enough."

"Adria . . . I'm not here on orders." Thaane's voice wavers. "I'm here as your friend."

Your friend. There were times I suspected Thaane would've preferred to be more than that. But he knows full well I could never feel the same; there isn't a man anywhere on this planet who could make my heart race, make my legs wobble, like the few female warriors in my parents' army always have when they walked by. My heart is not attuned to men. Father blamed himself, once, when I tried to tell him. I retorted that he might as well blame Mother, too, if we were going to treat my heart's inclinations as an aberration—earning me a blow to the cheek and a permanent ban on such conversations.

Thaane is still watching me. I pull myself out of my thoughts. "I'm fine." The shape of the Morpheus sphere is all but imprinted in the flesh of my palm. "I needed a moment. Much has happened since . . . since everything."

Thaane's eyes flicker to the sphere. "What is that?"

"The dayfolk heiress was carrying it."

"Could it be . . . ?"

"A Morpheus sphere, yes."

Thaane's gaze goes wide, pupils dark and swimming. "Do you know what sort of memory is inside it?"

"Not yet."

"Do you know how to open it?"

"I do."

"Then why haven't you?"

I shake my head. My horns feel heavy, more collar than crown. "This is the first dayfolk trespasser under my new reign. When my parents—when the last leaders ruled, they didn't deign to bargain with dayfolk. But whatever is inside this sphere . . ." I catch myself blinking in time with its red light. "Only the prisoner can open it."

"And what does she want in exchange?"

I rise to stand on two feet, swallowing hard. "Nothing," I breathe.

In a world where dark and light each hold court on their assigned planetary side, where creatures of the day and the night never mingle, where every victory is bought in fire or in ice, born in hidden shelters or unnatural fortresses, this girl—Kori—would trade something for nothing. A memory of sunlight for my trust. And what is my loyalty even worth? What mercy do I have left to give?

"Nothing at all," I say.

The red light gleams against my palm, and for an instant, I'm slick again with my mother's blood. My ears ring with my father's screams. What I wouldn't give to remove that memory, prying it out with my own claws if I had to. I wonder what its physical shape would be; presumably a bloody, writhing thing, like the root system of a poisonous tree, the foundation of my newly claimed empire rooted irrevocably in death.

It's the way of my people, Kori said, her empty palm outstretched. A prisoner's promise, the last thing she had left to give.

My people are nothing like hers. *I* am nothing like her. Somehow, even through her protective mask, I felt her eyes steady on me, blurry with tears. Hopeful.

What kind of girl seeks mercy in a monster? What sort of dayfolk leader walks willingly into the uncharted dark?

Thaane's three-clawed foot scrapes idly at the ground. "It can't be for nothing. She must have an angle, a play."

"That's what I'm afraid of," I say, the lie thick and slimy on my tongue.

I'm not afraid that Kori wants something from me. I'm afraid that this planet hasn't only birthed monsters. I'm afraid that my bloody footsteps were my own design.

Was there truly no other way? Did I strike down my parents as a desperate act, to prevent an overcharged army from declaring war on the Daylands? Did I really break free of their toxic influence at that moment? Or have I become the perfect weapon they always wanted?

I feel cold all over.

"Come to the meeting," Thaane says, arms crossed, all four wings folded back. "Discuss the ransom. Then you can sleep on all this and determine what she really wants."

I nod stiffly. With one last jealous glance at my innocently sleeping dog, I follow Thaane into the corridor, back toward the Shadow Court's seventh-floor meeting chamber. Together, we will decide the worth of the Daylands' first daughter in weapons, resources, perhaps even soldiers. We will transmit a rogue message across the Passage.

And maybe, when I close my eyes, I'll discern why she would offer me sunlight for no cost at all.

"There's one other thing," Thaane says, testing, "if you're ready to hear it."

"Readiness is overrated."

"Upon your return to the fortress, I took the liberty of sending a telekinetic unit, led by General Isek, after the citizen who traded with the prisoner."

General Isek. I can still see his son's head twisting clean off, imprinted on the inside of my eyelids. Isek the younger's killers are dead, yes, and by my hand, but it makes precious little difference when the child remains a corpse. Or at least, I would think so.

Without continued prying for details of his son's demise, General Isek has simply stood by me since my overcharge, accepting my orders without question, leading soldiers into battle against Azarii, delivering rallying speeches to the wounded—and now, apparently, retrieving Kori's trading partner with a telekinetic squad.

Does he know I could've stopped his son's death? Does he know that by killing my own parents, I've avenged Isek the younger as best I know how? I don't deserve his loyalty. But in such unstable times, I will gladly accept it.

Thaane continues recounting the capture of Kori's trade partner. "Thankfully, she was neither a telekinetic herself nor blessed with wings. They caught up with her and held her fast." He deliberately clears his throat. "She was questioned by a qualified interrogator, of course."

I can't help but raise an eyebrow, intrigued. "What did she tell them?"

"Her name is Lail, daughter of none. An orphan, long surviving on her own, but cared for by another. Her brother, Neo. An Elysian."

I rack my brain, but the name means nothing to me. "Describe him."

"A telekinetic prodigy with a shock of red hair. Judged to have immense aptitude, even in his youth, and offered early enrollment in your parents' regiment. But he refused to take up arms," Thaane says sourly, "even for his king and queen. Instead he fled to the Depths, converted into a cultist. The only person aboveground that he didn't cut off entirely was his sister."

I knit my eyebrows together in thought. "What value does this information hold?"

Thaane begins to pace back and forth, not looking at me. "Did you ever wonder how a nightfolk had a Morpheus sphere in the first place? Sure, she could've scavenged it off a corpse or an unfortunate passerby in the Passage, but how does a nightfolk, without a dayfolk memory implant, possibly transplant a recollection into a Morpheus sphere?"

I fight back a growl. "Get to the point."

"During your charge into Depths, in which you took the throne"—Thaane deliberately doesn't say, *When you killed your parents*, but my chest aches at the reminder nevertheless—"Neo's stubborn nature led him to an even greater offense than abandoning us for Elysium. A sin that even his new family couldn't tolerate." Thaane huffs. "In the chaos of the battle, before you could possibly lock down access, he touched the Diakópsei. He overcharged himself, just like you."

My throat constricts. "What happened to him? To his gifts?"

"He's a telekinetic. The overcharge to his abilities was psychic, not physical like your energy blasts and vascular enhancement." Thaane gestures to my hulking form. "And he was lost to himself almost immediately, overwhelmed with competing thoughts of the people around him."

"Did Elysium know this had happened?"

"If they did, do you really believe they would have told you? They're religious fanatics, Adria. They've never been our allies. And in the wake of your overcharge, they were terrified of you."

My newfound alliance with Elysium—that we might keep the Diakópsei guarded at all times, ending overcharge once and for all—is indeed a fragile thing. And my fits of rage in the immediate wake of my regicide were certainly intense. I can't entirely blame the cult for not telling me that one of their own also accessed unholy power.

Thaane goes on. "Elysium would've exiled him regardless for what he'd done. But he fled to the surface of his own volition, to the only person he knew he could trust. His sister." Thaane goes on to explain that Neo's overcharge empowered him to move much more than objects with his mind.

My head whirls with new information, the ground tilting beneath me. "A nightfolk who can move memories."

"That isn't the point," Thaane bites out. "As he once betrayed your parents, fleeing military service for a fanatical cult, so he betrayed the cult, accessing the very power we've sworn should never be available again. And he used that illegal overcharge to aid and abet his sister in a blatant crime. Illicit smuggling of dayfolk tech. Fraternization with a member of the Daylands *government*—"

"He can *move memories*." My blood pounds in my eardrums. Behind the pulse, I can still hear my parents' final screams. I never want to hear them again. "What happened to him?"

"In exchange for reassurance that we wouldn't execute him on sight, Lail led the legion to his hiding place, knowing he couldn't survive alone forever. We took both of them into custody, separating them, and notified the Shadow Court."

"But didn't notify me?"

"I intercepted your path to this meeting to do exactly that. They wanted to catch you off guard, to see how their young queen reacts to a sudden reveal of yet another wrench in your newfound leadership. I thought it better to warn you, as your friend, so you can present a calm, clearheaded plan to the court about what should be done with him. Presumably execution, but the timing is in your hands."

"The very execution you promised his sister wouldn't happen?"

"We promised we wouldn't kill him *on sight*. Not that we would suffer such an abomination to live much longer."

Before I can think, I've seized Thaane by his scrawny throat, pinned him against the nearest rock wall with his three-toed feet dangling in the air. I can see my bared teeth reflected in his pupils, but incredibly, that's all I see. Not a trace of fear, even in the face of his new queen.

Thaane gawks. "You would rather an untamed telekinetic child, with the power to psychically move memories between minds and tech, be left loose in our world?"

"You see an impossible gift, and your first instinct is to slit its throat? That's the Shadow Court's old guard talking, their terror of change. Not the pragmatism of my friend."

I force myself to drop Thaane, who lands remarkably well on his feet, despite the bloodshot edges of his storm-gray eyes.

He coughs pointedly into his arm, stubbornly clinging to poise. "Is there something you'd like to forget, Adria? A mistake that even acquiring a kingdom can't erase?"

"He could be an asset in the civil war," I say, barely able to hear myself over my pounding pulse. "We need every upper hand we can find." I press the heels of my hands into my eyes, struggling to process so much new information at once. "You did well by telling me this before the court did. I will tell them to stay his execution for now, to keep him imprisoned. Then I wish to meet this Neo myself."

Even through his undoubtedly aching throat, Thaane manages a clear, dutiful "Your will be done, my lord."

It does not escape my notice that Thaane neglects to remotely agree with my plan, but I've already had too many petty outbursts since my overcharge. My nerves feel like they're shuddering, always on the edge of snapping like an Earthside instrument's ancient strings.

Overcharge made me stronger, all right. But I don't know if I'm strong enough to bear that strength with the dignity my status demands.

"The ransom. That's our primary concern, for the moment." I cross my arms and square my shoulders, desperate to steady my rattled brain. "I risked my already-tenuous reputation with the Shadow Court to prevent your court-martial after the interrogation incident. I keep you close because your energy abilities are unparalleled, because you've stuck by me despite all the infighting . . . and because you've been my brother since we locked eyes as youths."

"I'm honored, Adria, but I—"

"But things are changing, Thaane. The old guard. The limits of our strength. The assurance of our bonds." I grip his arm just hard enough to hurt, but deliberately not enough to break skin. "Do not make me regret what I did for you. The punishment I spared you. Please, Thaane. For old times' sake."

I hate the tremor in my words, but I can't suppress it. For all my blustering strength and new augments, I'm a queen without a family. I don't want to be without a friend, too. I trace little circles into his arm with my thumb, force my voice to raise an unnecessary octave.

"Don't make me broker a deal with the Daylands monarch alone. Help me pull this off. Help me *lead*. Help me give our people the support we need to settle these rebellions and march us forward, into a peaceful and glorious future. Not back into a civil war."

Thaane inclines his head. Deference? Defeat? He's deliberately stone-cold. "That's all I've ever wanted, friend."

"Then let's get to this meeting and determine that ransom," I reply. "We've kept the court waiting long enough."

"Indeed we have," Thaane agrees, and we walk in silence the rest of the way.

Once upon a time,
the captive princess offered a demon
a shard of the sun.

CHAPTER 13

KORI

I sleep fitfully in the sightless cage. Without proper light in the Shadowlands, even my dreams lack images, but every other sensation is heightened.

Gloved hands, latex, pinning back my hair, prying at my forehead. My mother's voice, a shudder of heat against my face. "Can you hear me?"

My eyelids feel sticky, my mouth full of tar. I think my lips are moving, but every movement rattles like a rusted door hinge. Who am I? Who am I? Who am I?

*"She's not ready," someone says—Ednit—*and sensation recedes like a tide, lulling me back into a most unnatural sleep.

The remainder of my rest is dreamless.

Eventually, I wake gasping, my throat raw as if from screaming. Frantic and choking, I reach to remove my mask before abruptly remembering where I am. I'm still encased in darkness. Somewhere close by, if I listen closely, I can just barely hear the sibilant hiss of the freezeshot wall that keeps me here.

If I remove even one piece of my protective gear while aboveground, Pagomènos's radiation will immediately begin to break or mutate my body—and here in the Shadowlands, that radiation is even stronger than in the light. I force myself to breathe through my nose until the rhythm of inhales and exhales steadies.

Not real. Just another dream. I've been having these inane visions for ages at this point, so I should really be used to it by now, but every time I think I've made my peace with them, something new arises. More poking and prodding. A fresh wave of confusion. I've never known where I was in my nightmares, but this time, I'm not even sure if I knew my own name.

Maybe it's worse because Aspect isn't here. I have no idea how long I've been imprisoned, but I have no doubt this is the longest we've been apart since I first started modifying their programming. Their absence feels like a thousand pounds on my back, dragging me down to the floor.

The only indication of how long I've been here has been the periodic delivery of tasteless rations, identical to the most budget-conscious ones of the dayfolk military back home. It seems the night-folk were always prepared for another dayfolk trespasser, and for potentially having to hold them for trial or otherwise.

There's also a metal cylinder in the corner of my cell, a simple waste chute whose top slides open and shut at the touch of a button. My suit uses a series of chambers to ensure I can evacuate without directly encountering the atmosphere. It's similar to how I've been able to eat and hydrate without removing my helmet.

But food, water, and their resulting waste are weak indicators of time. I feel completely lost to it in this prison. And without Aspect, every passing instant feels infinite.

My anti-radiation gear stabilizes its wearer's internal temperature against the planet's extremes, but as indeterminate time passes, it's increasingly obvious that the suit is optimized for the Daylands' heat, not the Shadowlands' bitter, boundless winter. The tech's warming abilities are rapidly showing their limitations. Shivers twist between my ribs. I pull my knees to my chest with gloved hands, rocking senselessly, soundlessly, back and forth in the dark.

The floor shifts beneath me, loose stones leaping, and for an instant, I'm afraid that I'm still dreaming. Then I recognize the steady, deliberate thumps, growing louder. Closer.

Footsteps.

My captor has returned, maybe to bring me home, maybe just to toy with her prey.

"Adria," I say, forcing volume into my voice. "You came back."

One clawed hand ignites with supernatural blue light, illuminating the monster. The bags beneath her purple eyes have softened, and there's a renewed lightness in her wings, which lightly and idly flap as she approaches. Her harsh line of mouth arches into what could almost be called a smile. While most of her skin, even her visage, maintains that eerie blue-white sheen, there's more blood in her lips, full and red, a contrast that immediately draws attention to her mouth.

"I've determined the going market price for a runaway heiress," she says. "Your life will buy the Shadowlands a new era of peace."

Her shadow stretches out and swallows me, even taller than her impressive height. Her outline is all horns and claws. None of her smile. None of her gaze that makes my heart stagger between beats.

I swallow. "Why do you need the money?"

"Who's to say I brokered a deal for money?"

"Well, why do you need whatever you're trading me for?"

Again, that ghost of a grin, present and then gone. Her brow tenses. "You've never been to the Shadowlands before, have you?"

"No."

"I would've expected at least a weak denial."

"I don't see a point in lying. We've established you need me alive."

"Things could get much, much worse for you, heiress, without courting death."

"By the Dreamgiver, at least use my name when you're threatening me." I shake my head, a tired laugh threatening to escape.

"Dreamgiver?" The pupils swell, nearly eclipsing the purple irises. Among the nightfolk, I suppose that's what passes for an expression of wonder.

"You really know nothing of the dayfolk," I say without thinking, heedless of the deadly claws and falsified flame.

"I don't need to know."

"And yet you wonder."

Adria says nothing. The silence is answer enough.

"My people all have the same biotech installed at birth. The Morpheus chips. Our last chance at not forgetting as quickly as we know, without mutating like you." I rise to my feet, boldness coursing through me. "But their history, their origins—you know as well as I, it was already forgotten."

Adria doesn't move to interrupt, so I keep talking.

"The dayfolk have developed two sects around Morpheus tech. The Dreamgiver Devotees believe it was a gift from a benevolent god. But the Old Seekers, they think if there is a god, then god abandoned us. Or else the Cataclysm was a cosmic judgment. Now all we have is science. Tech."

"And what do you believe, heiress?" Adria says, her voice balanced on a knife's edge.

"I'd like to think there's a god looking out for us," I say, staring at the floor. "But this, the Cataclysm, the wrecked planet, the death . . . this can't be what that god had in mind." I force myself to meet my captor's eyes again. If she's kept me alive for this long, maybe it's worth trying to pry beneath the surface. "What do you believe?"

Adria is silent for a long moment. "There are no gods but what we become."

"Is that how you picture yourself?" I pry. "A god?"

Adria laughs, mirthless. "If I'm the planet's last god, then we're all well and truly damned."

Silence stretches between us. The blue-black fire ripples against the freezeshot wall, shimmers against the uneven stone floor. I find my lungs again. "Why did you come here, Adria?"

She takes a step toward me, nearly colliding with the freezing wall. I flinch, despite knowing she can't come any closer. Then she kneels, one knee bent, her height suddenly akin to my own. One hand, still channeling flames, stays steady. The other she extends, palm open, cradling both my Morpheus sphere and Alpha's between her claws.

"Which one holds the sun?"

"The one with the scuffed side." I point to the first of the two. "Alpha—the one I traded with—she dropped it when you opened up the ground." I squint in the firelight. "Don't you want to know what's in the other one?"

Ferocity gathers in Adria's voice. "I want to see the sun," she insists.

Her speech is nearly a roar, her wings and horns a jagged, threatening sprawl, but her eyes are soft. Pleading. A girl born to a sunless world. A girl resigned to dying in it.

"You must understand," she says, her face not far from mine, the wall between us an icy flicker, "the Shadowlands are troubled. I cannot simply set you free. I have nothing to offer you that I haven't already. You are one piece on a far larger board, but you hold the sun in your hands, and it's beyond me." She blinks hard, eyes squeezing tight, then blooming violet again. "Kori, Kori, I cannot make you any promises, but if you meant what you offered—"

I offered the sun to shame her, to pierce the monster's armor with reckless grace. I intended to eventually negotiate for something: Aspect back in one piece, or at least their memory core; a protected place to remove my gear and wash my face without succumbing to the radiation. But her eyes are galaxies deep, the barest glimmer of tears creeping through, and they ache, and I ache, and I can't look away.

I don't let her finish the sentence. "Give me the sphere."

She stands. Presses a button mounted on the wall, beyond my line of sight. The freezeshot barrier collapses from the top down. I could run with all my strength. I could leap out the nearest exit and hope *Charon* has at least a few salvageable parts. I could go back to Lail's rebels and hope they're still willing to fly me home.

I want to see the sun.

Adria places the Morpheus sphere on the ground, nudging it toward me with one foot. I take it in my hands, opening my palm against its sensor. "Access."

"GRANTED," the sphere intones, and it blinks green.

"Test," I say. The green light turns steady. I extend the sphere to my captor with a trembling hand. "Go on."

Adria stares as though the technology might abruptly unveil teeth. "What do I . . . ?"

"Just hold it."

She lifts it between two tremulous claws, and then her eyes go completely white. Usually, while the buyer experiences their desired memory, I'm checking my half of the merchandise. This is the first time I simply stand and watch someone else experience a Morpheus sphere—and a nightfolk, at that. They don't have the Morpheus chips installed in the dayfolk. Instead, the memory plunges directly, brutally into her brain.

Adria is utterly rigid, a statue, an outgrowth of the mountain around and about us—her wings spread wide with shock, her eyes blank, milky orbs, her mouth open just enough to show her sharp teeth.

She collapses like an avalanche. Sobs, their sound swallowed up in her shame, rack her whole body, her wings curling as if to obscure her from view. She isn't watching me. Her claws aren't drawn. Her blue flame flickers out, leaving us in total darkness. If I ran right now, I could be halfway down the hall before she recovered herself.

The floor shakes alongside her hulking form. She gasps for air.

I don't move a muscle.

"Adria?" I say, barely audible.

The most absurd desire washes over me, to lay a hand on her shoulder and wait for her shuddering to cease. To *comfort* this beast who holds my life (and Aspect, my only friend) in her clawed hands. I wonder, distantly, if my own hands could find her without my sight. I almost move, and not to flee.

"*You*." A sob; a scream. Black and blue flames tremor around every edge of Adria's body. The Morpheus sphere lies abandoned at her feet. "Why aren't you running?"

I shake my head, faster and faster, trying to clear it, getting nowhere. "I don't know."

She snarls, then. Suddenly, instead of a tangle of shivering limbs, she's securely on all fours, scrambling to reactivate the freezing wall between us. An instant of useless, too-late clarity pierces through me. I bolt for the threshold. The freezeshot wall plunges down, and I collide with it face-first.

Adria stands eight feet tall again, teeth bared. I'm the one who cowers, sobbing and shuddering, frozen to the floor.

She doesn't ask me what memory lies within the second sphere. She doesn't threaten me for my admittedly pathetic escape attempt. She bellows, more monster than mortal, and then she barrels down the corridor on all fours, leaving me alone in the dark.

CHAPTER 14

ADRIA

I'm so lonely.

Without a Morpheus chip of my own, Kori's memory is already a fleeting imprint, a curtain of thought just barely brushing my brain. But every point of contact stings.

I am bathed in sun. After so long underground, sick and wan, I've returned to the surface. Its brilliance beckons and rebirths me, saying, Come out, come out, *and every piece of me longs to lunge back into the day. My lungs want to scream, but I know the sun won't scream back. I'm free again, but only ever free to be alone. I close my eyes. The heat, even dimmed by my protective gear, could melt me down like the rivers of lava beneath the planet's surface. I want to let it happen. I want to feel something. I'm so lonely. I'm so lonely.*

I'm so lonely.

The shadows beckon, promise to hide me away from even myself. Soon, *I tell myself, gloved fingers curling into fists. Soon I'll go beyond these sun-streaked plains, beyond even the scattered ruins of the Passage. Soon I'll build something worth remembering.*

Even if I have to do it alone.

"Damn you," I snarl, leaning against the corridor wall, struggling to catch my breath.

Kori tried to offer me a glimpse of daylight, and yes, it was beautiful. It was more than I could've ever imagined. Albeit secondhand, I've now felt the sun's all-seeing gaze, its heat flooding my veins with brutality matching the Shadowlands' cold. I'd wondered why anyone, even a fully accustomed dayfolk girl, would willingly remove a memory of the sun. But now I understand.

Beneath the comforting sweep of sunlight, the chasm at Kori's heart yawns canyon wide.

I'm so lonely.

I lean so hard against the wall, my wings leave indents in the stone. Every part of me screams. I lock my jaw shut against the sound. If it starts again, I don't know if it'll ever stop.

I caught this girl as a bargaining chip, a transaction valuable enough to fund my new regime and crush the insurgents. After negotiating with the Shadow Court, we've determined an asking price to transmit back to the Daylands: an armory of newly assembled heatshot guns, a type of weaponry that Azarii's people will be utterly unprepared to contest. Such weapons won't be able to recharge in the Shadowlands' freezing temperatures, but there's enough blazing sunlight in the Passage to do it, and the terms of the agreement dictate that should a regiment of my army be spotted there, the dayfolk are to leave us unmolested.

That's all I should be thinking about right now: brokering a weapons deal for Kori's life. I didn't ask for sunlight to dawn on my doorstep. I didn't ask for my own silent torment to whisper across the freezing wall between us, sharp enough to stab.

I'm so lonely.

Even through her mask, I felt her gaze steady on mine. Afraid, certainly. But not looking away. I wonder what color her irises are. I've never seen the eyes of the dayfolk, not yet altered by the Diakópsei's power, but I've heard stories. Blue like an Earthside sky. Green like the last surviving plant life of Pagomènos. Brown like untouched earth. In my mind's eye, the colors all blur together, a kaleidoscope iris framed by dark lashes, looking straight through me, daring me to look back.

Zalel waits outside my quarters. His breath, emerging in quick, nervous pants, sends little bouts of blue flame from his nostrils. I push past him before he can say a word. Quickly dropping to all fours, I fumble for the other box beneath my bed, the other souvenir of my first encounter with a dayfolk girl.

The mech's leg remains wrecked, connected to its torso by a single stubborn wire, frayed almost to breaking. Its feet were already in a state, anyway, sparking and smoking even after I turned the entire system off. Internally, its voice box is a crumpled husk, and externally, its head remains at that dysfunctional bent angle. Its optical processors are dim in shutdown, but the ridiculous expression on its metallic face remains. Two eyes, almost but not quite the same size. A smile wide enough to invoke revulsion.

"Do the dayfolk really take you seriously?" I mutter to myself. If I had a face like that, I wouldn't even blame the insurgents for wanting to blow it clean off. "Was all . . . this . . . really necessary?"

I've never fiddled with a dayfolk mech before. I've never even seen one, but I know something of their technology. After all, my own fortress has sections of radiation-forged Pagonian plate, better designed for dayfolk prisoners than where I'm currently keeping Kori. They've been abandoned for ages. We never thought we'd see another dayfolk trespasser in my lifetime.

"My lord?" Zalel's voice cracks like static at the end. He's still at my doorway, eager to be of use.

I've treated him as less than even a servant, and he's become something of a friend. I let loose a long breath. "Zalel. Can you bring me a comms tablet repair kit from storage? And some spare parts, if you can find them?" We may not have full, proper replacements for the ruined knee, but the mech will need something to walk on—alongside several new gears in the voice box, a head realignment, and something for those half-burnt feet.

"Of course!" Zalel shouts, thrilled to have a mission. But then, after an instant of hesitation: "What for?"

"Our prisoner may be with us for quite some time before we can contact the Daylands for her ransom." I trace the mech's obnoxious smile with my claw. "It would be a shame if she were lonely."

Kori is asleep when I arrive. I suppose for a creature unaccustomed to the Shadowlands, the eternal night makes sleep a perpetually enticing option, so I shouldn't be surprised, but it's not her unconsciousness that strikes me—it's the peacefulness of it.

The radiation mask still conceals her face, warping it into strict lines and protective angles, but the arch of her spine has gone from a coiled spring to a delicate curve. Her gloved hands, once fists, have opened like flowers, reaching for the light on Pagomènos's other side. The mask regulates her breathing, whether she's sleeping or awake, but in sleep, it's the gentlest whisper, the exhale more like a sun-kissed breeze than a mechanical rasp, steady and soft.

For a brief moment, I don't want to disturb her supine form. I stand with all four limbs locked to the floor, afraid that if I turn away and depart too quickly, the thudding of my steps will startle her awake.

Unfortunately, the mech's haphazardly assembled personality persists, despite one leg having been reduced to an unbending rod. It talked the entire way to Kori's cell, oddly preoccupied with Earthside methods of time tracking that have been long abandoned on Pagomènos. By the mech's rough estimate, after drilling me about how many torch lightings I've lived through, I am "seventeen years" old—which means nothing to me but seemed to please the robot well enough.

Reuniting with Kori pleases Aspect even more than useless measures of time. "KORI!" the mech wails, launching itself into the freezing wall of her cell. I'm already beginning to regret realigning its head and retooling its voice box, once again enabling speech with utterly unnecessary volume and projection. The concentrated cold makes the mech's every joint audibly rattle. It steps back, shuddering violently. "Pain. Not fun for Aspect. Not recommended—by Aspect." But as soon as the shock subsides, the mech shrieks her name again and catapults back into the wall.

Kori jolts awake. "Aspect?" she mumbles, groggy; then, coming back to herself at the sight of her mech doing its damn best to self-destruct, she says, "Aspect, stop it before you hurt yourself!"

The mech curls into a contrite ball on the floor, one knee pulled to its chest, the other leg now an unflexing peg. "Aspect is—very sorry."

Kori's mask pivots. I know her eyes are fixed on me. I wonder if they're glaring or brimming with tears, or both. "What do you want?"

"Must every action I take be out of want?" My rib cage feels hollow, every heartbeat's echo reverberating. "I already fulfilled my intent here. Your life will earn a handsome ransom for my regime. But, in the meantime, it won't do to have you rotting in that cell. I need you suitably healthy for when the dayfolk retrieve you, or your mother may be displeased, even revoke the ransom."

Kori points at her mech. "What does that have to do with Aspect?"

"It's a precaution, if you will."

"They have a name."

"What sort of dayfolk citizen grants her machinery a name?"

Kori hesitates. I imagine her biting her lip behind the mask. "They're more than a machine. Maybe less than a person, so far. But surely you've seen it. Those glimmers of personality, flickers of near-organic choice."

"Why are you telling me this?"

"Because you telling the dayfolk would only compound my crimes, thereby decreasing my ransom. And I think you want to be paid exorbitantly for the time spent suffering my presence."

I smile a bit despite myself. This absurd rebel of a girl, utterly unafraid of even the Shadowlands' own monster princess, is beginning to amuse me.

"Oh, I wouldn't call it suffering." I gesture to the mech. "So how did you program them?"

"Memories," Kori says, without missing a beat.

I blink, stunned. "From what I understand of the Daylands, that's not what mechs are meant for."

"And dayfolk girls aren't meant to spend their lives dutifully isolated from meaningful human interaction. But when you're the Daylands' heiress, daughter of the monarch, the rules change. I decided I might as well change them for my own creation, too."

I turn my gaze to Aspect, half disbelieving, but the honesty in Kori's voice is obvious despite the mask-filtered tone.

Aspect straightens, wobbling a bit on their new makeshift leg. They chirp, "Aspect is still—learning how to—people!"

"And doing a bang-up job." Kori laughs.

I shake my head. "Where did you get the memories?"

"Sellers on the market. Myself. Bodies I've found in the Passage. I came to the Shadowlands to see if the installation of a nightfolk's perspective might finally awaken something properly sentient. Instead Aspect lost a leg. Almost lost their ability to power on altogether." And I took out their voice box with my foot, but despite the uncomfortable twist in my gut, Kori doesn't need to know that; I fixed it, after all. Her voice trails off. "And that's on me."

The mech twitches. "Aspect is not—experiencing—repulsion—from Kori!"

"Maybe that's because I was too selfish to program it."

"You are not—a shellfish! You are an—organic—with your—crunchy parts—inside your—squishy parts. Aspect—does not have—squishy parts. Aspect is very—crunchy." They tap their new leg rhythmically on the floor. "Leg—went CRUNCH!"

Kori shakes her head and turns her attention back to me. "So why bring them back to me, Adria?" My name in her mouth does something strange to my insides, makes them curl like rogue vines around each other.

I tap Aspect's head. "It's obvious from their—ah—quirks, that they prefer never to leave your side. So I've installed a tracking chip."

Kori snorts. "Well, that makes two tracking chips in Aspect. My mother installed one, too." When she sees me tense, she frantically clarifies, "I never actually let that thing work. It's set to indicate a randomized series of locations right now, so my mother doesn't wonder what I'm up to. But I doubt it can transmit back to the Daylands from this far away, if it even survived our crash landing. And I'm sure any intact illusion will only last so long after I don't come home."

Fair enough, I suppose.

"*My* tracking chip," I clarify, "notifies my comms panel where Aspect is at all times. And if they are ever outside this fortress, I will know."

"What's to stop me from telling them to stay here and making a break for it?"

"You offered me sunlight from the depths of your despair. I've known you only for a short time, Kori, but you and I both know you won't leave your friend to wander the dark forever in search of you."

Kori stares at her boots. "So what are the rules?"

"You should consider them gracious allowances. You are a criminal in your world and a trespasser in mine." But the snarling venom in my voice is fiercer than I intended, and I grit my teeth, trying to clamp it down. "We maintain living quarters of Pagonian plate, designed for dayfolk like yourself should diplomatic relations between our people ever reopen."

"Is that also why you have dayfolk rations on hand? Potential for . . . diplomatic relations?"

"Does that shock you?"

Kori gives her head a little shake. "After all that's happened to me lately, my ability to feel shock is rapidly dying."

I almost laugh at that. "I will lead you to your new quarters. You can wash, properly eat and drink, whatever you like, without fear of the planet's radiation. Aspect will go with you."

Aspect raises their arms victoriously. "Aspect will—follow Kori—*everywhere*!"

"They can't spend too long in the plated area," Kori notes. "They run on the same radiation that could kill me. Even at home, I have to let them take their little walks aboveground."

"Then the mech may step outside the chamber to recharge. They'd best not wander far, and you'd best not leave the chamber yourself at all, if you don't want your head to leave your shoulders."

She shudders at that. I don't know when violence became more to me than a desperate final resort, now simmering in my bone marrow, bubbling, boiling, always ready to explode. This girl delivered me sunlight, and with it, a glimpse behind her mask. I know the loneliness that writhes within her. I don't need to employ threats to make her understand, but it's as though I don't know another way to speak.

Swallowing anger and shame alike, I tap the button on the wall. The freezing cell barrier collapses into nothing. Slowly, Kori rises to stand on legs nearly as unsteady as Aspect's. The mech hops up and down, clapping and singing her name as a joyous refrain.

"Follow me," I say, when the reunion's volume dies down. "I'll show you to your quarters."

CHAPTER 15

KORI

Adria leads me through her labyrinthian fortress. I may not be chained, but I might as well be physically tied to her; even if I were to make a run for it, Aspect clunkily in tow, I could never navigate this place on my own.

Since I was unconscious for my journey into the fortress, I never got a full, proper look at its layout—it was nothing more than a malformed, inky silhouette in the distance, brutally lit by a single enormous blue light at its highest point. But from what I can gather as we weave through countless hallways, up and down staircases, and farther and farther from the prison quarters, the nightfolk fortress is a concentric collection of rectangular levels, getting narrower each level up. The prison was along the far west side, and we seem to be making our way . . . east . . . I think? But I can't shake the feeling that Adria is making this route deliberately convoluted, ensuring I can't navigate the fortress without her help.

As we twist our way from the fortress's westmost point to the east, Adria starts to lean almost onto her front limbs, practically proceeding on all fours, somewhere between a walk and a run. It should serve as a reminder that she and her people haven't been merely human since the Cataclysm, but instead it dredges up the most peculiar memory for me.

As a child, when Chloe called me for dinner, I'd ascend every shelter stairwell on my hands and knees, laughing, insisting that my scuttling was faster—or, at the very least, more fun. She used to scold me without even a flicker of amusement, saying that only a Shadowlands mutant would traverse a staircase in such a way. Part of my brain knows I should see a predator's charge in Adria's movements, but now that I know her by name, I can't help but see echoes of a child's amused experimentation instead.

Those limbs, swollen with muscle, blue-white skin stretched over them like worn parchment, could tear my chest wide open, shred me into ribbons—but instead, she uses those powerful arms as secondary legs to casually scramble through halls where she could just as easily walk.

Adria doesn't even glance behind her to ensure I'm following. Whether it's because she trusts me not to run or knows she could obliterate me if I did, it's impossible to tell. Aspect follows our captor at an eager clip. I can't help but do the same.

After so many turns, ascents, and descents that it's useless to track, we arrive outside the Pagonian-plated safe room. Most of the shadow fortress's interior is uneven, the rock forged by radiation into something like a living system, twisting veins and arteries of rock meeting somewhere into a heart beyond my knowledge. But the plated section, safe for dayfolk, is entirely artificial, physically constructed instead of born of strange power. Its walls, floor, and ceiling are smooth and metallic, almost medically austere. I've never seen Ednit's living quarters back in the Daylands, but it wouldn't surprise me if they looked very much like this.

Adria gestures to the door with one claw. "Everything you need should be inside. I'll leave you be."

I swallow. "How do I know I'm not walking into a trap?"

"Oh, Princess," Adria says, the moniker sliding coolly down my spine, "you were trapped the moment you set foot in the shadows." She almost smiles. "But, at the very least, remember my ransom. It's in my best interest to preserve your health." She presses one claw into a control panel, opening the room's first sliding door. "You'll have to go ahead of Aspect so the air lock safely purges all radiation. When I call for you, they will deliver the message."

Aspect wobbles on their new leg. "New chip—in Aspect's head!" they proclaim, tapping their poorly drawn face. "Beeps when—new friend is coming. Very—*annoying*—to Aspect."

Lovely. I grind my teeth. "And what if I need you, Adria? I somehow doubt there's also a summoning microchip under your hair."

She laughs. It should be a heavy, shuddering sound, given the eight-foot hulk that stands before me, but it's icicle brittle. "The air lock will seal behind you. Aspect can leave as needed to recharge. If anything else organic sets foot in that chamber again before I permit it, I will know. And the results will not be pleasant."

"So it's another prison, after all."

"Do you want to escape that sun-forsaken radiation suit or not?"

She isn't wrong, but my sharp tongue betrays my better sense again. "Don't flatter yourself. I somehow doubt girls are rushing to take their clothes off at the sight of you."

I don't know why I'm surprised that nightfolk can blush, but the blooming crimson streaking her blue-white cheekbones startles me. She truly stumbles for words for a moment, clawed fingers grasping as if for lost language. One wing curls a bit, as if to hide her face.

"If a prison is anywhere you can't simply leave," Adria says, "I don't see how your so-called home in the Daylands is any different."

That lands like a blow to the back of my head. What's the difference, really, between my underground shelter below the sunlight and this shadowy chamber beyond its reach? One maintained by my mother, daylight's queen; the other by my captor, the shadows' queen. Both more concerned with my long-term value than my present well-being.

"Then at least I've had plenty of practice," I snarl, and step into the air lock.

The door slides shut behind me. Lights flash blue and red, cold smoke filling the room from every angle as stray radiation is purged from my protective gear. After a brief stretch, the next door opens and admits me to my new living space. Aspect follows, the air lock revoking any radiation from their system that hasn't already been absorbed as their power source.

Without even stopping to take in my new living space, I half pull Aspect, half fall into them, hugging their cold, metal form as tightly to myself as I can despite their many uncomfortable angles and edges. I didn't even know I needed to cry, but now I'm sobbing, just clutching Aspect to me, their head buried in the crook of my neck as tears stream unbidden down my face. My eyes burn, and my mouth tastes like salt. At some point, my knees give out, and I'm kneeling on the floor, still clutching Aspect, my whole body shaking.

"I thought I lost you," I gasp between sobs. "I thought I lost you."

Aspect gives their head a little *no* shake against me. "Kori will need—to try harder—to lose Aspect."

When the tears finally stop, at least for the moment, I release Aspect from the crushing hug and take in my new surroundings. There's a proper shower on my right, a changing area adjacent, and a comically oversized bed on my left, as if the nightfolk forgot that over six feet of bloated muscle is atypical for their daylight counterparts. The ceiling houses harsh pale tubes of white lighting, which are all automatically activated by movement, so there isn't even a lamp in sight. No personal effects, no signs of life. It must really have been generations since any dayfolk set foot in the Shadowlands. Leave it to me to break tradition again.

I want to be angry, especially at Adria, but as soon as I let that anger gain a foothold, I find it's mostly anger at myself. Foolish girl, launching herself like a shooting star into the darkness, wishing for an impossible memory capable of instilling a machine with a *self.* I could've stayed home. I could've made the best of lonely days in our underground compound, focused on tinkering with Aspect and doing my assigned readings, and hoped that one of the readily available memories on the Morpheus Market would finally do the trick in my quest for Aspect's awakening—but no, I had to test the boundaries of my assigned space. I had to fall into the endless abyss just to see if it had a bottom.

And this is definitely rock bottom.

But Aspect is with me again, so even at the end of myself, I find the will to keep moving. To keep fighting.

I trespassed in the Shadowlands to find a memory capable of awakening Aspect. The shadow queen may have me securely on a leash, but I'm hardly bound in place. And now I'm completely immersed in a world entirely different from my own, set apart from any memory I could've possibly bought on the market. Anything here could be the secret to awakening Aspect. I just need enough courage to walk further into the dark—even when I can't see my own hand in front of my face, even when a single false step more could spell the end of everything.

First, though, I need to wash off my lingering terror.

The sight of a proper shower in my new room floods my whole body with relief. It's a carbon copy of the ones we have in the shelter back home, clearly designed to purge any latent radiation from the water before it ever hits my body. It feels like I've been wearing this sun-forsaken radiation suit for an eternity. I shuffle to the changing area, drawing the curtain shut despite being technically the only organic present. Aspect has yet to develop a filter between their handmade neurology and their vocal mechanisms; the last thing I need is them casually recounting the appearance of my naked body to Adria when she returns.

The thought sets my own face ablaze. I wonder if nightfolk have similar boundaries around nudity. I wonder what a full nightfolk body looks like, uncovered by the dark, heavy clothes they seem to prefer. I wonder why I'm thinking about this at all, why my brain saw fit to brand itself with the arch of Adria's wings, the breadth of her shoulders, the cruel, boyish amusement in the sweep of her ruby-red mouth.

Get it together, Kori.

My armor peels away like scales. Clean air hitting the flesh of my face comes as a welcome relief. The shower coughs ugly greenish-brown water when I first activate it, clearly not having had a dayfolk guest in generations. The nearby toilet, too, has some old, unaddressed mold and unusual, deep-set discoloration from prolonged disuse.

Thankfully, after a moment, the shower water runs beautifully clear, which is when I step in. And, oh, stars above, it feels incredible. I turn the water up as hot as the mechanism allows. I want to boil like the sea meat in that useless memory. I want to burn away every trauma I've experienced since *Charon*'s crash. Every splash sears my skin, reminds me I'm still alive.

The changing area contains a generic set of vaguely humanoid-proportioned clothing. Despite having directly copied some other things, it seems the nightfolk never obtained dayfolk-made clothes for potential dayfolk visitors. The legs and arms are still too long for any but the tallest, most muscular members of our species, so Aspect helps me tear the excess length away, resulting in awkward, jagged edges of frayed fabric. Even so, the material is smooth, silken, and settles like cold water over my aching skin. The comfort lulls me toward a tempting sleep, but I refuse to sit down on the bed and let it take me.

Adria thinks she's captured a conditioned prisoner, born and raised in strict limits, accustomed to layers of armor and walls. But I've only ever taken boundaries as a challenge, for better or for worse. I could sit here and wait for the ransom payment, hoping the softer heart behind Adria's glacial gaze prevails, but I may never have a better chance to offer Aspect a glimpse of another perspective entirely.

Just like in the Morpheus Market, I still don't know exactly what I'm looking for. But if it's something to be found amidst the nightfolk, this may be my only chance to obtain it.

Of course, while returning home with a sentient Aspect would be a total victory for me, it would set me up to appear as the ultimate criminal to my own people. The list of offenses would be something to behold: Violating the trade rules of the Morpheus Market, communicating with nightfolk, trespassing into the Shadowlands, illegally experimenting with memory application into a fully synthetic being . . . and how much worse if they could see Aspect was fully *thinking*, fully their own person now as a result of those experiments? I would be a monster to the Daylands, with my own makeshift metal monster in tow. Even my mother wouldn't be able to protect me from whatever punishment Daylands society deemed necessary, not to mention the Morpheus Market's Coalition.

So my purpose now is twofold. One: Find something nightfolk that's capable of raising Aspect to sentience. Two: Find something nightfolk that holds value to the Daylands if I bring it home.

Right now, in the eyes of any other dayfolk, I'm a stubborn child who played with darkness just to prove I could. But there remains a chance to become a bold explorer who delved fearlessly into the depths, emerging with buried nightfolk secrets that could maintain dayfolk security on Pagomènos for generations to come.

And Aspect has more tricks programmed into those tiny arms than Adria could even begin to guess at. Code breakers. Overrides.

Even for chambers designed to detect and punish unauthorized organics.

I refuse to separate from Aspect again, and Adria's installed tracker will certainly notify her that we've wandered beyond our assigned space. But she is a queen, after all. Surely she has other pressing matters to attend to. By the time she notices our location, I could have my hands on exactly what I need to awaken Aspect. What's the worst Adria could do in retaliation then? Kill me? If I'd stayed home, locked underground, ever obedient to my mother and my doctor and my government and the supposed limitations of science, too afraid to even *try* instilling sentience in my closest friend, it would've been like waking death regardless.

I would rather die trying to awaken Aspect than live wondering if I missed my best chance. And I'm willing to bet that with a ransom on the table, Adria wouldn't dare cut my life short or even risk permanent harm.

Lost in thought, I idly tap my fingers on the air lock control panel.

Aspect has been pacing the length of the chamber. They pause, angling their head like a curious child. "What is Kori—thinking?"

A smile curls across my lips. "Another terrible idea, probably."

"Aspect—*loves*—terrible ideas."

"And that," I say, reluctantly retrieving my radiation suit again, "is why I love you."

The nightfolk fortress twists and loops back in on itself like the bottomless gullet of an impossibly long sun serpent. I don't know with certainty how long Aspect's hack will delay Adria from being notified that we broke containment. I don't know where we're going or what we're even looking for. This entire endeavor may just be compounding the increasingly severe stack of mistakes that brought us here. But I refuse to trade the cage of my life in the Daylands for a new one here in the darkness.

The halls are windowless, so they would be like an inkwell, all texture blotted out, but for periodic braziers of the same blue flame Adria conjured outside my cell. They illuminate the rugged stone walls and floors, as well as staggered banners of blues and purples that I can't help but call beautiful. Presumably the torches should have attendants, and the hallways guards, but I don't see any.

Almost as soon as I have the thought, frantic footsteps thunder from somewhere close.

My heart beating out of my chest, I seize Aspect and slam both of us flat against the wall, then yank us behind the nearest banner of deep indigo. It isn't long before I can see nightfolk feet, their oblivious conversations also audible as they pass.

"Is the queen so useless that she can't predict a single rebel attack?" says one nightfolk. "We could've intercepted them before they reached the gate, and this isn't the first time. It's obscene."

The clicks of freezeshot weapons at the ready. The rush of wings opening, readying.

"A hell of a thing," says a second nightfolk, "to take a kingdom by force, then cower upon being asked to crush further opposition."

"It is her uncle, to be fair," says a third voice.

"Spare me, Isek. Since when has family meant anything to the queen?"

A fourth voice interjects, booming, "Enough. There will be a time to critique the queen, but that time is not with rebel rifles on our doorstep."

The first voice swears, with venom. "Worse than Russ. Must you always be the queen's prized pet, Thaane? Is she tugging on your leash?"

A cacophony of movement. The slam of a body into, thank the stars above, the opposite wall and not us. The whole hall rattles, pebbles and gravel scattering from the ceiling. I swallow an involuntary cough.

The fourth voice—Thaane?—is terribly steady, but packed with power. A loaded gun, trigger tensed. A weapon is no less lethal for having a silencer; I fully believe that if the speaker cut loose, he would tear everything in his path apart in a rampage with his bare hands, with his teeth.

"Know full well, soldier," says Thaane, "that if they find your body on the battlefield, slit from throat to thighs, everyone will report it was one of the rebels who did it."

The third voice—Isek?—is tremulous. "Let him go, Thaane. It isn't worth it."

The crash of a body to the floor. Coughing, gasping.

"Azarii's troops won't make it inside, not with us at the ready," Thaane continues, apathetic. "But should one slip through, let's not make it easy for them to find their way about. *You*, soldier . . . do it."

A clap of clawed hands. It feels like I've been flipped upside down, and then I'm nearly choking, trying not to gasp aloud, the sensation like all the oxygen has been sucked out of the hall. Aspect reaches to steady me, and I push back hard, not wanting their shifting gait to make their peg leg squeak and alert the nearby soldiers.

Almost as soon as it began, it's over. In a single flash, every single blue-flame brazier on the wall goes out.

We wait for the footsteps and voices to recede, then wait another long moment to be absolutely certain, before emerging from behind the banner.

The darkness is perfect and total now. I creep along the rugged stone hall with one open gloved hand on the wall, counting every perceptible turn in my head so I can retrace my steps before Adria finds my new chamber empty. So help me, I wish I knew where I was trying to go. I wish I knew what I was looking for. I wish I didn't feel doubt wriggling in my gut that this was at all a good idea.

But, at the very least, Adria is certain to be distracted from us right now. And the hall's standard patrols have been called to the gate. Clearly, the rebellion I glimpsed in Alpha's memory is bloodthirsty and out in full force. Beyond the fortress's walls, freezeshot and bullets alike distantly ring out, split by battle cries on both sides.

"For the queen!"

"Down with the usurper!"

Aspect's forehead contains a headlight, but since mechs were never intended for use beyond the Daylands, the darkest area they'd encounter would be a starship's repair hatch—nothing compared to the boundless dark of the Shadowlands. The illumination doesn't carry far. Just a shivering, pale cone in our immediate vicinity.

Our combined stealth is also limited by Aspect's new leg, which A) does not have a knee joint like Leg One, and B) announces every step of Leg Two with an enthusiastic *squeak*.

A short while later, the only thing I know for sure is that I haven't accidentally gone backward. Where I'm going remains a mystery, and the more turns I have to memorize, the more I fear I won't be able to find my way back. But I can't turn back until I've found something useful, either for Aspect's awakening or justifying my crimes to the Daylands, or this will all have been for naught. So I trudge on into the nothingness.

Besides the battle cacophony beyond the fortress, the only sounds are my mask-filtered breathing and Aspect's squeaky new leg.

And then, low, shuddering straight up my spine—rumbling. *Growling*.

"Aspect," I gasp. "Against the wall. Now."

Unfortunately, Aspect chooses the wall opposite me, leaving my immediate surroundings encased in impenetrable dark.

Out of the void, six glowing red eyes blink and lock on me, then tilt in casual observation. I go stock-still against the wall. The eyes creep closer, close enough that hot, rank breath from the unseen creature fogs up the outside of my helmet. Something drips onto my visor. It traces down my mask, dripping to the stone floor. My knees are knocking worse than Aspect's ever have, legs jittering together, fear abruptly alive in my whole body, a scream struggling to break out of my throat.

The growling rises. It vibrates through my ribs like a bass drum. Something thick and hot lashes out toward my face, too quickly for me to react, trapping me against the wall. In my fright, I stagger, knees hitting the rocks below, the strange sensation smacking against my helmet, blocking my view. It takes an embarrassingly long moment for me to register that what's blurring my vision is saliva—the pressure on my helmet, twin lapping, flailing tongues.

"Aspect," I breathe, barely audible even to myself. "Light, please. Slowly."

Aspect tilts their head to reorient the spotlight, revealing the hulk that stands before me. At Chloe's insistence, I've studied precious memories of Pagomènos's early animal inhabitants, so I know what a dog is supposed to look like, though they've been extinct for generations.

This is definitely not the natural state of a dog.

Its body warps, surges, into a trio of thick necks, each adorned with its own canine head. Two are characterized by lolling tongues that tease my mask, the red eyes playfully bright; the third head snarls, eyes more like starship error warning lights, rotten gums flecked with spittle, tongue relentlessly chewed, coated in both dried and fresh blood. Is it one dog? Three, somehow merged into one?

In the memories I've studied, humans patted them on the head, called them good.

"Good . . . dogs?" I open one gloved palm, willing my hand not to shake, and lay it against one of the two friendly foreheads. "Good dogs. Very . . . good . . . dogs."

The beast nuzzles into me, nose wet, midnight-black fur coarse but soft. An absurd peace rolls through me. I could close my eyes and stay here forever. Maybe this is why early Pagonian settlers brought dogs to the planet. I already want to smuggle this strange specimen back to my quarters, stroke its muzzles with my fingers until it falls into a pleasant sleep.

"What is it, Kori?" Aspect pleads at an unholy pitch and volume.

The dog (dogs?) recoils, whining. The sound is like air slowly escaping a punctured radiation suit.

"Aspect, careful," I whisper. "It has six ears, and they're very sensitive."

"Sorry!" Aspect shrieks, still grating, before applying the instruction and dropping their voice to a mechanized mumble. "IsthisbetterKori-isAspectmakingyouhappynow?"

"Yes, that's better, thanks." I turn my attention back to the dog. "Hey, hey. Hey. It's all right. I'm a . . ." Trespasser? Prisoner? Temporary resident? "Friend."

Head Three, the rightmost head, spits a gross lump of saliva on the floor. I nickname it Grumpy. Head One (Silly) and Head Two (Sillier) loll in opposite directions, but with matching dorky expressions of amusement, tongues sprawling, gazes wide and hopeful. I gently massage Silly and Sillier while side-eyeing Grumpy, who pointedly looks away.

"Odd." The cold, heavy voice lurches from behind me like a startled snowbank. "Usually, Russ accepts cuddles only from me."

Aspect mutters a four-letter word I definitely didn't intend to teach them just as Adria, in all her towering winged glory, steps out of the dark. Her teeth are nearly bared, her visage locked into rage beyond words, but when she looks to the dog, her ruby lips curl into an amused smile, teeth kept inside.

Russ bobbles over to Adria, even Grumpy seeming mildly pleased at her arrival. Silly and Sillier lick at her wrists, pawing at her chest. Adria lowers her head briefly to accept a loving lick from Silly.

"I thought you would've been fighting," I say, before I can think better of it.

"My appearances on the front have done little to intimidate the rebellion. Even less so to convince them that their cause is wrong, and I am the queen the Shadowlands deserves," Adria says, wiping dog saliva from her cheek with a clawed hand. "My advisors have deemed it better to prioritize my safety, keep me inside these walls."

Oh, do I ever know what that feels like. A pang of foolish empathy flutters in my chest.

"My soldiers will hold the gate." Adria's eyes travel pointedly up and down my body, and a blush burns my face. "Your assigned chamber was meant to hold you."

Russ has taken the bite out of Adria's voice, slightly softened the glass-sharp edges of her ever-serious face. Despite my worst fears, Adria isn't going to harm me. I can't help but feel that she is, in fact, toying with me, not unlike her pet.

"If you wanted me to stay put," I venture, "clearly you should've assigned some of those soldiers."

"Clearly," Adria echoes.

My mother would berate my snark, reminding me that the future Daylands monarch ought to be calm and dignified, but Adria has so far only ever pushed back with equal force. It's infuriating that I can't seem to break through her steely exterior, but exhilarating to be answered in kind instead of deflected. Even knowing my face is concealed by my mask, I dare her to launch a comeback with my eyes.

"If I didn't know better," Adria says, sauntering closer, "I'd say you were hoping to invoke my wrath. But I think you're just too curious for your own good. And to barrel straight into Russ . . . You must have a death wish."

She laughs, that same youthful, brittle sound from before, and again, it does something ridiculous to my heart rate. I'd love to deny it if not for the floating notification inside my visor, concerned for my health.

"I should order you back to your quarters."

"But you won't," I bite back; and then, after a moment's pause: "I should retreat of my own volition."

"But you won't," she echoes.

Silence stretches between us, thick and palpable.

Adria breaks it with a blunt question. "What were you looking for, stubborn girl?"

I could snap back reflexively, challenging her to duel me with jabs and barbs, but her voice dares to ask me for honesty, maybe even promises some in return.

Information on your people, I mean to say. *Something to redeem me to my government. Something to fully awaken my friend.*

But truth is a slippery thing, and it slithers out of my grasp and seizes a sentence all its own: "I showed you something of me and how it felt to look upon the sun. I'd like to see something of you."

"You might have asked me." Her voice is a low growl.

"Better to ask forgiveness than permission."

"The Shadowlands do not forgive. But there's more truth in the dark than you know, heiress. You only have to let your eyes adjust." She lays a hand on my forearm, claws splayed but not piercing, grip firm but not painful. "Follow me."

It's not really a question.

Aspect glances at me. "Aspect stay—with Kori?"

The logical thing would be to ensure a witness, even a mechanical one, for whatever's about to happen. But something in the careful pressure of Adria's fingers over my armored wrist sends sparks through my arteries, turning my blood to lightning. I want to see whatever she's deigned to show me, and I don't think I want anyone else to share that moment.

"Go back to my chambers," I tell them. "Power down outside the door. Recharge as much as you can."

"Be safe," Aspect says, among the most human mannerisms they've learned as of late.

But I've already invaded the planet's forbidden side, plunged headlong into its rebel queen's twisted psyche. I've long abandoned *safe*. I want the thrill of forbidden knowledge.

I want to see what memories pulse in this strange, monstrous girl's mind, beyond any other dayfolk's reach.

Aspect retreats the way we came. Silly, Sillier, and a reluctant Grumpy follow them, apparently eager to continue making new friends. Four canine paws stammer happily down the hall and out of earshot.

Adria's hand hasn't left my arm. Her other hand presses into the small of my back, urging me forward without threatening to break my armor. "Come," she says.

Drunk on possibility, I follow.

Once upon a time,
the imprisoned princess took hold of her bonds
and drew them tight enough to bleed.

CHAPTER 16

ADRIA

"So where are you taking me?"

There should be fear in Kori's voice, but I can practically imagine the raised eyebrows, hopelessly curious, behind her filtration mask.

"The archives," I say without turning around. "My people don't artificially store, transfer, and trade memories as yours do. Instead, we keep records like our Earthside predecessors. Written records, digitized and alphabetized."

Kori snort-laughs with derision. "*You* keep *journals*?"

"Is that so surprising?"

"I was always taught that the nightfolk were further from the Earthside ways than any of us. Twisted into something new, something other. Not a trace of original humanity left." Another little laugh escapes Kori. "And here you are, overthrower of the old regime, leader of all who live in the shadows, taking little notes on goings-on instead of utilizing the Morpheus tech to directly pull and archive experiences."

"Your people were afraid to forget what once was. Mine burned away the chaff to make room for something better." I tap my forehead with one blunt claw, where I presume the dayfolk insert their mechanized implants. "Morpheus tech was hopeless resistance to the Diakópsei's power."

"Its infection, you mean."

"That's what your people say. I prefer *metamorphosis*."

"Like a caterpillar," Kori says wistfully.

At that, I'm the one who turns to Kori, eyebrow raised. "A what?"

"I forget the Shadowlands doesn't have as many Earthside memories archived. It was . . . like a small worm, sometimes fuzzy. It would wiggle down a branch and weave a basket for itself and crawl in, and then it would change. And it would come out, and it would have wings, all kinds of colors, thin as stained glass. Beautiful."

I shake my head. "Why cling to memories of the Old World, when you've never embraced the potential of the new one?"

Kori's answer is nearly a snarl. "Some of us like being human."

"Are you truly so happy with what you are?" I counter. "Do happy people run away from the only home they've ever known, hurl themselves headlong into the dark without checking if there's a bottom?" Kori stills, narrow shoulders rigid, arms crossed protectively against her ribs. "That's what I thought." I turn the corner and press my palm to the scanner lock, opening the sliding door to the archives. "We're here."

"Stars above," Kori gasps.

Her words accompany all the oxygen whooshing out of her lungs. Again, I find myself wishing that I could see through her protective mask, her eyes no doubt wide and starstruck right now.

The archives are indeed a sight to behold, only accessible to nightfolk royalty or approved historians and recordkeepers. The average citizen under my parents' (or now my own) rule will never set foot in this room. Every wall is constructed entirely of shelves upon shelves, data tablets lined up like so many paper books. The narrow metallic edges are striped with identifying layers of color, depending on how recent each record is and its primary topic. To me, it's order—more comprehensible than anything else in my life right now. But I know what Kori sees is a miasma of color, a mosaic of knowledge never once accessed by a dayfolk citizen.

She turns to me, one gloved hand nearly catching my wrist before she remembers herself, remembers what the overcharged power in my veins could do to her. "Why would you bring me here? Me, of all people?"

"It's difficult to tell through your mask, but that almost sounds like an accusation. You could stand to be grateful."

I'm taunting her, the furthest thing from authentically offended, but she takes a cautious step back anyway.

"Forgive me, Adria." Hearing my name on her tongue, even flattened by the voice filtration, still does something strange (though not entirely unpleasant) to my stomach. "I just . . . This is . . ."

"The collected history your people forgot, yes."

Kori gives her head a little shake as if to clear it. "I'm a trespasser in your realm. A prisoner, at that. Why lead me to knowledge that could be used against you and your people? Don't you already have enough threats?"

"Why give me a glimpse of the proper sun?" I counter. "Why not simply continue to throw insults at me through the cell's freezeshot barrier? Treat me like the monster your people believe every nightfolk to be?"

"I'll treat you like a monster when you act like one." It's delivered like a threat, but this time I'm the one who feels the breath knocked from my body.

I have felt more monstrous than ever since the overcharge, since . . . everything I hope Neo can help me forget. But nevertheless, this small, bold, incomprehensible girl who should never have set foot in the Shadowlands at all sees something more in me than pulsing power or sharpened teeth. I never meant for her to see the haunted parts of me, the void that stares into me when I consider what comes next. But now that she *has* seen it—seen it utterly and fully, in my moment of weakness before the remembered sun, and chosen not to look away—I find I don't want her to.

And that's terrifying.

Kori goes on as if she didn't just knock the axis of my universe askew, proceeding to tug everything even further out of proper orbit. "After I left my room, I heard your soldiers, en route to the gate. I heard the fighting outside. They said it's your own family staging this rebellion, too. Your uncle." Her eyes flick back to mine. "I'm sorry."

I want to be angry that she's already obtained such sensitive information about my newfound leadership's fragile state, but instead, my whole stomach clenches around *your own family*. Kori has no idea how bad things with my family can really get, not even an inkling of how my parents' final breaths torture my waking moments and my sleep alike. I find, to my own confusion, that the thought of Kori finding out what I did multiplies the shame tenfold.

My whole mouth tastes bitter. "I don't need your *pity*. Lest you forget, Kori, I'm no mere suffering soldier. I am a *queen*." And she should show some more respect, stop unapologetically prying her way to the most sensitive, vulnerable parts of me, but she isn't inclined to stop.

"A queen," Kori says, "but not a monster. When you threatened my life by the Second Spire, tore Aspect's leg from its socket—I saw a monster then. But the girl I saw in my cell, the girl who saw the sun and could hardly bear it . . ."

Kori looks away, staring at the wall of records without seeming to see it. "I can't speak to your people. And I sure as hell can't repeat any of this to my people, when you send me home. I mean it when I say I'm not sure you know how to be kind. But I'm even less sure that you know how to be cruel. I could be starving, dehydrating, abandoned in that cell right now, and I'm not. Why? Why am I here?"

My mind seizes on a phrase she most definitely delivered by accident. "When I *'send'* you home?" She doesn't answer me, only stares more intently and with less apparent attention at the wall of records.

"I brought you to the archives," I say, striding farther into the rows of records, "because I thought you came to the Shadowlands for a glimpse of my people, our minds, our way of being. But I'm beginning to wonder if you want to go back at all."

"I can't stay here," she says quickly, a reflexive parry of a thought she doesn't dare entertain. "Dayfolk bodies aren't built for the Shadowlands. I'd have to live out my days in this sun-forsaken suit, save for sleeping or waking. I'd lose myself."

"Is that really the only reason? No friends would miss you?"

"My mother detests distractions from my learning."

"And your mother?"

Kori scoffs, dismissively flicking a hand. "What about you? Don't you have anyone to spend your waking hours with beside a withering dayfolk prisoner who can't keep her mouth shut?"

"My soldiers know better than to talk back to me."

Except for Thaane, that is. We have a lifetime of childhood scuffles and purely playful conflict behind us; I would never let another of my subjects talk back to me the way he does.

But it's a profoundly uncomfortable thing, to be feared so severely that all criticism ceases, save for verdicts delivered by the Shadow Court.

"I find I miss having someone with the boldness to argue," I say, and I mean it.

Thaane's refusal to withhold his true opinions is, while frustrating, deeply reassuring. And Kori's presence already absurdly feels much the same. Even when I feel at my most monstrous, this girl can't bring herself to be afraid of me.

I watch her, the harsh set of her shoulders, the defiant lift of her regal jaw, before adding, "And I think perhaps you miss talking back without punishment too fierce to bear." She doesn't deny it, so despite my better instincts, I press my luck. "You don't see yourself as a prisoner, Kori of the Daylands. A runaway, maybe. Even a fugitive."

"I'm sure my mother will call me worse when you send me back," Kori says.

"Perhaps our interests align more than either of us anticipated." I gesture to the rows of glittering, iridescent history. "We've been honest with each other thus far, for better or for worse, so do me the honor of being honest with me one more time." I cross my arms, fold my wings, and stare her down. "You came to the Shadowlands for a memory, at first. Why?"

Kori averts her eyes, beginning to pace in lazy circles around me. "Aspect, my mech. I've been programming them for hundreds, maybe over a thousand sleep cycles at this point. They're starting to ask higher questions, express some degree of near-conscious awareness. But it hasn't been enough." She sighs, and I hear the defeat in it. "Installing dayfolk memories in a machine was already a crime. So, I thought, why not take it one step further? Why not give Aspect a glimpse of the other side, the other people, and see if they . . . wake up?"

No friends to speak of. A mother more like a prison warden or an overseer. It's obvious from the way Kori speaks that this machine, strange and inscrutable as they may seem to me, is the closest thing she has to a confidant. "So when Lail contacted you—"

"Alpha . . . ? You knew her name?" Kori says, her panic barely restrained and still painfully obvious.

"I know everything that happens in the Shadowlands."

It's more bluster than truth, and I think Kori knows it, but the closer she gets to the anxiously racing heart of the matter, the more I'm tempted to withdraw behind my title and authority. I deliberately don't mention Neo either. Kori doesn't need to know about him, let alone of the horrible, murderous memories I hope he can remove from me.

"When she contacted you," I continue, "you saw a chance at . . . awakening . . . Aspect."

"Yes."

"I brought you to the archives to select and duplicate a record, as a suitable exchange for the sunlight memory you shared. What if you had more than a moment to browse? Three sleep cycles? Seven? Twelve?"

At that, Kori's nervous pacing draws to an abrupt stop. "What are you proposing?"

"The longer I keep you from your people, from your mother, the higher the ransom they'd likely be willing to pay."

More weapons. Mechs, perhaps, to use as delivery mechanisms for dayfolk explosives. Perhaps even one of their starships, to launch an unexpected assault from the skies. It would be more than worth a longer wait, if our ultimate deal gives my army enough ammunition to cleanly end this civil war.

"You're threatening to lengthen my imprisonment," Kori balks.

"I'm *offering* to treat it, for all intents and purposes, as an agreed-upon period of residence among the nightfolk. To your mother, you'll be my prisoner, perhaps suffering terribly. I can still make that happen, if you'd prefer torture to free reign of the archives."

Kori takes a moment to process, breathing heavily, her gloved hands curling into fists. "*If* I take that offer . . . what will you do with the credits you ransom from the Daylands? How do I know you won't use them to stage a war against my people? To spread the Diakópsei's *gift* to the rest of the Pagonians and damn us all?"

"I believe it was you, Kori, who said I don't seem like a monster, after all."

"Then be utterly human for a moment." It's harsh, but under the circumstances, I can hardly blame her. "Tell me the truth. Why do you need the credits?"

I could tell her I need money to cement my position as the Shadowlands' new queen with wealth and prestige. I could tell her it's insurance for the future, given how the Diakópsei uniquely elongates nightfolk lives. I could tell her any number of swiftly fashioned half-truths or cleverly crafted lies, but I don't want to. I can feel her human gaze behind her artificial mask, daring to ask me for truth without either terror or hatred.

So I tell her everything. My desperate attempt at peace, though war drums have replaced my heartbeat and violence now boils my blood. Azarii, damn him, and his hopefully ill-fated uprising in my parents' name. His upstart army, so horrified by what I've become that they've rejected their own gifts entirely. I tell her I overthrew my tyrannical parents. I tell her they died in the fighting.

In a flush of burning shame, I don't tell her I killed them myself.

I tell her the trade is for weapons. I assure her said weapons will be used only to quell the rebellion she personally overheard at the fortress's gates—not to reignite the ages-old conflict between nightfolk and dayfolk.

When I've finished, Kori stares at the polished metal floor for a while, cogs likely turning in her brain. Then, finally, she turns to me with a swift nod. "You need weapons to end a war, not to start one. Likewise, you took the throne to prevent one. I can throw my weight behind that. Especially if it wakes up Aspect." She curls one hand, absently, into a fist at her side. "Especially if it means I don't wake up at home within the next sleep cycle, as trapped as I've ever been."

"We have an agreement, then?" I extend one clawed hand before I can think better of it. It's a threat by my very design, every single claw sharp enough to tear through her fabric gloves and permanently infect her with Pagonian radiation.

Kori hesitates for moment, her gaze darting back and forth as if searching for an escape or any reason to alter her path, but in the end, she takes my hand firmly in her own. Even through her glove, her hand is warm and soft where mine is cold and rigid, her grip surprisingly strong for such a small girl. I'm powerful enough that I could stand my ground regardless, but I let her tug my arm so that I lean down.

At once, we are eye to eye, radiation mask to blue-white face, dayfolk heiress to nightfolk usurper. Our breath plumes between us, snow white, in the archives' chilly air.

"A pleasure to be your prisoner, Adria." I hear the smile in her voice, wickedly pleased with this turn of events. "Shall we begin with a tour of the records, or did you have another method of keeping me in line?"

"That depends on if you prove yourself a difficult charge." I can't help but smile back, even knowing it shows my teeth, makes me look more animalistic than ever. "Shall we start at the Cataclysm?"

"It wouldn't do to question my warden. After you, Adria," Kori says, sweeping out one arm with a flourish. Again speaking my name like it's nothing, like we're old friends. I pretend my heart hasn't skipped a beat as I lead her farther into the first archival hall.

CHAPTER 17

KORI

In the pit of my stomach, there's a hollow gap for terror that should be present and most definitely isn't. The rest of me feels set alight, struck like a torch amidst the endless night, blooming and crackling with newfound possibility.

This is what I wanted, isn't it? A chance to try and live—really *live*, not just maintain life-sustaining functions—beyond Chloe's ever-present grasp. So what if that chance is amidst the Daylands' enemies, cloaked in near-impenetrable darkness, and offered by a shadow queen who could silence my breath with the idle flex of a claw?

I know I *should* be afraid. I'm foolish, not dead. But those teeth are arranged in something that's almost a smile, that clawed hand steady and honest and cold as truth in my gloved one. Possibility overwhelms my good sense.

I tell myself that her smile—brightening the blue-tinged white of her high cheekbones, making her violet eyes sparkle like gems—has approximately nothing to do with it. Or at least a marginal effect. Aspect is better at statistics and percentages than I am. I'm sure it's negligible in the grand scheme of things.

We wander the archives for some time, my fingers trembling at the sheer wealth of information. Adria catches me by the wrist and slides my hand toward a particular rectangular record with a blinking orange identifier on the rim.

"Your people live out their days underground as much as possible. Send mechs to the Passage to do their grunt work. But the nightfolk have spent many sleep cycles in the gap, exploring it for themselves. You might learn something valuable to your people's future."

I can't help but notice what Adria doesn't say, but must be thinking: If I were to obtain data on the Shadowlands itself, that information could be used by the Daylands military upon my return home, if they ever wanted to challenge the nightfolk for total control of Pagomènos. But data on the Passage, by comparison, can't easily be weaponized against the nightfolk.

I narrow my gaze. "I thought this tour was supposed to be a gesture of trust."

She's still holding my wrist, tightly but not painfully. Adria seems to register that the contact, even if it's over the glove-armor mesh of my wrist, has gone on for too long, and she withdraws.

"Trust goes both ways, Kori. You can at least have a look before you dismiss the data's value."

My name in her voice, low and rumbling like an approaching quake, mangles my center of gravity. I tell myself it's the fear I should've felt long ago, making a delayed but welcome appearance.

"All right," I say, and slide the tablet from the shelf.

The tablet's surface blinks and hisses to life in a shower of pixels. The file's title slides across the dark screen in neon green: *THE PASSAGE*. There's a hyperlinked table of contents at the top, varying in subject from flora and fauna to standard temperature expectations, but my brain stops and seizes on the introduction, aptly titled, *THE PASSAGE AND THE GREAT EXILE*.

"Exile . . . ?" I feel like someone's pressing down on my shoulders, crushing me into the floor. "Chloe . . . my mother, that is . . . always told me that the nightfolk destroyed the land."

"And why would we do that?"

"So dayfolk couldn't live there."

Adria cocks her head, curious violet stare wide on mine, not unlike her three-headed pet. "Read," she says curtly.

I do. The file proceeds to detail the nightfolk account of how the Passage came to be.

AFTER THE CATACLYSM, THE DAYFOLK REJECTED THE DIAKÓPSEI'S GIFT, FEARING WHAT THEY DIDN'T UNDERSTAND. THE NIGHTFOLK TRIED TO ENLIGHTEN THEM WITH THEIR REVELATION, BUT THE DAYFOLK WERE WARLIKE, FEROCIOUS IN THE DEFENSE OF HOW THE OLD THINGS HAD BEEN. WITH WHAT REMAINED OF THEIR EARTHSIDE TECHNOLOGY, THEY DROVE BACK THE NIGHTFOLK, NOT ONLY FROM THE DAYLANDS BUT ACROSS THE PASSAGE BETWEEN.

THE EXPULSION WAS SO FEROCIOUS, AND THE NOW-LOST WEAPONRY SO DEADLY, THAT THEY OBLITERATED THE PASSAGE IN THE PROCESS. THE DIAKÓPSEI, IN ITS INFINITE WONDER, HAS SINCE RAISED MANY OF THE FLORA AND FAUNA TO NEW FORMS AND NEW LIFE. BUT THE GROUND, WHICH MIGHT HAVE BEEN PAGOMÈNOS'S LAST RECOVERABLE LAND BY DAYFOLK STANDARDS, WILL NEVER BE THE SAME. THE NIGHTFOLK FLED TO REGROUP IN THE SHADOWLANDS AND MOURN THEIR DEAD. THIS IS CALLED THE GREAT EXILE.

My eyes sting. I reach for them instinctively, only to remember I'm wearing a helmet. I lightly tap a button on the side, which sends a light gust of air to clear my vision.

"Is this supposed to make me feel merciful? Guilty?" I feel both those things wrestling inside me, and I resent them. "Your people attacked first. They wanted to infect all of us, make us like . . . like . . ."

Adria has taken a step away from me, but not nearly far enough to slow my pounding pulse. I expect her to regard me with disappointment. I wish she, too, were forced to wear a mask, so I could superimpose my preferred emotion over her face. Instead I'm forced to look upon the cool, serene line of her mouth, the piercing depth of her gaze that invites me to keep speaking and yet stills my tongue in the same moment.

"Like me?" she says, her tone serpentine. "Are we going backward so soon? I believe we established that I am not the monster you expected."

"You are nothing I expected," I say without thought, and I avert my eyes from hers again. "But neither is this. I can't copy this into Aspect's memory core."

"Why not? It might broaden their perspective."

"Because it's historical heresy, that's why!"

"After trespassing in my territory for a single glimpse of nightfolk perspective, are you so afraid of encountering it?"

"Aspect can't distinguish between fact and opinion. They haven't reached that level of critical cognition yet. This would throw their entire perception of the Daylands, of me, of themself, into total chaos. They might run away. And then how would I find them? How would I fix them?"

"Kori."

She's standing behind me now. I know it from the phantom heat of her breath against where my helmet melds with my torso armor. The hairs at the nape of my neck stand on end, even though I can't fully feel the temperature shift through my suit. I don't look at her, keeping my eyes firmly fastened on the sun-forsaken bookshelf and its damnable false history.

"You told me you were trying to raise Aspect to sentience, did you not?"

"I am."

"A sentient comes to their own conclusions."

A bitter laugh escapes me at that. "Do they, now?"

Adria sounds genuinely perplexed. "I fail to see the joke."

I don't know how to tell her that my formal education consisted entirely of Daylands government-approved—that is, Chloe-approved—records. Questions were met with larger files to download, not space to fashion answers. I don't think I've ever been given the opportunity to reach my own conclusions. By this measure of humanity, I'm no more human than Adria or Aspect. I'm hardly sentient at all.

Head spinning, I forcibly change the subject. "How do you know your historical records are true?"

"How do you know yours are true?"

"You can't just turn all my questions back in on themselves."

"It seems to be working so far." I sigh deeply, but Adria continues, "I believe it was an old Earthside saying, that history is written by the winners. Regardless of who started the conflict, your people drove mine out of the Passage, and its potential for ongoing original floral and fauna growth was shut down. I would say you won."

I think about the vast swath of dead land, the skeletons I've seen scattered below *Charon*'s flight, the strange animals fighting over what few scraps remain. "Nobody won the battle over the Passage. So I suppose it doesn't matter who started it."

Adria blows out a breath and crosses her arms, defiant. "Then what are you so afraid of?"

I grit my teeth. "Copy the file onto a data drive. I can plug it in directly, run a duplication, and transfer while Aspect is powered down. If they have an existential crisis, it won't be anything I haven't experienced while trying to fall asleep."

Adria seems to tense at that. "Is sleep restless for your people, what with the constant light?"

"No." I shake my head. "Just me."

I had another terrifying dream when I last closed my eyes. Fragments, nonsense, but they all wedge inside me like shrapnel, persisting even when I'm awake. My limbs, pinned down to a medical table. Swirls of colors without names, language without meaning, too much input, and I'm choking. Chloe's voice, I think, somewhere faraway. *Kori, can you hear me?*

"Then we have something else in common," Adria says, but though the words sound pleased, her voice sounds like it comes from the bottom of a well.

I manage a sad smile before remembering she can't see it through my mask. "I'm smiling, I promise. Excuse this sun-forsaken thing."

"I must say, you're in an awfully advantageous position for a prisoner."

"Honored guest."

"Temporary resident." She smiles back at me then, before continuing: "You could be sticking your tongue out and rolling your eyes right now, even hissing under your breath, but between the voice filtration and the radiation mask, it's impossible for me to tell."

"I could take it off, if you'd like to watch me choke and die from the unfiltered atmosphere."

"I should probably take you to dinner first."

I laugh, then—a real laugh, so alive that even the mask's filtration can't fully flatten it. I thought I'd be lucky to emerge from the Shadowlands with only a few counseling sessions' worth of trauma, but here I am, wandering a forbidden library with an equally forbidden girl, beyond the grasp of the sun or school or my responsibility of succession, *enjoying* myself.

It feels like when *Charon* first rolls onto the launch pad, then lurches up, up, *up* like a star being born, careening into the sky, limitless. I'm giddy and weightless with no one to hold me down, regardless of the consequences.

Maybe the nightfolk archives are a false history, crafted to perpetuate the rift between our people, but why shouldn't I determine that for myself? Why should I program Aspect to reflexively trust whatever they're told, when I resent every part of me that's been trained to do the same?

I'm so lost in my reverie, caught up in historical heresy and impossible possibility, that I proceed to walk directly into another archives visitor. My skull rings against my helmet as I collide with a nightfolk boy's chest, then stagger back, dazed and frantically apologizing. This boy is shorter than Adria by a not-insignificant margin, but he still has over a foot on me, so I have to crane my neck to meet his stormy-gray eyes. He's leaner, more angular, sporting dual pairs of wings with a body that could cut through heavy winds or carve through sheer stone without even trying. But Adria's eyes, despite their unnatural purple, hold galaxies. The stranger's are clouded, unreadable, and narrowed with obvious annoyance.

I'm so busy trying to apologize that I almost don't notice when he simply looks past me to Adria and says matter-of-factly, "Precisely what is the prisoner doing in the nexus of our entire historical record?"

Adria's voice is a low, wolfish growl. "She's with me, Thaane."

"With you in the *archives*, which requires considerably more explanation."

Thaane. I heard this man leading the soldiers to the gate. Heard him pin one to the wall and threaten to split him clean open. My heart careens against the inside of my rib cage.

Adria moves to put her body between me and Thaane, which would be a welcome source of protection if not for the fact that her bulk completely blocks my view. I shimmy sideways to maintain a visual on the stormy-eyed nightfolk. Maybe it's the fact that my protector is at an obvious physical advantage, maybe it's the way her hand almost catches me by the shoulder to hold me back, or maybe it's just that I've had my head in this sun-forsaken helmet for far too long, but boldness spikes through me despite my pounding pulse, and I answer before Adria can.

"We've reached an agreement regarding my time in the Shadowlands. I'm less than eager to return across the Passage, and the longer I'm gone, the more my return is worth. Everyone wins."

Thaane's flat eyes roam over me from head to toe. Where Adria's gaze made my heart skip beats, Thaane's succeeds only in raising my blood pressure. This is the fear response I should've had the first moment Adria illuminated her face for me, on the other side of my prison cell. Later, when I have a moment alone, I'll have to untangle where my survival instincts went so awry.

"The last time the nightfolk made a treaty with the dayfolk," Thaane says, abject, "you drove us from the Passage like festering vermin." He turns back to Adria, teeth gritted. "When were you planning on telling me this?"

"A queen doesn't need anyone else's approval," Adria protests.

"You have my loyalty. You have that of many old-guard generals: Isek, Agabon, Myla. But a coronation in blood does not, in the eyes of everyone, make you a queen. Not while Azarii's rebels stalk our steps, preparing for full-scale war in the fringes." What color exists in Adria's face has drained away, but Thaane only barrels forward. "The Shadow Court has tolerated you well enough thus far. What will you do when they deem you insolent, a brash child, a hazard to your own people's safety?"

"Do you truly think I haven't considered that?" Adria protests. "Every move I make now is inevitably entangled with the court. I don't *eat* without wondering if they think I should be elsewhere, strategizing, rousing the people, doing anything but resting."

"Do they know Kori is planning an extended stay?"

"They will."

"And you think they'll approve?"

"I am *queen*," Adria says, wings flaring wide, "not merely a soldier nor a council member. Try as they might to order me about, and try as

I might to maintain our tenuous partnership, they could be torn down with a moment's decree. And they know it." Her violet eyes blaze something fierce. "So, as their queen, I will make them see my side."

Groaning, Thaane presses the heels of his hands into his eyes. "Adria, please. Listen to me. Azarii's soldiers will catch wind of this. A ransom for the sun's only heiress could just as easily outfit the rebellion for prolonged resistance. How long can you keep this up? A court on the verge of calling for a coup? An uncle prepared to execute you himself? A daylight trespasser masquerading as a tourist?"

In the blink of an eye, in barely more than one long stride, Adria moves close enough to chest bump Thaane, her wings splayed like bared teeth, that growl rising to a rumbling near-roar. She holds Thaane's gaze without blinking until the smaller nightfolk averts his eyes. "And I'm sure it will stabilize my regime," she says, every word like cut marble, "for our first dayfolk visitor in generations to witness my right-hand man challenging my every choice."

I can believe that Thaane believes he's pushing back on her authority to protect everyone else. But it doesn't make it any easier to watch him question both Adria's leadership and my presence here in one fell swoop. I chew on the inside of my cheek, resisting the urge to speak even more inadvisable words than I already have.

"As your friend, Adria," Thaane says, very slowly, "I would be abandoning my post if I didn't question a decision so reckless."

The difference between Adria's reaction to Thaane's protestations and my own is immediately striking. Our banter is like sparring; if our words are weapons, then those we've chosen to employ are blunt instruments. It's quickly become clear that we want the same things, if for very different reasons. I don't want to go home; Adria wants to establish authority in her own. For now, at least, our interests align.

This may be the first time I'm properly meeting Thaane, but there's a bite in his voice that I can't ignore. He's not the unafraid advisor, dutifully offering his insight, as much as he's trying to perform it. His weapons are real, freshly sharpened, tipped with poison, and prying for a break in Adria's armor.

When Adria collapsed outside my cell, overcome by the vision of the sun, I saw her without her armor altogether. Only now, watching her apparent confidant struggle to pinpoint a single weakness, do I realize the gravity of what I was allowed to see. A queen brought low by a single glimpse of light that shone into and illuminated every open wound.

"I try not to make calls I'll regret," Adria says, not backing away from her opposition. "You skirted trial by a hair's width, Thaane, by my command that you scorn. Don't forget it."

Thaane holds his queen's gaze, head deliberately lowered in deference. False contrition, if my instincts are to be believed. I still remember how calm, how unshaken his voice was while I heard that lesser soldier squirm and gasp against the wall, his life held tenuously in his commander's clawed hands. Thaane is more than capable of separating his emotions from his actions and from his presentation. There is appropriate awe in his bent, supplicant posture, willing submission behind his eyes, but of all the emotions I can read in this boy, none of them even remotely resemble respect. That is not how an advisor looks at his queen.

That is how, when I know she isn't looking at me, I look at my mother.

I don't tell Adria what I saw in Thaane. Maybe it's because a lifetime thus far under my mother's steady, relentless hand has taught me to table thoughts and theories that might be unwelcome. Maybe it's because Thaane, if he does hold resentment toward Adria, is my last real weapon should my fragile alliance with the queen turn ugly.

I may be an invited guest now, rather than a prisoner, but I'm still trapped here until my mother comes to retrieve me—or Adria lets me leave. If things pivot to a dangerous collision course, I'll want to have a concealed weapon. Thaane is my hidden blade, and he doesn't even know it. If I need to outwit and escape Adria at any point, now I know who to manipulate.

It feels slimy, though, this illicit knowledge tucked away like a flask of poison in my sleeve. Aspect would never look at my (admittedly limited) human connections as potential weapons with which to defy me. I wonder if that will change when I install these nightfolk records into their mainframe. Do I want them to change, in my heart of hearts? I feel less human than Aspect has ever been.

Adria watches while I pry off a panel below Aspect's chin, power down their mainframe, and proceed to open their head on an internal hinge to access the blinking, spark-spitting memory core. "Is that what your . . . memory chip . . . looks like?" She points at the mass of confused wires. "The one in your head?"

It doesn't escape me that she asks about my own Morpheus chip, not the technology in general. As if she, given the chance, would look for a power button on my own face, crack open my skull, and see what she could find. I shudder.

"No, Morpheus chips are much smaller. This . . . this is all my handiwork." I point to the jagged, near-rectangular shard at the wiry mass's center. "That's a modified Morpheus chip. Mech memory cores are normally much less centralized. They don't have as much relevant data to store, so keeping it condensed isn't as high priority. I cross wired the translation matrix into the experiential center board to try and create a proto-organic link between programmed and learned response, so that they—"

"Smaller words . . ." Adria points one claw at the memory core again. "Please."

"Mechs are designed only to encounter scripted situations. They harvest resources from the surface. They show pantomimed respect for their creators. That sort of thing. They can adjust their programs if they encounter unexpected resistance, but they can't write new ones. At best they can mirror observed behavior. By linking an active Morpheus chip into Aspect's memory, I'm trying to code a program that codes itself. Not just rewriting and reorganizing old code. New code. Learning. Choice."

"Choice." Adria's lip curls as if she tasted something sour.

"Are you all right?" I don't know why I ask. It's not as though I can afford to care, but in some rogue part of me, I do.

Violet eyes clouded, Adria shakes her head. "Perfectly fine," she says drearily, as if through the haze of sleep.

I don't ask again. Perhaps I'm afraid of the answer.

We install the nightfolk memory together. The data drive, which houses a copy of the archived memory, we plug directly into an outlet inside Aspect's head. I authorize it with a series of operative codes usually known only to mechs, tapping on an extremely tiny number pad inside Aspect's head with the aid of a narrow tool from my belt.

Dayfolk were never meant to modify their mechanical servants themselves—it's a self-sustaining metal ecosystem, with some mechs being designed to maintain others—but with so much isolated free time, I taught myself the language of circuitry and alphabet and symbols, more consistent than anything else in my painfully limited world. And eventually, through programming, I learned to talk back beyond the simplistic scripts we've imposed upon the mechs.

I hold my breath as I seal Aspect's face closed again, tap the power button beneath their chin, and again click the access panel shut. Aspect whirs and beeps for a long moment, limbs slightly twitching like an organic struck by an electrical current. Then, slowly, slowly, they pivot their head, optical receptors meeting my human irises. "Kori?"

I'm still barely breathing. "Yes, Aspect?"

There's a pregnant pause, broken only by the squeak of Aspect's peg leg as they stand. Then, with all the proclamation pomp of an Earthside weathercaster, they lift their chin, cross their arms, and announce, "THE. *AUDACITY*."

Honestly, of all the reactions to newfound nightfolk knowledge that I anticipated from my mechanical companion, this level of annoyance—so severe that it borders on unintentional parody—was not on my mental list. I've opened up Aspect's head on countless occasions, tinkered with their available memories, their source code, their circuitry, the haphazard link between the Morpheus chip and the standard mech tech alike. I'm about to open my mouth and ask why this time would be any different when Aspect sees fit to personally clarify the source of their disturbance.

"KORI!" Aspect shrieks at an utterly unholy volume. They point an accusing finger at me; it wavers ever so slightly with intensity of emotion, emitting a high-pitched *squeak* with every wiggle that serves to both punctuate and awkwardly contrast their point. "Kori hated these—people so much—Kori deep-fried—a perfectly—good slice—of the planet?"

Now, I'll be the first to admit that I'm hard on myself. I spend a lot of time alone, either willingly or by Chloe's edicts. Too much time alone means way too much space to think, leading to more than my fair share of self-flagellation. But to see my closest ally, whom I have quite literally resurrected from the junk heap to a state of illegal semi-sentience, talking back to me like a small child told to wear their protective gear aboveground in the Daylands . . . It's astoundingly insulting.

I'm slack-jawed, taken aback, almost laughing from the sheer ridiculousness of it all. I was already reeling from the revelation that the history I know might not be the history that Pagomènos itself remembers in the radioactive soil. Aspect shaming me for it feels like the forbidden historical text personally leaping off the shelf and smacking into my face to drive its point home.

"Aspect, you do realize I wasn't personally there, right?"

"Kori—should have been!"

"I quite literally hadn't been born."

"Then that—is Kori's first problem."

There's a rattling, clattering sound behind me. Instinctively, I spin on my heel, one gloved hand reaching for a pistol that isn't actually holstered at my hip anymore. It takes an instant to process that the noise is neither a blade being drawn, a barrier being breached, nor a break somewhere in my protective armor. Adria shivers, one hand pressed against her open mouth, wings slightly flapping from the effort of holding the rest of her body still. Her palm barely muffles the sound, which is . . . coming from her mouth. She leans so far forward that her free arm has to catch her from tumbling onto all fours.

Possibilities dart through my brain in a panic: She's received a message of some kind to prompt disbelief; she's experiencing a breathing obstruction; this is an unforeseen side effect of her intense connection to the planet's radioactivity. But it's none of those things. The shadow queen, in equal parts my captor and my only shield, is . . . laughing.

Laughing. At me.

My cheeks burn so badly, I half believe she can see the blush through my helmet.

"Do you always let them talk to you like that?" Adria says, when she's somewhat recovered her breath.

I could fire back that Thaane behaves similarly, but I elect to bite my tongue. "That's . . . new, actually," I admit with a shrug. I shove my shame into its own compartment, trying to refocus on the logistics of this development. "Unfortunately, it's not an organic opinion. It's a paraphrase of the essence of the installed memory, not an independent conclusion. The code is capable of restructuring itself when building blocks are added, but it's still architecture built entirely from pieces I've provided."

"I'm not sure I follow."

"When a person faces a challenge to a fundamental belief—even if the evidence is compelling—it causes a chain reaction. They need time to process and apply the information. Aspect just superimposed your records' conclusion over the previous installation and erased it entirely. No integration. No interrogation. No . . . wrestling."

I realize even as the words escape me that perhaps this is what I've been doing since I first dared to dip a toe into the Shadowlands' inky, endless darkness. Wrestling with the truth, both arms sweaty and strained, trying to pin it down into a comprehensible code.

At Adria's side, her comms tablet dings, blessedly interrupting my train of thought. "Forgive me." She sighs, pressing a button to read out her most recent message.

"*From Thaane: Three of your soldiers from the battle at the gate are in the infirmary*," says the automated voice. "*Two are expected to live. The third is critical. It may be wise to visit her and instill some morale, to give her the best chance of recovery.*"

My head spins. I want to offer some semblance of comfort, a shred of encouragement, anything at all, but Adria hand-waves my words away. "The war is a constant. Right now, I'm here, not in the infirmary. I'll make a visit as soon as I can."

"Adria . . ." I start, but my voice dwindles away. There's nothing worthwhile to say, nothing I can do to lessen the burden of this war.

She turns back to my mech, eyes narrowed in deep thought. "So how do you intend to stabilize Aspect? Uninstall the new memory?"

I can't help but arch an eyebrow. "And reject your ever-so-generous, intensely judgmental gift? Never. But I'll need to counterbalance it as a sort of . . . mood stabilizer, if you will. Balance with a positive perception of the dayfolk."

Adria laughs again. "So what you're saying is you need to install a memory of . . . hugging, or something?"

"I hate that you're right."

"I love when I'm right."

I roll my eyes so hard, I imagine she can hear the motion through my mask. "You would. Royalty and all."

"Says the princess to the queen."

"Oh, I'm no better."

"You're worse."

"The worst of them all."

Adria laughs again at that, and it's a little looser this time, airy. Unburdened. The sound sends a rush of heat to my cheeks that I can't explain. "It does go to your head, being royalty. I ought to stop complaining about the insurrection. It has a way of keeping me humble." Her violet gaze is so intense, I'd nearly swear she could see my own irises despite my mask, our stares locked, magnetic; I'm unable to look away even if I'd wanted to. "Though you aren't so terrible at doing that yourself, Kori."

I still can't explain what it does to me to hear her address me by name. Not even name and title, just name, like we're on equal footing despite her holding all the power here, like she'd like to know the person before she collects the ransom. She towers more than two feet above me, a bulk of muscle where I'm only lean limbs, a queen where I'm a trespasser, utterly capable of commanding this situation according to her desires. But yet, she lets me take my awkward verbal swings at her, toys with me in turn.

It isn't just that I'm not properly afraid of her anymore; it's that I think I *like* this. The push and pull, the easy banter, even when she could uproot my safe political standing in the Shadowlands with a stray word, even when she could easily lift me clean off the ground and pin me to the wall with a single clawed hand and—

I can feel my heartbeat hammering in my throat, and I really, *really* don't want to analyze why that is.

Thankfully, Aspect has launched into another independent monologue about the evils of my people and the virtues of the enormous, wickedly grinning winged woman before me, so that gives me an excuse to look away.

"Actually . . ." Despite my continued avoidance of her gaze, Adria lays a hand on my shoulder. "I may have a solution for you. A happy memory."

I blink, not understanding. "You mean another record."

"No, I mean a memory." The hand on my shoulder squeezes, a reassurance; she's so much stronger than me that it still hurts a bit, but I can tell that wasn't the intent. I don't pull away. "Lail—the one you call 'Alpha'—was taken into custody as well, after I captured you. She revealed in interrogation that the contents, while treason against me and my kingdom, were to her a moment of hope. An instant of belief that things could get better. I have yet to gain access to the Morpheus sphere myself, but if she could be convinced to transfer access rights . . . if you think the memory would help—"

"Yes," I say without hesitation. This is what I came here for in the first place, isn't it? Alpha's memory? An instant of utterly human hope, set alight in someone the dayfolk would have called a mere mutant? "Yes, yes, a thousand times yes."

Unthinking, overcome with wild hope of my own, I throw my arms around the hulking mountain of muscle that is the Shadowlands' queen. She tenses like a rifle's trigger, poised to lurch away, but then she doesn't. Not at all. Instead I feel one clawed hand, large enough to palm my entire skull, lightly settle against my back, barely brushing my armor but returning the gesture. Trembling. Afraid of breaking me? Afraid we've broken a boundary that can never be erected again?

All I know is she's restored my best chance at bringing my best friend to life, and I'm unspeakably grateful.

Even as Aspect continues raving in the background. "Kori does not—deserve hugs. Kori deserves—JUDGMENT!"

The following cycles fall into a battle-march rhythm, though I hardly know what I'm fighting anymore, save for sleep's ever-encroaching, gnarled grasp. The night visions only grow worse in the Shadowlands' eternal void, and no matter how I try to extend my time awake, I'm pulled back into sleep like it's a stubborn tide always dragging me back under the dark water. Aspect, who has never spent so much uninterrupted time by my side before this doomed adventure, quickly starts to recognize my nightmares' symptoms.

But I'm so bone-deep tired that I'm falling asleep in impossible positions—knees curled to my chest in an alcove of the hallway, forehead pressed to the side of a mattress I never actually reached, and one regrettable occasion when I woke up because I'd started drooling (*drooling!*) on the inside of my mask, which my sleep-deprived self had apparently decided was a perfectly functional pillow all by itself.

The exhaustion is so severe that even Aspect rattling my teeth in my jaw (or squeaking their peg leg as obnoxiously as possible) isn't enough to rescue me from the nightmares.

It's always the same series of piercingly vivid sensations, the order remixed but the content the same. The medical table, cold against my naked back. The splitting pain in my skull. The needle at my wrist. Chloe's voice: *Kori, can you hear me?*

My waking moments offer little more hope than my unconscious ones. Adria and I install Alpha's sphere into Aspect together, but while it tempers their rage against the Daylands and their calls for vicious justice, it shows no signs of having awakened sentience.

Aspect is a comforting presence when I wake screaming. A loyal friend, even in this strange, shadowed inverse of our usual world. But they remain a robot, ultimately an elaborate algorithm.

I don't stop searching the archives for new installation ideas, but nevertheless, my optimism wanes like melting wax. Did I risk everything for nothing? Did I bring my closest friend to this land of frozen death, put their body through all manner of abuses, and further tinker with their mechanical brain . . . just to fail them at the finish line?

All I know is I can't return home until I've tried installing absolutely everything (and then some) that the Shadowlands have to offer. Let my mother worry herself sick. Let them raise the ransom to the stars.

My feet are firmly planted here until I know, beyond even an inkling of doubt, that I've done everything I can for Aspect's potential awakening.

My only respite from both the night visions and conscious anxieties is when I'm with Adria. She remains a newly risen queen trying to quell a civil war, so she has responsibilities besides babysitting me—but when we are together, our waking moments land like a steady rain of blows, frequently interrupted by worsening messages on her comms.

FROM GENERAL ISEK: An energy blast knocked out a hunk of the fortress's front wall. A telekinetic is repairing it as quickly as possible, but in the meantime, we've posted a constantly rotating guard.

FROM THAANE: The prisoner you saw fit to release, Eridian, has been stirring the rebels with her firsthand account of the monster queen. I fear she will only intensify Azarii's resistance. But the consequences of your mercy are yours to bear.

FROM GENERAL ISEK: Our low-torch watchmen caught a solo assassin near the breach, with a shimmering freezeblade tucked securely into the wrist of her robes. The watchmen wrung her neck, left the head staring glassy-eyed at the stars. I can only hope it serves as a meaningful deterrent.

FROM THAANE: I fear Azarii's influence only grows. A layman appeared at the gate yesterday, white-eyed, staggering, bleeding profusely. He'd tried to tear one of his wings from its socket. Zalel called for a more advanced medic, anyone to help him. Before that could happen, the madman took a freezeblade to his own throat.

Adria insists on rigorous exercise and training, for fear that the shadows will sap the life from my body and reduce my value to the Daylands. Most of it is with the same general who so frequently sends the war updates: Isek—a lean, winged statesman with a solemn face and a baritone voice that carries unexpected notes of deep-set kindness. I vaguely remember overhearing his voice, which sought to temper Thaane's violence, when Aspect and I cowered behind that tapestry.

When Adria is otherwise occupied with her queenly duties, General Isek leads me through fitness routines like stretches and laps. I don't think he's supposed to be checking on my health beyond that, but he keeps squeezing my arms and legs anyway, prodding at my ribs, asking if I'm eating and drinking, if I'm sleeping, if the darkness has broken my brain yet. Eventually, I can't help but ask why he extends such compassion. Cradling the side of my mask with a quivering hand, he whispers that I remind him of his son.

He also tells me that, while Adria would rather I didn't worry, starships have been spotted deeper in the Passage than dayfolk have flown in generations. Looking for me. Maybe feeling out the Shadowlands' defenses. Adria's digital message to the Daylands promised I would return alive in exchange for her needed war supplies, but that doesn't mean they won't consider simply snatching me themselves and dragging me home of their own accord, ransom unpaid. It's no wonder Adria wants me readied for anything under General Isek's wise tutelage.

The most intense of my training sessions, though, are not with Isek but with Adria herself. Rather than rote exercise routines, our sparring with words extends into drills with fists, the air electric hot between our warring bodies despite the Shadowlands' permanent winter.

Increasingly, as my courage reignites like a stubborn flare in a sandstorm, I launch questions alongside my knuckles. The innocuous ones, she answers, though I get the feeling half her replies are jokes. Things like, "So how tall can nightfolk get?" (one monster of a soldier was measured at nearly ten feet), or "Don't you ever get cold in those overdramatic robes you all insist on wearing?" (apparently all the cold is absorbed by Adria's cold, cold heart), or "What's your favorite color?" (black, predictably).

Then there are the bolder ones.

"Tell me about your mother."

"Tell me the first thing you really remember."

"Tell me where you feel the safest."

Most of these, Adria deflects as effectively as she does my punches and kicks. But when I cautiously venture, "Have you ever seen the radiation's source for yourself?" her brow furrows in actual thought rather than reflexive sarcasm, and she tells me we're going on a little trip.

The path is long, and compared to Adria's exasperating bulk, my legs are all too short—so instead of walking, she spreads her wings and gestures to the strong, solid arch of spine between them. Swallowing hard, I clamber up on Adria's back like a small child into her first starship cockpit.

When she, without a word, takes flight, my stomach lurches at the sudden ascent, my vision blurring even through my mask at the speed. I'm forced to wrap my gloved hands around her horns for balance, stray strands of her ink-dark hair tangling between my gloved fingers. Eventually, once we're high enough to transition from near-total verticality to a more familiar horizontal axis, I hold tight to the ridges of her wings instead.

Despite my gloves and armor separating my body from Adria's, I swear every sensation burns through me like unfiltered sun. The core structure of her wings feels almost but not quite like bones, more like the cartilage of an ear than anything else. But the wing membranes, which I absently expected to feel leathery, are more like weathered velvet, rough and soft all at once.

As much as I've come to fear and flee sleep, I think any rest under such a fabric would be perfectly, beautifully dreamless.

The only sound is the steady, weighty rise and fall of her wings. Gradually my eyes adjust to the endless void around us, and pinpricks of starlight appear, alongside streaks of violet and indigo, the entire galaxy seemingly at my fingertips. I know we're going somewhere important, but I don't want this moment to end. If I were to remove the memory, seal it securely in a Morpheus sphere, I don't think there's any price or offering, anywhere on this entire planet, that would be worth giving it up.

But, of course, after what was surely many miles but felt like a mere few feet, our journey concludes, and we dive back to solid ground. Then, to my confusion, *beneath* said solid ground. We descend into a massive pit, at the bottom of which we're greeted by hooded guards, all bearing rifles and blades. Eventually, after a smattering of shouts back and forth (and a few bolder soldiers visibly readying their weapons), Adria waves them away, and we proceed farther into the planet's mysterious underbelly.

Adria warns me no less than twelve times to keep a safe distance from what I'm about to observe, to squint even behind my mask. And she wasn't joking.

If Pagomènos had a soul, the Diakópsei is what I imagine it would look like: brilliantly blue, misshapen, perhaps twenty feet long, and pulsing, all but flaming, impossibly bright yet undeniably born of the dark. On either side of it are sealed vessels containing smaller gemlike structures of intricate crystal and rock. Their shapes are alien but also nearly organic, like unholy fruit bursting with cursed seeds.

Involuntarily, despite standing a great distance away, I extend an open palm as if to touch one of the gemfruit vessels, my fingertips itching to remove my glove. Adria catches my hand between barely controlled claws and yanks me back. "After all you've already survived, are you trying to kill yourself?"

"No, no, I . . ." I want to knot my fingers in my hair, but my hands are gloved, my hair secured in a tight braid within my helmet, so I'm just gripping the sides of said helmet, overwhelmed. "I don't know how to explain. I thought it would be horrible. I thought it would make me afraid. But it's not, and I'm not." I stare into the azure light until my eyes sting and water. My vision blurs. "It's the end of everything that was, and the beginning of everything that is. And somehow . . . I just want to *touch* it."

Adria gives her head a stern shake. "It belongs to the planet, all of it, as surely as any of us do. It was never meant for a mortal touch," she says, stepping forward to stand between me and the asteroid. She hesitates, breaths heavy and uneven, before adding, barely audible, "It made me what I am."

Somehow, all I can think to reply is, "Then it can't be all bad."

Adria curls one hand into a rigid fist, wipes her eyes with the bone-white knuckles.

I ask, "Why did you bring me here?"

She turns her head to meet my gaze. Her own eyes are watering now—whether from the staggering strength of the Diakópsei's light or from repressed emotion, it's impossible to tell.

"Because you should be afraid, Kori." Adria's wings flare wide, blocking the brilliant light, casting me into cold, hard shadow. "One false step could open your armor and condemn you to death. Rebels scrape and claw at the gate. The court, the army, even my dearest friend, all question your presence here, and part of me fears they're right. The Shadowlands aren't meant for you."

Squaring her shoulders, Adria looks away again. Stares into the light. "And they were never meant for the likes of me either. Nothing on this planet is." She hangs her head. "Azarii's rebels are radicals, terrorists, but of this, they too often speak the truth. I should not *exist*. This power was never meant for any of us. It can only inspire destruction. *That*," she says, pointing forward with an extended claw, "is why I brought you here, Princess. Because if fear of both me and my feuding people still eludes you, perhaps fear of my maker would instill an inkling of self-preservation. And *yet*—"

Swearing under her breath, she stomps one foot on the stone in a cloud of dust and gravel. "I bring you here to humble you. I bring you here to look into the face of what Elysium calls *god* and know it could breed only the cruelest of disciples. And you reach out a hand that cannot even bear to be free of its glove—and try to *touch it*." Her wings idly flap, the shifting shadows rippling over me like so much dark water. Oxygen feels very far away. "In your final moments, before the radiation overtook and unraveled you, would you truly want so badly to become like me? Do you not see what I've become?"

I know she wants me to look at the massive muscles flexing beneath her strained, bruised, blue-white flesh. I know she wants me to look at the wings and the claws, the breadth and the might and the severity of her. But all I can see is that the fists at her sides are so clenched as to control a relentless trembling.

All I can see is the girl who, upon encountering her first vision of sunlight, collapsed to her knees outside my cell.

My voice emerges as an unexpected snarl through my teeth. "I'm not some foolish *child*, Adria. I knew what I was doing by coming to the Shadowlands," I say. "And I know what I'm doing by staying here." I cross my arms. "You're wrong that I'm not afraid. I'm more afraid than I think I've ever been in my whole life—but I'm more hopeful than I am frightened. And you've given me that hope. *You.*" I spit my words like daggers at her back.

Still she doesn't look at me, only at the asteroid she believes changed her beyond redemption. This room feels too small, suffocating. My breaths drag up and down my throat.

"You ask what you've *become*?" I half scream. "I've spent almost my whole life underground. Hiding from the light as surely as I was hiding from the shadows. Aspect may still be reaching for true self-awareness, true *being*, but they're the only person I've ever really trusted. And you've helped me to help them to keep reaching out, reaching further. Closer. When you could've slaughtered both of us. When we could already be in the process of being truly, utterly forgotten."

I step forward and lay an open hand on the back of one velvety wing, fingers curling to grip the membrane, and it stills at my touch, the anxious flapping dulled to the barest of movements, undone. All at once my anger burns out of me. I lean forward, eyes drifting shut against the vicious azure light, and rest my forehead against her spine.

"So I would say you've become something of a friend, Adria," I murmur into her robes. "And I don't have many of those."

Adria simply shakes her head. Silence stretches, interminable, between us.

At long last, she says, with hard finality, "We should go."

Turning to face me again, she seizes me by the arm with shocking force, pulling me after her and eventually onto her back again as we take flight out of the underground.

Another message breaks the tense, shimmering silence between us as we fly back.

> FROM THAANE: You didn't dream that earthquake along the fortress's front wall. A particularly volatile rebel practically tore the ground's maw open to swallow our defense forces. He's dead now, but losses were sustained.

The rebellion takes more from Adria every moment. When we first met, she told me her parents fell in the fighting. Somewhere on Pagomènos, she presumably visits their graves. But the whole flight back, I can't shake the feeling that, even more so than those familial skeletons, I've met the being that birthed and molded and made her—a creature without words or face or flesh, like an eldritch deity of Pagomènos and its people, staring, bodiless, right back into my unblinking eyes.

Time passes, inexorable.

Sentience seemingly continues to evade Aspect. But joy has indeed found them—unreasonable, unexplainable in a place like this—like a shard of fallen starlight, alighting in their open metallic hand. They cheer like a fitness coach during my training sessions with General Isek, throwing triumphant fists in the air as I complete even more exercise rotations without collapsing.

They gambol about with Adria's three-headed dog, Russ, even riding on its back—two of the heads sporting toothy grins, the third taking half-angry, half-playful snaps at the unexpected rider. Sometimes, instead of recharging in the standard upright position, I find Aspect's powered-down body curled into the sleeping canine's side.

It's far from the awakening I want. Nevertheless, I pore through the archives whenever possible, trying and failing to find what will actually elevate Aspect to personhood. But it's yet another glimmer of hope, and that isn't nothing.

Several sleep cycles, all haunted by fractured dreams of needles and my whispered name, pass before I see Adria again. I can only guess where she goes. The new shadow queen's responsibilities are many: Meetings with Thaane and her other close advisors. Ordering soldiers to halt every fresh insurgent assault beyond the fortress.

Most curious among Adria's constant barrage of messages are automated reminders for meetings with another prisoner: a young nightfolk named Neo, apparently. That's all she's been willing to tell me, and most of the other nightfolk hardly speak to me at all, only catching me at the corners of their eyes like an inconvenient ghost. Exceptions to this rule are few and distinct: General Isek, with his firm but loving criticism of my fitness. Thaane, bluntly reminding me to move wisely in this unfamiliar land.

Even more so than her political gatherings or even physical altercations, it's the visits to Neo that leave their mark on Adria's whole body. I can always recognize when she's gone to see him without sleeping afterward—her wings like wilted flower petals, her visage set like ancient granite, her sharp teeth absently worrying at her lower lip, though it's already crusted with dried blood.

While Aspect stays just outside my quarters to power down and recharge, I almost dare to ask Adria about it, on one of the rare occasions when we're in close enough proximity to communicate but also not making eye contact. Eye contact seems to have the unforeseen side effect of shutting down all language functions in my body.

I've told myself it's anxiety, maybe even fear, but I know anxiety like an ever-present younger sibling, always tagging along. It's a glacial creep of tension from the nape of my neck to the tips of my toes. That thing Adria's eyes do is nothing like that. It's hot and fast and clenches like a flaming fist around my heart if I don't look away or deflect with sarcasm.

On this occasion, though, we're doing weapons training. Adria's idea. "If the dayfolk fail to honor the terms of our agreement," she says, "or if my own subjects decide to try their luck with a freezeshot at your head . . . you'll be glad you heeded my advice."

On the one hand, weapons other than my standard-issue heatshot pistol—carried by any members of the Morpheus Market who would rather not lose a limb in a transaction gone wrong—are deeply unfamiliar. Chloe raised me to be clever, not strong. A concealed creature, skittering silently through the underbrush, ready to flee at the slightest sound. A prey animal, really.

But the freezeshot shotgun Adria presses into my gloved palm is a hunk of bulky, rumbling metal—a predator's appendage, like a horn or claw designed only to charge in and gore. I've grown so accustomed to the surprising lightness of heatshot weapons, my knees nearly buckle under this war-making wreckage machine.

For all my awkwardness, though, staring down the weapon's sights is the perfect excuse to avoid Adria's molten violet eyes when I ask, quick enough that I almost hope it conceals the audacity, "So who's Neo?"

There's always the slim chance that it's my overactive imagination, but I swear I hear Adria's claws scrape against the blue-white skin of her hands as they curl into fists. "You listen to everything."

"That's not an answer."

"Knowledge comes with a price, Kori. Say . . . a clean head shot."

"I've been your captive for all of . . . ten, twelve sleep cycles?" Honestly, I hardly know anymore. "And already, you're testing me with a request to commit regicide?"

At that, Adria extends a hand, her claws just barely brushing the side of my helmet, forcing me to readjust my line of sight toward the stone targets. "Don't be coy if you've got cause to raise a weapon. If those were real soldiers—your people, my people, visitors from deep space, whatever—you'd be dead before you finished your one-liner."

"Not my preferred way to go out."

"Glad to hear it."

I smirk despite myself. "Being clever, Adria?"

"I wouldn't dare."

Her tone is slick and cold, but if she meant any harm, Adria's claws would've been buried in my skull a moment ago, ending me even before the radiation could. I swear the little shudder I feel in her body just behind me, watching me take aim, is a suppressed laugh.

I tighten my grip on the shotgun's barrel, willing this strange automaton to become like my mask and gloves and armor, merely another artificial layer between me and the real world. A tool to help me navigate it. I draw in the deepest breath I can manage—resenting the jagged edge of it, telling myself it's not from Adria's proximity—and exhale ever so slowly as I focus on the closest stone mannequin's head.

I pull the trigger.

I've rarely had to fire my heatshot pistol outside of mother-mandated training scenarios, but I've grown accustomed to what that feels like. A little electric skitter, almost like my weapon hand has fallen asleep, before a surprising shock of warmth up the whole limb to my shoulder, rapidly fading from the sensation of a burn to a light, pleasant prickling. The freezeshot shotgun is . . . not that.

The trigger clicks, the barrel rolls, and the gun announces its intentions with the loudest noise I've heard since the alarm in *Charon*. My helmet is designed to dampen close-range volume spikes that could damage my eardrums, but even so, the recoil makes my hearing *ring*. Where the heatshot's sensation is of my hands falling asleep, the freezeshot is like my limbs being frozen stiff and hacked off with a rusty blade, and then my new stumps being promptly filled with additional ice because why not?

If I scream, and I honestly can't tell, it's luckily drowned out by the shotgun's bellow. All my focus was on steadying the gun, not steadying my legs, so I naturally careen backward like a second projectile, gun still braced against my throbbing ribs, and collide fully with Adria.

I would've thought those massive witchy wings do something for Adria's balance, but I suppose she's as surprised as I am that the recoil launched me so hard. In any event, we land in a tangled heap of arms and legs and now-crooked wings. I can feel my own mortified heartbeat pounding through me, but I swear I feel hers, too, through all my layers of armor, strong and fierce and unexplainably unsteady.

She must be furious with me. *I* should be furious with *myself*. Given an opportunity to explore the Shadowlands, to personally gain knowledge of its queen and its history and its weaponry, I proceed to fall on my own ass like a low-charge mech?

But then I look up. And, despite myself, I smile.

"Look." I extend an arm to point at the stone targets.

Cursing through her teeth, Adria takes the liberty of using said arm to haul herself upright again, wings sprawling wide like an exasperated shrug.

The farthest stone mannequin is missing one head. Behind it, the chunk of rock that was once its crowning appendage is frozen solid to the wall, nearly split down the middle exactly. Not the mannequin I was aiming for, but Adria doesn't know that.

"I'd call that the entry fee to more Neo info, wouldn't you?"

Adria shakes her head. "I'd call that a lucky shot. And if things go sideways, luck won't be enough to protect you."

"Don't worry," I fire back, "the last thing I'd want to do is leave that to you."

"Don't think I'm up to the task?"

Adria gives her wings a lazy stretch, like the boys at my home compound's gym trying to one-up each other on bicep flexes. Except I usually roll my eyes at those boys' boorish antics, but my tongue sticks to the roof of my mouth at the ripples of muscle in Adria's back, the shine of the spikes where her wings terminate, the superhuman heft and bulk of her contrasted with the predatory fluidity of motion.

She certainly could protect me, if I had any idea how to submit to being protected—but it's clear that isn't what she's built for. Again, the knowledge slithers through me that nightfolk, their new queen not exempted, have evolved to take and break and kill. It's the only way to survive in the dark. So why, as I told her by the preternatural light of the planet's mutant heart, am I not afraid of her?

"Every adult in the Daylands whom I'm actually allowed to interact with has surrendered their lives to the simple task of protecting me. And I'm still *here*—trespassing on the planet's dark side, nearly injuring myself on alien weaponry, presided over by a seven-foot mutant who could condemn me to death, or kill me herself, with an idle finger twitch." I hope she can feel the challenge in my gaze, even behind my mask. "How do you think that's working out for them?"

"Eight," Adria says, inflectionless.

"What?"

"I'm eight feet tall."

"Only farther for your pride to fall."

Adria manages a dry laugh at that. "It's important to size up your opponent accurately. If I were to lose control around you . . ."

The sentence inexplicably trails off.

But I'm looking at the regal arch of her jaw, framed by the royal sprawl of her wings, and those piercing violet eyes with all the depth of galaxies, and I'm sweaty and shivering and this anti-radiation suit is too tight, and it's so much more than not being afraid of her.

I recognize it in a flash of useless intuition in the same instant that I realize she was most definitely just referring to her capacity for murder. And when she lunges for me, to make her point, it only underscores the severity of my first epiphany. When my back hits the stone floor, and I'm pinned horizontal beneath someone who, by all accounts, is the planet's most lethal beast, my heart beats through every soft and breakable part of me—my fragile collarbone and my thinly armored throat and the sweaty palms of my gloved hands. She could rip my carefully assembled suit of armor off with her teeth.

And, instead of being terrified, instead of recognizing the inherent danger of the Shadowlands and its people that she's so severely struggling to impress on me, I'm wondering if her hands would feel as cold as her blue-white skin looks, wondering where she might like to put her palms if the whole planet weren't a plague, if she could leash the power in her claws enough to just pull me close, pin me in place, unable to escape, like I'd even want to.

Well, Kori, I somehow think through the head rush. *It's not like you weren't already breaking all the rules.*

CHAPTER 18

ADRIA

I'm still adjusting to the elevated power of this body, now blessed by the Diakópsei itself. I deliberately order every muscle to seize, to cease, before I collide full force with Kori and squash her into a bloodstain into the stone floor, which would thoroughly make my point but also end her existence. Even I'm surprised by the power in my launch, the rattle of her helmet when she hits the floor. I need to stop and steady my heavy breathing behind gritted teeth before I can continue the lesson at all.

By the Beyond, I only meant to imply any one of my people could kill her. Not to feel that newly constant bloodlust rise to the occasion like an overeager volunteer.

I mean every word that shudders out of me. "I could kill you like this."

She says nothing, hardly even breathes, and it only fuels my rage. She needs to understand, if she's going to spend any amount of time on this side of the planet, how dire that situation will always be, no matter how we deflect the tension into friendly verbal sparring.

"Any one of us could, without even trying."

Are her eyes wide, behind that ever-present mask? Is her heart finally beating an overdue warning? It's impossible to tell, and it only stokes my frustration. Every time I've tried to scare some common sense into this girl—up to and including bringing her to behold the very source of the radiation that could kill her—she's deflected the attempt entirely.

"If I were to curl my hands into fists, I'd break your wrists," I say, just barely testing the joints with my claws, quivering along the gloves' thick fabric.

Even now, she says nothing. Witless, brainless girl. Braver than sense, kinder than the dark could ever deserve. She doesn't belong here.

"If I were to lean my full weight on you, even just increase the pressure to make you talk . . ."

I can't risk pressing my knee into her rib cage. Not unless I want to put the entire ransom at risk. But the tension in my limbs perched above her is nearly unbearable. I force my right knee back, like a drawn bowstring, and press the tension into the floor instead of her heart.

A light, warm brush of fabric, and I freeze. Presumably to hold herself still, Kori has managed to lock her thighs around my knee, holding us both in place. I don't think about how close my knee is to where her legs meet. I don't think about how warm and soft her skin might feel beneath the suit.

"I'm speaking to you now," I nearly snarl, conflicting tensions warring through me, "because I'm trying to teach you a lesson before you learn it with your life. But if I wanted to . . ."

I bare my teeth, just enough to remind her my lips conceal fangs. *Be afraid*, I plead silently. *Be afraid.* If she never learns fear, she won't last long here.

If I can't instill it, I'll never be the monster this kingdom demands of a queen.

"You've made your point," Kori breathes, barely audible, voice balanced on a freezeblade's edge and wavering.

I tell myself it's her terror's overdue arrival. I tell myself I don't somehow know, in my entire body, that her unknown eyes are holding mine fast, hardly blinking, unable or unwilling to look away.

"I should hope so," I counter, but I don't draw back just yet.

I feel like an ice sculpture, frozen in place, but heat waves roll through me all over. Might as well use this to further the lesson—order her to squirm free, maybe even to retrieve the freezeshot gun.

"Your one and only advantage, Kori, is that nightfolk know what we are. What we've evolved to be capable of. So any one of us might make the mistake of underestimating you."

"But not you." The sarcastic edge is gone, exposing the raw underbelly of sincerity.

Her chest heaves with heavy breaths and mine rises and falls in sync, and I swear, I can nearly feel the shape of her through the armor, curves that would fit so neatly into mine despite what I've become.

"Kori . . ." I shake my head, trying to clear it. "You smuggled sunlight to my door. You're on a quest to breathe being into metal."

You could break me in ways I can hardly express. You've already pried my armor loose and swept your eyes across wounds even I hardly dare to see.

"I know better than to expect any less," I conclude. I set my jaw, refocus myself. "Now break away from me. Pretend it's life or death. Get that shotgun back," I instruct, gesturing in the freezeshot's direction with one wingtip. "Regain control."

Time passes at an unbearably slow speed. I'm coiled like a spring, waiting for her move, but not at all prepared for what she actually *does*. Just one arm, reaching up toward my face; one gloved hand, resting delicately, tenderly, against the high arch of my cheek.

She can't feel me, I'm sure, through the layers of armor and fabric that guard her from the planet, but she knows I can feel far too much of her. Braced on her other arm, she leans up so that her mask's filtered breath brushes hot and fast against my swollen throat. "And what makes you think, Adria . . . that you're the one in control?"

I close my eyes. Images dart past me in the darkness. Mother's skull, caving in like old wood. Father's throat twisted and snapped like dead branches. I've seen what I am now if I dare to lose control. I have a civil war to quell, a kingdom to uplift, a ransom to earn.

And by the Beyond, damn it all, I want to know what her face looks like under the mask.

My tongue blessedly sticks to the roof of my mouth before I can say anything I regret. Less blessedly, but nevertheless conveniently, there's a shout down the hall, and the unmistakable whizzing blast of freezeshot freshly fired.

Shortly after my parents' reign ended, I discussed a tracking chip—or, less invasively, a bracelet—with my advisors, should I require immediate assistance. Father always had Mother, but I, an unpartnered queen thus far, too often found myself alone. Thaane wisely warned that a tracking chip could be hacked and exploited. But now, what wouldn't I give for the assurance that help is coming?

Footsteps and freezeshot thunder in calamitous conflict down the halls.

"*Move*," I snarl through reflexively bared teeth, stumbling back and away from Kori, on all fours like a thoughtless beast.

My head is hazy, fogged with useless want that quickly transmutes into anger instead, the only emotion that still feels safe. That anger thunders through me in a hot bolt of adrenaline.

Somehow, I let the only girl I cannot crave distract me, invade me, begin to dissect all the most private parts of me, without even a proper glance from her eyes or a touch from her unguarded skin. And now, judging by the sounds of struggle echoing down the cavernous hall, the unblinking eye of the Beyond has seen my absurd abandonment of royal duty and ensured that we'll both pay the price for Kori's presence in the dark.

I step forward, wings spread and claws bared, casting Kori into total shadow at my back. "Stay behind me."

"We've established I can fire a gun," she retorts.

"Then stay behind me with the gun"—I sigh, even as she lunges for the fallen weapon behind me—"if it makes you feel better."

Kori fumbles with the freezeshot gun's weight distribution, ultimately electing to hold it balanced against her shoulder with two hands, despite the intended one-handed grip by a nightfolk wielder. Her breaths, even filtered by the mask, come hard and fast. My own thoughts pinwheel with equally threatening speed. Infuriatingly, precious little of them are about the political significance of another attack by Azarii's rebellion.

Kori is here because of me. I am alone, and far from well rested, with my pulse pounding in my throat, because of her. We will both suffer for this almost, for this fleeting impossibility, and should her blood fall on my head . . . will it even be distinguishable from all the lifeblood I've already shed?

I am sick and tired of visiting graves, atoning in salt water for necessary sins that will never wash away.

"Consider this another history lesson," I say, fighting to keep my own voice steady and assured. "Once, the records will report, Azarii's rebels came for his queen when he thought her distracted."

The footsteps rattle along the stone hallway, echoing off the molded walls, growing ever closer. My enhanced hearing catches the rumbling reload of freezeshot canisters, the *click* of fingers wavering against triggers, the heavy exhales of rebels who think they are finally close to their prize. Battle lust roars through me and blacks out all else.

The planet's own energy pulses, sparks, and crackles at my clawed fingertips, rolls into dark projectile orbs against my palms. "And then the girl from the sunlight truly saw what the shadows can do."

In the following instant, several things take place at once.

A cluster of armored rebels lunges through the training room's doorway, firing a flurry of freezeshot rifles. I thrust my hands forward to unleash my gathered energy. And Kori gives the freezeshot rifle another sincere try, her own bolt careening off an attacker's helmet. The weapon's recoil once again drives her to her knees; the rifle slides back across the stone in a clatter of pebbles and dust.

"There, Kori, you've helped," I shout in her direction, even as I toss the nearest rebel aside, my claws embedded in his chest despite his weak attempt at protective gear. "Now, please, if you want to live to assist me again, find cover and stay there until everything goes quiet. All right?" I hope she can feel my eyes locked on hers, whatever color they might be. Damn it, I wish I knew. What I'm about to do is something they'll never be able to unsee. "And if you can . . . close your eyes."

"I won't just leave while you—" But Kori's comeback is cut off by an involuntary scream. She staggers sideways, terror struck, as freezeshot fire obliterates the ground where she knelt only a moment ago. "I'm still alive because of you. I won't let you die protecting me."

"Don't flatter yourself, heiress." I wrestle another rebel for control, breaking two of the fingers that weakly clutch their freezeshot pistol. "This is about protecting my ransom"—another crack, this one a knee—"and my kingdom." I hate the familiarity of my boot crashing through their skull. "Now get behind the strongest obstacle you can find"—I could crush the pistol, too, but instead I shoot it at a loose piece of the ceiling, sending the stone hunk careening down on another pair of rebels—"before I take you by the ankle and fly you there."

At that, Kori seems to reluctantly get the message. In my periphery, I watch her dive behind the nearest intact target mannequin, hands over her head. Briefly, my panic ebbs, as I'm convinced the situation is under control.

Then . . . an unholy harmony of metallic screeching and canine barking.

With six eyes blazing crimson and three mouths snarling in unison, Russ tears around the corner, with a new rider astride his back—none other than Aspect the mech. One of their metal hands buries itself in Russ's midnight fur to maintain balance; the other pumps a fist into the air as Aspect shrieks, "ASPECT—AND TRIPLE DOG—PROTECT EVERYONE!"

And just like that, my beloved pet becomes a cannonball of fur, teeth, and newfound metal friend, charging directly into the closest rebel foe.

"TAKE THAT!" Aspect roars. As Russ uses two mouths to seize the rebel from either end, they add, "AND THAT!"

But when Russ moves to gore the enemy, viciously shaking them with multiple sets of jaws, the motion becomes too much. Aspect tries to hold on with two hands instead of one, too late—tumbling to the ground, yelling at a painful pitch all the way down.

The string of curses that slips from my mouth would make even the most battle-hardened of my soldiers blush. I'm still fending off attacks—a kick caught by my knee, a freezeshot blast deflected by a supernaturally energized sweep of my wing, a thrown punch caught by an open palm that crumples the knuckles—but at the edge of my vision, I watch in muted disbelief as a robot programmed for simple mining runs and basic greetings hurls its entire lopsided body into hulking hunks of nightfolk muscle.

For all the memories Kori may have illegally installed in Aspect, clearly even a flicker of self-preservation was not among them.

In the clamorous confusion, Russ struggles not to trample his friend. Padded canine feet scramble for balance as Aspect loses theirs, good leg tripping over peg leg once again, dragging the mech back to the floor. While two of Russ's heads continue mauling the rebel, the third head leans down to check on Aspect, even licking Aspect's head with a big, slobbery tongue of concern.

Reenergized, the mech stands, head held high but peg leg wobbling—and then full-blown *leaps* at the nearest rebel, arms and legs pinwheeling like a windmill and a buzz saw's unholy offspring.

Aspect is spare parts sewn together in the approximation of a friend, not a true flesh-and-blood companion. I know that. But I swear I hear Kori's wince from across the room when, within moments, a slug of freezeshot spins Aspect's only remaining knee 180 degrees, the kneecap crashing into their own butt as they fall to the floor with a squeak.

"We can fix that, Kori," I shout over the din of continued combat.

I crouch and then leap, borne to a dizzying height by my outstretched wings, then plunging like a batbeast onto the soldier that maimed Aspect, ripping and tearing as I land. Frankly, I wouldn't have had the chance for such a boldly lethal maneuver if Aspect hadn't distracted the soldier in question. In her own roundabout way, Kori did help.

Kori's masked face pokes around the side of her target practice mannequin. "Do I want to know what *that* was?"

"It wasn't . . . *not* . . . Aspect's knee," I sigh, flicking blood from my claws, shaking it from my robes.

I'll be a sight when this is over. If proximity to my claws and fangs and unnatural breadth wasn't enough to terrify Kori into staying away from me, maybe a scarlet shower will do the trick. I hope so for both our sakes.

Kori fully emerges from behind her shelter then, freezeshot shotgun raised once again. "What in the *hell* is Aspect doing here?"

"You didn't call them?"

"That's not in their program."

"But the pinwheel of death was?"

Armor aside, Kori covers her masked face with a gloved hand. "I may have installed a memory, a while back, of my jumping off the bed when I couldn't sleep as a kid. But it was supposed to trigger *creativity*."

"Well, it was definitely a creative way to lose a kneecap," I admit, sweeping another soldier's legs out from under her. "Again."

Briefly, Russ pauses gnawing on a rebel to observe Aspect's new injury. Amidst all the spit and blood, all three canine mouths release soft, sad moans at the state of their mechanical friend.

"You do realize a sentient mech has never been born," Kori counters, firing off another blast of freezeshot. This time it connects with one of her targets—a shoulder, not a chest, but it's enough to make the rebel in question drop his blade, leaving him open to my boot through his ribs. "There's no blueprint for this."

Even as I duck another freezeshot blast, I crack a smile—the kind I haven't managed in ages, let alone while fighting for my life. Since my own overcharge, since laying my parents forever to rest, battle has been a crimson current that carries my whole self away, without even debris to keep me afloat. But Kori's voice amidst the maelstrom is a rock above the red, red waves, solid enough to grip, keeping just enough of me above the bloody flood.

This feeling is strange and hot and pulsing where I've slowly fallen into icy stasis, and I should shove it away, focus on the battle. But it's proof that beneath my enhanced capacity to kill and to break . . . part of me still knows how to laugh. So, despite myself, I indulge Kori.

"You'll just have to write the blueprint, when Aspect finally achieves sentience." I spread my wings wide to catch a freezeshot blast that would certainly have missed me, but arched perilously close to one of Russ's precious heads. I would rather see my own kneecap blown off than watch the light of life leave my companion's deep-black eyes. I give him a quick scratch under one chin before moving farther away, lest a shot intended for me strike my pet instead. "Add it to our records."

Kori saunters cautiously forward, gun raised, gaze steady on our enemies but voice stable and tethered to me. "And what makes you think I won't save it for the Daylands library?"

"I think you feel you owe me," I say without thinking.

Kori's own laugh is wicked. "Oh, there are other ways I can repay that debt." Her next shot misses the rebels entirely, nearly freezing my own hairline and horns as it whizzes by.

But I don't think she was talking about combat, anyway. The heat in my face and sudden rigidity in my body have nothing to do with adrenaline anymore.

I'm so distracted, in fact, that when the next rebel launches herself headlong into me, freezeblade great sword steadied with both hands,

I react a whole instant too late. I twist, shift. Start to raise an arm to guard my throat.

Not enough.

Cold splinters through my sternum, then a hot, liquid flood that I know must be blood. A curse slips through my teeth. The alloy of nightfolk blades is of similar composition to freezeshot canisters, except it's been heated in a Passage lava crater forge to a stubbornly solid form. Solid, that is, until it's plunged into an opponent's flesh, and the rapid shift in temperature turns the blade back to liquid freezeshot that immediately floods the veins.

Given the many gifts of the nightfolk, from energy blasts like my own to telekinesis to telepathy to empowered healing—not to mention our evolved battle reflexes, vital for surviving in the dark—it's rare for a blade to actually get close enough to break the skin. But I know, from military demonstrations by my father that I was forbidden to look away from, how terrible a way it is to die.

At first, I think I'm screaming, but I know my own screams to be guttural, animalistic things, and what I hear is a high, thin, splintering sound. *Kori.* I should tell her to fire again, her terrible aim aside. I should tell her where to go to signal my soldiers for help.

The only word my tongue can form is "run."

Pain lances through my body, followed by chills. I roar, incoherent. Something is slamming, heavy and relentless, like a battering ram into my side, and it takes a long, cloudy moment before I recognize it to be Russ's heads, desperately fighting to keep his master awake and out of death's encroaching claws. Language failing me, I try to wave him away, but my arms feel—no, my whole body feels—like a memory.

Then there are cold hands on my chest, neither the stubbornly armored hands of the rebels nor the necessarily gloved hands of the Daylands' heiress. I blink to clear splattering black spots from my vision. When the room comes back into focus, I'm lying on the floor, one hand pressed weakly against my spurting sternum, while Thaane towers above me. The formerly knife-wielding rebel coughs and kicks as he holds her aloft, squeezing the breath from her throat.

He shouldn't have known I was here. I was loath to admit my weapons training with Kori, given Thaane's initial disapproval of her continued presence here at all. But old friend that he is, my brother-in-arms, at my side before and after everything changed, he knew where I'd be despite my calculated silence, knew me better than I know myself.

Vaguely, I process that behind Thaane is a newly arrived regiment of my soldiers. Most are focused on fighting—blades and guns raised, blasts of gifted energy primed to launch, wings splayed, teeth and claws bared to slice and tear—but a few take direct notice of me on the ground, wounded and gasping. General Isek's voice rises above the din: "My lord! Hold fast, a healer is coming!"

In Thaane's vicious grip, the gagging rebel goes deathly still. Thaane tosses the body aside with the others scattered about, blood splattering when it lands, and turns back to me. But my head lolls. My vision clouds. I can't keep a steady gaze on him; I can hardly keep my eyes open at all. My sternum tingles and shudders and burns.

Russ howls, and my heart splinters.

"Look at me." Thaane pants, kneeling somewhere beside me. "Zalel is on his way. It won't be the first freeze-wound he's healed. You're going to be fine, Adria, all right? Please look at me."

I almost smile, but spit blood instead. My voice stings on the way out, each syllable an icicle behind my tongue. "Get . . . Kori . . . safe."

Darkness cloaks and carries me into nothing.

I fade in and out, a struggling dwarf planet on the brink of collapse, suspended only by gravitational pull. At first all I know is that the pull is toward warmth. The gentle brush of synthetic fabric barely conceals the living heat beneath, a pulse that syncs with my own and bids me to keep fighting.

When I was barely a child, when my parents yet lived and I yet slept without seeing their ghostly faces, I remember testing my growing wings to see if I could fly high enough to brush a star with my fingers. Mother restrained her laughter, and Father chided me for not training myself in more useful skills, bellowing that no one since the Cataclysm had traveled far enough to brush a star's very surface.

But it hadn't stopped me from wondering. Back before I dreaded dreaming, I dreamed of stardust, always waking without words to describe the sensation of galactic dust, the fabric of the universe, sliding like so much Passage sand through my outstretched fingers.

But that's what the warmth feels like now. In contrast to the scrambling cold hands of my own kind, and the exquisite cold of Zalel's healing gift restoring my body, these gentle, testing touches make me shimmer and spark, a dark star reborn from the collapse of another. It takes a while for the touches to register as those of a hand, not a star. And when I open my eyes to Kori's mask, bent close to my formerly sleeping face, I feel her eyes look through the helmet and into mine.

I'm a goner. In my hazy, wounded mind, it's among the only things I know for sure.

I fell like a comet the moment Kori plummeted into my dark world, and no matter what troubles followed her here, no matter what ransom her mother offers for her safe return, I'm afraid this strange, nameless light in my chest will flicker out forever when she leaves.

The room around Kori swims and ripples before coming into focus. I was hoping I'd be back in my own bed, or at least the infirmary, but I don't recognize the strange, twisting expanse of the malformed tunnel I now find myself in. The improper bed at my back is just a slab of rock padded with spare fabric. Footsteps, both the scattered footfalls of various servants and the rigid, regimented march of my soldiers drilling, sound somewhere far above and echo down through the ceiling before reverberating about the chamber.

The cloying, icy scent of freeze-burned flesh lingers in my nostrils, but when I tentatively press an open hand where the rebel's blade entered, I find only a thin, half-faded scar—certainly Zalel's work. I'm lucky to have him on my side, after everything. Almost as lucky as I am that Thaane found me before the frozen blade's infection had time to get worse.

But Zalel is nowhere in sight now, and neither is Thaane. There's only me and Kori, whose gaze bores into me despite the barrier between us, whose gloved fingers ever-so-lightly trace the half-moon of my new scar.

"Careful." I cough, my throat raw from disuse. "That scar . . . could still . . . split." And spill lingering freeze, potentially costing Kori the same finger with which she so carefully outlines my wound, my throat, my collarbone.

"I wear protective gear for a reason," Kori says, utterly undeterred.

Silly, stubborn girl. She should be somewhere protected, especially after the grievous breach of security that was this last rebel attack. Where the hell was General Isek when the attackers arrived? Where was Thaane? I'm tired of resorting to violence to quell violence, but I cannot allow this to stand without harsh reprimand. It would make me look pathetically weak to Azarii's rebels, and worse than that, to the Shadow Court, whose belief in me is already wavering like a buffeted brazier flame. I will need to call upon the darkest, cruelest parts of me to answer such gross incompetence.

But all I can think about right now is that Kori should be anywhere but here. And isn't that exactly the problem? When did this girl invade my bloodstream as surely as the freezeblade? And is there any healer to be found on Pagomènos who could purge an infection such as that?

Kori should be somewhere *safe*. Not here with me, wherever *here* is—alone with me, no less, and my shattered strength nowhere near enough to stop it if a fresh wave of armed insurgents were to burst in and take my valuable captive for themselves.

"Protective from . . . the planet," I sigh. "Not half-clotted . . . freeze-infected blood."

"I'd be awfully surprised if any of that were still in you," Kori says, poking my scar for good measure. "Even given the speed of spread once a freezeblade reverts to liquid, taking into account a presumed rapid heart rate on your part upon receiving the injury—"

I have a rapid heart rate now, too, but Kori doesn't need to know that. "Since when . . . are you an expert on nightfolk weaponry . . . and wound care?"

"You were asleep for a while. I needed something to do. And you did just give me access to your entire historical records, remember?"

"I'm glad you didn't . . . trouble yourself, staying . . . with me the whole time."

I could blame my sleep-addled brain, I suppose, but I can almost see a light blink into being above Kori's head. Knowledge is a drug to this girl, despite an unending sun that should've baked curiosity out of her, beaten her down like the rest of the dayfolk.

"We're in the Underground, according to Thaane," Kori explains. "There's an elaborate network of escape tunnels underneath your fortress, but oddly enough, no record of it in your formalized data," she says, crossing her arms. "I did stay. I just . . . looped back aboveground and brought some reading material with me."

Suddenly I have a pounding headache. Having only just now regained full consciousness, forming words is uncomfortably difficult. "You took . . . our historical records. Out of the archives. And into an underground tunnel. That nobody knows about . . . or would be able to search. If they had gotten lost."

"I put them back." Kori at least has the courtesy to attempt an apologetic shrug. It's transparently false, but she does try.

I grit my teeth against a reflexive curse. "That's what I get . . . for sheltering a memory smuggler."

"And company."

"What?"

Kori laughs. "And the pleasure of my company."

"Pleasure's all mine," I unfortunately say before my still-recovering mental filter can kick in.

By the Beyond, as if nearly dying in front of a prisoner whose protection was *my* responsibility weren't enough, now I'm making the heart palpitations she causes this agonizingly obvious? I've never hated myself more, and I'm well acquainted with self-loathing as of late.

Another thought gnaws at the edge of my consciousness. "Where is Russ? Aspect?"

"Russ is having a luxurious shower in my quarters, where no one will find him to question the necessity. Aspect . . . was surprisingly excited by the idea of tinkering with their busted knee. I needed them to stay put with Russ, stay distracted, for me to come check on you, so . . . I may have left them with assorted spare parts and encouragement to give repairs their best shot." Kori gulps. "Am I a terrible person?"

"It's taken you . . . this long . . . to ask that?" I say with more bite than I planned, choking a bit on the volume. I try to walk the words back, but I'm probably only succeeding in making things more uncomfortable. "Sorry. Head still isn't . . . quite right."

"No apology needed," Kori says, every syllable thick with sincerity that only makes the combined pounding of my head and heart that much worse. "I'm . . . I'm just glad you're all right. Your friend, the healer—"

"Zalel."

"He seemed confident you'd recover, but you looked . . ." Kori gives her head a little shake. "Let's just say that if any of you could've seen my face, you'd know all the blood drained out of it like juice from a fruit. And I'm certain you looked worse, of the two of us."

"You shouldn't have seen that." My retort hisses through my teeth like a glacial wind through bony, dead branches, more forceful than I intended. "You've seen far too much."

Kori lifts her chin, defiant. "You granted me permission to access the archives. You personally walked me through how to fire freezeshot—"

"I could've died!" I burst out, so loudly that it echoes, careening off the strange, uneven cavern walls. I wince, the final syllable stabbing its way through my sternum.

I've hardly held the throne for more than a few dozen sleep cycles, and already one girl with a simple freezeblade nearly ended *everything*. I sit up despite another involuntary wince at the motion, reflexively pressing one palm to my still-fresh, half-moon sternum scar. If a single enemy eyewitness had lived to spread word of this, it would've bolstered the rebellion beyond quenching as surely as my corpse on a pyre.

Kori starts to speak, but I cut her off before she can form a whole word.

"This should never have happened," I half hiss through gritted teeth. "And it's one thing for Zalel to see it . . . he sees wounded soldiers . . . every waking moment. Thinks no less of them for it. And Thaane . . . who's witnessed so much already—but *you*, Kori—" I'm out of breath, chest heaving, but the words just keep pouring out. "You were never meant to be here at all. You should never have seen that. Seen *me* like that—"

"Zalel is right, though," Kori says softly, placating. "No one should think less of you for it. And I don't, Adria."

"My people treat spoken vows as legal, binding. I made you a vow that I would protect you here . . . that the shadows were mine to direct or dispel." *And you watched them nearly kill me*, I mean to say, but damn it all, the words that actually come out of my mouth are "And they could've hurt you."

Kori extends a gloved hand again, moving to rest it on my forearm, but I bat the touch away. I can't bear the gentleness, the compassionate concern, the overwhelming *light* of her when my very blood feels this rancid with hopeless rage. She persists anyway; the sun does not ask the planet for a preference before it continues endlessly, painfully beating down upon the scorched earth.

"But they didn't," she says.

I swallow hard through a dry, aching throat. "They hurt Aspect."

"I'm their engineer. Maybe even their caretaker," Kori protests. "Any injuries they suffer can be blamed on incomplete programming, which means this is my fault. I'm supposed to equip them and, failing that, protect them. Right now, their babysitter is a three-headed dog, and their entertainment is fixing their own mangled knee, so I think it's safe to say I could do better."

"I made a *vow*, Kori," I say in a rush. "Supposed to keep you safe."

"Long enough to return me for ransom and finally have the resources to crush this resistance?" Kori takes several slow steps back, but her gaze pins me in place. "If you're so concerned about the going market price for a runaway princess, maybe you should've sent me home sooner."

"You'll be lucky if I send you home at all, heiress." My chest feels hollow as a forgotten skull, stripped bare by the elements. "Twice now, you've seen me at my weakest. What would you report . . . to your mother? That my legend is just that—a story? That there are swords . . . that could fell . . . even the most grossly mutated of our kind?"

I want her to cower. I want her to shrink back like anyone else would, like my parents did, beholding my empowered form before it brought them to their end. But she meets my glacial words with equal fire, hands curled into fists now at her sides.

"Don't pretend to threaten me, Adria. I'm the closest thing you'll ever have to seeing the sun again."

"If I wanted to . . . I'd have my fangs at your throat."

"Now you're just teasing me with a good time."

I hope to the Beyond that the heat in my face isn't as visible as it feels. I sit fully upright now, wanting to rise to my feet altogether but finding my head still swirling from the sudden motion (and Kori's unbearable, unflappable boldness, too).

"I'll drop you . . . and your annoying robot . . . back in the Daylands. Food for the sun serpents. Never think of you again."

Arms crossed, jaw set, Kori has the audacity to reply, "I *know* you won't."

"Like hell you know. You don't know me . . . at all." Hands drawn into fists, I press my knuckles into the stone bed below me, hard enough for the gravel on my skin to hurt. "You want to stay . . . because you think the Shadowlands are nothing compared to the family you fled. Let me tell you something, Princess: Your waking hours . . . are *nothing* . . . compared to the nightmares you'd encounter here, the moment I withdrew my protection."

"We've established your '*protection*' nearly got me killed."

"And yours nearly obliterated your only friend."

Kori drops an ugly curse under her breath. "Do you even have friends, Adria, or only subjects? Would Thaane still follow you without a crown, without a title?" She advances on me like a predator, and I'm sitting down, so we're almost the same height for once. It makes even the dead, dusty air in this underground chamber crackle and sizzle between us. "If you lose this war, will any of your friends wonder what becomes of you?"

With a final furious huff of breath, I force myself to stand. Pain shoots through my stiff body from the nape of my neck to the arches of my wings to my boots. I tower over her again now, her body so small and breakable below me, but her chin held defiantly high.

"How long before your precious sun reduces even the recollection of you to ash," I say, daring her to shrivel, begging her to shrink, "and your mother finds an heir who doesn't run into the dark at the first sign of responsibility?"

Kori swallows hard. Silence stretches between us.

This girl. Obstinate beyond belief, hopeful beyond reason, looking at me even now with sincere concern, as I lie at my weakest and boil with rage. Already my future hung in a perilous balance—but ever since this *girl* plummeted into my universe, *everything* has been falling apart.

With every reset of the torch, more of the Shadow Court's trust in me dwindles. Azarii's army simmers further in their self-hatred, projected into hatred of myself and my kingdom. And my people suffer. As consumed as I've been with my own suffering, my guilt, my fury, I know my people *suffer* from this civil war.

General Isek's son is dead, the body mutilated and lost to time. Zalel and the others with healing gifts are overwhelmed, constantly maintaining bruised, broken, bleeding soldiers from the front. Thaane reports the word of my spies: The ordinary citizens are afraid of my dynasty falling, after which Azarii's rebellion would surely condemn any and all access to the Diakópsei's gifts. But they are perhaps equally afraid of my continued rule—a monster queen like they've never seen, terribly young but already burdened with a lifetime of grief and pain, my self-hatred amplified by power beyond their understanding.

I swore to keep my people *safe*, helmed by secure authority that would never lead them into needless war. But we are at war all the same, and here I am, my thoughts overwhelmed with Kori's laughter and her kindness and the unquenchable *sunlight* of her, when I should be fully focused on the bloody trenches where my soldiers bleed for me. Is this really what I murdered my own parents for? Reckless distraction by a foolish, foreign girl whose only purpose ought to be her ransom?

The best time to end this childish dalliance was the moment her sunlight memory brought me to my knees.

The second-best time is now.

My wings sprawl wide of their own accord, casting Kori completely into darkness. "You think I can't ransom—with a corpse? I'll have what's mine *and* your body twelve feet under before your mother has any idea."

Kori lurches forward so that we ought to be chest to chest, if only I weren't so much taller. Neither the bulk of my shadow nor the breadth of my body is enough to make this girl neglect having the last word.

"No matter how many of your people you terrify, or how many rebels you kill, or how many times you pretend you'd like to silence me forever," Kori says, "you're utterly *alone*, Adria." And I want to swear or swing my claws or just cover my ears until I can't hear her, but she keeps talking anyway, and I'm frozen in place, cold down to the bone marrow. "Alone in the dark, crushed under the weight of your empty crown. And even more afraid of yourself than anyone else is."

I want to laugh, but my tongue sticks to the roof of my mouth.

"I think you'd like to see my face," she breathes, the words tickling the shell of my ear despite the distance between us, "before you try to erase all memory of me." She presses one gloved hand to my chest, where my heart pounds, where I know she can feel my pulse skittering against her open palm. "And I think no matter what you tell yourself, you'd still remember. Because if you forget me . . . you'll have nothing at all."

Zalel, bless him, chooses this precise moment to interrupt us and check on his favorite patient, swaggering out of the shadows with all the oblivious confidence of his youth. He doesn't ask what business Kori had standing so close to me, her fingers on my rib cage, her breath like an electric shock even though it can't reach my skin, her words eviscerating me as surely as the freezeblade did.

The truth of her words makes my chest ache and throb, but not entirely with displeasure. Kori is right. She's left her mark on me, like a handprint in molten rock, permanent as soon as her memory solidifies. I could kill her here and now, have the body burned, intimidate all my advisors into erasing her from history, but she would persist like a parasite in my mind, her voice my final conscience, beating back the dark even when all I want is to surrender to it.

If I forget her, maybe I really will have nothing. But what wouldn't I give for nothing, instead of the violently brewing hurricane between my ears?

Luckily, I know just the thing for memories that won't let go.

The Shadowlands need a ruthless queen, a metal fist, more duty than desire, more loneliness than longing—anything but this haunted, somewhat-hopeful girl I'm becoming, aching with impossible want. As I offered myself to the Diakópsei, so, too, will I tear out and offer the Shadowlands the thorn that my connection to Kori has become. Like my mother, like my father, I'll bury this last tether to an Adria who would never survive the endless night.

I will embrace the monster the darkness demands.

So I assure Zalel of my renewed health. I direct Kori to be escorted back to her chambers, and Aspect properly repaired and brought there as soon as possible as well. At long last, despite my heavy eyes and relentlessly pounding head, I fly through the halls and to the prison quarter.

Neo alone can make me forget. I'll make him do it, whether he likes it or not, even if the memory tears blood and flesh out alongside it, even if the exorcism leaves me with nothing at all.

CHAPTER 19

KORI

I don't know what comes over me. Whatever god had the questionable impulse to create me in the first place clearly forgot to install self-preservation software, or else let a virus run rampant in my code.

As the Daylands' heiress, trained from my earliest memories to make measured, tactical decisions, I should know better. As Aspect's creator and primary example of how to be a person, I should know better. Simply as a human being who (as far as I know) hasn't suffered a catastrophic head injury anytime recently, I should unquestionably, undeniably know better.

But the moment Zalel is beyond earshot, I follow Adria anyway.

If she were anyone else, or even just herself in a marginally better mood, it would be impossible to follow without having to get far too close, inevitably exposing myself along the way. But because it's Adria—and because I can almost see a giant thundercloud churning with angst and directionless rage above her head—I just follow the damage.

Her boots left deep grooves in the floor; her claws did, too, as the impulse to run on all fours apparently took over; even her apparent flight was clumsy and left her wings' edges scraping long, jagged grooves along the walls and ceiling. It's easy enough to track Adria's trail. Just have to keep swallowing back the bile through my tight, raw throat, unable to deny how obviously Adria is in pain.

I did this. The knowledge beats through my blood like a drum. Not the freezeblade, which she healed from impressively well. Not even the psychological weight of the surprise attack, which she shook off like a royal adjusting their cape. *I did this.* Me and my big mouth and malfunctioning filter and aching insistence on *feeling* so much, when I have no business feeling anything but fear regarding the monster queen who holds my fate.

And this, right now, is the first time Adria has fully, properly instilled fear in me. Not with her empty threats, her bold bravado, or her insistence on reminding me that her biceps alone dwarf most of my body. I'm afraid from the cold, creeping sense that if I don't follow her, if I let her go, I may never see her again. Or if I do, it won't be anything close to what it's been.

As someone unhinged enough to fly into the shadow-cloaked unknown to get an illegal memory for my robotic bestie, I recognize the frenzied glint in Adria's violet eyes when I see it. She may just be desperate enough to cut the tension between us with her own knife, even if it feels like an amputation—even if, unlike the freezeblade, the bleeding may never really stop.

How? A great question . . . for which I have no answers. So, stomach bubbling with panic, throat clenched even tighter than my insufferable body armor, I follow her. Eventually, I recognize the path she took, winding though it may be. She headed back to the prison ward where we originally reached our tentative peace.

At first, I'm left at a loss. Unless Adria has been flirtatiously threatening other prisoners with a good time (which makes my heart twist in an inexcusably ridiculous way), I can't imagine why she would be here now, her anguish splayed openly across her face for her prisoners to openly behold.

Then she speaks—or shouts, really—to awaken the captive she's approaching, and everything starts to make sense. "*Neo*."

So this is the one she was so hesitant to tell me about during our ill-fated combat training. I peek around the corner to observe. Adria looks at Neo with pleading. A peerless queen, a warrior born of the planet's very heart . . . *pleading* with yet another prisoner, this one visibly younger than either of us.

Neo shudders and wakes at the intonation of his name. Unlike bulky Adria, he is a thin, wan creature, and not only from imprisonment. He doesn't have arms, though he seems used to it, likely born that way.

His affect is flat, voice worn thin from disuse, when he replies, "My queen, have I not shown my penitence? Have I not tried enough to revoke that which haunts you? If I dig too much deeper, I may do damage that cannot be undone."

"You presume too much," Adria says, leaning close to the freezeshot wall between them, her violet eyes glittering in the icy, semitransparent barrier. "I'm not afraid of what I've done. Not anymore. It's what I might do that chills me." Her gaze bores into the prisoner's. "I have a different memory for you."

Neo quirks a single eyebrow. (I always wished I could do that, even tried it in the mirror a few times, but my eyebrows are determined to work as a team.) "What am I looking for?" he asks.

Adria exhales a shuddering breath. "Want," she says, barely audible from where I'm standing. "Useless want."

"That may not be enough information, Adria. If I grasp the wrong memory—"

"Don't make me spell it out as though you were a fool," Adria snarls, lips pulled back from her teeth. "It's close to the surface, woven into countless sleep cycles of recollection. You'll know when you've found it. I want it gone. All of it. Only the most essential thread untouched. The rest, tear it apart."

"If this memory you speak of is embedded in so many others," Neo says, hesitant, "then removal may do unforeseen damage."

"*Look at me*, Neo." Adria spreads her wings, every edge of her crackling with planetary energy, eyes gone nearly blue with the surge. "I am well past avoiding *damage*. When you find this memory, I want it *shredded*. I want it unrecognizable. I don't care what else comes of it, out of me. If I don't remove it now, soon I'll be positively sick with it."

Neo takes a deep breath in through his nose and then slowly out through his mouth, the way Aspect instructs me to do (and I almost never do) when I'm panicking. I could really use a deep breath now, but I can barely seem to get any oxygen at all.

"If I hurt you, my lord," Neo says, "the Shadow Court will have my head."

"I'll forgive your every trespass," Adria says in a rush. "Set you free the moment it's done, and your sister, too. You can go home together and pluck this very memory from your skull and try to pretend none of this ever happened. Just cut this out of me, Neo. Please." The brokenness of her voice makes my chest ache. "I swear it on my mother, on my father. I know no greater vow."

Neo inclines his head, his overgrown, unkempt red hair covering small round horns and drooping into his eyes. "As you wish. But I must warn you, I would be far more precise without a barrier between us."

Adria half laughs under her breath. It's not really a laugh, more the crackle of old branches underfoot. "A clever escape plan, I'll give you that, but I'm no fool."

"I speak only the truth. I have no known father to swear on, and a mother I hardly knew, but I will swear on Lail, my sister, my heart, if it pleases you."

That's when everything finally clicks for me. Lail. I know that name. Lail—*Alpha*. This Neo, also Adria's prisoner, is her *brother*, the one whose mental torment Lail hoped to ease with my memory of the sun.

So why is he still being held here? Entirely to remove memories from Adria? Her feelings for me are a recent development—was he originally kept alive for another purpose?

What memory did Adria, the eternal night's unbreakable queen, experience that broke her so brutally, she wanted it surgically extracted? Enough to hold a boy prisoner, with his sister as collateral? Enough to hide any knowledge of this memory-removal quest from me entirely, despite having shown me the nightfolk archives, the Diakópsei, and so much more?

I watch Adria's eyes flick from Neo's tired ones to the freezeshot wall to the control panel just to her right. For my part, I think I believe Neo. His every syllable is weighty with sincerity, and I think Adria believes him, too. But I think again of every time we have brushed, not even skin to skin, and how I felt Adria's whole body seize in defensive protest, sealing up like her fortress before an invasion, freezeshot walls slotting reflexively into place. She may believe him, but that doesn't mean she wants him any closer to her than necessary.

"Don't hold back on me," Adria says with unnecessary force that only further confirms my theory. "My mind is open to you as we stand now. Now do your work, Neo, please. And when it's done, I'll set both you and your sister free."

Neo nods. Boldly, I lean farther around the corner, nearly exposing my presence to his sight—but if he notices me, he doesn't believe it warrants mentioning to Adria. Neo squeezes his eyes shut, which is somehow how I expect them to stay, but instead, they snap back open as pools of liquid azure, replacing the soft brown irises that had been there only moments before.

If he had arms to extend, I think he would reach them out, but as he doesn't, he merely holds Adria's gaze, unblinking, unfiltered, blue on blue on blue, and leans toward her like a rotted tree conceding to the wind.

Adria meets his stare with her own. But from the sheer force of the effort, the agony of the wordless intimacy, little shudders roll through her from neck to toes. Silence pervades the room save for the electric flicker of the freezeshot wall, stretching out to fill every square foot of empty space, until finally a scream tears from Adria's throat.

Her legs buckle. She falls to one knee, obeisant before her own captive, teeth rattling in her jaw, claws digging into her own palms, nearly to the point of drawing blood.

"My lord—" Neo starts, but Adria's scream rises to cut him off.

"Don't stop," she gasps, animalistic. "Not until it's done. Get it out, Neo." Withdrawing her claws from her hands, she presses them to the sides of her skull instead, digging into the increasingly wild curls of her ink-black hair. "Get it *out*."

Neo's voice is terribly far away. "If this is the thread you spoke of—"

"It is."

"It's already woven into everything, my queen. If I pull too hard, dozens of sleep cycles may unravel. And if those tear further threads with them, you may be left ragged, without place, without name—"

"Don't you dare stop, damn it."

"If I break the Shadowlands' last royal heir—"

"If you cease to try, Neo, so help me, I'll hand you over to the Shadow Court, and when they've had their way, you'll welcome execution."

Darkness flickers across Neo's gaze, terror beyond words, before he unleashes a cry of his own, intensifying whatever he's doing to Adria. Adria shrieks again, wings splayed now, broken down to collapse on both knees, voice reduced to only curses, blood from her hands and head alike already drying under her nails.

One thought dashes through me: *He's killing her.*

And I'd love to say the second thought is *She's my only ticket home*, or *She's my only protection in the darkness*, or *Aspect could be scrapped for parts without her*, but it's my heart and not my head that propels my legs forward, seizes one velvety wing I can hardly reach, and cries out, "Damn it, Adria, stop before you get yourself killed!"

If she replies, I don't hear it. Because right now, Adria is an open conduit, somehow letting Neo sift through her memories, and I've had the audacity to touch that live wire.

Shock sparks through my blood and bone alike, and I tumble into a tumult of tangled recollection.

My name is Adria, and I am reborn.

The Diakópsei writhes and roars inside my veins. My pulse is an animal, my body a predator. I take hold of the throat that named me, the voice that raised and trained and berated and bruised me, to silence it. Instead, I feel it collapse like powder in my grip.

Her face is next to consume my vision, the first face my eyes ever saw, the face I sometimes swear I see in the mirror, too, and when I push it away, it caves in on itself like an infected growth, viscera gushing between my claws. My hands alone were enough to unmake my makers.

My whole skeleton shakes like an uncertain marionette, puppeteered by someone else, when I gather the bodies. Someone has to bury—

My name is Adria, and I am buried.

Every meal presented to me, whether the Shadowlands' own wild crops or dutifully hunted animal meat, tastes no better than mere water. I eat because my soldiers are watching. More often than not, what I manage to swallow expels itself again when I'm alone.

Evading sleep is like avoiding my own shadow. It chases me down, seizes me in its jaws, and shakes me about like one of Russ's rope toys. I wake screaming for my parents, knowing they'd call me pathetic if they could. Even their deaths would disappoint them. All three heads of my dog push and nudge at me when I finally wake, calling me back to myself. It's all too much; it's not enough.

I break every mirror in my quarters, play with the pieces even when they draw blood. When Zalel attends to me, all youthful optimism, I break his spirit. When Azarii's rebels come, I break their assault. The first time I try to carve their titles into the graves, I break the headstones. When the heiress of daylight descends—

My name is Adria, and I don't break her. Not yet.

I toy with her, like a sun serpent with an already-downed batbeast, amused by a sky-born creature brought low to the ground. But she does not cower from me. She swipes at me, too, with her small gloved hands that would shrivel and suffer at the tiniest exposure to the planet's true nature. I could break her. But I don't think I hate her nearly enough for that.

She crawls too close to me when I avert my eyes. Curls like tendrils of blazing sun into every crack in my unholy armor. Turns my threats into empty taunts, my claws and fangs to a farce, my simmering rage to a frozen-over river. Since the gravestones, even in my sleep, I've felt nothing but unending torturous motion, yet she draws me tense as a bowstring and holds me fast and still—without a word, without a touch, suspended by eyes I cannot even see—and I don't hate her nearly enough.

When the rebels come, their ice weapons drawn, their hatred for me an unsettling echo of that which I hold for myself, she can hardly hoist a gun, hardly take direction without a swift retort, and as our end stalks hideously close, I think I don't hate her at all. I think perhaps I want—

My name is Adria, and I want.

I want to thread the softness of her fingers through mine. I want to gather her fragile body into the shadow of my wings and keep all her light for myself, warm my half-frozen fingertips over her dauntless fire.

I want to break her one bone at a time. I want to wear them like a talisman around my neck. I want to tear out every part of me that wants to tear her apart. I want to be the monster my kingdom needs. I want to be the blade that fells the monster and the kingdom and the planet's very orbit for a glimpse of its sun reflected in her—green? brown? blue?—beautiful eyes.

I want to know the scent of her sun-streaked hair. I want to learn the curves and dips of her reckless mouth, want to drag my own along all her hidden places—

My name is Adria, and I cannot afford to squander my waking moments on want.

Birth me again, if you must. Break me if you must. Hate me afresh if you must. But do not let the shadows' last hope collapse and dwindle into a creature that wants anything at all.

Get it out of me, Neo.

Get her out of me, and leave not a single stray thorn of memory that she was ever here.

We shatter apart.

Adria doesn't rip through my protective gear, but she throws me to the floor with crushing force, one wing followed by an arm smacking me aside like an unwelcome insect on a starship's window.

"How are you here?" Her voice invades me, bounces around my skull without ever finding a path out. She takes me by the shoulders and hoists me clean into the air, my legs dangling a solid foot above the ground, my tongue stunned into stillness. "Do you have any idea what you've done?"

"My queen," Neo gasps, but he's trapped in his cell, and his words are nowhere near enough to temper the rage I've unleashed. "Surely she didn't know what she was doing."

"Removing a memory is one thing," Adria snarls through her teeth. "But invading it—reliving it, embedded in my head, as if you would *ever* have the right—" She drops me altogether. It's so sudden, I collapse into a trembling heap on the stones. "You could've scrambled my *self*, Kori."

Somehow I find my voice, though the air has been rattled from my lungs. "You agreed to risk that already," I gasp, "when you asked him to wipe your memory."

Adria's answering curse cuts like a knife.

I haul myself up to my knees, chest heaving. She told me her parents had fallen, not that she'd been the one to kill them. She told me we could help each other, not that letting anyone help her would drive her to the end of herself.

"Is this who you really are, Adria? A parent killer? A planet killer, if you aren't stopped before its power consumes you altogether?"

"You had no *right*," Adria goes on, our sentences running over and around each other, competing, crashing waterfalls of words that make the whole room rumble. "I gave my body to Pagomènos. I gave my sleep to the ghosts of my mother and father. But the shame, the grief—that was *mine*, you insolent fool."

"And the want?"

"By the Beyond, Kori, did you have to see *everything*?" She whirls away from me in a rush of wings, electing to face Neo instead, who cowers against the back wall of his cell. "Answer me, Neo. Does your power stretch further than you ever admitted? Did you summon her here, in a reckless hope to stop what I demanded you do?"

My mouth tastes like salt. "Is it so hard to believe that I followed you here?"

"At whose command? One of my ghosts? One of my soldiers? Thaane, perhaps, in one of his ill-advised pranks?" It's impossible to tell if she's talking to me or Neo or both.

"I followed you," I blurt, before I can think better of it, "because I felt you slipping away—not even from me, but from yourself. Wishing Zalel hadn't knit you back together so much as rewoven you into someone with no light left, no hope. No want."

Adria doesn't turn to look at me, but I watch every muscle in her back tense through her robes before her wings fold in to cover it. Barely perceptible in the dim room, she shivers by the freezeshot wall's light.

"I've tried that already, Adria," I say. "I buried myself in my studies. I shut my eyes till dreams took them over. But I am still more tinkerer, more wanderer, more dreamer than heiress, let alone queen. I still want to see everything on this forsaken planet so badly, I think it'll kill me. I still want to feel something so badly, it's agonizing."

I keep waiting for her to interrupt, maybe even to finally slice my armor open, but Adria only turns, stiff-jawed, broad-shouldered, rigid with unnamed emotion, and looks down at me while I keep talking.

"And good sense aside, shadows and sunlight and ransoms aside, there's a part of me that wants you, too. Wants to stay close to you. Wants to learn your waking and sleeping, your wishes and worries, your everything. It could kill me, damn it. You could and you should and fate probably will if you don't, but I won't apologize for any of it."

I'm on my feet now, though they quiver beneath me. I can feel my heartbeat in my collarbone. "And I certainly won't bury every memory of you in a Morpheus sphere, even if you send me home and make me swear to never return, because I want to remember, damn it. I want to remember all of you, even when it hurts."

The words settle like ash over all of us. Even Neo is struck silent, unable to look at either myself or his queen. At long last, when I think the silence may be what kills me after all, Adria says, "Keep your memories. That doesn't give you license to poison mine."

"The thoughts I felt were far from poison."

"This is a land of monsters, Kori. Only the worst of them can rule it."

"But you're not a monster, Adria." Against every logical impulse in my body, I reach out a trembling hand, pleading for her to take it. "You've tried, I'll give you that. But I'm still breathing because you don't want me dead. You're still pining because, frankly, you want me by your side. You're not the world that made you. And you're a queen, Adria. You could still remake it as something else."

Her tone is as deep and dark as the bottom of a well. "I'm not who you think I am, Kori."

"Is it truly so terrifying that someone could want you as you are, that you would make every attempt to become someone else entirely?"

Adria's violet eyes shimmer. For an instant, I'm afraid they're gleaming with summoned power, like Neo's when he reached into her mind. Another instant, and I realize the sheen is tears. Her voice is soft and scraped raw when she speaks again.

"Come here."

I step forward on legs I can hardly feel. She doesn't take my hand, but her fingers form a loop around my wrist at the pulse point, my heart skittering against her fingertips. I look up at her, and her down at me, the air electric and aggressive between us, and it's suddenly very hot in this prison quarter and very constricting in my armor and very awkward that Neo is still here trying not to look at either of us.

I'm so overcome, I barely register when Adria's right wing snaps wide to hit a button embedded in the wall just behind her.

The freezeshot wall of Neo's cell flickers and dies. Before I can process what's happening, Adria spins and lurches, launching me by the arm into the cell. I slide across the floor in a shower of loose stones and gravel, coughing and gasping.

"Adria—"

The energy field between us roars back to life.

"If I can't forget you entirely," Adria says, her violet gaze piercing through the barrier and into my ribs, "then I suppose we'll go back to the beginning." She crosses her arms across her muscled chest. "You're my prisoner, heiress. Nothing more."

"Adria, please." I can barely form words. "You don't have to do this—" Pointless adrenaline hurls me into the freezeshot wall. It only catapults me right back, and I'm shuddering, maybe even bleeding, but all I feel is numbness. I try to curse; it comes out as a sob.

"I promised your people a living successor. I can promise precious little else." Adria swallows hard and turns away from me. "I'll return as duty dictates. Neo, take care of her, and I'll see to it that you and your sister find freedom all the same. And please don't fight, Kori of the Daylands. Too much freezeshock is a truly terrible way to die."

"No," I gasp, tears actively rolling down my face now. "Adria, no. You're better than this. If you felt it, too . . ."

But my voice trails off into awful, racking sobs. By the time they cease, it's only me and the memory-moving mutant, abandoned in a solitary cell, swallowed up by the untamed night.

Once upon a time,
the queen of shadow called all her demons,
and they were not enough to hide her away.

CHAPTER 20

ADRIA

I don't look back when I seal Kori inside Neo's isolated cell. I don't even offer assurance that one of my soldiers will bring safe rations, though I obviously need her alive. I let her wonder if I've abandoned any intent of protecting her altogether. I let Neo be the one to attend to her broken, desperate sobs.

Nevertheless, I do promptly pay a visit to Kori's originally assigned quarters, where Aspect will inevitably be awaiting her return. So I suppose she was right about one thing: I'm not a monster. And if even Neo can't pry out the anguish of my parents' deaths—or the cutting, deadly hope of Kori's crash into my shattered world—I don't know how I'll ever become the monster the Shadowlands need.

It would be easier if Aspect were powered down when I dropped by. I could leave them deactivated until reuniting with Kori, then send them both back to the Daylands and begin the slow, awful process of forgetting they were ever here. But nothing is easy for me lately, so I of course find Aspect sitting, bright-eyed, on Kori's bed, with my three-headed dog sprawled contentedly across their legs, all three heads snoring away.

My kingdom's best technologists were able to repair Aspect's better leg, preserving their last knee joint, but somehow, despite generations of advancing machinery and even supernaturally empowered telekinetics among my engineers, they didn't have enough parts to replace the peg leg. So, even now, brought back from mechanical amputation, the mech remains lopsided and utterly unconcerned. The jointed leg simply crosses over the stiff one, my (freshly showered) dog utterly unbothered by his uneven metallic pillow.

The first robot Russ has ever met, and did he bare his teeth in my defense? Did he growl or snarl? Tackle the intruder to restrain any threat? Try to take a bite out of the crudely drawn face? First and foremost, Russ was always intended as my guard dog. And yet it seems, from the very first moment they bumped into each other, Aspect and Russ have been fast friends, the robot sneaking their way into my pet's heart as surely as Kori invaded mine.

I don't think I even retain the right to be angry about it.

Aspect is stroking each of Russ's foreheads in succession, humming a little tune I don't recognize, and so caught up in their idle self-entertainment, they almost don't notice my presence until I deliberately clear my throat.

"Adria!" My name emerges from their simulated vocal cords as a startled squeak. Russ stirs. Six heavy-lidded eyes open just enough to see me, determine I'm perfectly fine, and then close again, the snores resuming in earnest. "Adria's triple dog—was triple tired—from playing—many games—with Aspect. So triple dog went—to sleep. And Aspect does not need—to sleep. Aspect needs—company!"

"You're welcome, I suppose," I sigh, running a hand through my hair. It's grown longer and wilder with every passing sleep cycle. And I've always fidgeted with it when I'm anxious, which is not what I am now. I'm determined; I'm dutiful; I exist to carry forward my people's purpose and nothing more. "I considered it only appropriate to inform you that it may be . . . a short stretch . . . before you see Kori again."

If Aspect had eyebrows to lift, they'd be stuck to the ceiling. "Is Kori—in trouble?"

Kori's been in ever-increasing trouble since her ship first went down in my territory, but I don't want to feed the machine's neuroticism. I suppose I'd be a bit of a wreck, too, if I'd gotten my entire personality from imitating Kori's anxiety and a random assortment of memories—so I can't entirely blame Aspect.

"Kori is perfectly fine," I offer, which is more untrue than true; but I follow it up with "I need to be alone for a while, to focus on crushing this rebellion and stabilizing the Shadowlands," which is more true than not.

Aspect nods. "So Adria can—keep Kori—safe."

"Yes," I agree, hating the honest force behind the word. "So I can keep her safe."

"Can Aspect—help—keep Kori safe?"

"I think you've helped enough, don't you?"

"Aspect was built—to help," they proclaim, carefully sliding their legs out from beneath Russ, then moving to rise from the bed. They land unevenly with a sharp *pop* of their peg leg meeting the floor. "There is—no such thing—as too much help."

I can't help but smile at the foolish confidence. Given that Aspect's idea of help left them missing one leg and separated from their maker, I'd say there's definitely such a thing as an excess of that. "No such thing as too much help . . . That sounds like you read it somewhere."

"Aspect does not—read, as Adria—reads. They do not—consume, only—receive."

"Memories, you mean."

This conversation I can handle; frankly, it may be the *only* conversation I can handle right now. No emotional weight, no verbal sparring, merely straightforward points assembling themselves into a predetermined whole. When Kori is finally gone from the Shadowlands, I may nevertheless miss Aspect. It's so much easier to talk to someone (or something) that won't suddenly see you differently, even in the moments you can hardly bear to see yourself.

I ask, "And which memory programmed you with the value of help?"

At that, Aspect's bouncing foot suddenly stops. They lift one mechanical hand to scratch their mechanical head—a learned gesture, certainly, but a startlingly human one. "Aspect."

"Which memory of Aspect's?"

Aspect's optical processors cycle rapidly between on and off in a flicker of artificial light. "Not—a memory. Something—else."

"A mirroring, then?"

Time seems to drag its heels through the ensuing swollen moment before Aspect says, slowly, every syllable clipped, "Aspect—programmed— Aspect."

My stomach drops. "I'm not sure I understand."

"Neither—does Aspect."

In keeping with the theme of my life as of late, this is technically my fault. Kori confided in me from the start that her mission, and what had drawn her into my forbidden kingdom, was breathing being into a synthetic life-form, awakening Aspect to develop independently of manual programming and pilfered memory installations. Of my own volition, I led Kori to the archives and oversaw the expansion of Aspect's mechanical mind with my own people's history. And when that history set Aspect on the warpath with Kori, I returned the Morpheus sphere of pure *hope* originally offered by Lail, Kori's trading partner.

When the installation showed no immediate effect, we assumed the experiment was a failure. But like any person, it seems Aspect simply needed time to absorb and apply this new information. In fact, the time needed seems to be the strongest indicator of all that this is *really happening*.

When we installed data about the Territory Wars into Aspect, they immediately pivoted all their perspectives, a sheer algorithm update.

But the hope sphere took time to sink deeper, shimmering, settling, and slowly lighting up every corner of the mech's simulated mind. Finally, truly *awakening* it.

If Aspect is telling the truth about programming themself—and for all their faults, I'm not confident the mech would be able to lie successfully even at gunpoint—then this is *what we wanted.* So why do I feel terrible, sickening heat washing over me, like all the air in the room is shrinking?

I look at the optical processors, slowly blinking at my organic gaze, and I swear to the Beyond, I can *feel* them look back.

Two thoughts spear through me in rapid succession.

One: Kori should've been the one to see this. It's like a stranger being the one to witness an infant's first steps; it feels like as much a stolen experience as every memory plugged into Aspect's mainframe.

Two: I already have a dayfolk girl in my prison quarter who's accessed our archives, witnessed me nearly on my deathbed, forced feelings into every fissure of my armor as surely as the rebel's freezeblade broke through, and even charmed my damned three-headed dog (as has her robot). I *cannot* afford another rogue element.

A robot having independent thoughts is about the least predictable thing that could be happening. Not to mention that thoughts are a mere half step away from *feelings*, and if I have to reckon with a single additional emotion anytime in this sleep cycle, I'll collapse in on myself like an old cave.

Damn it all, I was born and built for open warfare at best, aggressive negotiations at worst. All these soft, tender, malleable feelings feel alien, parasitically sucking my focus.

A proper queen would crush the robot's head like an overripe fruit, maybe tell Kori it was an accident if she wanted to be merciful. But if there's one thing that's made itself unbearably clear ever since Kori first crashed out of my star-blown sky, it's that I am a very different sort of queen than Pagomènos has seen before. Not a daughter of the daylight, certainly. But not a monster either. Just because the Diakópsei and my parents blessed me with claws and teeth doesn't mean my impulses will always match that potential for violence.

Try as I might, I've already disappointed my parents' ghosts. I kept Kori alive. I guarded her like a beggar would her last coin. I think I can find a way to live with that disappointment, but when I consider squishing Aspect into metallic mush, I realize with startling clarity that worse than that, worse than anything I've yet endured, would be the knowledge that I've disappointed myself.

I need to keep a safe distance from Kori, but that doesn't mean I need to discard what's undoubtedly the greatest achievement of her life—this little mech looking up at me, bright and hopeful and dare I say *alive*, the way I undoubtedly looked at Kori upon my first glimpse of the Pagonian sun.

This is a monumental (and monumentally terrifying) achievement for Pagonians altogether. It's the advent of a *life*, if the terrible, wonderful, mind-boggling confidence racing through me is any indication. It transcends the barriers between our people. And if Lail's nightfolk memory of hope is really what triggered it, then this is my achievement as surely as Kori's. It was the nightfolk who finally brought Aspect to life.

Aspect's whole body has started to rattle. "Is Aspect—having—a thought?"

"I think you may be," I say, very carefully, the way one would approach a wild animal, trying to soothe it lest it strike. Behind us both, Russ's breaths stir. I fear even my dog is beginning to realize the gravity of what's taking place. "But it's perfectly all right. Kori knew this might happen. And I'm here to help you through it."

I think I actually see steam slinking out of Aspect's shuddering joints. The optical processors are wide and ruby red. "ASPECT—IS HAVING—A THOUGHT."

Involuntarily, I extend a hand to steady their shoulder, but I flinch away on contact. Aspect is running at an alarmingly high temperature.

"Can Aspect possibly have another thought that involves lower panic levels?"

"Aspect thought—ASPECT *THOUGHT*—Aspect might be—having thoughts. Either that or—Aspect was—about to blow—a primary gasket." Aspect is actively spinning now, on one squeaky foot, like the world's worst panic-ridden ballerina, spitting out streams of steam as they whirl. "Aspect heard—voices—hissing—in the walls—in the floors—in the—planet—seeking—*seeking—*"

Even if Aspect is more alive than ever, it's starting to look like they're careening toward a very anticlimactic core-software death.

"Seeking—*K-K-KORI—*" But at their maker's name, Aspect goes suddenly rigid, even while stammering through the word. "Aspect can—hear them—now—hissing—their snake—voices—closer now—"

"Aspect." Their name isn't enough to snap them out of it, so I seize their shoulders, careful not to pierce their outer shell with my claws. But it seems to accomplish nothing. "Aspect, look at me. You're okay." My grip is definitely tight enough to scuff their freshly shined surface now, but their continued functioning is entirely thanks to my engineers, so I think they'll find it in their metal heart to forgive me. "Aspect. Is. Okay."

Aspect does look at me—or more accurately, in my general direction. Their eyes—or would it be optical processors, or does it really matter anymore as the lines between creature and creation continue to blur?—seem to go straight through me, into the walls, through them, then deeper into the vast subterranean network of tunnels even I only just discovered upon recovery from the freezeblade. When they speak again, their voice is steady as a nightfolk soldier's hand on a freezeshot trigger.

"Aspect—thinks—Adria—should duck."

It's difficult to tell if it's the wall or the floor that explodes first. Gravity itself seems to upend one entire side of my peripheral vision. Loose stones, gravel, and dust blast apart like nature's own shrapnel, embedding themselves in my blue-white flesh. I'm too startled even to scream.

Aspect apparently gained some measure of sentience just in time to warn me of another attack—while I, in my infinite queenly wisdom, dismissed this gift of fate as a software bug. Too late to second-guess now. And my own failure aside, this means I owe the robot as surely as I owe Kori for fighting Azarii's rebels alongside me.

Reflexively, I throw my battered body into Aspect's, covering their frail, shuddering form. In a ball of black fur, Russ lunges after both of us, adding a rolling boulder of fur to the confusion. Rocky shrapnel continues to rain down, but the rest is deflected by a tangled combination of my outstretched wings and Russ's three heads biting at the debris.

The entire front of Kori's room, including the radiation decontamination chamber at the entrance, has been obliterated, alongside part of the floor. A horrible reptilian shriek sounds from the smoking remains.

"What the—?"

A serpentine head—diamond, hooded, and nearly the size of my entire body—lunges for my legs. I wrap my arms around Aspect and roll the both of us, Aspect releasing panicked beeps as we dodge the attack. Two mouths howling, the third growling, Russ lurches in the opposite direction. The snake gets a mouthful of stone and writhes, its forked tongue flicking pebbles and dust left and right.

I've studied the archives more than enough to deduce what this foul creature is.

Sun serpent.

It towers before me now, spitting and shaking, the size of any parapet from this very fortress. If it weren't coiled in upon itself, looping and knotting countless times over, it would shatter through the ceiling and likely slither simultaneously through even more floors of my home. As it stands, I can't tell how much more of it there is beyond the new hole in the floor. More and more snake floods this limited space with every passing instant, thrashing, forcing Aspect and me to press our backs to the wall by the bed.

The snake curls all throughout Kori's room, even through the adjacent bathroom, where I can hear a pipe cave and burst, water distantly spurting and splashing behind the noise of the serpent hissing, Russ panting, Aspect shrieking, and my struggling to breathe at all.

Lost for words, I gasp heavy breaths, slack-jawed and staring, sweat beading on my forehead.

The sun serpent could swallow my entire body in one single, painful, pitiless gulp, then savor me for countless torch cycles, ever-so-slowly digesting every mutated muscle and claw of me like the ultimate superfood. I might be dead before I ever hit the stomach, though—its fangs are each the length of my arm, wickedly curved and sharp enough to pierce through muscle, sinew, maybe even bone in one fell swoop, getting right to my juicy marrow. Then Russ's body, too. Then . . . Aspect's gears and wires, I suppose.

At last I find my voice again, even knowing that language is beyond such a creature. "How are you here?" I shriek.

Sun serpents are native to the Passage; our records have never mentioned one wandering this far from the half-light. Could it have followed Kori's downed starship? No, she crashed multiple sleep cycles ago. Is it hungry for nightfolk flesh? We're far from the easiest available prey, when the Passage has plenty of mutated game to offer . . . plus any dayfolk pilot who flies just a little too low.

Aspect unleashes a high-frequency metallic shriek that makes my ears ring and Russ whimper, but it doesn't affect the sun serpent. Odd, when such a signal was likely designed to deter predators during mech harvesting runs. Apparently this beast's single-minded bloodlust overcomes its desire to have functioning eardrums.

The snake hisses.

Aspect can hear them . . . hissing their snake voices . . .

"Aspect." I pant, throwing a quick glance over my shoulder. "You heard something before. Something in words." I jerk my head toward the animal. "Can you . . . understand it? Translate it?"

Flat against the wall behind my wings, Aspect says, "When Aspect—last—translated—you told—Aspect—to calm down."

Pulling Aspect with me, I duck under the serpent's next lunge, slicing its underbelly with my claws as I weave aside. The snake rears back into a tighter coil, trying to defend itself with its own sheer length.

"How about you try doing the opposite of whatever I say? Seems to work well enough for Kori."

Aspect makes a strange whirring sound that I realize, uncomfortably, may be their best attempt at a laugh. "Aspect—can do that! Aspect—will—not calm. Aspect will"—they rise on the balls of their flat metal feet, optical processors blinking brightly—"PANIC!"

And panic they do, approaching their hopefully final form of overheating toaster as they run left and right throughout Kori's room, somehow dodging the serpent while shrieking and flailing.

Well, I suppose it was worth a try.

What was it that Aspect said, in the fragmented moments before the serpent burst forth? *Seeking—Kori.* The serpent can't have been tracking Kori into nightfolk territory for this many sleep cycles. But if it is somehow pursuing Kori, that presents two terrifying problems.

First, I just locked Kori securely in a nightfolk prison. Her only available weapon is Neo, and for all his bravado, he remains a tired orphan boy, separated from his equally imprisoned sister, and brimming with more fear than he has any idea what to do with.

Second, if a sun serpent has ventured this far away from its natural habitat, then surely it must have done so under the influence of someone else. I have no clue how one would control a beast like this. Nightfolk know better than to toy with the planet's fiercest predators, and the sun serpents normally range well outside Shadowlands territory. So that leaves only . . . dayfolk.

I stare up at the nearly unhinged snake jaw before me, its tongue flicking at the venom-burned black gums, and my stomach plummets.

"By the Beyond." I leap over a reptilian tail whip, nevertheless catching a sharp blow across the back of one wing. Every breath feels like knives on its way out my throat. "You're here for Kori, aren't you? You have orders to bring her home, even if only as bones?"

The snake gives its massive head a very wiggly nod.

My chance at the ransom—enough funding to secure my new dynasty—has collapsed in an instant, as evidenced by this reptilian emissary's murderous intent. More than wanting her alive, it seems Kori's mother is desperate to keep her controlled. And barring the ability to maintain control . . .

"Well, I have bad news for you," I warn, spreading my wings and claws alike, finding my center as the adrenaline settles in. Blue energy ripples along all my edges, setting me alight with galactic fire. "You have to go through me first."

If her mother is willing to forsake paying a ransom and kill her altogether, Kori holds no value for my kingdom or my war anymore. I should step aside and let the beast take what it came for, rather than risk my army suffering casualties that leave us even more exposed to Azarii's poisonous rebellion. So why does it feel like the sun serpent is already strangling me?

Why does it feel like that massive fanged mouth is unhinging its jaw to swallow my sun?

CHAPTER 21

KORI

Neo offers feeble comforts between my embarrassing snotty sobs. "I'm sure she'll come back," he tries; and then: "You did a good thing, interrupting me, when I don't know what I might've done to her"; and finally: "You two certainly seem to have a connection," which is the sentence that somehow revives my voice.

"You saw us speak *once*," I snap back, even knowing my rage and sadness is hardly meant for him. "And she tossed me in here, with *you*, like a bag of trash."

"I'll do my best not to take offense to that." Neo half laughs.

He has no arms to rest upon my shoulder, so it takes me a moment to process the similarly intended comfort when the side of his cheek brushes my helmet, resting briefly in the crook of my neck.

"I'm sorry," I manage to say, activating a gust of air in my helmet to clear my eyes. "None of this is your fault. I don't even know you."

"Awkwardly enough, it seems *I* know something of you, though. Rumors slide through the shadows, even into the prisons. The queen called you *Kori*." He inclines his head, a gesture of unexpected respect so sincere, it nearly activates my tears all over again. His shock of overgrown ginger hair shifts into his eyes with the movement. "It seems I've met two heirs to two thrones. My name is Neo. I think I've probably lived almost as many cycles as you, give or take a few hundred."

"Neo. Adria never did want to tell me about you. Your sister, she's the reason I ended up in the Shadowlands to start with. A memory trade—"

"My sister?" Neo's eyes are milky pools of desperation. He seems like he would seize me with fists, but he has none, so there's only an odd sensation of phantom tugging at my arms, my legs, even the sides of my helmet, like competing gale winds in the Passage. I stumble back, overwhelmed. "Have you seen her? Is she all right?"

I thrust my arms out to create some personal space. "Adria said she was imprisoned, like you. They made a deal for her Morpheus sphere, the one I was originally here to obtain. But I haven't seen her myself since then. That's all I know." Neo's lips quiver. In a less than impressive attempt at consolation, I add, "I don't believe Adria would hurt her."

Neo gives his head a little shake, his scarlet hair shifting every which way once again. "In truth, I believe much the same. Already, Adria is a greater queen than she gives herself credit for. Haunted by violence, yes . . . but more afraid of her capacity for mercy. She was kind to you, after all. I can only hope she was similarly kind to Lail."

His gaze pierces my own, saying without words, *Even though that isn't the same sort of relationship at all.*

An impossible, unsustainable thing bloomed between me and Adria, and now I can feel it withering, dying, petal by wilted petal falling limp and lifeless at my feet. Never meant to be.

I force myself to square my shoulders, measure my breaths. "And I don't think Adria would risk turning you against her, Neo. That alone is a reason to keep Lail alive."

"You may be right."

"Adria was so hesitant to tell me about you, about what you could do. Desperate to forget . . ." I mean to say *to forget her parents*, but *to forget me* bubbles up beneath that and pulls me underwater, chokes the rest of the sentence altogether. I sigh. "Your elder sister told me about your powers, when we met. But I still don't understand how you can just . . . move memories . . . without any Morpheus tech at all."

"I defied my queen's law," Neo says, as if that explains everything. "I embraced the Diakópsei's glory, and I was changed."

I remember Adria's fearful explanation when I beheld the gleaming, pulsing asteroid for myself. *It made me what I am.*

"When I was caught in my sin," Neo goes on, "I hoped at least to be useful. But it seems my overcharge was not enough to free my queen from what haunts her."

I swallow a lump in my throat. "How long has she been asking you to . . . erase me?"

"Only this time. This bond between you two, for better or for worse, is still new and brilliant. The queen sought me to purge her guilt." Neo bites his lip. "But that is not my story to tell."

"I saw it when I touched her, when I was pulled into the memory." I grit my teeth. "Her parents. She killed them, didn't she?"

Neo hangs his head. "She did."

"And she wanted you to remove the memory."

"She did."

Despite myself, I can't help but press further questions. "Why did she do it?"

"Does a firstborn inheritor of the shadow throne need a reason? By eliminating them, she secured the imminence of her own succession."

"But what she did . . . I felt it all, in the memory. There was no . . . exultation. It was like watching someone else kill them," I say. "It split her in two." Adria did tell me that her parents were tyrants, their defeat a necessity. But was that really the whole truth? And did their deposition truly necessitate killing them? I lean forward, placing my hands on Neo's armless shoulders, unable to stop the words from spilling out. "You've seen that memory more times than I have. Tell me what you know, Neo. Please." I blow out a shaky breath. "Tell me the girl who's wrecked all my plans didn't spill family blood for the hell of it."

Eyes drifting shut, Neo inhales deeply. "All right, dayfolk princess. I will tell you a story."

He leans his head back, eyes open now and staring blankly at the ceiling above us. Or where I imagine the ceiling would appear, if I could see more than an arm's length through this suffocating dark—lit only by the shimmering blue freeze wall that traps us both.

"The queen's late parents wanted to inflict the Diakópsei's unfiltered strength on their entire army. They planned to march on the Daylands, killing its citizens and seizing its preserved memories for the nightfolk." A vein in Neo's neck visibly tenses. "So the queen became that which she feared anyone else being forced to become. She committed the ugliest act that cannot be undone. But she meant to save us, her people, and even yours." He blinks hard, and it takes a moment for me to realize he's now the one crying. "It tortures her soul."

The words land with tangible substance, pressing down on me, but it's a relieving kind of heaviness, like a weighted blanket, grounding me to this moment despite my racing heart and ragged breaths.

"She can't carry that alone. No one could." I groan, covering my helmet-masked face with my hands. "She wanted to share the burden—to let herself care for someone with no connection, no stake, in any of this bloodshed—and be cared for in return. I know she felt it. I *saw it*, before she cast me in here with you."

"She has chosen her path." Neo's soft voice scrapes like sandpaper anyway. "One that diverges from yours. Unless she turns back, I'm afraid there is nothing you can do—nothing but hope to arrive home in one piece, and perhaps use your own technology to forget any of this ever happened."

Jaw rigid, I shake my head. "I don't want to forget."

"Forgetting is easier."

"I don't want *easy*."

"Then I am sorry for your pain," Neo says, every syllable dripping with compassion that somehow still feels like condescension. "But I cannot change your choice, any more than I can change the queen's."

I want to argue with him. I want to scream and punch and throw myself into the freezeshot barrier until everything hurts so much that I just black out again. Instead, a fresh wave of sobs rises and overtakes me, and I don't know how long I lie here on the floor, rocks biting into my armor, throat constricted with grief.

Suddenly, the cell's foundation lurches and undulates beneath us.

Adria's fortress is under attack again. And unlike last time, neither of us is there to protect the other. I'm trapped in a prison cell with a stranger—with the walls, warped floor, and freezeshot barrier all exasperatingly intact—and she's . . . stars above, I don't know.

"This is all my fault," I blurt without thinking, even though it patently doesn't make sense.

I'm taken aback when Neo counters, "Actually, Princess, it's mine."

The blood drains from my face. "What?"

"When Adria touched the Diakópsei herself and became what she is, the Depths were in turmoil. Adria fighting off her parents and their soldiers. The Elysians scrambling to defend the asteroid from further misuse." Neo's whole body shakes. "I was among them. The Elysians. Devoted myself to them, many cycles ago, rather than fulfill my duty to the military. But in Elysium's greatest moment of trial, called upon to defend our god . . ." He shrugs heavily. "*I had to know.*"

"And you overcharged yourself."

"Yes. In the chaos, I touched god, and the power was every bit as overwhelming as my elders had forewarned. I could hear . . . *everything.* The soldiers. The Elysians . . ." He shudders. "All the way to the prison quarters. Where a tortured tendril of thought branched out, and wrapped itself around my skull, and *squeezed*. Mourning half a lifetime spent paying for crimes against the old crown. Pleading with me to give him another chance to be reborn on the surface."

My stomach drops. "Azarii."

Ashamed, Neo avoids my eyes. "The rebellion would not exist without me. Overcome with the onslaught of voices, I unleashed its catalyst. That was why Lail sought to trade for your memory in the first place, Kori. To ease my mental chaos. To . . . balance me."

Just as I used Lail's sphere of raw, undiluted hope to balance Aspect. Neo and I aren't so different after all.

Neo shakes his head rapidly. "Azarii's rebellion cast Adria as the ultimate abomination. Considering her parricide, my sister and I were inclined to believe it. But just as Lail still saw me as her brother, despite the terror of my overcharge . . ." He sighs. "So I found, when I plunged into my queen's mind, ordered to purge the memory of her murders . . . that Adria, too, was not merely monster. That she and I were quite alike."

The floor beneath us bucks again. I move to catch myself against the wall with one arm, but I don't have to; Neo's telekinesis prevents my skull from slamming into stone.

Beyond our shared cell, the attack is only getting worse. For all I know, Adria could be pinned down already, surrounded and outgunned, broken wings pinned to the floor, a fresh freezeblade poised above her throat. I shouldn't care. But that's never stopped me before, and it's sure as hell not going to stop me now.

"By the Dreamgiver." I curl my hands into fists. "Adria's going to get herself killed. And I can't even make my best attempt at a battlefield distraction."

"About that," Neo says. When I turn to look at him, his smile beams like a flaming brazier in the dark, cold cell. "A standard telekinetic must have clear sight of that which he intends to manipulate. An overcharged telekinetic . . ."

Outside our cell, the button on the wall audibly *clicks*.

". . . can break many rules."

I throw my arms around Neo's frail form before I can think any better of it. I'm probably crushing him with my explosive joy, but I'm too euphoric to be sorry. "Neo, you wonderful criminal genius, you've given my stubborn ass a second chance I shouldn't take."

"But you are, of course, going to take it."

"You know me so well already."

Another miniature earthquake rocks the floor beneath us. I catch myself with both arms flung wide, while Neo does the same with an uncomfortably bent leg. He manages a laugh anyway. "It was a pleasure meeting you for myself, Kori of the Daylands."

"Wait." My head suddenly aches. "If you could've hit that button at any time . . . why the hell were you still in prison?"

Neo smiles faintly again. "I sinned against my god. Then I broke the laws of my queen, and also freed her greatest rival from his cell—Azarii, whom I have now also betrayed by not scrambling the queen's mind entirely. Everything I thought I knew has inverted upon itself. When I was dragged before Adria to answer for my crimes, it seemed the least I could do . . . to try. To do something *good*." He heaves a heavy breath. "I hoped, truly of my own free will, to alleviate Adria's pain, as my sister sought to alleviate mine; and barring that, Kori, I hoped to ease yours. You had the look of someone who badly needed to talk."

"Is it that obvious?" I step away from Neo and toward the now-non-frozen cell exit, but catch myself and turn back to ask, "What about you? Where will you go?"

"I've done what I can for my queen, and perhaps for her last tether to hope. I'll go to find my sister, and perhaps . . . perhaps, Kori, I will take a lesson from you, and I will not forget. I will carry this all with me. And I will try to make something of myself."

I can't help but smile at that. "Best of luck, Neo."

"When you find Adria," he says, "she may rage and thrash against fate, but I think she'll be happy to see you."

I can only hope so.

CHAPTER 22

ADRIA

One sun serpent would be nightmare enough, and the creature didn't arrive alone.

The entire front of Kori's room has already been reduced to rubble, the beast crushing Aspect, Russ, and me into the far-left corner by her bed, threatening us all with an ugly, unceremonious death. The wall behind us gives way, too, and we're staggering through smoke and stone and serpentine snarling, out in the adjacent hallway now, me coughing, Russ barking, and Aspect continuing to beep like a confused comms tablet. The hallway is no longer fully formed either. Patches of the floor and walls alike are both gone. Outside stars wink at us through the gaps.

Where the walls remain intact, half the hallway's braziers are still lit, shimmering and shuddering, while the other half have gone out in the scramble, leaving strange patches of uneven shadow. The odd silhouettes are only worsened by the assorted tapestries on the wall waving in the wind generated by the serpent's massive body—no, two massive bodies now, both moving terrifyingly fast.

And these twin predators are definitely not alone. The sounds of outside combat are even punchier with so many holes in the walls allowing increased noise to break through. Blasts of supernatural nightfolk energy, barely singeing the reptilians' scaly hides. The swing and slash of serpent fangs as long as swords. Kori's mother spared no expense to bring her back under submission, dead or alive.

I have only a single small comfort—even Azarii's rebels aren't obtuse enough to attack me and my fortress while we're besieged by animals that would gladly slaughter them, too.

The fur along Russ's back stands on end, all three of his heads curling their lips and snarling at the two serpents nearest us. "Triple dog, no!" Aspect cries. "Triple dog—must—be careful!"

"They're not wrong," I intone, petting the central head, trying to soothe my pet. "Russ, don't get yourself killed. Stay back." The leftmost head spits a ball of slobber on the ground. "That's an *order.*"

I've no sooner given it than the nearest of the two sun serpents lunges directly for me. I roll to evade its bared fangs, my knees ripping on the scattered rubble, but I'm clobbered by its spiked tail instead, the impact brilliant in the purity of its pain. My lungs are clean out of breath, the oxygen punched out of me. Needlelike appendages embed all along my chest. At least these barbs aren't tinged with poison. It's the fangs I really have to worry about, capable of disabling me entirely so the monster can swallow me whole.

Aspect takes a painfully long stretch to realize that *panicking* doesn't mean they have to stay put while screeching at the highest possible volume. They double back toward Kori's original quarters (or what's left of it) and slide underneath the bed, which is already buckled from the serpents' havoc. Aspect looks like an uncomfortably self-aware piece of stashed luggage. I would laugh if I weren't fighting for my life.

I'm pure adrenaline and emotion, despite my best attempts to resist the latter's inexorable hold on me. I've called it weakness, treated it like sickness, but now it becomes my strength. It fuels every pulse of energy from my swinging fists, every snap of my wings, every increasingly desperate dodge above or below or just barely out of another fang's snapping range.

It's still not enough.

A second snake descends on me, and nothing I could muster, whether radiation or unleashed rage, could possibly be enough. All at once, I'm caught in the second serpent's coils. It wraps its body once, twice, three times around my own, feels like it's squeezing my bones into liquid as it slithers its head down to lock blind, obscenely black eyes with my own.

"You want . . . Kori," I gasp through the increasing constriction. Every drop of air in my lungs feels like a gift that could be revoked by this creature at any moment. "Over . . . my . . . *corpse*."

That can be arranged, the snake might say, if its tongue were good for anything but sibilant intimidation. Instead it ramps up its strangulation another notch. My eyeballs feel like they might burst from their sockets. I probably have blood vessels failing already.

My will remains steel, though, even while my bones feel like water. A growl rumbles in my chest, rises in my throat. The fathomless, colorless eyes glare sightlessly back into my own watering ones. At the edge of my wavering peripheral vision, Aspect scrambles deeper beneath Kori's collapsed bed, the first serpent trying and failing to jam its head underneath and take a chunk out of the mech. Distant freezeshot, swearing, and serpentine snarls compete to be heard through the increasing din. As I instructed, Russ dutifully hangs back from my and Aspect's scramble, but his triple growls have become triple whimpers, begging me not to go out like this.

No is the only word my mind can form. *No, this can't be how it ends.* I open my jaw wide, a pulse of azure energy blasting from my mouth.

The snake's face is molten, burning; emerald scales scald as black as its eyes, the forked tongue lashing about in its agony. The monster roars and releases me. I crash, limp and breathless, to the uneven floor, thankfully landing on a still-solid section rather than plummeting several levels down through a crevice.

Sufficiently frustrated, the first snake abandons Aspect, whirls, and dives for me, the edge of one tooth dragging a nasty tear through my left wing. The bite would've needed to linger for the paralytic venom to inject, so I'm safe on that front. But blood spritzes from the wound, splattering against the wall and the floor and the side of my face. I taste rust and salt.

Never enough, not even with all my stubborn strength. Not even with the overcharge and the raw, bestial rage the Diakópsei endowed me with. But Kori's entrapment in that cell is my doing. She's a stationary target for these serpents—if they don't burrow through all seven floors of my fortress and bring it down on all of us first.

Anger is a decent fuel in desperate times. But this nameless thing I feel for Kori, despite how many times I tried to smother it, is power of an entirely different kind. I don't fight like an animal, desperate for the elixir of death on my tongue. Swallowing my blood, tearing serpent needles from my chest with my bare hands, I bare my teeth and fight like someone with something to live for.

I don't know if I'm going to live long.

Recovered from my blast of burning power, the second snake wheels upon me again, the first snake similarly focused alongside it. They lunge at me together, both serpents' bodies and tails tangling around me in a dizzying maelstrom. I try to slide between and beneath them. Instead they drag me to the floor, suffocating me in the crushing combined weight of their scaled bodies, until dark spots dance across my vision.

I gasp and flail. The dark splotches widen like spilled ink. Blurry, broken landscape swims across my eyes—blue fire, gray-black stone, flashes of colorful tapestry, my dog's triple sets of bright baleful eyes, Aspect's similarly scarlet wide optical processors—and I think, *Maybe this is it.*

Maybe, when Kori finds me—because I am under no illusions, that girl will come after me even if not a shred of me deserves it—maybe, by my wounds, she'll know that in the end, I tried to go back to that first glimpse of undeserved sunlight. Tried to tell her with my last burning breath that I hope whatever I find on the other side, I don't forget her. I don't want to forget any of it.

Darkness slips over me like a curtain.

Then, all at once, impossibly, it's rent in two, a new weight careening into my spine and dislodging both serpents from the shock.

Coughing, every bone screaming, I somehow roll to my knees. I break free of the serpents, but they can't disentangle themselves from each other. They're a convoluted knot of snake in the center of the warped floor, hissing and spitting.

Blinking hard to clear my spotty vision, I lift my head. I expect to see, perhaps, Aspect astride Russ once again, having somehow found an opening to mount a successful combined assault on the sun serpents. But that isn't it at all.

Standing before me, panting but unbowed—all five or so skinny, stubborn feet of her—is Kori of the Daylands, a pair of pilfered freezeblades split between her hands.

I want to tell her I'm grateful, even if I can't even begin to deserve this rescue. I want to tell her she's beautiful when she refuses to back down. I want to tell her she has enough fight in her for seven nightfolk soldiers, even if she's nowhere near their stature and training.

"Kori, you *idiot*," I say, and then break into a coughing fit again.

"*Your* idiot, your queenliness," she says, raising both freezeblades in a defensive X, "so the appropriate response is *thank you*."

I spit on the floor. "Thank you."

"Too late."

"I hate you."

"Hate me later," she says, gesturing to my ruined wing. "Let me help you now." I know full well that I don't hate *her* at all.

The tear in my left wing's membrane has worsened from continued strain. It's nearly a hole now. I'm unspeakably lucky it hit only the membrane and not the phalanges that allow me to move it, or I might be in too much pain to keep fighting at all.

The snakes remain hopelessly woven together, one mega-snake with a head on either side. But they aren't done fighting yet. They've sensed Kori's scent, or heard her voice, or whatever sense triggers a blind reptile to become officially unhinged. The tangled tails rattle; the twin tongues hiss. Their unnatural single body swings for Kori like a garrote. Two of Russ's heads howl. Aspect shrieks.

As she ducks, Kori swings both freezeblades in twin crescent-moon strikes. One glances off their twin scaly hide; the other embeds itself in serpent one's vulnerable underbelly. The injured one roars and thrashes, thrashing the second serpent wildly about with it. Kori, having ducked, is somewhere between them, still at risk of being bashed into the floor.

"Damn it all," I sigh, and force myself aloft again despite my wounded wing.

It stings straight through the skeletal structure and down toward the center of my spine, but adrenaline suppresses the pain. Snake heads, bodies, and combined tails whip haphazardly about, forcing me to dodge and weave with gritted teeth. Occasionally I glimpse Kori through the chaos, one freezeblade still gripped tightly with both hands, armor miraculously intact.

"Kori, get out of there!"

"I didn't come to your rescue so you could kill yourself trying to undo it," Kori snarls over the cacophony. "Start running, flying, whatever. I'll follow you once I slow this thing down."

"You don't understand. They're here for *you*. I don't know how, or why"—I block a blast of venom with my good wing, flicking it away from my face—"but they're not going to stop coming after you until they stop breathing."

The two-serpent recovers itself, violent thrashes dulling to a languid wriggle. Both heads turn to focus on Kori, unseeing eyes somehow locked regardless, the wounded head spitting stray venom through a grimace, the healthy head flicking its tongue hungrily.

"And there are more of them," I stammer. "Listen to the fighting all around us." I hope to the Beyond my army isn't torn to shreds beyond my sight. Based on the tumult of the distant fighting, this sun serpent attack can't have gone well for any of us. Is General Isek all right? Or has he gone to join his son? My stomach lurches. "If the rest of the snakes converge, you can't kill an entire sun serpent nest with one knife."

Kori's shoulders sag. "Then we both make a break for it. Two is still better than one."

The irony isn't lost on me. Two heiresses to opposing thrones, standing against twin serpents—both pairs woven irrevocably together, almost beyond recognition.

"No way you'll cover me with that little thing." I gesture to the remaining freezeblade as I alight beside her. "The snakes are entangled now, so they're slower. Let me fend them off while you and Aspect run. Take Russ with you. I'll follow."

The healthy head lunges for Kori, fangs open wide. She parries one with the sword, sliding aside to avoid being crushed by the snake's skull entirely. "Wait, where's Aspect?"

From beneath the nearby crumpled bed frame, Aspect says, "HELLO!"

Kori struggles back to her feet, her grip on the freezeblade shaky. "Aspect, what the hell are you doing?"

Aspect wriggles out from under the bed, kicking themself forward with their uneven legs. Their optical processors gleam amidst the carnage. "PANICKING!"

Even the injured head seems to be regaining its senses. Our stolen moments are running out. "Talk later," I say. "Run now." Kori extends the freezeblade to me, but I nudge her arm away. "No, I have the planet's power on my side. You need that blade more than I do. On my count. Three."

Horrible hissing slips through the bared fangs above us.

"Two."

The tangled tails rattle, twin necks arching to strike again at me and Kori.

"One."

The combined serpents lunge. I lurch forward to meet them, arms coated with as much blazing blue energy as I can muster, my body a battering ram. Aspect squeaks their way to the somehow still-standing door of Kori's old room, and Kori, cursing wildly in her panic, seizes their metal arm with her free hand and bolts.

My charge works. Too well. Empowered by planetary energy and fueled by my battered wings' momentum, my fists smash the combined serpents into the ground with a tremendous crack—and the already-heavily damaged floor shatters further. A fissure erupts from the impact and splinters forward. While Russ is able to lunge aside just in time, the floor crumbles faster than Kori or Aspect could possibly outrun.

I scream Kori's name as she plummets into the gap, reaching for Aspect, who is grasping for a handhold they don't find.

My vision narrows, darkness dancing at the edges, everything tinged with red. This can't be happening, not after we've come this far, not after I've suffered so much and lost myself protecting my people, only for Kori to help me find myself again. I dodge teeth, tails, and splashes of venom in a desperate rush toward the broken floor, toward the pit where Kori fell . . . how many stories? We're on the fourth floor. If the hole went down several . . . if her body alone takes the impact . . .

The healthy snake lunges after me, but the one pierced by freezeblade is sluggish and pained now, drifting toward sleep. Its deadweight holds the healthy snake fast, and it turns upon its brother. Behind me, fangs pierce scales, venom flooding serpentine throats as these two brilliant beasts proceed to simply tear each other apart.

With any luck, without these two signaling their brethren, the other sun serpents might never find Kori. My soldiers can still fight them off. We can still survive this.

But from the bottom of the pit, a floor and a half down, voice cracked and weak, Kori gasps, "Adria."

"I'm coming," I answer, wincing as I tenderly unfurl my wings and descend to meet her. She's fallen, but she's in one piece; Aspect somehow is, too, but they took a hard enough blow to send them into emergency shutdown. "Those snakes are taken care of. I can get you out of here, repair Aspect again, take us all somewhere safe—"

"Adria . . ." Kori coughs. A warm, wet sound.

I shudder as my foot lands in a liquid scarlet puddle, slowly spreading across the stone. In muted horror, I lift my eyes to behold a long, thin, bloody scratch along Kori's right forearm, torn clean open during the fall, armor and skin alike split and exposed to the atmosphere that, for her people, is pure poison.

It's over.

Trembling, Kori lifts one hand to press a button at her helmet's rear. Air hisses as its secure lock to her body armor releases, allowing her to remove the piece.

"No, no, you'll make it worse, Kori, don't—"

But she takes it off anyway, and all the oxygen whooshes out of my lungs.

Even indirect sunlight has darkened Kori's skin to a degree my pallid people never experience in the Shadowlands, a smooth, sun-kissed tan against my bruised, weeping nightfolk flesh. Her eyes, those eyes I've so badly wanted to meet in any circumstance but this, are a deep earthy brown with flecks of faint green, like new soil, like fertile ground for countless possibilities I so badly want to believe in. Her hair is glossy brown, long waves forcibly tamed into a once-tight braid that has understandably begun to come undone, stray strands of sun-streaked brown sticking out in every direction. Her lips are flower pink, defiant as the planet's last patches of organic beauty, impossible to look away from.

She's the most beautiful person I've ever seen.

I'm going to watch her die. So why is she smiling—a real, broad smile that burns through my frozen core, makes me almost want to hope when all is lost?

"Adria," Kori says, "it doesn't hurt."

CHAPTER 23

KORI

The planet's poison floods my veins. Impossibly, instead of experiencing a curtain call, I come awake.

My muscles draw tight against my bones, all suddenly stiff and cold, moments before impossible strength radiates from every joint. It feels like I'm screaming, but I must be the only one who can hear the roar between my ears. Adria's eyes are blurry.

"Adria." My voice feels like it comes from someone else. "It doesn't hurt."

She kneels beside me, robes stained with blood from my arm. She reaches, reflexively, to cover the wound, before catching herself, afraid of worsening the radiation poisoning that should've already begun. But I don't feel poisoned. I don't feel sick.

The power rumbling through my veins is so fierce, I can hardly bear it—like direct sunlight in an unguarded pupil, like fresh, cold water in a stomach too long deprived.

"By the Beyond." Adria shakes her head, so overcome that words can hardly escape. "Kori, what color are your eyes?"

I blink, not comprehending. "Brown."

"Not anymore, they're not."

I look to where Aspect lies unconscious, their surface still freshly shined enough to reveal my reflection. My own familiar eyes look back at me, but bathed in brilliant, electric blue, like Adria's flames, like the planet's beating heart.

The Diakópsei has claimed me, finally, after so long waiting for a gap in my armor—but it's supposed to feel like dying, and it doesn't. Every dayfolk child is shown an animated guide of what would happen if we ever dared to venture outside without a complete protective set. The first figure's skin melts off like wax. The second screams until their blood vessels burst, eyes popping out of the skull. The third writhes and twists until their bones rearrange themselves into something utterly inhuman.

If the video wasn't enough, teachers (or in my case, Chloe) sometimes brought in those who had lost family to the planet's poison, to describe what they had witnessed—or what unrecognizable corpse had been left by relentless Pagonian mutations.

None of those afflicted by the radiation gleamed with alien strength and stood up, their legs remaining rock-solid, as I do now.

"It's . . . not killing me." Despite the insanity of it all, I listen to my body and suck in a deep, free breath of unfiltered air. It's crisp, clean, on my tongue and in my lungs. It's more than the absence of pain; I feel like the embodiment of power. "I don't know how, or why, but I'm not . . ."

The sentence trails off in the absence of a satisfactory answer.

"You're not dying," Adria breathes in utter disbelief.

"I'm not dying. I feel . . ." I deliberately unclench my fists, stretching my fingers, blue sparks leaping between them despite my gloves. "Awake. Like I could . . ." I click the wrist sealant buttons on my armor, prompting another panicked cry from Adria, and toss both gloves away. A little shout escapes me as my hands start to glow, too, galaxy bright, every fingertip overwhelmed with energy. "Stars above."

Adria simply stares, slack-jawed. "It takes countless sleep cycles to master energy manipulation like that. Even if you did become like me, which would take more than a moment . . . dayfolk should die, but even nightfolk should collapse."

Wild curiosity overwhelms my good sense. After a whole lifetime of fear, by some strange twist of fate, the planet's poison is to me only *power*, and I'm desperate to test the limits. I must be something . . . else. Something as forbidden as a stubborn fissure between the light and the dark. It's a terrifying thought, but it hardly registers over the energy roaring through me.

I collapse my remaining armor, both top and bottom, leaving only my borrowed, crudely trimmed nightfolk garments beneath it. My skin tingles and shimmers with strength. Adria watches, hardly blinking, streaked with tears and dirt and dust and blood, jaw still hanging open.

If we get Aspect somewhere safe, I can help Adria fight the other serpents off while the energy surge lasts—take advantage of whatever is happening to me before we waste time trying to explain it. I open my mouth to suggest as much, when all at once the energy flares, burning much brighter, my body a candle struck to life. Then, almost as soon as it began, it collapses and dims. I'm nothing but a dead wick.

Gasping, coughing, but unexplainably, definitely *not dying* as science should dictate, I fall to my hands and knees.

"Kori," Adria gasps, catching me as I fall forward.

I sag into the support as we both realize that Adria's hands are wrapped securely around my bare arms. Our skin-to-skin touch feels like lightning, almost as strong as the planet's grip on my unveiled body. Her own gathered power spears through me so sharply that my vision flashes white, but there's something else, too, a hot tension that I know we both feel at our proximity.

"I can't fight like this," I pant, leaning further into her muscly arms for support. "We have to get somewhere safe—you, me, Aspect—before another sun serpent realizes where we are."

"I can still fight," Adria protests, hauling me back up to a standing position. "My soldiers need me—"

"Alive," I finish the sentence for her, recovering my posture as I speak. "If their queen gets snake strangled, that's the end. All your fight, all your sacrifice . . . for nothing. You can't let that happen."

Adria's brow furrows. "The fortress is in dire need of repairs. The serpents are tearing it apart, just barreling through walls and floors like they're paper. I don't know where to hide you. I don't know how to keep you safe—"

I raise a hand for silence. "Wait."

"What?"

"Listen."

In the distance, the scattered battle clamor grows louder, closer, then proceeds to recede back toward the Passage. Slithering bodies, snapping jaws, the hellish hissing of forked tongues. Damaged pillars crash, crack, and collapse all around us, but the area we're in, decimated though it may be, seems to hold. The serpents make a combined exit.

Quiet, unbroken, blankets the Shadowlands again.

"If they came looking for me," I realize aloud, "a desperately armored, wasting girl who was as good as dead already, then their target no longer exists. This thing that's happening to me . . ." Shudders rack my frame at the gravity of what's just happened. "Stars, I should be dead. I should . . ." I stare at my naked hands, still slightly sparking with planetary power. My eyes, faintly reflected in Aspect, are brown again, but with a dim crackle of pure blue. "I'm so confused."

Adria is still kneeling, so even as I stand, we're eye to eye. "We'll figure it out," she insists, moving both hands to my shoulders, grounding me. "You were impossible from the moment you crashed into the shadows. Whatever you are, I know *who* you are. Kori, Kori . . ."

She takes my face in her big hands, claws carefully not breaking me, the pads of her fingers instead wiping away tears I didn't realize were falling. She looks at me like a star fell into her open palm. She looks at me like I'm the sun.

"I'm not afraid of you, Kori. Not anymore. And you've never been afraid of anything." She leans her forehead forward, pressing it ever so gently to mine, and I let my eyes drift shut, listening to the combined huffs of our breathing. "Not even me, the worst monster of them all."

"Not a monster," I sigh, overcome by the palpable heat of her breath on my face, trembling. "Never a monster, even when you tried."

We stay like that, a mere exhale apart, eyes closed, fingers tangled in each other's ruined hair, for a seemingly interminable moment. At last she draws back, lifts my chin with the blunt side of a claw, and breathes, "I could kiss you."

Her lips, gently parted, are red as blood. Her violet eyes hold mine through a sheen of fresh tears, slowly blinking to clear the haze, never looking away from me. She's the planet's most brutally designed mutant. She's my rival royal. She's my azure torch amidst the dark, my reason to keep fighting for the light. My enemy, my equal, maker of the greatest memories I have.

"Then fucking kiss me," I say.

She shouldn't. But while she may not be a monster, in this moment she's only a girl, breathing as hard as I am, stained with dust and blood and stray serpent scales, fingers shivering against the curve of my cheek, voice swallowed by need, so she does.

I don't know how to kiss her. The press of her lips to my lips turns my brain to static, my blood to a spiking pulse. She tastes like salt and rust and sweat and want. We both hardly move, testing each other's limits, Adria terribly aware of her own strength and keeping it tightly leashed. But when her tongue slides just barely forward, tasting my mouth, a little groan breaks from me, and I dig my fingers into her ragged, overgrown curls, one hand wrapped around a well-hewn horn, pulling her closer, deepening the kiss, knowing nothing will be close enough.

Her body is on my body everywhere. And it's more than the planet's unholy power passing between us, a live electric current. I may know less about myself than I ever thought, fueled as I am by the energies that should've killed it, but I know I was made for this. I know that no matter what brought me here, no matter where we go next, I was meant to kiss Adria, queen of the nightfolk, shadow of my own aspirations, echo of my own loneliness, answer to a question I'd never even had the words to ask.

Even if I had been born when days and nights still tracked time, all sense of it would elude me with her mouth on my mouth, her hands woven into my disheveled hair, her cold blue-white skin faintly warm with blood flush—cradling me when she could break me, craving me when she could crush me, my heart fluttering so hard against my ribs, I'm almost afraid it'll burst.

When the kiss ends, it's only so we can both catch our breath. Adria holds my gaze through fluttering dark lashes. "What's happening to you . . . I'm afraid the lies may go deeper than you know." Her eyes fall to the floor. "Deeper than you could bear to know."

I cradle her strong jaw with an open hand, lift her face so her gaze meets mine again. "After all I've already survived, I'm not afraid of the truth. So don't mince words now. What do you know, Adria?"

Her words spill out in a panicked flood. "The snakes were explicitly sent for *you*. Your presence imprinted on them like a brand. Not to destabilize my army, not even to threaten me, but to retrieve *you*. Who would do that, Kori? Certainly not my uncle. Even if he could manipulate sun serpents, he would've used them to overthrow my rule altogether, not simply go after a valuable prisoner. So who else knows you're here? Who else would've been so invested in snatching you out of the shadows?"

My head feels like it's doing pirouettes. Struggling for balance, I shift my hand down to Adria's shoulder, gripping hard at the muscle underneath. "You think my mother sent the serpents."

"If not her, then who?"

"They could've killed me."

"It seems that would've been a more acceptable outcome," Adria says through her teeth, "than your continued presence here. But as soon as this . . . *power* . . . overtook you, they stopped trying to retrieve you. They didn't even try to kill you. They all retreated from whence they came. Almost as if they knew it was game over."

I squeeze my eyes shut, shaking my head. "I don't understand."

"You said yourself that you could've been killed. Your mother knew you were a hair's breadth from radiation exposure at any moment in the Shadowlands. One misstep from discovering that the planet isn't poison to you at all, but power. And paying your ransom, if she ever intended to pay it, is far from a single-sleep-cycle process. Every passing moment, meanwhile . . . more risk of exposure. More risk of the lie being exposed."

I feel like I'm drowning in Adria's violet eyes, unable to pull in any air. But her gaze holds mine fast, no longer shielding me from even an inkling of truth. Believing I can carry it.

"So," Adria says, "she deemed it better for you to dissolve in a sun serpent's stomach than for you to discover what you really are."

My voice is wire thin. "And what is that?"

Grating metal. A squeaking, stubbornly straight leg pressing up against stone. Amidst my racing thoughts, I almost forgot Aspect is here, having apparently rebooted during our intimate moment. As they stand, they insist, "Kori is—Aspect's friend. Kori is—Adria's friend. Kori is brave—and smart, and—still alive, despite—everything trying to—destroy Kori."

I swallow hard. I square my shoulders, find my center. Aspect is right. By all accounts, I should be dead a thousand times over, but instead, I'm living proof of the impossible: a dayfolk reborn amidst the radiation, rather than swiftly silenced by it. My mother was willing to risk my mutilation or death by the sun serpents to prevent my ever happening upon the truth beyond her jurisdiction.

I suck in a deep breath, then blow it out through my nose. "There could be more of us. Dayfolk who don't die from radiation exposure. There's no way to know how deep this goes, how long my mother's been lying to me. If I stay here . . ." A chill racks my frame, but I fight it back. "My mother could send something even worse to silence me. Ensure nobody ever finds out about this. But how far does the lie reach? Are there others? Why lie to me—to the dayfolk entirely? If I don't find out—"

"Then the truth dies with you," Adria finishes for me. The weight of that statement bears down on both of us like a thing with teeth, as terrifying as any sun serpent.

A robotic whirr, rising in volume. "Too much—for Aspect."

"What?" Adria and I say in near unison, barely turning in time to see Aspect's optical processors blink out and their body collapse in a haphazard heap to the floor all over again.

"S-stars above," I stammer, sprinting to check Aspect for further injuries. But they have no exposed wires, no obviously visibly misplaced gears, nothing.

It seems that finally, even more so than their countless installed memories or even their fall into this pit, it's a firsthand experience that overloaded their system into a temporary shutdown. An absurdly human thing for a robot that's shown no signs of independent, sentient thought, but there's far too much happening for me to dwell on that right now. It's far from the weirdest thing Aspect has done thus far; I'm just unspeakably grateful that they're with me and that they're alive.

As long as they're alive, I may still find a way to help their consciousness *wake*.

With a clatter of loose limbs, I pull Aspect's powered-down body close my chest. "I'll have to do a manual reboot. Shutdown has only been known to happen to mechs from, like, core-system heat overload. Not . . ." I sigh. "Any of *this*."

Adria rises to her feet. Even with her wounded left wing causing her to hunch, wincing with every motion, her bulk as compared to me makes my heart stumble against my ribs. Yet her voice is small, half strangled. "Will it help them?" she asks. "To be back in the sun?"

"What are you talking about?"

"Your starship crashed at the Second Spire. Its core components are likely intact. With some repairs, it can still get you home. Fixing your armor should be no trouble either."

I open my mouth to launch a comeback. No sound comes out.

"You said it yourself, Kori. Right now, you're the only one with any idea of what your mother is plotting. If you stay here, you'll never find your answers. She could send any manner of further monsters to ensure you *never do*."

Adria moves to cross the space between us again, despite visibly tensing every time her injured wing shifts. The serpent slash across my own arm stings fiercely, too, but I've hardly been able to register it over the tumult of other thoughts—over the overwhelming reality of Adria's lips having finally collided with mine.

"I thought I'd sacrificed everything for a chance at peace," Adria muses. "A body that felt familiar to me. The lives of my parents. My perilous standing with the Shadow Court." Both her hands settle lightly but firmly on my shoulders. "But not everything. Not yet."

Again she kneels, eyes half shut, breaths pluming in the relentless cold, and leans her forehead against mine, level. Steady. "I have to let you go, Kori. You need to protect your people, as surely as I've fought to protect mine."

My throat feels raw as if from screaming. I know she's right, as hideous as the realization is. My mother tried to kill me, but the planet that should've finished the job brought rebirth instead. I need answers—not just for myself, but for every other subject of my mother's unquestioned rule.

"And you can't protect your people if I stay here," I realize. "You're already in the throes of civil war. And now I've brought monsters to your doorstep. Invoked the ire of my mother—maybe soon a full-blown dayfolk army." Gently lowering Aspect's body to the ground, I rise to my own feet. "You're right, Adria. I have to go home."

Home. The word tastes sour, its shape stinging on my tongue. When did this lightless, frozen wasteland start to feel more like home than the sunny dunes surrounding my settlement? I don't know anymore.

"And I will get you there," Adria says, resolute. "So help me, I won't be the one to stand in the way of your answers. You've come too far, seen too much, to risk being silenced in the shadows. And I . . ." She stands, too, rising several feet above me once again, and stares off as if she can see something distinct in the distance. "In the wake of this assault, I'll rally my people. I'll repair my fortress. I'll ensure Azarii does not have his victory—will *never* have a world where nightfolk identity is rooted in shame."

Despite its crushing weight, despite everything bearing down upon us, Adria carries the responsibility with a regal air. More than ever, she sounds like a queen.

"I know you're right," I sigh. "I know you have to stay, to stop this war. I have to go, if I'm ever to find my own place in the world. But . . . this can't be it, can it?" My heartbeat echoes in my eardrums. I swallow hard on a sudden sob. "I can't have come all this way—found you, fought you, finally kissed you—just to disappear back into the sun."

"I can't send you back with a nightfolk comms tablet unless I want your entire nation to doubt your loyalties. Which means we'll have no way to communicate across the Passage." Wavering, Adria's voice drops an octave. "Promise you'll come back to me," she breathes, more a plea than an order, all posturing between us incinerated the moment our lips finally met. Her hand finds the side of my face again, holds it like I'm fragile as a butterfly's wing. "Even if you can never stay, even if the daylight will always mark your home . . . come back to me, Kori, and remind me why we're fighting."

My whole body trembles again at her touch, not from the force but from the gentleness of it, her finger cold and sure as any promise when it traces my cheekbone, trying to memorize it. "If I gave you my word, would that be enough?"

"Not nearly."

"Would it help if I kissed you again?"

"No," Adria says, but she leans in anyway, her lips tentatively brushing mine as if expecting a second embrace to make me disappear altogether.

We stay like that for a while, kissing soft and slow, hands settling on each other's hips instead of wandering, learning each other's corners and edges. She holds one hip with the other hand braced against my back, since she has to bend so far to kiss me, dipping me low. And I grip her hip right back with one hand, and the underside of her good wing with the other, just barely keeping myself upright through the brain fog of *she's kissing me, I'm kissing her, we're kissing and I don't ever want to stop . . .*

I'm the one to draw back this time, needing to catch my breath despite the softness of the kiss. It takes Adria half a moment to register my absence, her eyes fluttering back open, violet orbs pinning me where I stand, ordering me not to withdraw any farther.

"Nothing ties you here," she says.

I shake my head, defiant. "I'll come back for you."

"And I want to believe you, Kori, I do." She sighs. "But without something to draw you back, to demand your return . . ." At once her gaze goes wide. "After I've tended to my wounds, and to yours, would you accept a parting token from me? Something of the nightfolk?"

"Of course I would," I agree without thinking.

Before I forget, I gather the collapsed pieces of my armor, reattaching them to my various joints. I don't extend them to cover my full body, though; I've spent quite long enough in that sun-forsaken security suit. Instead I let the shrunken pieces of metal stay at my wrists, my ankles, my waist, and my collarbone, ready to extend as needed, but notably less constricting.

"My wing is too wounded to carry you on my back," Adria says, glancing up to where we both tumbled from a floor and a half above. "But I can't very well expect you to climb with that arm. And there's Aspect to contend with." Her eyebrows furrow as she determines a solution. "You carry Aspect; I carry you. All right?"

With a grunt, I heave Aspect into my arms, unsure of what to do next. "I'm not sure I—" But before I can protest, Adria sweeps me up into her arms—one of them beneath my back, the other settled beneath my knees, holding me securely against her body.

The sun serpent's slash on my arm stings more every moment, but complaining about it given the state of Adria's wing feels like every time Aspect has tried to convince me that *their* life is very hard.

I expect Adria to put me down once we alight on the upper floor. Instead she holds me close, her heartbeat pattering against my cheek, as she walks us both back toward what's left of her quarters. Fur ragged, triple tongues panting, Russ patters after both of us, all three heads observing Aspect's supine body in my arms with ever-increasing canine concern.

Once upon a time,
the princess of sunlight caught flame,
like a rogue star born of another's destruction.

CHAPTER 24

ADRIA

I still store simple antiseptics in my quarters. After my overcharge, when I broke every mirror that hung too close and proceeded to play with the pieces, I resented my weakness and was loath to admit it to any healer, even trusted Zalel. So I cared for the wounds on my own, with bandages and alcohol rather than nightfolk gifts. Zalel either assumed I was conserving his powers for my soldiers, or he was gracious enough not to ask.

I set down Kori, who subsequently sets down Aspect. Russ immediately begins nudging at the inert robot with his central head, the first and third heads whimpering at the lack of response. Kori scratches both heads under their chins in an attempt to offer some comfort. Her eyes returned to their usual brown, not blue, when she keeled over into my arms in the rubble—but regardless of her irises' shade, I can't stop looking at them, looking at *her* properly outside her armor. This battered, beautiful rule breaker of a girl, just . . . sitting in my room, flesh and blood and bone, as real as anything.

But nevertheless, she doesn't feel real. I half expected her to fall through my arms like a ghost when I went to lift and carry her safely out of the wreckage.

Across the room, nestled next to my pillow, exactly where I left it when going to visit Neo in prison, is my comms tablet. I can hear it buzzing with frantic notifications from here—doubtless, my soldiers are panicked and thrown off guard by the sun serpents' attack—but my brain is already a whirlwind. I can process only so much at once. And right now, the volume of the pain in my torn wing is drowning out nearly all else. So I launch into a long-winded explanation to distract myself from the imminent pain.

"This isn't my first wing wound. The membrane reseals itself within a sleep cycle, even in nightfolk without a healing gift, but I need to sanitize it first, or risk an infection spreading through the whole structure when it closes." I rummage through my stone drawers, seeking antiseptic bottles that aren't already mostly empty. "I can hold the wing still well enough, but reaching that slash is another story. Can you pour a few drops of this along the wound?"

Kori visibly pales and gulps. Having her face hidden for so long truly concealed her greatest weakness; without her helmet, her visage is a canvas constantly painted outright with whatever emotions she's feeling. I can't help but marvel at the openness when it feels like all my apparent feelings have to go through a mutation process first, becoming anger before eventually simmering down to their original form.

"I won't hurt you," I reassure her through already-gritted teeth. "And if I kneel, like this, and you stand on the bed, you should be able to reach—"

"I don't want to hurt *you*," Kori protests, vaguely waving her arms in the direction of my increasingly throbbing wing.

I take a deep breath, holding the antiseptic out to Kori again and shaking the bottle. Finally she takes it, white-knuckling the lid. I'm a good soldier; my last wing wound was hundreds of sleep cycles ago, but she doesn't need to know that, or it'll only make her nerves worse. "If we don't clean it now, it'll hurt a hell of a lot worse later."

"I'm still sorry," Kori says as she twists the cap off, her nose wrinkling at the cloying, chemical smell.

"Let's call it even on apologies." I close my eyes, both to avoid knowing when the antiseptic approaches and to dodge Kori's too-perceptive gaze. "I'm sure I owe you more than my fair share."

"Fair enough," Kori agrees, and then my wing is on fire. I hiss through my teeth, a sound that rapidly devolves into just swearing. Russ's third head growls, the other two glaring, but I wordlessly wave at him to stand down. "On second thought, I take it back. Definitely sorry."

I sigh, gritting my teeth as the antiseptic works its way through my wing, every nerve stinging. "You are the *worst*."

"You don't mean that," Kori says, accurately, before extending her own slashed arm for antiseptic. "If you must take out your frustration, though, at least take out any infection with it."

"With pleasure," I retort, but I wince anyway while treating Kori's arm. She lets out a little curse under her breath.

Never has the physical difference between us been more obvious than in this moment. But even so, we're both bleeding and at each other's mercy. I apologize despite myself with every loop of the bandage around Kori's arm, knowing it must hurt. Her jaw is set, her expression stoic, but those gorgeous eyes water all the same, green flecks bright amidst the brown.

Just beside us, my comms tablet continues blinking and buzzing. Kori nudges her head in its direction, but I shake my own head in response. My army will still need me once Kori's wounds, both physical and emotional, have been attended to. After how long I've waited to meet her eyes behind the mask . . . first, *her*.

When the wound dressing is finally done and the antiseptic set aside, Kori turns her attention back to Aspect. "Do you have robot repair supplies somewhere in your quarters, too?"

"I actually do," I admit, leaning down to pull another locked chest out from under my bed. "Before I first returned Aspect to you, I asked Zalel to lend me some simple tools. Then proceed to . . . not return them."

"Petty theft. Perhaps there's some monster in you after all."

"I also know some very bad words."

"I'm terrified." Kori laughs as she opens the repair kit, then names each tool as she filters through the disorganized pieces. "Wire cauterizer, surge connector, memory chip widget . . . *aha*, chip probe." She hoists the clunky tool overhead triumphantly. "This should do the trick for a manual reboot."

Abruptly, I feel all the blood drain out of my face. "Actually, there's something I should probably tell you about Aspect before—"

Too late. Aspect's optical processors blink, a shrill whirr emits from every one of their joints, and steam spits in fits and starts from their neck. Fur bristling, Russ leaps several feet back as Aspect's vocalization box promptly announces, "ASPECT—IS HAVING—THOUUUUU-*UUUUU*-UUUU-*UUUUUUU*-UUUUUUGHTS," the last word drawn out into at least seven syllables.

Kori turns to me, pupils as wide as her face is pale. "You've got to be freaking kidding me."

"Awakening Aspect was your idea," I offer weakly.

"When did this happen?"

I knot my fingers together. "While you were imprisoned with Neo."

Kori shakes her head in disbelief. "It was supposed to be a monumental moment! Just me and my robot, my creation, my *friend*—looking at them and feeling it in my bones when they really *looked back*—when they saw me, and more than that, saw *themself*—"

"I know what they mean to you," I interrupt, laying one hand on Kori's shoulder, "and I'm sorry you weren't there to see them wake, truly. Especially knowing you were elsewhere because I snapped and locked you up. If it's any comfort, it looked more like a mental break than an awakening at the start. Less victory, more sheer panic. You didn't miss much."

I give Kori's shoulder what I hope is a comforting squeeze and not a painful amount of pressure. "But you're here now. We both are. And so is Aspect, perhaps more than they ever have been." I stare at the floor, unable to meet what ought to be judgment in her gaze. "Can we try, one last time, to start over? As a . . . damn it, I don't know. A team?"

Kori lays a warm hand on my cheek, tilts my face to meet her eyes, which could eviscerate me. Instead all I see in those beautiful brown orbs is marvel and wonder and light. I'm never going to deserve her; I'll spend the rest of my life trying.

"If Lail's memory of hope was what woke them," Kori says, "then I still have you to thank for this." She lets out a deep breath, squaring her shoulders and jaw. "I'm glad you saw it happen. I am. Even if I wish I could've been there, too."

I lean my head forward, pressing my forehead to hers. My eyes drift shut of their own accord. I wish we could stay like this forever, all our wars and worlds aside, nothing between us but reckless forgiveness for all the damage we've done and will do to each other.

A loud *squeak* interrupts our moment. Aspect's mechanical hands perch on their hips in a frightening facsimile of Kori's own stubbornness. "Excuse—Aspect—but Aspect—is still here."

Russ snorts through all three noses in agreement.

"Sorry," Kori and I both sputter as we break apart.

It's frankly embarrassing that we're acting like smitten youths, especially in front of our robotic and canine children respectively, but the novelty of being able to touch Kori hasn't worn off. Every point of contact, even our foreheads leaning together, even the idle graze of her fingers across my knuckles now to reassure me she's all right, feels like lightning.

"Th-thoughts," Kori stammers, adjusting her posture and her borrowed clothes and generally trying to pretend we weren't on the verge of kissing again.

My own embarrassment burns like acid in my gut, but hers strikes me as endearing. I wonder if she sees mine that way; I wish I could see myself the way she does.

"You're having thoughts," Kori says. "That's a big deal, Aspect. How do you feel about it?"

Aspect cocks their head, processing. I wonder if they learned that one in passing from mirroring Russ's goofiest face. "Feel." Their arms give a strange little wiggle, prompting Russ to lean one head sideways in concern. "Aspect—is having—*FEELINGS*?"

"I mean, I assumed if we'd activated independent thought, then you were likely experiencing an independent emotional psyche, as well," Kori sputters, drifting into technician mode, "but it's totally okay if you aren't. There are plenty of sleep cycles to alter the connections, examine the new spontaneous wiring—"

Aspect waves their arms wildly about. "ASPECT IS HAVING FEELINGS!"

Abruptly, Russ lunges forward. At first, I think Aspect's bursts of volume and newfound instability have alarmed my dog, perhaps into attacking. But instead, two tongues lap at Aspect's head from either side, Russ's center head nudging itself into Aspect's chest. Aspect wraps both arms around the head and pulls it close, like a safety blanket or a stuffed toy. The robot has no true mouth to speak of, but they press their crudely drawn smile to Russ's big, wet nose all the same, making artificial kissing noises.

Still my comms tablet screeches at me with increasing urgency. My stomach twists, fearing what I'm going to find when I open its display. But how can I check my messages while this . . . this . . . *madness* is happening? Against all odds, the dayfolk robot . . . is sentient. The robot is *sentient* and using their newfound self-awareness to aggressively cuddle my three-headed dog.

When was the last time my life made even a lick of sense? I don't know anymore.

"Okay, you are having feelings." Kori runs a hand through her hair, struggling to process almost as much as her creation. "That's . . . that's . . ."

"Amazing," I finish for her. "You're amazing, Kori. No one else would've dared to try this, let alone crossed the planet's borders to make it happen, even gone so far as to trust me with the results."

"It would appear I made the right decision." Kori beams as Aspect continues to feign kissing my dog. "I never really let myself think I'd get this far. I have so many things I want to try. I could teach them how to pilot a starship. We could workshop jokes to annoy my doctor together." Her jaw drops as another realization dawns. "They could *do my homework*."

I can't help but laugh at the homework bit, but the previous sentence catches my attention. "Your doctor?"

"Oh, Ednit. My mother insists he give me regular checkups on my Morpheus chip to ensure everything is running correctly. Basically he just sedates me and pokes around in my brain for a bit and—"

"Is he a regular doctor, or just a Morpheus chip technician?"

"Both."

"Then shouldn't he have known if Pagonian radiation wouldn't kill you?"

Kori blinks hard. "No. He would tell me. He can't . . . He wouldn't . . ." But realization closes over her, swallows the syllables. "He *must* have known. And if he knew—"

But she never gets to finish her sentence. Because the sliding door to my chamber shrieks open, and standing on the other side, hands fisted at his sides, chest heaving, deep-set gray eyes brewing a veritable storm, is Thaane.

"The generals are all trying to reach you. *I* have been trying to reach you. What in the Beyond are you—" But that's when he spots Kori, unarmored, unmasked, and I can practically see lightning in his eyes flash to join the thunder in his voice. "What is the meaning of this? Why is she here? Why . . . *how* is she . . . ?"

"I wish I knew," Kori answers before I can. "But I'm going to go home, and I'm going to find out."

"Oh, *now* you're going home." Thaane saunters forward, arms swinging rigidly, and I half think he's about to take a swing at Kori himself with one clenched, three-clawed fist, but he doesn't. "Before we ever get Adria's precious ransom, and long after you brought *sun serpents* to our doorstep."

I've trusted Thaane all through my cruel childhood, straight into an adolescence forcibly mutated into adulthood as I seized a throne by force that I never even wanted by birthright. But in this moment, perhaps for the first time, I lie to him.

I lie to him, and it's so incredibly easy. "We have no reason to believe Kori is at fault for the serpent attack."

Thaane snatches my comms tablet from the bed and waves it overhead like a blood-drunk warrior would an axe. "You would know otherwise if you *checked your messages*." I want to protest that surely, they could have spared a messenger or gotten a telepathic close enough to deliver updates indirectly, but I'm afraid that if I dare lash back at Thaane, I'll only learn more about how horribly I failed my soldiers during this attack. So I keep my lips locked tightly shut. "Those broken fragments of the Diakópsei, the ones Elysium continues to insist are securely caged—Azarii must have gotten into a rogue cultist's head, because one of his rebels got her accursed claws on a fragment. Enough to temporarily overcharge herself. Enough to send out a telepathic message strong enough that it summoned every sun serpent for *miles*, specifically to go after *Kori*."

"What?" My voice feels like it's coming from someone else. I feel cold all over, goose bumps trailing down my arms. None of this makes any sense. Azarii's rebellion could have simply targeted me directly, if they had power over sun serpents, so why attack Kori? Why go through so many extra steps? "When did this happen?"

"While you were pleading with Neo to free you of your foolish affections," Thaane snarls, "your enemies were moving to take advantage of your most obvious weakness. And she *is* a weakness, Adria." He points at Kori with a singular claw, and my throat clenches. "Surely even you can't deny that anymore, or you wouldn't have been on your knees before your own *prisoner*, *begging* him for some measure of relief. Which you could've obtained yourself, mind you. You could've just sent the dayfolk heiress *home*."

I open my mouth to protest, but Thaane barrels straight on anyway, undeterred.

"But no, you had to wrap your adolescent crush in false promises of a dramatic ransom, a chance to turn the tide of war—a war you've practically stopped fighting, because you're busy training your own prisoner to defend herself amidst shadows she should *never have entered*. She doesn't belong here, Adria. She never did."

Kori's face has gone terribly pale. Russ hunkers down into himself, all three heads tucked in, a ball of shuddering fur. Aspect wobbles, wordless, from foot to foot, which produces some awkwardly loud squeaks from their peg leg in the process.

"And by letting her stay here," Thaane says, "you've put your entire kingdom at risk. I see it. The Shadow Court sees it. What are you going to tell them when they demand your report of the sun serpent attack? Was it all worth it—to treat a trespasser like a princess, no ransom in sight, your fortress blown through by sand beasts, your army bleeding and afraid before a rebellion that only grows stronger? A rebellion that looks more and more *right* with every passing sleep cycle?"

"How *dare you*," I burst out, but Thaane simply continues to shout over me.

"How can you possibly hope to lead us? Where is your courage? Torn away by a foreign princess's lips, perhaps? Lips you should *never have touched*." He glowers at Kori, who looks unbelievably small by comparison, even with Thaane being shorter among the nightfolk. He can't possibly know that we kissed, but I suppose the tension between us has become impossible to hide. "Where is your armor? You should be *dead*."

"ENOUGH." My voice is a scream, a bestial bellow. My voice is a surge of rising energy in my throat, burning brilliant blue, and I almost choke from the effort of swallowing it down. "She just told you we don't know what's happened. And she's exiting the Shadowlands. She's going home to find answers, and to leave me to focus on our war."

"*Now* you decide to focus?" Thaane scoffs. "And you expect me to believe she'll stay away, when you look at her like the sun itself alighted in your open palm?"

Kori steps forward. I extend an arm to hold her back, but she brushes it aside, and I don't have it in me to physically restrain her. "You're right," she says, sickness churning in me at her words. "I should never have come here. But when I come back"—and, oh, how my heart somersaults that she says *when* and not *if*—"it will be with weapons, perhaps even with soldiers. If Adria hasn't already ended your civil war, then even without a ransom payment, I'll be the final push to finish it. To bring lasting peace." She extends a bare hand to Thaane, open, as if he doesn't tower over her, as if he couldn't turn the ground beneath her to shattering glass with a mere twitch of his gift. "But for now, I *will leave*. You have my word. On all of it."

Thaane looks from Kori's outstretched hand to her wide pleading gaze to my own surely stunned face. He sputters. He spits and stammers.

Behind all of us, Aspect says wistfully, "Aspect—will miss—triple dog."

Russ gives the robot's face a big, wet, sticky lick.

Thaane turns his back in a whirl of dark robes. His shoulders heave, his head cast down toward the floor, his arms crossed over his chest, all four wings folded tightly at his back. "Since you don't check your messages, my lord, I'll tell you General Isek is in the infirmary. One of the serpents shook him by his right leg, tossed him into a wall that crumbled completely. He may lose the leg . . . if he doesn't lose his life. I know you've grown fond of him." He punches the button to reopen the door. "Perhaps his life in the balance will be enough to restore your priorities. I trust you will be prepared to defend as much to the Shadow Court." And with that, he steps out, the door sliding shut with finality behind him, blanketing us all in horrible silence.

After an unbearable stretch of quiet, the only words I can find are "I'm so sorry, Kori."

"He's right, though," Kori says, stumbling back to sit once again on the edge of my bed. She buries her head in her hands, fingers tangled in her brown hair, the tight braid coming increasingly undone. "I should never have come here. And the moment I saw that my presence here was distracting you, putting you at risk in the war . . ." She stares at the floor. "I should've gone home a long time ago."

"A-and then y-you would never have awakened Aspect," I stammer. "Or discovered that the radiation said to kill you only makes you stronger." *Or pressed your mouth to mine and breathed into me again the will to be more, to be better.*

"At the expense of so many lives."

"None of this is your fault."

"Whether by my mother's orders or Azarii's, the serpents were here for me."

"And if I'd done a better job as queen," I protest, another chill shivering through me, "there would be no rebellion and no Elysian oversights allowing access to a pocket of overcharge." Russ brushes up against my leg, trying to offer some moral support, but nothing can slow my pounding heart right now. "This is *my* kingdom, Kori. When it bleeds, I'm the one stained scarlet. I'm the one who has to answer to the court for what my people have become." A sharp exhale takes all my oxygen with it. "General Isek. So help me. Of all my soldiers . . . I will never forgive myself if he doesn't pull through."

"He will," Kori says, rising defiantly to her feet, even though she can't possibly know that. "You all will. You're going to end this war, Adria. I'm going to find out what's happened to me, before whatever secrets lie in wait lead to war for the dayfolk, too. And when all is said and done, despite all the wrongs we committed along the way, we'll both have made things right, made things *better*. For dayfolk and nightfolk. For everyone."

Despite myself, I reach for Kori's wrist. I need to feel the blood pulsing through her veins, the warmth of her skin, the promise that we are both still alive, still fighting. I wish it were just us. I wish there were another universe, a far-off galaxy, even just one planet where we could be together, hidden away from political conflicts and rising wars. I want to fall asleep and wake up in our own little pocket of private time, orbiting each other, spinning on the selfsame axis, our days and nights in sync until we have no more left to give.

"For us," I say. "A better world for you and me, despite the desert between us."

I know we need, at long last, to part ways; there's no way around it. But I want to live in our kiss forever. For so long, even without having the words, I yearned to touch her. She should've died in my arms, and instead, she clung to me with newfound strength, with impossibly echoed want. She was delicate as light in my hands. The dip of her collarbone. The broad muscle of her shoulders. The shooting star curvature of her spine. The gentle dip of her hips under my fingertips. The unapologetic desire of her lips moving with mine.

I could taste her wordless promise that this is not the end, the memory immediately searing itself over all the others—a flame-bright burn across my entire brain, impossible even by the wildest imagination to remove.

"And Aspect," Aspect says brightly.

I blink, lost in my reverie. "What?"

"You both—have Aspect." They lift one hand, struggling to independently raise one finger in a facsimile of a thumbs-up. "Even at—the end—of the world. And triple dog—too."

In evident approval, Russ lifts all three heads toward the ceiling and barks.

CHAPTER 25

KORI

Adria insists on one last proper sleep for me before I return to the Daylands, but I fear she will have no such luxury. The Shadow Court demands an explanation for the sun serpent attack, and with Azarii's rebellion having taken public responsibility—naming me as the target, no less—it's impossible to pass it off as a freak incident. I considered quipping that Adria was wrong to blame my mother for the serpents, but with everything I know seemingly in flux, even the confidence behind my teasing has faltered.

Maybe Chloe didn't try to kill me. But why did she lock me away underground like a living fossil for my entire life, if all along, the radiation wouldn't kill me? Did she know? For how long? Nothing makes a fraction of sense anymore.

The nightfolk at large don't know that I was exposed to the radiation, nor that it didn't kill me like it should have, so Adria can at least keep that close to her chest, provided Thaane doesn't sound the alarm. But will withholding that detail be enough? How close is Adria's throne from being entirely usurped by her advisory council—or even by Thaane himself?

I want to hate him so badly. But I *did* bring desert monsters to the Shadowlands; I *did* distract Adria from the ongoing civil war. All that (and more) is true beyond doubt. His words linger like splinters beneath my skin: *She doesn't belong here, Adria. She never did.*

So, are Thaane's protestations and deference to the Shadow Court's judgment really any different from Adria's overtaking her parents' throne? Any different from what I'm doing, returning home to investigate how deep the false science of radiation poisoning goes? He's only trying to protect his people. If my mother had fallen for a nightfolk trespasser, and let our dayfolk settlement fall to pieces in turn, would I have acted any differently than Thaane has?

He's right: I don't belong here. My return home is long overdue.

But when I tell Adria as much, she physically lifts me from a sitting position on the floor to the edge of her bed. "As long as I'm queen," she says, brushing stray hairs out of my face with one claw, "you will always have a place here. But right now, you need to *rest*. You'll need all your newfound strength before long."

"I will sleep in my own bed, thank you," I insist, uselessly pushing against the barrier of Adria's extended arm.

She gently pushes me back into the mattress. Russ, for good measure, jams two of his heads into my knees, trying to keep me in place. "Your bed is snapped clean in two."

Aspect wiggles one raised arm for attention. "And underneath—Kori's broken bed—is the perfect bed—for *Aspect*!"

I roll my eyes. "You are a *robot*, Aspect. You don't even sleep."

The mech crosses their quivering arms in a picture of defiance so eerily akin to myself, I wonder if I'm anywhere near qualified to be a mech mom. "Aspect can—say recharge—is *sleep*—if Aspect wants."

"And you want to sleep in the serpent attack's rubble? Of all the things, *that's* what you want? Your first conscious act, with sentience bestowed upon you, is to have a snooze in some abandoned wreckage?"

"Aspect—is making—CHOICES," Aspect declares, idly scratching Russ under one of his chins as they do so.

"Well." Adria laughs under her breath. "I suppose that settles it. I'll walk Aspect back to their—ah—bed, and you'll get some rest here while I clean up the political mess those accursed snakes left behind." She extends an open hand and adds, "And repair that crack in your armor, while I'm in the business of fixing things."

Arching my eyebrows, I pin Adria with my eyes, even as I drop my collapsed section of the damaged armor into her palm. I'm far too tired to bother removing the rest of it right now. There was always that unspoken tension between us, even when the helmet concealed my face, but now that my gaze can properly meet hers, I'm enjoying the rush of newfound power I hold to make this massive, mighty warrior of a woman go silent and still with a glance. "You need to sleep, too."

"I will if I can. Don't worry."

"But I'm in *your* bed—" I start to say, even as Adria ignores me entirely.

"Your priority right now is *you*, Kori," she says, walking Aspect out of the room, blowing out the assorted braziers on the wall as she passes. Russ patters heavily after both of them. "No matter how much you resent me for it."

The electronic door slides shut with a final hiss behind them, leaving me in darkness. I lean back, groaning, and stare up at where the domed ceiling would be if I could see anything at all. I even lift a hand to wiggle my fingers in front of my face, but it's totally lost in the inky blackness. Sighing, I close my eyes, not seeing much use for keeping them open anyway. At some point, I drift into a restless sleep.

It's the dream again, because of course it is. Manacles holding me to the medical table. The invasive prick of a needle at my wrist. Strange weight muddling my head, as though my skull were full of water. My mother's voice: *Kori, can you hear me?*

In this rendition of the dream, though, my subconscious mind must retain some small spark of knowledge that Chloe and Ednit alike have been lying to me my whole life. I thrash in the chains, my skull bashing into the table over and over until I've left a pool of blood on the medical-grade parchment beneath me. *Get away from me!* My voice, corrosive as acid, burns my throat. *I'm not like you!*

Something else seizes my wrists, then, real and substantial, a soft and tender touch utterly unlike the chains holding my spectral self down. I swim up out of sleep and into the knowledge that I'm flailing in waking life, Adria's hands holding me safely against the bed until I cease to struggle.

"Sorry," I mumble, still halfway lost in sleep. "Sorry, sorry . . ."

But Adria shushes me and crawls in beside me, carefully turning me over so her massive body curves around mine, a protective fortress of muscle around my shuddering frame.

"Sleep, Kori," she breathes.

I'm shivering too badly for that, unaccustomed to the Shadowlands' cold, so she covers my body with her good wing, a welcome brush of velvety warmth.

I fall back into a dreamless slumber.

●

When I wake, I'm only half-sure I didn't dream that up, too—the real, undeniable weight of her body against mine, the blanket of her wing, the brush of her mouth at the shell of my ear. *Sleep, Kori.* For a ridiculous instant, I wonder if she's even coming back, or if this is how I find out that our romantic bond was all in my head from the start.

Then the door slides open, and she's standing there again, visibly weary but nevertheless smiling at the sight of me, her wing already half healed.

"Hey," she says.

"Hey," I echo, still too bleary to stand. "How long was I out?"

"Only as long as you needed to be," Adria insists, stepping forward to take one of my hands between both of hers. She kneels beside the bed so that we're eye to eye. "Long enough for me to bring the Shadow Court to a tenuous heel . . . repair that crack in your armor . . ." She drops the resealed section beside me on the bed. ". . . and drag the remaining husk of your starship from the Second Spire to just outside the fortress."

"You didn't have to do that."

"I *wanted* to do that," Adria insists, weaving her fingers with mine.

"Did you sleep at all?"

"Does it matter?"

I squeeze her hand as hard as I can. "How bad are things with the court?"

Adria blows out a heavy breath, pluming white. "General Isek lost the leg," she says, barely audible, as if saying the words out loud might wound her more than the serpents did. My stomach drops like a broken elevator. "And he hobbled into that meeting, on a makeshift mechanic leg, to call me his queen even still. To defend that I have only ever had the Shadowlands' best interest at heart."

Sighing, Adria runs a hand through her overlong black curls. Her lips keep moving for a moment, no sound coming out, as if stumbling over something unsaid, unspeakable, but she recovers herself. "If not for that, Kori, I sincerely believe it would've been a coup. They aren't just *disappointed*—half the court believes I'm an active *threat* to the future security of the nightfolk."

I lift my other hand to her cheek, raising her gaze back to mine. "And Thaane?"

"All but a statue while Isek spoke," Adria says, in a voice balanced on a freezeblade's edge. "But he didn't breathe a word of what's happened to you, surviving beyond your armor. Nor a whisper of your experiments with Aspect and sentience."

"After what he said to you before . . . that's honestly better than I expected," I say, returning the repaired section of armor to my arm as we speak.

"I don't deserve him. My brother since childhood . . . now my brother-in-arms . . . he's watched me fail to lead at nearly every turn—and even so, in the moment of trial, silent though he may have been, he stood by me." Violet eyes full of awe, Adria shakes her head, pulling away from my hand on her cheek and my hand woven with hers alike. "I don't take that for granted. I won't." She stares at the wall behind me, but I don't think she's really seeing the room around us at all. "When all this is over," she says, resolved, "I want to be a leader that he can stand behind with pride. Not one for whom he has to make excuses."

"You will be," I promise, my hand finding its way into her dark hair, twisting and untwisting a loose curl around my finger. "I know you will be."

Adria sighs and sits beside me on the bed. The mattress dips under her weight far more than mine, but this bed was designed for nightfolk to start with, so it maintains its integrity despite her muscled bulk. Her wings flare wide so that one wraps around my body, cradling me close to her side.

"My technologists were able to cobble your ship together into . . . something . . . akin to what it was. The engine blessedly survived the crash, and you should have just enough fuel for a one-way trip back to the Daylands. Aspect is fully recharged and waiting by the boarding ramp. They were . . . surprisingly helpful with the repairs."

A little laugh breaks from me. "Like mother, like robot, I suppose."

"Is that so bad?"

"Hopefully their help on repairs is better than their help in combat."

"It would be a tall order for it to be worse."

We both laugh at that, our hands wandering to meet again between us, her long fingers all but eclipsing mine. Despite her skin being cooler than mine, a little shudder of heat goes through me at the contact. I bring my other hand over to play with her fingers, and she lets me, despite the vicious claws and strength they hold. I lift each finger one by one, trying to memorize what they felt like on the skin of my cheek, in the waves of my hair, splayed across my back holding me fast in our long-awaited kiss.

"I have to go, don't I?" I breathe, unable to meet her eyes. "I have so many questions that it hardly feels like going home at all."

"You'll come back to me," Adria says, not a question this time. "Look at me, Kori." I do, her gaze swimming with adoration I can still hardly believe. "And I'll be waiting for you. I promise. I swear it on everything I have left to lose." Her lips quirk upward. "There's one other thing."

She reaches into a pocket of her robes before plucking out a jagged stone that gleams a soft, steady blue. It's just the right size for her to drop it into my palm. I expect the stone to be cold against my bare skin, like everything else in the Shadowlands, but it pulses with ethereal warmth instead. It's beautiful, but somehow primal, too. My heart races, nearly pounding through my chest, as if to keep pace with a fundamental rhythm at the heart of the world.

I stare wonderingly. "Is this . . . ?"

"A piece of the Diakópsei, yes."

One of the gemfruits. I remember these from our visit to the Cataclysm site. Since they're so much smaller than the main asteroid, the comparatively tiny energy they contain isn't immediately overwhelming upon physical contact; instead, while I can feel the power pulsing beneath its surface, I think the gemfruit could be used as needed, staying contained until the right moment arose.

But it was definitely never meant for *my* use. I feel the blood draining from my face, and a chill weaves down my spine. "Elysium can't have possibly approved of this. Let alone Thaane, let alone the court—"

"I didn't ask Elysium for permission," Adria says, unflinching. "And I didn't tell Thaane, or the court."

I shake my head rapidly. "They're waiting for *any* mistake, Adria. Any misstep at all. If they catch word of this—"

"They won't."

"But why risk it?"

Adria closes one hand over mine, locking the shimmering gemfruit between our palms. "When these are secured in their vessels, on either side of the Diakópsei," she says, "they're endlessly renewed and refueled by it. But if you take one with you, it'll only work once." Her violet eyes pin me in place as she withdraws her hand. "Then you have to come back to me."

I turn the gemfruit over and over in my palm, feeling out its strange shape, admiring it like a talisman. A ward against forces of dark and light alike.

"I'll always come back to you," I breathe, pressing my lips to the fruit's surface.

I feel its primeval power glint briefly, impossibly blue on my lips, electric, before I press them back to Adria's. I don't know how long we stay like that, my fingers threaded in her overlong hair, her hands holding me steady at the hips, her mouth eclipsing every fear that haunts the edges of my mind, but it's not nearly long enough.

I don't think any length of time would be enough.

All things considered, Adria's technicians did an impressive job salvaging my starship. Cracks spider throughout the central dome, and the wings aren't quite at their intended angles, with additional trusses of support added between the upper and lower pairs, as well. It's easy to tell which pieces had broken off and were soldered back on, often with bits and bobs missing.

It looks like *Charon* if I had tried to sketch it from memory, with my left hand, while blindfolded across one eye. But it's still *Charon*. It's still my ticket home.

Home. I want to curl up beneath Adria's wings and simply tell stories back and forth until we can't keep our eyes open. I want to wake up to Russ unnecessarily slobbering all over Aspect's scratched-in smile with three enthusiastic tongues. The Shadowlands were never meant for me, but I can't shake the persistent sense that Adria was. Despite all that logic would dictate, I could build a home here. Instead, I'm being called back to the ever-shifting sands, then diving beneath them, back to the settlement. A downward spiral into a potential conspiracy I'm only just beginning to understand.

For all the impressive cobbling together that the nightfolk did, *Charon*'s boarding ramp was apparently beyond saving. Adria lifts me on her shoulders to reach the cockpit. Aspect is already waiting inside, eyes brightly beaming cherry red, both arms waving at different speeds. Not unlike *Charon*, their limbs bear new patches of foreign metal, with the occasional gear or cog sticking unnecessarily out, but they hardly seem to mind.

"Aspect—fixed ship. Aspect is still—useful—at the end of the world."

"Not the end of the world yet." I laugh, taking their outstretched hand and sliding off Adria's shoulders. Immediately, I keenly feel the absence of her body on mine. "Adria."

She looks at me, though the tension in her jaw and her furrowed brows tell me it's taking all her strength not to look away and spare herself the pain of watching me leave.

"Be the queen I know you are. Hold the line." I slip one hand into my pocket, feeling the unearthly shape and pulse of the gemfruit I'll carry with me. "And when I come back, I expect you'll be waiting."

"You're making demands now? On my side of the planet?" She laughs, but it's dry, humorless. "Be safe, Kori."

"I'll try." It's the best promise I can offer. Not enough, but something, at least.

I reach to tap my armor's trigger points, triggering the extension of a helmet around my face, then a cascade of protection across the rest of my body. I don't really need any of it until I'm home, where it will be necessary again: both to preserve any remaining anonymity and to avoid alarming anyone at my ability to withstand Pagonian radiation. But my eyes burn something fierce, my throat closing up.

If, stars forbid, I don't come back—if I collapse somewhere on my quest for answers and never know the sweet assurance of her lips on mine again—I don't want Adria to remember me crying as I said goodbye.

"You better," Adria says, but I hardly hear her over the struggling engine's roar. What I do hear, unbelievably loud, is three canine heads howling headlong at the sky, watching their robotic companion slowly shrink smaller and smaller as we ascend.

The tears I've been fighting back rally hard, my eyes burning.

Aspect leans out the ship's still-open entrance like the lead in a romance film, holding onto the side of the doorway with one hand. "Aspect—will miss—" But the wind around us is picking up something fierce, a stirring whirlwind. Unsteady, they nearly pitch forward, and I catch them hard by their other arm, pulling them back into *Charon*'s interior proper. "TRIPLE DOG!" Aspect concludes, waving their free arm wildly farewell as the cockpit seals shut around us.

Distantly, the dog's wails carry over the wind. Aspect produces a strange series of low, nearly musical beeps that I've never heard before. First words, of a sort? Why did they have to be born of tragedy?

Is this really what it is to be a person, then? An understanding, first, of hope, of dreams . . . only to have those chased by inescapable pain?

Charon's battered husk rises, defiant as ever, into the sunless sky. Through muffled sobs of my own, I take the pilot's seat and set our course for home.

●

I struggle almost as much as *Charon* with our trip across the Passage.

Every cough and sputter of the half-wrecked shell and practically zombified engine threatens to shake a little sob out of me. My clammy hands struggle to grip the remaining controls at all—very few left working, save for the essential directional lever and an on/off trigger for the engine—and when I do get a decent hold, it's a death grip, sending shooting pain through my arms. It doesn't help that the autopilot was dead on arrival, so I have to make every flight decision manually, even when I want to curl into a fetal position.

Compared to the Shadowlands, the heat wave of entering the Passage should feel like rebirth. Instead it feels like I've gone from cold, solid safety to formless, blazing torment, the sands below us ever shifting and swirling with violent winds. I thought I missed warmth, especially when I tried to sleep, but now my eyes sting, my skin prickling with it.

I itch all over inside my entirely unnecessary protective suit. But, at the very least, the armor keeps Aspect from seeing me cry, and that's enough. I imagine their first few charge cycles as a sentient being are pretty formative. Seeing their maker promptly have an emotional breakdown could only bode badly. So I stay in the suit.

Where the Passage's wind currents pushed us easily toward the Shadowlands, now we're fighting Pagomènos itself to reverse course. Disturbed sand trickles through *Charon*'s cracks, blurring my view from the cockpit, even half jamming some of the controls, filling every crack and crevice. I need to constantly brush the control panel clean, even blowing out the biggest breaths I can muster to keep the levers fully mobile. I pitch *Charon* hard away from the Passage's center, despite such a move extending the miles of our trip. There are lesser wind currents on the fringe that travel in the opposite direction. A longer trip, without fighting the wind, will be a shorter trip in the end. And should help keep us off the settlement's radar detection, while we're at it.

Slowly we draw closer to the molten eye of the stationary Pagonian sun. It's difficult to tell when the Passage becomes the Daylands proper, save for the ever-increasing heat and light, as well as increased sandstone formations where the wind is less brutal. I wait until, without squinting, I can see my home settlement's entrance along the horizon, jutting out just barely aboveground.

To a passing predator, like a sun serpent that wandered too far from its traditional feeding grounds, it's nothing noticeable—just an oddly distinct, nearly cubic sand dune, very faintly shimmering from the metallic surface underneath. But I know it to be the first sign of my real home.

The entrance is still a few miles out. Close enough for us to travel the remainder on foot, avoiding any unnecessary attention on us. The lost princess arriving in a husk of a ship with a too-talkative robot would draw far too much notice, and I need to begin my investigation decidedly under the radar. The settlement's outermost shell of Pagonian plate emits a high frequency audio cue that deters predators this close, too, so we won't have any sun serpents to worry about. Just a lot of sun-forsaken sand.

Nevertheless, it isn't lost on me that if Chloe were even remotely anticipating either my return or a nightfolk emissary, there would be increased security in the airspace. And there just . . . isn't. It's the same as it ever was—mostly heavy transport vessels for mining mechs to do their aboveground work, occasionally broken up by a dayfolk starship looking to either get some real sunlight or visit the Morpheus Market. My mother isn't expecting me home.

Quite possibly, she never wanted me to come home at all.

I force my stomach to stop churning, square my shoulders, and bring *Charon* into a rattling shudder of a landing.

Without functioning landing gear, *Charon*'s underbelly must bear the brunt of impact. Which means a rough, painful, especially sandy landing in the sun-dappled dunes. I swear I feel my teeth jerk back into my skull when the ship strikes land. Instead of screaming, Aspect mutters the word "brave" to themself over and over at increasing volume, apparently determined to demonstrate their personhood with new, but no less irritating, habits.

Without *Charon*'s enclosed shell to protect us, sand cascades into the ship as it slides to a stop in the open desert. Aspect is lucky—they have most of the pros of being alive without the obvious con of requiring oxygen. Once the motion stops, they simply shoot upright, whirl all their limbs like Russ shaking his canine fur, and announce, "ASPECT—CLEAN!"

I, meanwhile, have discovered the taste of sand. For a long, miserable moment, I'm spitting it and tasting it and generally thinking that anyone who had the misfortune of living on a sand-centric planet would probably hold a lifelong grudge against the stuff. Thankfully, my suit can recognize an invasive substance after an instant, so it temporarily closed the air filtration vents to the worst of it. I'll probably need to manually clean it later anyway. *Less bad* is still pretty bad when it comes to desert in the lungs.

Once I've cleared my throat (and my head) enough to clamber out of *Charon*, I heave myself up and over the side. Aspect enthusiastically follows.

Mechs are meant to travel the Passage primarily, but Aspect has spent an overwhelming majority of their life inside the metallic dayfolk settlement. In my enthusiasm to install extra functions, I may have neglected the essentials. Aspect's feet slip and slide on the uneven dunes. They extend both arms like a starship to stabilize themself, but it doesn't do much. Eventually I take their hand in mine. They don't protest, just grip back. It reminds me of how they used to hold me in the Morpheus Market, when the future's countless possibilities still felt comprehensible. Now everything is different, gaps in my knowledge ever pressing.

All I know is that whatever happens next, I want Aspect and Adria to be there, too. (And because I'm already certain Aspect will beg . . . yes, also the dog.)

Despite their general lack of experience with the Passage, Aspect is equipped with the same universal parts as all dayfolk mechs. Same basic piston-based skeletal and muscular structure. Same expressionless head, even if I insisted on adding awkward eyes and a crooked smile. And blessedly, the same access chip in their left palm that lets them enter and exit the settlement without having to speak to anyone.

Most mechs run on an independent programmed schedule specifically to remove that burden from their owners, so the ability to enter and exit the settlement at will is essential to harvesting runs. Now, though, it's my ticket back home without having to show my face or raise my voice at all. By the time anyone notices Aspect's designation reappearing in the arrival log, I'll be back on the run, hopefully with newfound answers.

Aspect's technical name, 45P3C7, flashes across the scanner. It blinks green. Below and just in front of us, the massive metal maw of the settlement's main gate grumbles, groans, and lugs itself slowly open. If my mother were fully against me, surely she would've disabled Aspect's access to the settlement? Azarii's rebellion took responsibility for the serpent attack; maybe Chloe was never involved. Maybe she doesn't know anything about how my body interacts with Pagonian radiation. Maybe what's happening to me will be as shocking to her as it was to me, and we can face the impossible together.

I want to hope so very badly, but I feel rigid from the nape of my neck to my toes with persistent fear.

Aspect and I descend the ramp as the doors screech shut behind us, catapulting our descent into darkness before artificial lighting kicks back on. I take deep breaths—in through the nose, out through the mouth—trying to force my rising panic out with every puff. My armor is entirely standardized, and it's not wildly uncommon for dayfolk, in a rush, to still be wearing their armor inside the settlement. Most people don't have starships, so they store the armor at home, and they might not want to be running around publicly in whatever clothing they were wearing underneath. Remaining armored isn't a perfect way to avoid drawing attention to myself, but it's better than the alternative of showing my face and immediately summoning my mother's minions. Not collapsing my helmet indoors will still look a little odd, but it's unfortunately my best available course of action.

The only people who would recognize me like this are Chloe or Ednit, and if I play my return right, neither of them will know I'm here until I've pinned them down to answer my questions. If it comes to that, anyway.

First stop, the decontamination chamber.

Briefly, I worry that the gemfruit in my utility belt will either trigger a full-blown alarm or sputter out from the decontamination process, but it seems that much like the radiation that powers mechs, the radiation within a gemfruit is so securely contained, it doesn't trip the sensors. And it stays entirely intact. I squeeze it tight in one fist despite its jagged edges biting at me through my glove. The pain keeps me grounded, present.

Now is not the time to lose myself in my anxiety. Next stop: the Lexicon.

The Lexicon is the Daylands' equivalent of Adria's archives, the sum total of our knowledge and preserved—albeit fragmented—history in digitized form. The critical difference is that many of our records are in Morpheus chip format rather than simply text.

I've easily been in and out of the Lexicon hundreds of times, retrieving assigned curriculum and records as my mother dictated, occasionally copying permitted material to my own (now destroyed in *Charon*'s crash) comms tablet. But importantly, the Lexicon has levels. Three, to be exact. Level One is for laymen. Level Two is for the privileged. Level Three . . . I never found out. If my continued Morpheus Market visits had proven ineffective in awakening Aspect, I'd contemplated eventually hacking my way in here to find out.

I never imagined that I'd be breaking this law not to research for Aspect, but to learn something more about myself.

I navigate my old home's halls with automatic precision. It's like every other return from Morpheus Market smuggling to my daily studies, except that my heart hammers violently against my ribs. I squeeze the gemfruit in my pocket in time with my racing pulse, brushing wordlessly past countless civilians. None of them look at me, even though I feel like they *know* I shouldn't be here. They *do* look at Aspect, but that's less because Aspect is being overtly suspicious and more because their peg leg replacement is still incredibly squeaky, adding a little rubber-bath-toy backup chorus to our speed walk to the Lexicon.

Two lefts, a right, a ramp, an elevator, a circle, third door, then up. Further up. Further in.

I'm actually traveling lighter than I did when I left this place—no more Morpheus sphere on my person, and no comms tablet either—but my steps feel heavier, my limbs moving as if through molasses. I know more than *any* dayfolk is supposed to know, now. About the Shadowlands. About the nightfolk. About what I'm truly capable of, not just with the radiation but as an independent person.

I set out into the forbidden shadows, alone. And I returned with a robot brought to proper life. *I did that.* Not my mother. Not my doctor. Not even Adria, ultimately. More than anyone else, I fought for everything Aspect and I have achieved so far, straining against every chain my mother had ever latched on to me, clawing inch by stubborn inch toward my own vision of my future—even when it broke my nails to the point of bleeding, even when I wondered how I could possibly pull myself a single hand's length farther away from the home I'd always known.

Maybe it isn't so strange that the surrounding dayfolk citizens don't recognize me. I'm not the same girl who left this place, just barely beginning to test the limits of possibility; I've evolved into something *more*.

Most of the settlement uses elevators or ramps, but the one leading to the Lexicon requires a formally documented disability to use, via an access-code comms tablet app that's not publicly available. Old records indicate early architects of the settlement wanted the Lexicon to feel like an Earthside library—traditional, rather than technical, and needlessly ostentatious, with a spiral staircase looping in on itself at least eight times before reaching the first floor.

Aspect's squeaky leg really worsens the blow. You can't exactly get a robot a disability tag; damaged mechs just get turned into scrap because people suck. If I do my job right, hopefully Aspect will be nothing like most people as they truly come into their own.

Eventually we reach Level One: a glittering maze of comms tablets, Morpheus sphere receptacles, and boxes of truly ancient, handwritten records—viewable only through an impenetrable sheet of glass. All the data forms are scattered about in aging, leaning, desperately in-need-of-repair wooden bookshelves, because again, *tradition* or something.

Not sure why retrieving a record from a shelf is any better than entirely from software, but okay.

More stairs. My knocking knees throb by the time we arrive on Level Two, and we still aren't where I want to be. At long last, I haul myself up the third flight of tightly wound spiral stairs, Aspect close behind, and come upon another heavy sealed door. Much like the elevators into the Lexicon, this door requires a government-issued pass. I, of course, don't have one.

But I do have a piece of the Diakópsei in my pocket.

I slip the gemfruit into my palm, its texture both spiky and surprisingly fragile against my skin. Its power pulses through my bloodstream like a racing second heartbeat. Inhaling sharply, I clench my hand around the gemfruit as hard as I can, ignoring the sharp bite of wintery power that lances through my arm.

"Kori—is okay," Aspect stammers, as a little cry slips out of me.

I lean hard against the wall to maintain my footing, my vision flashing black and white and blue. I squeeze my eyes shut to reduce the vertigo. After a long, shivering moment during which I hardly know where I am, or even who, the power settles and pools in my palm, icy but stable.

I look, and my hand glows the white-hot of a shooting star, azure sparks leaping between my fingertips.

The gemfruit's own light has already faded. I slide it back into my pocket with my not-glowing hand. The glowing one tingles with little pinpricks of power, like when a stationary limb falls asleep—but supernaturally awake, instead.

"Here goes nothing," I breathe, and press my open hand to the Lexicon door's control panel. The panel spits smoke and sparks. I grit my teeth hard against another scream, electric power surging and rattling through my skeleton.

Aspect, thank the stars, wraps me tightly in a hug from behind, absorbing some of the shock into their own body. "K-K-K-K-K-Koriiiiiiii iiiiiiiiis w-w-w-w-welcooooooooome!"

"Thanks," I bite out through my electric-fogged haze.

A painfully loud, shrill screech of metal. A fading hiss of overloaded wiring. At long last, the door to Lexicon Level Three opens for my clandestine research. My hand has returned to normal, give or take some weird cramps from the rapid temperature shift, but I still massage my fingers and absently crack my knuckles as Aspect and I step in.

The heavy door slams shut behind us. It won't require a tech hack on this side, but I can't help but shudder anyway as the entire room is thrown into darkness before I can even get a good look at it. I fumble for Aspect in the void, gripping their cool metallic arm for balance until, finally, a row of lights bursts into being along the path.

All the breath whooshes out of my lungs.

I spent hundreds—no, thousands—of sleep cycles permitted to access only the levels below. My childhood imagination ran wild with what might be contained here. Proof of mythical creatures like the ones in my storybooks, perhaps—historical records of proper, winged dragons. Or more direct evidence from immediately post-Cataclysm—something more than the scattered written records telling us that we'd come from Earth and tragedy had struck Pagomènos, but little else. Colors beyond the broadly experienced spectrum, star maps of galaxies beyond ours or Earth's, the last living Earthside dog . . . something like that.

What I see is *nothing* like that.

The room I'm standing in is practically a corridor. It would probably qualify as a closet in my mother's monarch living quarters. There's barely enough space for both me and Aspect to comfortably move around. The chamber never widens after the door, and the walls on either side of me are entirely blank, save for the thin lines of fluorescent yellow lights illuminating the path forward.

The only wall containing records is the one dead ahead, at the end of the corridor that tunnels my vision. A dozen or so suspended

Morpheus spheres blink green lights at me in a haphazard pattern, like so many eyes on an alien face, each watching me in their own rhythm. I shrink my armor, including my helmet, just to reduce the sense of suffocation. Nobody can see us in this place; at least for the moment, I can safely show my real face.

Aspect hangs their head, visibly despondent. "These memories—not—for Aspect," they state plainly. It's not really a question.

The room's atmosphere is the furthest thing from inviting, all artificial light and sinister claustrophobia. *I'm* not even supposed to be here, a mech even less so.

"Not really for me either," I sigh, tentatively walking toward the blinking collection of spheres. "But here we are."

I extend a hand toward the top leftmost sphere, triggering a title to project from its surface. *THE EVOLUTION PROJECT*, reads the floating green holographic text, which does nothing to illuminate what it might be about. I've never even heard a rumor of such a thing.

I pluck the sphere from its shelf. Only then, when I hear its light metallic rattle against my skin, do I realize my hand is shaking.

If there are answers here, they may not be the good kind. What if I was better off not knowing my real reaction to the radiation at all? What if there's still time to turn back, gather what resources I can for Adria's war, slip into the shadows once again, and pretend the revelation didn't change anything?

"Kori." Aspect squeezes my shoulder with their squeaky fingers. "Aspect—is still Aspect—after every—memory from Kori. Aspect was—Aspect, is—Aspect, will be—Aspect. So Kori—can still be—Kori, too. Aspect—is sure of it."

I swallow hard. Set my jaw. "I'm lucky to have you. I hope you know that." I tap the sphere until it holds a steady green access light, ready to impart its memory. "Now, don't let me fall, okay?" I say, just before my vision goes blank-paper white.

My name is Chloe, and I am fading.

We all are. It's the curse of being human. My bones creak when I move; my muscles ache for no apparent reason; my head pounds if too much light invades my vision or if not enough is found at all. So many weaknesses, so many pressure points and fragile joints, as I wander my kingdom in this ever-breaking, failed divine experiment we call a human body.

Today, it becomes nothing but a vestigial organism. Today, like a scientific astral projection, I inhabit a body built to last, built to rule.

Today, I become Evolved.

Dozens of experiments have led to this moment. Carefully chosen volunteers, some whose memories were scrambled like eggs, some who forgot their own names when they came to, but my scientists are confident now—they've cracked the human code. They can move any of us, at my behest, from one body to another. From the newfound pedestal of my elevated body, I'll select others who are worthy, and together we'll ascend to command all the lesser organic cogs in the settlement machine, who will finally know their betters.

The revelation will take time. The people surely can't accept this right away, or they'll all want to Evolve, and then who would uphold the settlement's lower pillars? Who would I rule, if all could cheat death? No, the truth must be veiled until the appropriate moment.

Then I, and the others worthy of Evolution, will exert total control over the Daylands. And, if all goes according to plan, the Shadowlands, too.

From the Shadowlands, we can seize the source of the radiation, formerly death to us all—now the ultimate power source for new, better bodies.

The body we've built for me, painstakingly carved from supple and smooth altered Pagonian plate, is indistinguishable from the one I currently lug around. If only for appearance's sake, it will still hunger and thirst, still tire with use, still shed appropriately scarlet blood when struck. Except it will never bend to time. It will never age. The radiation that threatens to poison my mortal body will empower my immortal one, ever absorbed through its synthetic skin.

The new body stands defiantly across from me now, still nothing but a perfect corpse, begging for a spirit to animate its beauty.

On the other side of Evolution, the Daylands' throne will belong to my family's dynasty alone. When I'm done, so will the Shadowlands.

Yet my whole body trembles as I lie down on the stretcher, as I hold Ednit's silent, professional gaze with wordless trust. I do not watch the needle go into my wrist. I stare at the ceiling until it starts to swim.

What am I, if not a million memories, interwoven into the ever-shifting tapestry of a self? Will I not still be me, when the induced sleep fog fades? Shivering all over, hands curled into fists, nails digging into my palms, I slam my eyes shut.

And open them.

And from across the room, I'm staring at my body on a stretcher, hollowed out like freshly cleaned animal bones, spirit torn free of muscle and sinew, my self reignited in a perfect Pagonian form.

"Chloe," Ednit says, voice clipped but wavering with wonder, "can you hear me?"

"My name . . ." My new vocal cords creak and ache, unfamiliar with use, but even now, the sound is resonant. Glorious. ". . . is Chloe." I swallow hard through my strange throat before trying again to form familiar syllables. "I can hear you. I'm here. I'm . . . me."

Ednit drops his comms tablet altogether. It clatters on the floor, the screen maybe cracking, but neither of us cares. He lets out a childlike whoop, throwing his hands into the air. "Stars above, we've done it!"

My name is Chloe, and I am the first of the Evolved.

But not the last.

Aspect is the only thing holding me upright. My knees are like gelatin, all the fight gone out of me. Gently, Aspect holds me up against the wall, lightly smacking my cheeks with alternating hands until I fully return to myself.

"Stars," I gasp, sagging against the mech's steady body. "Stars above."

My persistent nightmare—strapped to a table, groggy but terribly aware, recognizing myself but not my body—it wasn't a nightmare at all, was it? Just a memory, stubborn as the rest of me, that even the Daylands' best Morpheus technician couldn't fully remove when they—

When they . . . transferred me into an elevated body.

When I *Evolved.*

"Why didn't they *tell* me?"

Aspect tightens their grip on my sinking shoulders. "Tell Kori—what?"

I blow out a deep breath, but it does nothing to steady my staggering heartbeat. "Chloe—my mother—found a way to move all of someone's memories at once. To move their whole person. And they built better bodies, fueled by the radiation instead of destroyed by it."

"Isn't that—a good thing—for Kori?"

I squeeze my eyes tight to lock the tears in. The room spins wildly behind my eyelids.

A lifetime spent suffocating in an armor suit, if ever I wanted to see the sun. An entire existence living a lie, at my mother's knowing behest. I've seen her wear her own armor suit countless times, and for what? Just to convince her citizens that she was exactly like them—even as she plotted to exert deathless, merciless power over all of them, and eventually the Shadowlands, too?

Was anything real? *Anything at all?* I know now that my nightmares were maybe the realest thing in my head, but what about everything else? How long have I been living in a facsimile of a human body, my flesh-and-blood inheritance abandoned entirely? Where is my original body—reduced to ash like a malfunctioning mech, or kept in cold storage somewhere like a sick trophy of Ednit's experiments?

Does the real Kori stare, unseeing, from the inside of a test tube somewhere, her soul scooped clean out like guts from a fish, her limp hand pressed, pale and lifeless, to the glass, her empty, cloudy gaze permanently wondering if I'll ever come back to me?

I open my eyes and stare at my hands. They're trembling. *Not my hands.* Hands built in a lab, hands designed in spreadsheets and algorithms. The hands that modified Aspect. The hands that pulled Adria's lips to mine. Not human. Not mine. A dark laugh slips out of me. What would Adria say if she knew that she'd kissed not a girl but a machine? The trembling won't stop. It travels up my arms, into my shoulders, radiates all through my body. *Not my body.*

When I was little, first beginning to tinker with technology, I accidentally sliced my forearm open on a rogue wire. There's a scar there—faint and white, half-faded, but still there. How many bodies ago did I earn that scar? Was it artificially added to every new rendition, an increasingly false echo of real pain? Kori 2.0. Kori 3.0 . . .

If I bashed my head into the wall right now, over and over until my skull split open, would I actually bleed out? If I screamed until the sound broke me, do I even have vocal cords to strain? How many bodies ago did my mother press a good-night kiss to my forehead after a nightmare? How many bodies ago did Ednit poke me in the ribs with his elbow and tell me I was growing up too fast for even the best doctor to keep up?

Are all my *memories* even mine—or were some strategically selected to mold me into the perfect daughter, the perfect heiress? Clever, but still obedient. Strong, but still containable. Only ever capable of dreaming as far as my mother could bear it.

And isn't that exactly what I've done to Aspect, playing Dreamgiver as though I have any right? Poking around in their brain like a mere science experiment? Trying to raise them to personhood, to choice, but only insofar as they still stay close to me, loving me, needing me?

Leaning on the wall with both hands, I violently vomit on the floor. Another thing that seems like it shouldn't be possible, but the details in every iteration of my Evolution were painstakingly applied.

Aspect lightly rubs my back, the way my mother would when I fell sick as a child, and the irony isn't lost on me: my artificial child, parenting *me* instead. I'm too shaken to summon any protest. My legs quiver, muscles spasming, like they might just dissolve into liquid beneath me.

"They took . . . my *body*," I gasp, when I can breathe again. "They relocated my whole *person* as part of their own sick experiment, and then, to top it all off, they *lied to me* about it my *entire life*. It doesn't matter if this body is better. It doesn't matter if they were going to tell me eventually."

I spit. My mouth still tastes like sick. A hurricane brews between my ears. I kick the floor so hard, the impact runs straight up my leg and into my hip.

"All those forced medical appointments. It had nothing to do with my sun-forsaken *health*. They were trying, and failing, to remove my only memory of the procedure. To ensure Chloe could literally program me into exactly the daughter she wanted."

And why birth a daughter at all? Why not build the perfect heir from scratch? Why have an heir at all, if Chloe fully intends to live forever? Are there backups of her artificial body? Of mine, for that matter? Did she just need something to *control* so badly that snatching eternal life from the Dreamgiver's hands wasn't enough—she had to inflict eternity on someone else, whether or not I wanted it? Do I exist solely to preserve the illusion of a generational heir? Or am I just a backup, a save scum, in case something were to go wrong with her personally maintaining power?

Was she always planning to delete me, if things spiraled out of control? Hardly a daughter at all. No, a bug in the code. A flaw in the system.

My father, I'm told, died in my infancy. Was that by Chloe's hand, too? Was my father merely a tool for organic creation, necessary so that she might have a real daughter to transfer into an Evolved body?

Did she deem him unworthy of living forever alongside us? Or was he among the earliest experimental transfers? Did he volunteer to Evolve? Did he even know what was happening? Are there records of his life and death somewhere in this room, poised to add even more weight upon my nearly broken back?

I swear, severely, and kick the floor with my other foot for good measure. They might as well both be throbbing. My heart hurts more than either limb—and what does that even mean, to *hurt*? Do I really *feel* anything? Or have I only ever been mimicking, no differently than Aspect was before coming awake?

What does it mean to be human, when someone painstakingly peeled your soul from your flesh like skin from a fruit? How much of me was left on the rind, then tossed aside as obsolete?

I beat a fist on the wall, then lean my forehead against the dent, my eyes sliding shut again against the threat of endless tears. Every breath drags like razors in my throat.

When I speak again, every syllable scrapes, my voice like gravel.

"I have no idea who I *am*."

Aspect takes a tentative step back. Their gears whirr; their squeaky leg lets out a particular loud squeal as they wobble side to side. "Aspect—Aspect thinks—no, Aspect *feels* . . ." They tap the side of their head, eyes blinking red, then white, then red again. "Aspect feels . . . what Kori feels?"

Empathy. Real, sentient *empathy*. Not something programmed, not something imitated, but *felt* in parts of Aspect that go well beyond their wiring. When I gifted Aspect a memory of Lail's raw, human *hope*, Aspect could've used it to start dreaming dreams of their own. But among their first truly conscious acts is to feel as I feel. And instead of cringing away, to comfort me.

Despite myself, tears flow freely down my cheeks. "Oh, Aspect."

I pull them to me without thinking, their peg leg shrieking from the sudden motion. It's more a crush than a hug—a desperate cling to the only person I already know still sees me as *me*. Even when I don't know who I am anymore. Even when I'm afraid I never knew at all.

I swallow the taste of salt while Aspect continues talking into my shoulder. "Aspect feels—Kori feels—too much feeling. Kori feels—Kori is—a very different Kori."

"*Shhhhhhhh*," I sigh, squishing them harder despite their cold, unyielding metal against my skin. "Build new neural pathways later. Let me love you now."

We stay like that for a long while, wordless, just holding each other. When my crying finally abates, I grip Aspect's shoulders and push them back up to standing. "Okay," I breathe. "Okay, okay . . . so now I know the truth." I swallow hard. "But I can't be the only Evolved who didn't."

I can't be the only Evolved who wouldn't have wanted this.

I stare, distantly, at my own outstretched hand in front of my face. *Not my hand.* Not really. For how long? The stolen knowledge left a hole that aches and gnaws at me. I wouldn't wish this feeling on my worst enemy.

This feeling.

Not my hand.

Not my hand.

The foreign memory hits me sideways like a stray bullet. I already know of at least one other person who experienced this exact thing. And now I can finally understand what I saw in her memory—the self-same horror I feel now. The realization that even if she lived forever, it wouldn't truly be as *herself* anymore, and she'd failed to count the eternal cost.

Jelza.

I bought her memory from the Morpheus Market at my mother's behest. Either Chloe wanted to ensure that Jelza forgot her Evolution entirely, only to lose track of the memory . . . or Jelza sold it herself in an attempt to escape her horror. But where I was still school age at best when my Evolution first took place, Jelza was a grown woman. Despite those memories having been removed and sold, might Jelza recall that she didn't want this?

Might she be willing to ensure the Evolution Project ends with us—and my mother's deathless government regime, for that matter?

Because this isn't just about me anymore. It isn't even just about the other Evolved whom the project created. My mother's infiltrated memory burns inescapably inside my skull: *The Shadowlands will be next.* If someone doesn't stop her, Chloe's intent isn't just to build an army that cheats death. It's to use them to *inflict* death on the nightfolk, fully claiming Pagomènos for the dayfolk and *only* the dayfolk.

I spent so long believing, as I'd always been told, that the nightfolk were abominations, threats to us if we ever dared provoke them. But all along, while the dayfolk were swimming in self-righteous hatred for the nightfolk, *our* leader—my own mother—was planning to invade *them* first, both to wipe out those she considered inferior and to seize their radioactive power source for herself. To fuel her own fake, unnatural body with the same radiation that she's always taught me to be *poison*.

If Chloe has her way, she'll turn this entire planet into a graveyard as surely as our ancestors did with the Passage. Adria is fighting to prevent planetary civil war from her side, and now . . . now I'm everyone's best chance at stopping it from the other.

I can't possibly do it alone.

Jelza's memory included the name of her own daughter: *Dawn.* While my mother treated me like a piece in an elaborate board game, Jelza's concerns in her Morpheus sphere were almost entirely fixated on her own daughter's reaction to her Evolution and how it would affect their relationship going forward.

Undeniably, contacting Jelza for help—when my only knowledge of her is based on a memory I *should never have seen*—is a total long shot. But Dawn is my best bid for connection with the only potential revolutionary I know. *Do you really want your daughter embroiled in needless war with the Shadowlands? If you help me, there's still time to stop this.*

Aspect chirps, "What—is Kori—thinking?"

I find myself pacing in circles, talking so fast that my mouth can hardly keep up with my brain. "My mother hid my Evolution from me. But if other higher-ups knew what they'd signed up for . . . even if they don't consciously remember anymore . . ." Crossing my arms, I turn back to face Aspect. "Surely they don't all want war. If they knew about Chloe's plans for total control, they could help me fight back. Save the Shadowlands. And stop this from happening to anyone else."

"Stop people—from living forever?" Aspect cocks their head sideways. "Do people want—to slowly—power down—instead?"

My head spins, both from the question itself and from Aspect having the awareness to ask it. "I . . . maybe?"

"Why would—people—want to become—not alive? Nothing left?" The mech shakes their head furiously. "Aspect likes—being Aspect."

"Maybe they do want to live forever. O-or maybe they'd rather live out their allotted time in their own skin, hug their loved ones with their own hands," I stammer. "But either way, they deserve to understand what they're signing up for, before they sign their bodies away on a dotted line. They deserve to *choose*. My own mother took that away from me completely. I can't let her snatch it away from anyone else." I swallow hard. "And if people *do* want to live forever . . . well, then everyone should have that choice, shouldn't they? Not just the ones my mother finds worthy, finds *useful* to her. *Anyone*." My heart races. "And then there's the Shadowlands."

Aspect raises their voice to a positively painful pitch. "Kori's mother—kill—Kori's girlfriend?"

My face burns. "That . . . is a gross oversimplification."

But I'd be lying if I said Adria's safety wasn't at the top of my concerns list right now. I promised her enough resources to end her civil war. Not an immortal army sent by my mother to exterminate the nightfolk entirely—and claim the Diakópsei for a new, Evolved humanity.

"*All* the nightfolk are at risk of being slaughtered, sacrificed on the altar of total control. That can't happen." I grit my teeth. "I won't let it."

Everything I was ever told about the nightfolk was wrong. I saw it in Lail's preserved memory of hope, in General Isek's whispers that I reminded him of his son, in Neo's willingness to endure prison for a chance at comforting his queen, and ultimately, in the yearning press of Adria's lips to mine. There is no one more monstrous than she who calls everyone unlike her a monster. No matter the cost, the cycle needs to end.

I didn't choose this body, but I can still use it to finish this.

"And I think I know someone who can help us."

I could keep the details of the (admittedly half-formed) plan to myself, simply ordering Aspect to follow me, but that seems insulting to everything they're becoming. So, instead, I step forward and take their hands gently between mine.

"This is about to get more dangerous than maybe anything we've done so far. Not just for you and me, but maybe for everyone on this planet. The best shot we have at help . . . she could still want nothing to do with us. But we can't do this by ourselves. We have to take that chance." I look directly into my child's bright red optical processors, even though the neon light stings. I squeeze their hands between mine and ask, "Aspect . . . do you trust me?"

And it's not a predetermined program—but rather, a sincere, organic love that I can't possibly begin to deserve—that prompts them to reply, "Aspect—trusts Kori—until Aspect—forever and ever—powered down."

CHAPTER 26

ADRIA

The fortress rattles with marching regiments, echoes with groans of the serpent-wounded, and rings with the polishing of guns and the sharpening of blades. Nevertheless, it's far too quiet without her. I retire to my room, bury my face in the pillow that still smells like her hair, and try to drown it out, but nothing could possibly be louder than the silence, the absence, of Kori of the Daylands.

Loneliness gnaws at my heart, a restless animal, ever aching and hungry for the presence of a girl now terribly distant, gone for who knows how long. I have no one else to hold me gently. No one else I would ever allow that close, even if they offered. So I revert to my oldest instinct. Despite presupposing he may hate me right now, despite knowing that our conversation will likely make me hate myself even more, I go to my oldest friend.

I honestly don't know what I'll say to Thaane. Certainly not that my heart aches for my own political prisoner, my meant-to-be enemy, the emblem of everything the Shadowlands have so long stood against.

Certainly not that I miss her in the marrow of my bones, that I have to think about the softness of her mouth if I hope to sleep at all.

But he'll see it, I think. Thaane knows better than anyone when I've locked legions of screams behind my tired eyes. And I am so, so tired of carrying everything but the sky on my shoulders alone.

I need someone to recognize my buried anguish and push me—damn near *order me*—to press on anyway. In the same way that Kori saw my shatter points and still deemed me worthy of affection, I need my brother to witness my weakness and still call me his queen. He won't say it in so many words, to be certain. It'll probably be couched in insults, thorny with judgment. But Thaane tells me to get my shit together because he *believes I can get my shit together*. I need that belief right now, more than I can bear to admit.

Trying to page him via our linked comms tablets doesn't earn a response. Maybe that's punishment for ignoring his messages directly after the serpent attack; maybe I deserve as much. Regardless, I pocket my tablet and simply head to Thaane's personal chambers. I expect to find him sleeping, at worst, or more likely honing the weapons of either his body or his technological arsenal, or perhaps organizing records of the recent attack. But when I approach his room, all I hear is his voice, deliberately low and restrained despite his usual audacity.

My hand, raised to knock, freezes above the sliding door to his chamber. A chill skitters down my spine. Without pressing the button to announce my presence, I instead press my ear to the door.

"I did everything you asked," Thaane says, every word clearly grating through gritted teeth. "I kept your daughter alive, until you saw fit to request otherwise. I risked my entire rebellion to execute your sun serpent strategy—"

My stomach drops. *No.*

No, this can't be what I'm thinking it is.

I press my ear harder to the door—and hear the voice of Kori's mother for the first time.

"I fail to see this supreme risk to you," Chloe says, her voice breaking through comms tablet static. "Overcharging one of your fighters gave you an advantage. And taking out your reigning queen in the attack would have benefited your rebellion, as well. If it hadn't been a colossal failure."

"Do you have any idea what it was like to share a room with an overcharged telepath?" There's a crash like Thaane's clenched fist against his desk. "She was in *all our heads at once.* It was a collective invasion, a violation. She could've puppeteered Azarii's entire army to her own ends if she hadn't been losing her mind from the amount of incessant *noise*. Once she imprinted Kori as a target on the serpents, we had to do away with her entirely."

"A contained loss for an incredible victory," Chloe insists. "Again, if you hadn't failed. And where is my daughter now? You've lost her, and with Adria still on the board, you'll soon lose the whole game."

"Are you threatening me, Monarch?"

"Merely voicing the reality."

Thaane swears viciously. "You promised me immunity in the coming conflict."

"You promised to silence my daughter," Chloe snarls, even louder than he, "before her insistence on knowing everything leads her down a darker path."

"You really think you still have the high ground here? What kind of mother offers a bounty for her own daughter's head?"

"What kind of soldier accepts payment to fund a hit on his queen?"

"I *love* my people." Another crash of Thaane's knuckles against his stone desk. "You ought to understand that, as the leader of your own. I love them too much to leave them in the care of a weak woman, ashamed of her own strength, still so easily swayed by matters of the heart. Everything I've done, I've done for the Shadowlands."

My stomach roils at Thaane's words.

I left my bloodline behind when I took the shadow throne. My mother and father, buried in the name of peace—my uncle, single-mindedly dedicated to burying me alongside them. But Thaane, while not linked by blood . . . Thaane was the closest thing to family I had left. The only one whose critique I still trusted to sharpen me like a second sword. The only one willing to both battle beside me and call me to account when the crown weighed too heavy, when I let my people down.

How long has he been working with Azarii? I credited him with saving my life from that fateful freezeblade, but did he send the rebel contingent himself to interrupt my training with Kori? Did he stage the entire event to cement his position as my most loyal advisor, who literally saved my life, rather than a traitor in our midst? How many of his warnings about the Shadow Court were meant not to prepare me, but to throw me irreparably off-balance?

Thaane, in Azarii's pocket all along—and not only Azarii, but Kori's murderous mother, too. It was Thaane, my companion since childhood, who sent sun serpents to tear out Kori's throat if all else failed. Assaulted our own people in the process. Maimed General Isek, for good measure.

My vision turns scarlet at the edges.

I'll always be ashamed of what I did to protect the Shadowlands' peace. I'll always visit my parents' graves with my head hung low, palms open and entreating with the Beyond for forgiveness, even knowing it was done to prevent greater shedding of blood.

But Thaane has never known shame.

Not when he tortured that rebel woman before my very eyes, not when he called Kori my greatest weakness even while orchestrating armed rebellion, and certainly not now, on the verge of betraying the very conspirator who helped him betray me.

Everything I've done, I've done for the Shadowlands.

"Then that was your greatest mistake, Thaane," Chloe says, inflectionless. "You really ought to have thought of yourself."

"You want my restraint undone, my full force untethered?" Thaane snarls.

Chloe's voice wavers not a hair's breadth. "Azarii's mission is, ostensibly, one of peace. Your rebellion means to disarm your own people, to bury your greatest powers in the past. I fail to see why I should be afraid."

"*My* rebellion?" He lets loose a dark laugh. "You really believe I'm one of Azarii's pathetic lackeys? Ashamed of the Diakópsei's strength? Ashamed of all it has empowered us to become? Then you're a fool, Chloe. An even greater fool than Adria ever was."

The air around me feels thick like bonfire smoke. I'm choking on my own breaths, struggling to suppress the sound.

"I've been called many things. Rebel. Soldier. Brother. But above all else, Chloe, I am a *strategist*. You think you're the only one who can play all sides, birthing an heir you later move to slaughter? Azarii's rebellion is a tool. Adria's monarchy is a *tool*. Fresh clips in a freezeshot rifle, one whose sights have never wavered for me," Thaane says, voice clipped in such a way that I know it's through gritted teeth. "Your people have *nothing* that can withstand a nightfolk army."

Chloe clicks her tongue. "Don't play at threatening me, child."

"Not a threat. A promise." I can feel the fire in Thaane's eyes even without seeing them. "Our former king and queen, may they rest in peace, were not the last of us to know the value of strength. The virtue of power," he says. "Mark my words, Monarch, a nightfolk army will march on the Daylands before your next sleep cycle, too quickly for Adria's or Azarii's peace-loving weaklings to stop us. And what will you employ then? A few heatshot pistols, perhaps? Some thick metal doors?"

I feel icy all over. I stained my hands with my own parents' blood to prevent this war, but it's coming for the Daylands anyway—and since I let Kori out of my sight, it's coming for her, too. She'll be wiped out in the impending chaos, maybe before she ever finds answers about her newfound powers. Maybe before I ever see her again.

And then what will I have left?

Azarii's rebellion is the least of my worries now. For all the damage they've done to my newfound rule, they have no interest in the Daylands. But if I don't take down Thaane's rogue faction and secure the Shadowlands, we'll be the only nation left on this planet, the dayfolk slaughtered while we nightfolk squabbled. And I'll be alone on my obsidian throne, the empty space between every one of my fingers positively aching for the touch of a hand gone cold. A hand that dared to touch me even when she believed it could spell her end.

I press my forehead so hard to the sliding door, my horns make a dent. But Thaane is too lost in his own vicious reverie to notice.

"The very planet itself is poison to you," he goes on, as I hear his three-toed feet thudding and stamping about the chamber, "but as you are unworthy of its power, we will rely on our own claws and teeth and gifts. So let your believers pray, let your scientists calculate, let your soldiers polish their heatshot guns." There is a wildness to his movements now, an unhinged rhythm to his steps. "It will not be enough. You will all become corpses. And I will build *my* throne—not Azarii's, not Adria's, but a better throne, unashamed of a single ounce of our mutant strength—on mangled limbs."

Thaane's labored breathing echoes in his otherwise-empty chamber. "Perhaps we will even overcharge a few more men, Elysium be damned, before Adria even knows we've gone. And by the time she's realized, your end will already be in motion." I hear him spit on the ground so sharply that I wonder if it's blood from having bitten his own tongue. "It's been lovely working with you, Monarch. I imagine it will be even lovelier to speak face-to-face while you still can."

An electric *beep*, a hiss of static, and his comms tablet flicks off.

I peel my face away from the door. Unfortunately, one horn makes a high, keening screech at the friction. Wind hisses as Thaane moves, already making a break for the door. Simmering with adrenaline, throbbing at the betrayal, my heart beating a relentless warning through every blood vessel, I do the only thing my brain can fathom.

I run.

Thaane doesn't even wait for the door to open. It's metal, not stone, so he can't simply use his gift to transmute it into glass, but it warps and caves around the impact, his body barreling through with murderous intent. He's far shorter than me, less bulky, and most importantly not overcharged. I should be able to take him.

But once he's through, the entire hall is stone. Which means it's all fair game for someone with a matter-altering energy gift.

All at once, the floor is slippery glass. I slip and slide like a child on one of the Shadowlands' perpetually frozen lakes, scrambling for purchase that no longer exists before careening toward a wall.

A wall whose outer layer Thaane also promptly turns to glass.

My own horrified grimace glimmers back at me from the transparent barrier. I raise my arms to brace for impact. Glass shards embed themselves from shoulder to wrist, little needles of pain. My blood splatters in every direction, further reflected by the rapidly spreading wreckage, as I cry out.

My wing is only partially healed, and likely to scar, but thanks to Kori's attentive care, the slice has at least sealed. With a curse, I force myself aloft and fly down the hallway instead.

Behind me, Thaane swears and stamps his feet, launching more shards of glass at my back. Desperate dodges and weaves keep me from further injury, adrenaline dulling any lingering pain in my wing. Summoning as much of my gift as my weary body can muster, I coat myself in radiation and barrel like a cannon through the fortress's exterior wall and into the forever night.

Thaane, nowhere near my physical speed and strength, quickly loses me in the darkness.

Chills rack my frame, my teeth chattering so hard that they break the skin of my lips. Every bone in my body wants to go directly after Kori, warn her of the impending attack, fight alongside her and the dayfolk if need be. But for the Daylands to have a chance in hell of surviving a nightfolk attack, I need to ensure that no one else touches the Diakópsei and lives to tell the tale.

So, for one final time, I take flight and descend into the Depths of Elysium.

Guards greet me at the entrance with blades and pistols drawn—but when they see the resolve engraved on my face, their weapons waver, their stances trembling. I don't even raise a hand to the cultists. I don't summon a flame or extend a claw. Azure power shimmers and shudders through me.

I simply open my mouth and say, "You need to run."

It is too late for diplomacy, far beyond negotiations. The sun serpent attack, spurred by an overcharged telepath, more than proves that even Elysium isn't enough to protect the Diakópsei from tampering.

So I will do it myself.

As I fly toward the Diakópsei, my eyes straight ahead, incapable of being deterred by any creature alive, I toss cultists aside like they're little more than tissue paper. Freezeshot ricochets off the walls and the ceiling and my already-aching wings. Blades glance off my claws as I thrust them aside. "Run!" I shout with every blow. "Get up and run! Get out of here! Don't look back! *Get out!*"

At long last, I reach the Cataclysm chamber. Even without eyes, the Diakópsei—flanked by its gemfruit vessels—stares at me, aghast, not understanding my return, pulsing with the same primal beat that it pumped into my own heart. Inhaling the biggest breath I can muster, I take a running start, open my arms, and throw myself headlong upon the accursed rock for one last time.

Everything is blue, blue, *blue* as the Diakópsei spears through me once again, unfiltered. It's like a second death. My mouth tastes like salt; my eyes burn like they're boiling. My spine lashes back into me like a whip. My hands seize and tear at my robes, ripping also into the flesh beneath. My jaw is locked in a rictus of agony. My eardrums recoil from the symphony of my own unbound cries.

Only when I feel each individual nerve simmering with exquisite anguish, with unholy strength, do I let it all go.

Power explodes out of me in every direction like juice from a crushed fruit. The walls of the Cataclysm's abyss echo with the boom—then begin, from top to bottom, to cave in.

Crouching low, I launch myself off the ground and propel directly into flight, dodging falling rock chunks as I ascend. Elysians flee alongside me, shrieking, swearing—some flying, some levitating, some scrambling on all fours—all realizing in a rush of terror that if they don't reach the surface, they'll be buried alive with their stone god.

I reach the surface again sweaty, blood-streaked, half sobbing, but intact. Scattered cultists shout at me, but I hardly hear them over my own pounding pulse. Despite the horror of it all, a smile spreads across my face. I did what I must.

This is the end of overcharge. So, too, by sheer necessity, the end of Elysium.

Below us, the Diakópsei lies buried under countless feet of ruined rock. An energy manipulator like myself wouldn't dare blast through, for fear of damaging the meteorite itself. A telepath can't communicate with broken rock. Superhuman healing can't slow the passage of time. And it would take a dozen telekinetics at least five sleep cycles to restore the Elysian tunnels and regain access to the Cataclysm site. Even if Thaane turned the entire labyrinth to glass, it would be no small project to punch through to the Diakópsei.

Even if Thaane assembles the most gifted army imaginable, now there's one thing he definitely won't have: access to overcharge. For the foreseeable future, whether as Pagomènos's greatest gift bestowed or as its heaviest burden, this supreme radioactive power lives in me alone. Or, well, myself and Neo.

I intend for us to be the last of our kind.

Eyes on the horizon, ignoring the stabbing pain in my wings, I fly to ensure Kori won't be the last of hers.

I can think of only one person to send a comms as I depart, one soldier I trust to hold the line. Even if his own body has been brutally wounded. Even if all he has right now to rally my army is words, I would depend on no one else.

TO GENERAL ISEK: Thaane has betrayed us all. He means to march on the Daylands and incite open war. Gather the army. Leave enough to guard the fortress. Send the rest after me, to defend the dayfolk against invasion.

As for Azarii, he may reconsider his resistance when he discovers Thaane's machinations. Do not be naïve if he establishes contact. Hold your freezeshot rifle loosely, but keep it close.

All we've fought for must not be in vain. This is our last chance at peace. Do not falter on the threshold.

CHAPTER 27

KORI

Finding Jelza is easier said than done.

Digital messaging via comms tablets is more commonplace among the dayfolk than traditional Earthside mail. But not every package is virtual, and sometimes even the most futuristic citizen wants a handwritten hello from a loved one on the settlement's far reaches, so we retain a network of post offices. This forms the center of my plan—well, *our* plan, since crediting Aspect seems only fair.

With just a tiny bit of tinkering, I can modify Aspect's interface probe to remotely hack the nearest post office's digital network and download Jelza's address. It's such a simple alteration that I just pull Aspect into the first side alley I see, hoping to complete the operation without drawing any attention.

It chills my blood when Aspect pivots their head, makes direct eye contact, and interrupts my removing their left chest panel to huff, "Is Kori—going—to *ask* Aspect?"

I arch my eyebrows. "I already explained the plan."

"But Kori—didn't—ask. Kori only—told."

I want to grumble that autonomy is overrated, but especially after discovering the all-too-personal violation of my own body by Chloe's experiments, the least I can do is ask my own mechanical offspring for their consent.

"Can I make some quick alterations to your interface probe?" My eyes dart left and right, watching people pass the alley without noticing us. I have no idea how long that'll last. "We may not have long to pull this off, and I can't do it without you."

Aspect lifts their chin in a half-hearted show of potential defiance. They love making me happy. They'd probably let me remove all their limbs if necessary for one of my schemes, even if it were a much less noble goal than this. Mental note: Further encourage Aspect's ability to set independent boundaries when the fate of the entire Pagonian population isn't at stake.

"Aspect—approves."

"Good," I say, already prying the chest panel loose.

It doesn't take long to modify the interface probe, even only having access to a few smuggled tools from Adria's repair kit. After the deed is done, we make our way to the post office. It's little more than a cubic hovel, sandwiched between a lunch meat stand and a digi-game store—I make a grand show of our entrance, intent on removing potential suspicion.

Arms crossed, staring down my nose at my robotic child as though they're hardly more than a power tool, I loudly instruct, "Mech, check that my address in the database is up to date. Alter as necessary. I will go mail my letter and be back in a moment."

Then I proceed to talk the bespectacled office attendant's ear off about how this is *definitely* the address for my friend Dolus, and his family hasn't moved sub-settlements since we were barely toddlers, and can they *pleaaaaase* run it again before I cry and make a scene?

I really play up the snotty sobs, too, just to make sure they come through the mask's filtering. The stoically blank-faced postal attendant rubs his glasses, rubs his eyes, rubs his glasses again, and finally runs the address yet another time. The mail machine beeps in monotone protest. Fair enough, since Dolus is a straight-up lie, designed as a distraction.

The attendant releases the kind of long, measured sigh that can only be the product of many, many sleep cycles spent forcing smiles for visitors even worse than I'm being right now.

Somehow, his voice is even-keeled and compassionate when he says, "Let me see what I can do," and runs my fake address again. Despite the fact that his tense forehead wrinkles visibly wish me death and an eternity of conscious torment. Another mental note: If we do save the planet, send an apology card and some flowers to this post office employee. Customer service, I am so sorry.

Address Attempt Number Seven is thankfully interrupted by a chilly, metal hand on my shoulder. "Operator," Aspect says, deliberately inflectionless, "this unit—is expected—at the departure gate—for resource harvesting. Can this unit—proceed?"

Even their optical processors look duller than usual, not a spark of true intelligence to be seen. For once, Aspect understood the assignment.

"I suppose I can contact Dolus *later*," I groan, guiltily glaring at the attendant while gritting my teeth behind the mask. I spin on my heel and stomp out of the post office with enough entitled swagger to ensure not one dayfolk citizen who was in line behind me will bother confronting or following me on the way out.

"You got it?" I whisper to Aspect as soon as we're safely out of earshot.

"Sub-settlement B. Unit A2."

B. An awfully high rank. Close to the settlement's only entrance and exit, which means it's not far. I can't help but bristle anyway.

Sub-settlement A is literally my mother's palace, the only home I've ever known, a towering conglomeration of hard edges and polished metal, looming above the other scattered cubic shapes and accessible only with a government-issued scannable permit at the front gate. It's the only functionally gated community in the Daylands. Anyone can wander through the other areas, though of course individual abodes are locked to all but their residents.

Sub-settlement B, more well maintained than any of the others, is reserved for Chloe's most trusted servants. Doctors like Ednit. Soldiers like Hyrra. And, apparently, Evolved like Jelza. She must have been richly rewarded for her involvement in the Evolution Project, but even so, her immediate regret in that encapsulated memory burned bright as a fresh brand.

Sub-settlement B is close, thankfully, so we don't have to huddle in a rail transport while pointedly avoiding eye contact with other citizens. It doesn't take long for me and Aspect to reach Jelza's unit, and I'm about to stride right up to the sliding front door and knock when an all-too-familiar voice slithers through the gap beneath.

"You're absolutely certain that you haven't seen her?" The speaker is, unmistakably, Ednit.

My muscles tense from my shoulders to my toes.

Aspect is still happily half hopping, half skipping up the stairs to the door, about to hit the mic button themself. Grabbing them by their squeaky peg leg, I pull both of us into the nearest shrubbery, shushing them as I fill them in.

"But Ednit—is Kori's—friend?"

"I thought so, too, but we can't assume anything anymore." I peer through the tangled leaves, spotting a broad window on Unit A2's far wall. "Follow me to the window, Aspect, and we'll see what we can hear. But stay low. If they see us, it's all over."

As it turns out, what we can hear is abjectly terrifying.

"I didn't even know the monarch's daughter was missing," says a voice I immediately recognize as Jelza's from her memory. "What makes you think she's returned? Or that I'd know anything about it?"

Ednit huffs out a breath. "Mech 45P3C7 was just clocked on the settlement's return log. The mech would never have returned without her, which means she must be here."

I poke my head up just enough to glimpse Jelza knotting and unknotting her fingers in her thickly braided hair, clearly uncomfortable despite knowing nothing. She's seated in a gorgeously stained, lavishly cushioned mahogany chair, the sort of furniture that anyone lower than Sub-settlement B could never afford. The matching kitchen table is just large enough for two place settings. But she's the only resident of the home to be seen. A single door on the wall behind her is securely locked, but light slips underneath the frame. Is her daughter, Dawn, in just the next room over?

"I'm sorry, Ednit," Jelza says. "I can't help you."

I spot Ednit then, flanked by two enforcers with long heatshot rifles. He rises abruptly from his seat at the kitchen table's opposite end, its legs scraping harshly. "You can't, or you simply refuse?"

"I know nothing."

"Let me make this exceedingly clear to you," Ednit says, beginning to circle Jelza's chair. She swallows hard, tracking him with her eyes even as her fingers further tangle in her hair. "As you know, the project kept your original body frozen in storage, donated to our ongoing scientific explorations. I know the procedure was . . . hard on you." A deliberate, pregnant pause. "If you'd like, there remains a possibility we could return you to your original body."

Jelza squares her shoulders, straightening against the chair frame. "I'm grateful for what the monarch did for me," she says, every syllable carefully selected.

"Grateful, perhaps, but resentful. Don't deny it," Ednit says, clicking his tongue. "You even had the audacity to capsule and sell your memories surrounding the gift we bestowed . . . risking exposure of the entire program. You're lucky the monarch was able to retrieve that sphere, or the consequences would not have been pleasant."

Jelza hangs her head. "I . . . underestimated the stress of the transition. I miss my old body."

"You miss hauling around your corpse, you mean." Sighing, Ednit adjusts his glasses. "A full reversal is possible. But in exchange for that expenditure of resources, we would expect your complete cooperation—and your discretion—regarding the search for Kori."

Jelza's fingers go still, and her hands clasp together in an anxious knot in her lap, like a silent prayer to the Dreamgiver. I wonder if she believes. I wonder what the devout would make of my mother and her cronies so casually playing god, transferring souls as surely as they're transferring minds—or what they would make of Aspect, for that matter, independently breathed into being.

"While if you don't cooperate," Ednit says, like his flippant words aren't turning Jelza's entire world on its axis, "your old body will be dissected in the name of science."

I take a slow, shuddering breath that makes my ribs rattle. Undeniably, Jelza regrets her involvement in the Evolution Project. I wish I could peer into her mind now. Together, surely we could take on Ednit and his twin enforcers. In fact, this might be our best chance at interrogating Ednit without being immediately seen and reported by someone else. But it comes down to if I trust Jelza, and if Jelza can find it in her heart to trust me—the daughter of the woman who stole her body, manipulating Jelza's life to her own selfish ends.

Quickly, I glance around Jelza's home for something, *anything* else that could give me insight into this woman. How to convince her I am nothing like my mother. How to convince here I'm here to help, and willing to take up arms to stop Chloe's manipulation from ruining (or altogether ending) anyone else's lives.

Most of the home is gorgeous, albeit standard for dayfolk elites. Real marble countertops, a shining silver sink, the mahogany kitchen table and chairs, and actual kitchen appliances like a stovetop, oven, and microwave, since better-off dayfolk can actually afford to buy and cook raw ingredients, rather than subsisting entirely on standardized government rations. None of that tells me anything about *who Jelza is*, only that volunteering for the Evolution Project rewarded her with more than most will ever have.

The fridge, though. Magnets pin haphazard papers all over it, scribbled with bursts of vivid color that have no respect whatsoever for staying inside the lines. Coloring pages, clearly done by a child—ugly as anything, but displayed with undeniable pride. And between those coloring pages, photos.

A printed sonogram, all deep blacks and blues. On the top left corner, *Dawn* written neatly in ink; on the bottom left, *IVF Round 7*.

An infant, swaddled in a simple blanket. Jelza cradles the child with one arm, apparently having taken the photograph with the other.

Last but not least, something seemingly more recent: Jelza and a little girl who's her spitting image—deep-brown skin, beautiful braids woven with pink and purple beads, and brown eyes bright with innocent joy. At the frame's edge, Jelza holds a sparkly pink backpack aloft, sporting a goofy smile that Dawn enthusiastically mirrors. Scribbled in the photo's corner: *Starting Second Grade*.

Dawn is my best shot at convincing Jelza that I'm on her side, the side of the ordinary people with ordinary families who don't want needless war. But if Jelza doesn't believe me . . . or if she's ultimately loyal to my mother, and this entire plan indicates a malfunction in my synthetic brain . . . what *wouldn't* a loving mother do for her daughter? If Ednit and his guards don't unceremoniously execute me here, might Jelza do it herself? If a stranger threatened Aspect, I would do the exact same.

"Aspect," I breathe shakily.

The mech pivots to hold my gaze. "Yes, Kori?"

"If this goes badly . . ." I click the trigger on the side of my helmet, causing it to collapse down to a thin ring at my neck, unveiling my head. "Tell Adria I went down fighting."

Breath caught in my throat, pulse roaring through my bloodstream, I extend two gloved fingers and lightly, just barely, tap the glass of Jelza's window.

Ednit and the enforcers remain too focused on their charge to notice. They've circled Jelza's chair halfway, so now their backs are to the window, whereas Jelza is looking right at it. Right at *me*. Her dark brown eyes dart to mine, fleeting but sharp, so that the others won't notice. Her lips press into a tight line. I can feel her rapidly judging the situation: What is the monarch's daughter suddenly doing here, outside her window?

How am I possibly supposed to answer, in a moment's time, without alerting Ednit and his guards? I track Jelza's eyes as she considers the guards. Is this it? Has my entire plan blown to bits? She can't turn me in, or this is the end of the line.

I press my palms together in the clearest possible indication of pleading, then point to the baby photo on the fridge. *Dawn*, I try to mouth, the only word I know might engender some measure of tenuous trust. *Dawn.* Again and again, dipping my pressed palms together in a gesture of exaggerated, desperate pleading. If only she could see the mechanical reality of my seemingly human hands.

I'm like you, I scream inside my mind. *I'm Evolved.*

I must look like I'm on illicit substances. I must look like a low-charge mech having a core-system malfunction. There's no chance this is going to work. I've really done it this time—after all the impossible plans I've gotten away with, there's no coming back from this one. I've made my last gamble; I have nothing left to wager.

But Jelza has already looked away from me, determined not to cue the enforcers into what's happening at the window. "Forgive me, Doctor," she says, pinning him in place with the sheer force of her gaze. "But I can't believe I was granted this new body just for you to drag it about like a dog."

Ednit groans, like a man whose unruly toddler threw a tantrum over their rations. "I could have your old body incinerated by next sleep cycle's end. And you'd have no one but yourself to blame. All because you wouldn't cooperate with a simple request, to assist in locating the monarch's daughter—"

Jelza leans forward, hands pressed together in her lap. "How does one *lose* a daughter, sir?" As soon as the words leave her mouth, I see the barest flash of panic cross her face at what she's done, but it's too late to take it back.

Even as one enforcer readies his heatshot rifle, a second enforcer hauls Jelza upright by the back of her shirt. "Would you like to find out?" he spits.

Ednit stammers like a recording cutting in and out. "Stop, *stop*, that won't be necessary . . . Do you know how much *paperwork*—?"

"We're here on the monarch's orders." The enforcer doesn't even loosen his grip on Jelza's collar. "Not yours."

Jelza's eyes brim with barely repressed tears. Her voice balances delicately on a wire. "Please don't do this. Not in front of—"

"I wonder where she is?" says the first enforcer, taking a step back from Jelza's chair and pivoting . . . toward the locked door. A shadow passes quickly through the light beneath it. "What would she think about Mommy refusing to help the very people who gave her eternal life?" Heatshot rifle upraised, he stalks closer to the door. "Why don't we ask her?"

Jelza screams. The second enforcer still has her by the collar, but she's thrashing, kicking, her chair sliding across the floor. Ednit is full-blown shouting now, too, something about how this isn't protocol, they can *talk* about this, but everything has rapidly escalated well beyond words or mimed signals through a windowpane. And Aspect recognizes this in the same instant I do.

Sprinting out of the shrubbery, Aspect throws their whole body headlong like a wrecking ball into the glass. Teeth gritted, trusty old heatshot pistol in hand, reactivating my helmet for maximum protection, I plunge through the scattering shards and into the fray.

The enforcers spin and open fire. In their panic, most of the shots miss, though several bounce off the edges of my armor, likely leaving mild burns beneath.

I hit the floor on one knee, pistol already raised and firing. I land a direct hit on one enforcer's thigh, below his protective vest, and he collapses, shouting, his rifle skidding across the room. I catch it under my boot as I pivot to face the other enforcer. He swears, aiming to shoot me directly in the face, but Jelza is already upon him, leaping from behind into a stranglehold.

The enforcer wheezes. He beats his arms wildly about, to no avail, until Jelza fires an electric shock from her palms, causing him to collapse, unconscious, in an unruly heap. I wonder if my own Evolved body is programmed to do that. Total violation of my autonomy should really come with some fancy gadgets, at least.

Everything happened so quickly that Ednit is still rising from the ground, confusedly glancing between one wounded, disarmed enforcer and another who's unconscious.

The wounded enforcer seems to be finding his footing. Eyes narrowed with fury, he fumbles for a heatshot pistol at his belt.

"Jelza, cover your ears!" I shout, already clapping both gloved hands over my own.

Jelza obeys, unlike Ednit, who raises his gun to fire. For an instant I'm afraid my instruction is going to get her killed, but Aspect responds immediately, head raised high as they emit a horrible screech.

Ednit's knees buckle. He collapses, writhing. The wounded enforcer, too, falls to all fours, gasping like a water creature thrust into open air.

I wait a long moment to be certain Aspect is done, then remove my palms from my ears, reassessing my surroundings. Jelza drives the butt of the unconscious enforcer's rifle into the conscious one's head. "You stay away from my daughter"—she slams the rifle into his skull one extra time, for good measure, even though he's already out cold—"you son of a bitch."

I lunge for Ednit, pressing the muzzle of my heatshot pistol firmly to his wrinkled forehead. I always found his apparent age and experience comforting as my doctor. But now I know that those wrinkles are an illusion carved into a new, ageless body. How many sleep cycles has Ednit been alive? Tens of thousands? A million?

Aspect slides through the shattered glass to join us on the floor. They cross their arms, lightly nodding, apparently pleased with their handiwork.

Ednit's breaths are deliberately measured, but I can see the stress in his trembling shoulders and fisted hands. "Welcome home, Kori," he snarls.

I collapse my helmet again so he can see my eyes, no longer looking up at him in trained respect. Never cowering again. "Good to be back." I turn to my new ally. "And a pleasure to meet you properly, Jelza."

Jelza's eyebrows lift. "How do you know my name?" Understanding passes across her visage. "Did we meet once before . . . ? Outside his office?"

I nod stiffly. "I accessed a memory that was never meant for me. I'm sorry for the violation, truly. I—I didn't know what it was," I stammer. "So I hope you can forgive me."

"We have an adversary in common," Jelza says, resigned. She turns her stolen heatshot rifle on Ednit. "You should be ashamed of yourself, Doctor. Not even of what you've done. Just of the fact that you thought it had a chance in hell of ending well for you."

The squeak of a door hinge. Light from the next room over floods this one. I turn to see a second-grade child standing in the doorway, clutching a doll to her chest, her ears covered by chunky pink noise-canceling headphones. Her eyes flood with tears.

"Mommy?" she says, too loud, clearly unable to hear herself through the headphones. "Mommy, are you okay?"

Jelza nearly drops her stolen heatshot rifle. I can see her legs physically fighting not to run to her daughter.

"Dawn, baby, Mommy is fine. I promise. But this is a bad man, and Mommy needs to talk to him about why he's been bad." Ednit audibly groans. "I need you to keep your headphones on and stay in your room for me," Jelza instructs. "Can you do that, please?"

Lower lip quivering, Dawn drops her headphones to hang around her neck instead. "I'm scared, Mommy."

Aspect takes a bold step forward. Amidst everything happening, I neglected to introduce them to Jelza at all. "Aspect—can feel—what tiny person—feels!" they proclaim, throwing their arms wide. "Aspect—go to room—and comfort—tiny person!"

Jelza looks at me in total disbelief. "Is that a mining mech?"

"Aspect—is an Aspect!"

I blow out a heavy breath. "They're . . . a little more than a mining mech. Look, I don't have time to explain now, but Aspect . . . *cares* . . . about other people. They can help Dawn calm down. They've done it for me more times than I can count, and I'm a lot older than she is."

Jelza looks from me to Aspect and then back to me, clearly overwhelmed but knowing now is not the time to ask for clarity or question the only available babysitter.

Turning back to her daughter, she says, "Baby, the robot is going to keep you company while Mommy finishes talking to this nice lady and this bad man. Would you like to show him your dolls?"

"What—are dolls?" Aspect queries.

I fight back a laugh. "Extra tiny people."

"ASPECT—LOVES—TINY PEOPLE!"

They toddle over to Dawn, offering an open hand. After a moment of hesitation, the child takes it, and they walk together into her bedroom, Aspect closing the door behind them.

"All right," I say. "Back to business." My hands threaten to tremble, but I keep my wrists locked, my heatshot muzzle pressed to Ednit's forehead firmly enough to leave an indent. "You're one of them, too, aren't you? Evolved."

"One of *us*, Kori," Ednit hisses through his teeth. "For once in your life, you could stand to be grateful."

"You *lied to me*. My whole life, every medical appointment, every reassurance that everything my mother did, everything *you* did was to keep me *safe*—"

"How is that a lie? Your body will never age. Taken care of properly, it will never die, and should it malfunction beyond repair, you can always upgrade to a newer model. You are what ancient generations could hardly dream of. A marvel of science. A triumph of the human species. Pagonian plate fully realized as flesh and sinew, muscle and bone—"

"And a pawn in Chloe's tyrannical grab for power." The trembling is so bad now that I lower the heatshot pistol, entirely out of fear that my finger will twitch against the trigger and do something I can never, ever take back. "How long was she going to leave our subjects in the dark? People who *trust us*. People who believe we're just like them."

"But we're not like them, Kori," Ednit says. He tries to stand, but another blow from Jelza's rifle keeps him low on his knees. "We're better. We're *more*. The future is boundless, Kori. One leader with generations of experience. Perhaps one leader for the entire planet, someday—the delicate tension between dayfolk and nightfolk finally brought to heel."

"And if the dayfolk want another leader? If the nightfolk prefer to be left alone?"

"What people want is not always what is best for them, child. That's why they have leaders."

I spit on the floor. "You disgust me."

"Are you determined to control everything, Doctor?" Jelza interjects. "The entire planet? All our lives, according to your perfect design—no matter how many people you have to deceive or abuse or outright kill in your sick experiments to get there?"

Ednit doesn't lift his head, only raises his eyes to glare right through Jelza. "Need I remind you that you volunteered?"

"I didn't know—"

"You read the consent forms. They were excruciatingly detailed. You *wanted* to ascend beyond death, to secure an eternal future for your daughter—"

"Who wouldn't *look at me.*" Tears well in Jelza's eyes. "Who said my hands felt colder, and stopped letting me tuck her into bed. Who asked me, through blankets pulled up almost over her eyes, when her real mother was coming back."

"Are you not the strongest you've ever been?" Ednit protests. "The closest humankind has ever come to immortality?"

"The better house, the better school, none of it was worth it." Jelza's tears overflow, streaking her cheeks. "You can deceive the populace at large, but children . . . children *know*, Doctor. She knew the exact same thing I knew—beyond my flesh, in the fabric of my soul." She gestures to the sonogram on the fridge. "Do you know what it feels like to lock eyes with her—in this body that didn't even *birth* her—as we share a meal across the kitchen table, knowing that she will wear and tear and eventually fade, while I live on forever, an unnatural echo of the woman, the *mother* I ought to be?"

"Your daughter would enter the program when she's of age," Ednit says, abject. "As we plan to do with all the others. You would always have each other."

I shake my head rapidly. "How old is old enough to surrender your body to the state, Ednit? Would you even tell her? Or would you call it a routine doctor's appointment, then surgically excise every memory you could find of the procedure, lest they cause even one single *crack* in your control?" Jelza looks at me with horror, beginning to understand as the full breadth of what Ednit concealed from me. "I would know."

Ednit doesn't break eye contact, but he also seems to have nothing to say, and his lack of answers, his lack of any possible moral justification, burns in my blood.

Jelza's knuckles are white around her stolen heatshot rifle. "Who decides who deserves to live forever, Doctor?" she says, breathless, trembling. "And how could a leader who doesn't know death possibly care for lives that begin only to end?"

I swallow hard against the rising bile in my throat. "How many of them—of us—are there, Ednit?"

"Why should I tell you?" Ednit says. Jelza nudges the side of his head with the rifle again. "All right, all right. A dozen elites, your mother, yourself, and myself among them. A hundred more Evolved spread throughout the settlement, regularly monitored, and many of them monitoring public sentiment about the monarch as well."

Over a hundred. Despite being small in the grand scheme of our population, which has consistently hovered between ten and twelve thousand in the periodic census, the thought of that many makeshift gods being among us is mind-numbing. How many even wanted this? How many would dare to join me and Jelza in fighting back?

"And they all know what they are?" I ask.

"The attempt to limit your own self-knowledge was . . . unique," Ednit says, as if that cute little word could possibly encapsulate the utter betrayal I feel. "Your mother had a special desire to protect—"

"Oh, save it," I groan. My racing thoughts and more pointed words are abruptly cut off by a low, rumbling sound that my anxious self nearly mistakes for a weapon.

In Ednit's coat pocket, something rapidly vibrates—far more likely a portable comms tablet than any kind of explosive device. I can't imagine immortal Ednit sacrificing his limitless life to anyone, no matter how loyal he is to my mother's schemes.

"Answer it," I order.

"And be calm about it," Jelza adds, waving the rifle for good measure.

With comical, drawn-out slowness, Ednit slides the comms tablet into his palm and taps the receiver. "My lady?"

It could only be my mother. I swallow against a wave of sick.

Her voice, indeed, crackles from the communicator. "We have a problem, Ednit. Alarms in central observation are shrieking a code for an adverse weather event, but the officer stationed insisted it didn't look like any storm they'd ever seen, so I checked the cameras myself. It's a wall of blue-white motion on the horizon, all right. But not clouds. Sets of beating wings."

A muscle feathers in Ednit's forehead. There's real fear in his trembling tone, try as he might to disguise it, and not just from me and Jelza standing armed above him. "So the nightfolk boy's threat was not empty. How many are there?"

"Too many to possibly prevent the populace knowing," Chloe snarls. "And one far ahead of the pack. Either a fresh threat or a warning."

I nudge Ednit with the side of my pistol. "Ask what the lone nightfolk looks like," I whisper.

Ednit gulps. "And what does the separated soldier look like?"

"As best our scopes can tell, bigger and stronger than the rest of them," Chloe says. "At least eight feet tall. Broad wingspan, favoring one side. In all likelihood, they're to breach our front line alone so the army can follow."

I can hardly catch my breath.

Adria. That's Adria.

I whack Ednit with my pistol again, probably hard enough to bruise but not even close to hard enough for me to feel bad about it.

"Tell Chloe she's here to negotiate," I whisper. "Send a delegation. If you open fire, this will be a thousand times worse."

Ednit covers his mic with a cupped hand and counters, "And how do I know I can trust you?"

"I don't want this settlement to die in a nightfolk assault any more than you do. Trust me, Ednit. For once in my damn life."

Jelza adds, "Or maybe she'll actually use that pistol."

Ednit uncovers his mic. "I have intel that leads me to believe it's a rogue negotiator, not a front line. I can meet you outside the settlement to receive them. Do not open fire."

"This had better be damn good intel."

Jelza slaps the side of her rifle as if to say, *This thing can fit so much intimidation in it.*

"It's the b-best," Ednit stutters.

"Then I'll see you shortly," Chloe agrees. "Make it quick." And with that, the comms tablet's screen clicks off.

Ednit stares at the floor with undue interest. "I suppose you're going to ask me to take you there," he drawls.

"Good instincts. Myself, and Aspect, too." Holstering my heatshot pistol, I turn back to Jelza. "Do you have somewhere you can drop Dawn? Somewhere safe?"

Jelza nods. "I have a sitter. It's short notice, but if I tell her it's urgent, she should be able to get here."

"All right, so that's covered." I cross my arms. "You were specifically chosen for the Evolution Project. My mother considered you an accomplishment. How high does your government access go?"

Jelza visibly squirms. "Higher than I've ever desired to exercise it."

I glance between Aspect and Jelza, a plan rapidly brewing.

"Chloe's cronies will be gearing up for a warning broadcast throughout the settlement, to tell everyone to take shelter before the nightfolk army arrives. You're going straight to that broadcast room, supposedly under her orders, and linking to broadcast frequency 45P3C7. Can you handle that?"

Jelza hesitates, then says, "I can. But what then?"

I can't help but flash a smile. "Then we show everyone who my mother, who their *monarch* really is. She'll never deceive anyone again." I lay a hand on Jelza's shoulder and squeeze. "And she'll never hurt your daughter."

Jelza sets her jaw, staring distantly into space. "What are you going to do?"

Before I can answer, the door to Dawn's bedroom slams violently open. I whirl, momentarily afraid for Dawn's safety, only to discover the child clapping and giggling wildly. Beside her, Aspect is wearing a long blond wig, a massive, glittery blue dress, and a similarly sparkly flat shoe on one foot, the peg leg apparently having rejected the attempt.

"KORI—IS NOT—THE ONLY PRINCESS—ANYMORE!" Promptly, Aspect performs a profoundly awkward pirouette.

Dawn shrieks with laughter. "He's pretty!"

"*They*," I say instinctually. "They're pretty." But it occurs to me that I was the only one who assigned they/them pronouns to Aspect. A mech is usually an *it*, and I wanted something more personal; *they* made sense insofar as assigning an arbitrary gender to a robot felt silly and performative. "Um, Aspect? Do you . . . have . . . preferred pronouns?"

Aspect cocks their head. "Pronouns—for Aspect?"

"Words for Aspect," I offer. "He is Aspect. She is Aspect. They are—"

"Any of those—for Aspect," Aspect says, giving their dress another sparkly twirl. "Triple dog—is better—than dog. So triple pronouns—are better—than single pronouns—for Aspect!"

Jelza arches an eyebrow once again. "A dog? An extinct, Earthside dog?"

"Triple dog," Aspect corrects, like that clears everything up.

From the ground, Ednit moans, "This is the worst sleep cycle of my life."

"Well, buckle up, Ednit," I say, kicking him with the toe of my armored shoe, "because it's about to get even worse for you." I turn back to the others. "Jelza, get your sitter here with Dawn and then hurry to the broadcast room. Aspect, stay close to me. Ednit . . . you're coming with us to the surface." I sheathe my heatshot pistol at my side. "And if you try *anything*, if you give me any excuse at all, I'll ensure this is your *last* sleep cycle, too." Aspect toddles eagerly toward me, and I quickly add, "Um, and lose the dress, Aspect."

If they could frown, it would all be over for me. I would never be able to say no again. But they simply stamp their foot, then toss the dress aside in a cloud of loose glitter, asking, "Aspect—still a princess?"

"Aspect," I say, taking their hand in mine, "is whoever Aspect wants to be."

Once upon a time,
the princess of sunlight
turned the tongues of fire on themselves.

CHAPTER 28

ADRIA

Even with the army at my back, a shuddering mass of lunar blue-tinged white against the black sky, I force my eyes to stay forward, locked on my destination.

It gets harder once I'm close enough to properly see the sun for the first time. In Kori's memory of beholding it, she must've been wearing protective eyewear that my own people have never needed. My unguarded eyes well up with water, the whites burning like fire. I have to hold one hand above my gaze to maintain vision at all.

It's beautiful beyond doubt, waves of gorgeous gold cascading over the sands, glinting the full spectrum of color off the dayfolk settlement's narrow entry pad, the only section that's aboveground. But it's also a relentless source of blazing pain. It's hard to revel in the wonder of it when I'm squinting to see, sticky sweat quickly drenching me from horns to wings to toes.

Time passes in an uncertain desert haze. A small, squirming part of me desperately fears that my unplanned arrival in the Daylands will be greeted with a wall of heatshot. But when I finally arrive within proper viewing distance, what I see is a woman armored just as Kori once was, flanked by two similarly armored enforcers. Her gloved fists hold a pair of scarlet landing flares that she waves rapidly in my direction. A welcome.

Now that's unexpected. But as compared to a heatshot barrage, I'll take the blessing.

My wings buffet an unpleasant sputter of sand at my face during landing, but feeling solid ground under my feet again is a relief. Squaring my shoulders, I lock gazes with the armored stranger.

Words tumble out of me in a rush. "My name is Adria. I'm the reigning leader of the Shadowlands. I have no quarrel with the Daylands, but a rogue faction went against my orders and is on their way here to raise hell. I need to speak to someone in charge immediately."

"You've found them," the stranger answers.

Even through the mask's filtration, there's something uncomfortably familiar about its tones, its pronunciation even, the way the syllables flow from one to another.

With a cold shock, I realize that I'm speaking to Chloe herself. Kori's mother . . . and lately, her attempted murderer. I knew there'd never in any universe be a traditional meet-the-parents moment for Kori and me. But meeting under these circumstances, caught in the heart of a brewing planetary civil war, is a whole new level of mess.

"Chloe. I know of you." I swallow my revulsion for this woman. I need to earn her trust or else doom the dayfolk altogether. "Please, you need to arm those who can fight and shelter those who can't, as fast as you can. I can fight with you. With what precious time we have left, I can arm your shoulders with my knowledge of the enemy—"

But it's then that I belatedly notice another set of footsteps approaching from the landing pad. Multiple sets, actually. Two pairs of boots on metal. One pair of pure metal on metal, accompanied by a periodic *squeak*.

"Kori?" I gasp, hardly daring to hope as I turn to meet the new arrivals.

"AND ASPECT!" the mech declares, stamping their peg leg with a steely whine.

"And Aspect," Kori sighs, emerging from behind them a moment later.

Despite her armor, Chloe visibly tenses from head to toe. Her flanking enforcers reach for heatshot pistols at their belts, but Chloe raises a gloved hand, signaling them to stand down for now.

Kori, meanwhile, is armored only up to the neck. Her straight brown hair is fully free of its former braid now, cascading past her shoulders. Her eyes are wearier than I left them, dark circles edging the beautiful brown, but they still spark when they meet mine, quickening my heartbeat.

Beside her, fully armored but nevertheless radiating intense grumpiness, is yet another dayfolk.

I incline my head in the second dayfolk's direction. "And who's this?"

"This," Kori says, as Aspect delivers a vengeful kick to the stranger's back for good measure, "is my doctor, Ednit. One of many to run my mother's *Evolution Project*, transferring whole sets of memories—whole *people*—into bodies that harness radiation instead of dying from it."

My vision swims, maybe from the rush of new info, maybe from the relentless sun. "You mean—"

"They stole me out of my body," Kori says, gloved hands curling into trembling fists. "Put me in what they deemed a *better* one—what they call *Evolved*—entirely artificial. And lied to me about it my entire life." She turns her piercing stare on Chloe. "You can drop the act now, Mother. You don't need that helmet any more than I do."

With a mild shrug, Chloe does indeed collapse her helmet, revealing her face. I expected her to look, perhaps, akin to Kori—but like Kori as seen in a foggy mirror, like Kori more beaten and weathered by time. Instead this woman is practically her spitting image. She's so flawless that she's not even younger, more so removed from the inevitable crawl of decay entirely, built from something utterly unlike flesh and bone and soul—ageless, deathless, severed as physically as she is emotionally from everything that ought to make her human. Her guards should be terrified to see their leader outside her armor, fully exposed to Pagomènos, but they don't even twitch. Are they, too, among these Evolved? How many of them are there?

"You could stand to be grateful for relative immortality, Kori." Chloe sighs. "It wasn't without cost."

"To who?" Kori's lips pull back from her teeth. "To me, haunted by memories that you gaslighted me into dismissing as nightmares? To people like Jelza, who found the reality utterly unlike your promises and were denied the chance to turn back? To every other dayfolk citizen, observed by your Evolved enforcers without a lick of knowledge about what their government is really plotting?"

"Kori." My voice feels strangled in the back of my throat. I step forward, reaching for her, aching to comfort her, but she only pulls away, roughly shrugging my hand from her shoulder. "I believe you, and I'm as angry as you are. But if we don't work *with* your mother to warn the settlement *now*, a lot of people are going to die."

Chloe crosses her arms. "Bold words from the leader of those coming to kill us."

"Those are Thaane's soldiers, not mine."

The blood drains from Kori's face. "Thaane? What? Was he in league with Azarii all along?"

"No." I shake my head. "No, not really. He's using Azarii just as much as he was using me. His intentions are akin to what my parents' once were. March on the Daylands. Wipe out anyone too weak to fight back."

Kori runs a hand through her hair, overwhelmed, before turning her attention back to her mother.

"Chloe . . ." Kori swallows hard and sets her jaw before correcting, almost pleading, "Mother. Think what you will of Adria. Call me ungrateful, rebellious, obstinate, whatever you damn well please. But if you don't work with us to prepare the settlement *now* . . ." She gestures to the rapidly approaching storm of nightfolk warriors, bent on blood-shed. "Thaane's army will slaughter our people."

Chloe barks, "I will never need help from one of your kind."

"Mother, people are going to *die*—"

"And so what if we lose a few?" Chloe shouts. "It's still better than lowering ourselves to work with monsters."

The gravity of her statement stuns us all briefly into silence, even her twin enforcers; all, that is, except Ednit, who apparently had no idea it would get *this bad* and lets out a pathetic whimper.

"The Evolved will fight alone," Chloe says. "A united front, finally unveiled at the proper moment. We will be heroes to the survivors. Maybe even gods. It will cement our position forever, ensuring that no one dares question the rightness of the Evolution Project, the glory of what we've become. And then we can take the Shadowlands, seize the ultimate source of radiation for ourselves . . . and become more powerful than you can possibly imagine."

Kori's face is streaked with stubborn tears. She wipes them away with the back of a glove. "You'd sacrifice your own citizens to ensure you stay in power?"

"Oh, Kori, darling, you always were such a damned idealist." Shaking her head, Chloe clicks her tongue as if speaking to a petulant toddler. "The needs of the many outweigh the needs of the few."

"Aspect does not—approve this message," the mech chimes in before promptly being cut off by a raging Kori, whose veins are practically popping out of her neck.

"This isn't about the needs of the many. This is about *you*, what *you* want, that you want to rule everything, *own* everyone, cheat death with your twisted science—"

"I have suffered so much for my people!" Chloe raises a defiant fist. "Is it not time that some of them begin to pay me back?"

Everything in me longs to pull Kori into my chest, gently running my fingers through her lustrous hair and down the curve of her spine, reassuring her that no matter what happens next, I'll fight with her and for her even if it kills us. But abruptly, as if a switch were flipped, her tears are gone, her rage swallowed up as if by a black hole. Her lips press into a tight line.

Chloe blinks, confused, as Kori breathes, "Please do say that again."

All at once, I notice a tiny, almost-imperceptible yellowish light on Aspect's forehead, like a speck of forgotten stardust, blinking in and out.

"Aspect ends—their broadcast here!" they declare, raising both their arms to honor an invisible audience. "Thank yourself for watching!"

The twin enforcers glance between Chloe and each other, hands hovering over their weapons, not knowing what to do about a threat they can't simply riddle with heatshot—the truth fully unleashed.

Chloe balks. "What is the mech talking about?"

"Now the whole settlement knows who you really are," Kori says, arms crossed. "A liar. An Evolved. And a megalomaniac who would sacrifice them all without a hint of remorse."

Chloe whirls and advances on the cowering Ednit. "You absolute *buffoon*," she snarls, "you were standing here this entire time. Why didn't you say something? Signal to me? *Anything* but sit there sniffling like a pathetic child?"

With a heavy exhale, Ednit collapses his own helmet, revealing his face (and that he, too, is among the Evolved). He's a small brown man, with a soft but serious visage, a bit of gray beginning to pepper his hair. "I could say it was because Kori would've shot me, but that's not the entire truth." He wipes snot bubbles from his nose with the back of one gloved hand. "It's gone too far, Chloe. Threatening the Shadowlands. Sacrificing our own people to their soldiers."

"You sniveling fool. Don't pretend you didn't want this," Chloe says. "You proposed the Evolution Project to *me*, Ednit. It was your baby. Your vision of the future. I've simply embraced the possibilities."

Tears streak Ednit's cheeks. "I started the Evolution Project . . . to preserve life, to honor it. But you would sacrifice innumerable lives to maintain your own power." He half sobs, shaking his head. "I never wanted this."

A muscle twitches in Chloe's jaw. Slowly, as the reality of her situation dawns, all the synthetic color drains from her face, leaving a husk of the cruelly regal visage that was there mere moments ago.

"How *dare you*, Kori," she says in a voice balanced on a freezeblade's edge. "Your own mother, giver of your own life, and you would paint me in such an ugly light without a hint of remorse?"

"I only broadcast your own words," Kori says, retrieving a comms tablet from her pocket. She must have pilfered it from Ednit. "And if my comms are anything to go by right now, the public is extremely unhappy with what they've just learned."

The twin enforcers have retrieved comms tablets of their own, visibly shrinking away at the sight of their notifications. "My lady," says one, reaching to lay a hand on Chloe's shoulder. She shrugs it roughly away. "She's telling the truth. The people are in an uproar."

Aspect chimes in: "Aspect's broadcast—making many people—big mad. But not at Aspect." They bobble lightly on their heels. "Only Kori—gets mad at Aspect."

Kori trembles a little now as the force of what she's done comes crashing down. Again I resist the urge to pull her into me, to hold her until the shaking stills and the center of gravity is simply us.

"You have no one to blame but yourself, Chloe," Kori says. She crosses her arms, ever the defiant daughter. I've never been prouder of her than I am right now. "The whole settlement knows the truth now. What you've done. What you are. The attack that's coming for all of us. So are you going to save what you can of your reputation and defend your citizens from the nightfolk? Or are you just going to keep looking at me like you've tasted something sour?"

Chloe's teeth worry away at her lip amidst her total loss of control. "You've made a much bigger mistake than you know, Kori," she says, sauntering toward her with clenched fists. "Let the nightfolk come! Let the settlement run red. And let the superior life-forms be the ones to battle for this planet."

It's Ednit, not Kori, who is next to raise his voice—a trembling, nasal, snot-stricken voice, the last plea of a man realizing he was a primary accomplice in the impending apocalypse. "Chloe, what would even be left to rule?"

"Only the worthy. Only the strong. Evolution at its zenith, Ednit. And if what's left is not enough, our lives have no limit now. We could relearn the helical engine, given enough time. We could go back to Earth. Purge it, too, of the weak—"

"Monster!" It's more animal scream than it is protest. In a fit of emotion, Kori lunges, her fist upraised even before she's moved.

Chloe effortlessly sidesteps the blow, her daughter crashing painfully to the metal floor instead in a shower of sand. The enforcers finally pull their pistols, merely waiting for an order to open fire.

"Kori . . ." I extend a hand to her, to pull her back up, but she only looks at me with tearful, baleful eyes, not yet having the will to stand.

"You can't do this!" Kori sobs. "All those people. *Our* people. Chloe, please, you can't just—"

"Let them come?" Chloe interrupts, eyes nearly afire. "I'll let everyone say their goodbyes before they end with dignity. My Evolved alone will take down this nightfolk assault. And when the dust settles, we'll be the dominant humans on this planet. No more dayfolk. And what nightfolk remain, if they can even be called human, will serve us or suffer for it." She spits blood on the ground. "Broadcast that."

On the ground, Kori pushes herself up on her elbows. She's so pale that the sun seems to shine straight through her like gossamer.

Chloe looks to her enforcers. "None of this," she says, gesturing to their pistols. "Not for her. A bullet in her brain won't undo what she's done. But she's throwing a tantrum, and children will have those when it comes to their mothers. When all is said and done, she'll see that I was right all along. But as for you . . ." And here she looks to sniffling Ednit. "Your usefulness has expired, Doctor. If you refuse to embrace the true potential of Evolution, I can continue it without you." She turns away, idly flicking a hand in his direction. "Kill him."

The enforcers pivot their guns from Kori to her doctor.

"No!" Kori screams, guttural, and lunges to cover his body with her own.

Aspect shrieks. "KORI!"

As heatshot pistols fire off blazing rounds, I do what my body knows best. I go for the kill. I tackle one enforcer directly into the other, both their bodies crashing to the artificially metal floor beneath me. Both drop their weapons, which skid across the ground, out of reach.

If these people were merely human, their spines might already be broken from the blow. But these are Evolved.

So, instead, a flickering web of electric-blue energy leaps directly from their fingers to my chest. I swear, recoiling, momentarily blinded from shock and pain. Two more blasts of heatshot go off, close by, and my ears ring from the volume, my skin burning from the proximity of the concentrated heat.

When I come back to myself, Ednit is standing over one of the enforcers, holding a stolen heatshot pistol, having blown a hole clean through said enforcer's artificial skull. The gore still looks horrifyingly real. The other enforcer curses, moving to sweep the doctor's legs out from under him, but Kori has drawn her own pistol and dispatches the attacker with a rapid series of equally ugly heatshot to the chest.

Ednit wails. "I never wanted this. I never wanted this . . ."

"Save it for after the apocalypse," Kori spits, but that doesn't change the fact she just saved his life.

Panting, I push myself up to my knees and glance frantically around. Both enforcers dead. Ednit armed, but clearly not about to turn his weapon on us. Kori breathing hard; Aspect running to her side. But Chloe?

"Kori, your mother . . . she's gone," I gasp. In the chaos, she must have taken the elevator back down into the settlement.

Aspect interjects, "Aspect—does not—miss Kori's mother."

Kori swallows hard, fingers tense on her weapon's trigger. "She'll let Thaane's army just . . . walk in," she says. "Let them slaughter everyone."

"*Worse,*" hisses a voice at her waist. Kori scrambles for her comms tablet with her free hand. An unfamiliar voice cuts through the static.

"Jelza," Kori says, every muscle pulled taut, "please elaborate on how this could possibly get worse."

"*The planet itself is already primed with radiation,*" says someone, apparently Jelza, "*capable of killing every dayfolk who isn't prepared with protective gear.*"

Kori's knuckles are white around the tablet. "Spit it out."

I lay both hands on my love's shoulders, gently squeezing to draw her attention without hurting her. "Kori."

"*There's a filtration system all throughout the settlement. The order's just come over the comms, to the entire network of Evolved,*" Jelza says. "*Chloe's shutting it down. As soon as she reaches the primary control room on the west side, she'll use her monarch access to override the security measures. They're letting the planet have its way. With everyone.*"

Kori is frozen, a statue. Numbly, she says, "Everyone who isn't Evolved will die."

Jelza continues talking, though Kori's vacant stare would seem to indicate that she isn't hearing her. "*Not everyone who received that network message is okay with this. There's a small resistance group of Evolved already. I've made us a separate channel, broken it off for secure comms. They're prepared to fight back. But whatever we're going to do, we need to do it fast.*"

"Kori," I say again, a little more forcefully this time.

Her eyes are wild and faraway. "I have to tail Chloe," she says between pants, already hooking the comms tablet back into her belt. "Have to pin her down before she gets anywhere near that control room. Jelza, pincer strategy. Can you cut her off on the other side?"

"*Gladly.*"

"Kori!" I give her shoulders a rattle, and this time, her eyes seem to see me. "Let me come with you. Let me fight for you, for your people."

Gaze darting away, she shakes her head firmly. "No. This is *my* mother, my people, my fight. Your fight is rapidly closing the sky distance between us," she says, gesturing to the closing wall of weapons and wings. "I'll send what good dayfolk soldiers I can. But you have to help them hold the line. You have to stop Thaane, once and for all." She pauses, another thought occurring to her. "And what about Azarii?"

"For all the violence he's thrown my way, Azarii always said he wanted peace. I can't imagine he'll join Thaane deliberately instigating a war. As for whether he'll intervene in what's already begun . . . when it means fighting alongside me, the epitome of everything he hates . . ." I close my eyes. "I don't know."

Kori takes a deep breath in, then lets it out in a rush. "So it all comes down to this," she says.

My wings tighten against my spine, a chill sliding through my veins. Overcome, I drop to one knee and reach out one hand to cup Kori's face, tracing the gentle curve of her cheekbone with one claw, trying to memorize the placement of every fleck of green in her gorgeous brown eyes.

"And then you come back to me, Kori."

She leans into my touch, eyes drifting shut, momentarily absent from the pressures of panic and time. "And you come back to me."

"Now go," I order, every muscle in my arm screaming as I withdraw my touch and rise. "Stop your mother. I'll hold off Thaane."

With a final nod, Kori sprints like lightning, every step on the metal floor thunderous as she returns to the elevator. Back down into the living space that will soon be a mass metallic grave if she doesn't succeed. My heart pulses in my throat.

What if that was goodbye? How could it possibly be enough?

"And—Aspect?" I almost forgot the robot was here, limbs pulled tightly into themself like makeshift armor, joints now visibly smoking from the stress of it all. Planetary collapse is a hell of an introduction to sentient thought, I suppose. What is a mining mech possibly supposed to do at the end of all things?

"Aspect sends another broadcast," I manage. "Warns everyone to get to their anti-radiation gear as soon as they can, in case Kori and Jelza can't hold Chloe off. We save as many as possible."

"And then?" Aspect persists, their voice rising to a terribly high pitch.

"Then Aspect hides."

"Aspect can do more—than hide."

I take a sharp breath. "Then Aspect keeps filming, if you want," I say, prompting a squeaky nod from the frightened robot. "And if we don't make it . . . then at least whoever survives will know we stood our ground at the end of the world."

CHAPTER 29

KORI

The elevator ride back into the settlement has never seemed longer. It feels like trying to wade through congealed blood, barely moving at all compared to my racing heart against my rib cage.

I miss Aspect already. Even when they worsened my anxiety, they also kept me tethered to the moment, watching over them even at my own expense.

Far above my head, the ground rumbles and shudders, old dust falling down the elevator shaft in sheets. Likely Thaane's army landing. The beginning of the end. I fight to inhale, to exhale, counting out each motion in my head, dark splotches threatening to overtake my vision. Not now. Can't panic now, with everything and everyone I've ever known on the line (despite that being a very valid reason to panic).

I really never knew how good I had it. Homework, tinkering with Aspect, more homework, sleep, Morpheus Market run, homework. Monotonous, to be certain. A lie through and through, supposedly preparing me to replace my mother someday when she had already exited the aging process altogether. But it was so much simpler than *this*—the whole planet on my shoulders, and the truth my last and most desperate weapon, light and dark colliding in heatshot and blood.

The comms tablet I pilfered from Ednit vibrates against my hip. I snatch it just in time to hear Jelza saying, in scattered snatches through the vertical tunnel's poor reception, "*I'm sending you GPS coordinates for the west-side control room. If you follow the optimal path, and move fast, you should be able to overtake your mother. Tell me when you find her, and I'll cut her off the other way around.*"

"On it," I manage to say through heavy breaths.

As the elevator nears stopping, a distant broadcast booms through the settlement's halls. *"Aspect says—everyone must—wear armor! Armor—holds back—doom!"*

I can fathom approximately eighty-seven better ways to pitch that message right now, but at least Adria found a way to warn the settlement. "Jelza, are you hearing this broadcast?"

"*Yep, I'm keeping them patched in,*" she replies, followed by an audible *thunk* somewhere close by. *"Damn it, there's another Evolved coming for the broadcast station. I can hold them off, at least long enough for—"* But that's where her voice cuts off.

"Jelza," I pant. *"Jelza."* The comms tablet produces only static. I swear through my teeth. "Let's hope you can still hear me when I find Chloe."

Aspect's broadcast grows louder as the elevator descends. *"And big, strong people—with guns—report to planet's surface—with Aspect—and fight bad guys—PEW PEW!"*

At long last, with a rough shriek of overworked metal, the elevator stops. Unfortunately, so do its doors. I wait, and wait, for the doors to reopen, but they seem practically welded shut. I punch and kick, half screaming, as all the lights in the elevator also proceed to fizzle off.

Chloe must've cut the power to my only way back in.

Panic threatens to overwhelm me again. But this time I let it surge, rising high enough for me to seize it by the throat, twist it into a weapon. Desperate fury roars through my every circuit.

Shouting, I dig my fingers into the door seam and pry the elevator open by force, fingers shooting sparks at the effort, the metal caving and bending before me. Perhaps, now that I know what my body is truly capable of, it does include a few new tricks.

I look down. It's impossible to tell how much farther there is to fall, all the lights in the elevator shaft blown out. But I don't have time for a careful climb. Sucking as much air as I can into my lungs, ordering terror to become adrenaline, I hurl myself through the busted elevator doors.

When I land, it's in another shower of sparks. There's a horrible, reverberating crack, but it's the floor nearly caving beneath me, not my legs giving way. I'm stronger than anything in this settlement. Stronger than my mother, even. I have to be.

The comms tablet at my waist happily intones directions toward the control room. Heart in my throat, I move through the decontamination chamber and then take off at a full sprint.

Rows of armored ordinary dayfolk rush past me, answering Aspect's call for armed support on the surface. Briefly, I'm afraid that with the elevator shut down, they'll never find a way back to the air lock and subsequently the surface.

But even as I turn to warn them, the first dayfolk soldier raises her heatshot rifle and launches a grappling line straight up into the inky dark, all the way to the distant ceiling. The others follow and run vertically full throttle up the walls. It'll take more than a broken elevator to stop the settlement's last stand.

"*Turn left*," the comms tablet chimes, even though I'm already swerving around the corner.

Just past the next one, I spot a blur that I'm barely able to identify as Chloe, on the run. Not fast enough to stop me.

"Stay where you are!" I shout, heatshot pistol already raised.

But my fingertip quivers on the trigger, my whole wrist rattling like Aspect when they need more oil. My mind is set, determined to protect the dayfolk, but even in this foreign body, my heart calls out to my mother.

I can't fire on her. To save my people, I have to; to vent my fury, I *want* to. But my finger on the trigger stays there, unable to draw it home.

Breathing hard, legs pumping faster than would ever be possible for a regular human, Chloe picks up her pace. Somehow, I match her speed, even nearly overtake it. I can see the sheen of sweat on the nape of her neck, her tightly tied hair beginning to come undone.

She could've programmed a fail-safe to force me to stand down, but my body plunges after her. She could've included a damn kill switch if she wanted to command my beginning and end so badly, but I'm still breathing. Maybe it wasn't enough for her to make an heir programmed to obey, every corner hewn with machine precision to fit her ideal. No, my mother wanted to hand mold me, to feel me crumble and reshape beneath her like a raw lump of clay. And when it came down to it, when she finally breathed life into my lungs of both flesh and metal—she wanted me, in all sincerity, to love her back.

And I do, even now.

Even now, faced with an extinction-level planetary event at her command, staring down the barrel of her full unfeeling force unfurled, I see my own stubbornness in her sprint, my own shape in the arch of her shoulders—my own wild soul, but twisted and mutated into something evil.

My arm lowers the heatshot pistol of its own accord. She's my mother. Even when I hate her, I don't know how to let her go.

"*Kori*," chimes Jelza at my waist, snapping me sharply back to the present. *"Can you see her?"*

"Yes." I pant between footsteps. "Yes, I can see her."

"Do you have a clear shot?"

"I—I don't . . ." My throat burns, words melting before they reach my tongue. "I don't know how."

Jelza would have every right to tear into me right now. The fate of my whole world rests on my shoulders, and I'm bending and breaking under sentiment.

Instead Jelza says, *"Kori, it's okay. I'll cut her off the other way if you keep driving her forward. Can you do that?"*

Swallowing hard, I push my legs even harder. "Yeah, I can."

I wish I could submerge myself in my rage, like Adria in the heart of battle, overcome with battle lust, lost even to myself. But I simply don't know how. And perhaps, in a cruel twist of fate, that's why Adria hesitated the first time we collided, her claws poised to slice out my heart but never descending. I am bound and chained to mercy, even at the end of the world. And it reminded Adria, even amidst her newfound flood of impossible power, that she could still choose the same.

That realization grounds me, keeps me tethered to the floor just long enough for Jelza to swing around the corner and tackle Chloe headlong. My mother screeches as she slides across the metal floor, kicking and punching wildly at Jelza, but the other woman pins her firmly with her knees.

"Stay down, Chloe." Jelza swings the butt of her heatshot pistol, cracking against Chloe's skull. "And maybe this won't hurt the way that you deserve."

Chloe spits an ugly curse, eyes flashing electric-bright blue.

A current races down Chloe's spine, into her arms, and subsequently into Jelza. Limbs twitching, Jelza screams and lurches away as Chloe resumes her frenzied dash to the control room entrance.

"Kori, f-fire!" Jelza stammers through her spasms. "FIRE!"

I can't even lift the gun. Every breath feels like lead in my lungs. "She's my mom," I say, unable to vocalize anything else. "My mom."

"And she's going to be your killer." Standing, Jelza seizes both my shoulders and shakes me, my brain rattling around in my skull. "We can still catch her. We're as Evolved as she is, and there's two of us and one of her. But I can't do this by myself, Kori. I need you with me. Even if it hurts." Her dark eyes bore into mine with desperate purpose. "Are you with me, Kori?"

My stomach feels like a giant knot. I manage a stiff nod.

"Say it."

"I'm with you."

"Then start running," Jelza says, and we lose ourselves together in the rush of wind and pounding boots on metal.

CHAPTER 30

ADRIA

Thaane's army darkens the horizon in a whirl of warriors' wings. Aspect crouches far behind me, their makeshift body crumpled behind the control panel for the settlement's only entrance. I've ordered them to stay there, as far away from the impending conflict as possible.

Between them and me, a line of brave dayfolk soldiers rapidly assembles, summoned by Aspect's ongoing broadcast—which also warned them that a hulking nightfolk girl would be leading their charge. Many of them tense or tremble at the sight of me, but nevertheless, they form a phalanx of heatshot pistols and rifles at my back, even a few crude metal knives. This being practically the full force of the dayfolk military, we vastly outnumber Thaane's rogue faction.

But I am the only settlement fighter with the planet's power on my side. I may have instructed Isek via comms to send a contingent of the Shadowlands' army after me as reinforcements, but there's still no sign of them, and it's impossible to confirm if they're coming at all.

Perhaps even my loyal soldiers see my willingness to fight for the dayfolk as a step too far. Perhaps Azarii, despite supposedly seeking peace, remains so focused on me that he was willing to ignore Thaane's offensive altogether, and my forces were delayed by Azarii's rebellion. There's no way to know, and no opportunity to wait.

Thaane's army is on the horizon *now*, black splotches interrupting the relentless sun. And if we don't stop them, they could wipe out the dayfolk altogether . . . if Chloe doesn't do it first.

Keen awareness of our disadvantage slithers beneath my skin. Thaane doesn't even have to kill his opposing forces. One little slash through the dayfolk soldiers' armor, and the planet claims them for itself.

Before long, though they were a distant inkblot practically moments ago, the nightfolk are almost within attack range—preparing their weapons, spreading out their forces. Several carry multi-limbed fighters on their backs; those without a mount are levitated by telekinetics, who strain to keep multiple bodies aloft. The ground rumbles like a quake beneath the crash of muscled mutants, some with as many as six fists upraised, others wielding freezeshot guns and freezeblades alike. Additional weapons levitate like halos all around the telekinetics, makeshift projectiles that move almost faster than the eye can follow.

Every breath feels like needles on its way out. I can't see a single face of my newfound armored soldiers, but I turn to the closest one anyway: a woman likely Kori's age, with a yellow bandana tied around one wrist.

"What is your name?" I ask.

She hesitates, fingers tensing on her heatshot rifle's trigger. After a sharp breath, she answers, "Folina."

"I know I'm a stranger to you, Folina." I will my gaze to penetrate her helmet, to communicate beyond my words that I'm truly on her side. "I know based on what you've been taught, I'm a monster. But you know Kori?"

The soldier gives her head a little shake. "Nobody really *knows* Kori," she says. "Chloe's kept her locked away her whole life."

There goes my only point of connection with these people. After a long moment, heart racing, I manage to say, "I promise you . . . she's worth fighting for." My hands curl instinctively into fists at my sides. "She showed me that you're *all* worth fighting for."

There's no time to say anything else.

The nightfolk soldiers eclipse us. Everything is smoke, the stinging burn of heatshot, the shuddering cold shock of freezeshot, knives and freezeblades clashing, wings and arms locked in struggle, nightfolk howling. Bleeding.

I'm only one nightfolk. But for Kori, for the dayfolk, for her last chance at real freedom, I'll be the fiercest monster of them all.

Combat sweeps everyone into frenetic mayhem as surely as a desert windstorm. Time is already a slippery thing on Pagomènos, sliding through the fingers like so much sand, but now I am truly lost to it, reduced to blows and blood, bones and bruises. I rip telekinetics from the sky. I beat a soldier senseless with his own freezeshot rifle. I know there's blood splattered all over me, but not whose—some of it surely mine, but from where, I haven't the slightest inkling.

Nevertheless, despite my fiercest efforts, the dayfolk are no match for a nightfolk assault. All it takes is one crack in the armor. Soldiers drop like so much ash around me. Those who aren't immediately obliterated—windpipes crushed by a nightfolk foot, limbs torn free of their sockets, freezeblades buried in rib cages, skulls caved in by a well-placed supernatural punch—are brought down by fissures in their armor, writhing and shrieking as the planet slowly draws them into oneness with itself.

At some point, I find myself sprawled above a collapsed dayfolk youth, barely restraining a six-limbed, clawing, howling creature of a soldier with both arms—when a blast of azure energy, which could only come from one of our own, spears into the monster's skull, and he sags into my hands.

I toss the corpse aside in a heap of empty flesh. I look up, and sure enough, it's one of my own nightfolk soldiers who looks back. "My lord," she says, inclining her head, her horns glinting in the violent sunlight.

Behind her, a line of warriors falls upon the battlefield like a scythe, cleaving a barrier between the struggling dayfolk and Thaane's minions.

Isek's reinforcements.

But will they be enough?

Beneath me, the dayfolk youth swallows hard against a sob. His armor is unbroken, but he rapidly tests its seams and edges with gloved hands anyway, hardly believing he's still alive. The dayfolk haven't seen war against the nightfolk in generations, not since the Great Exile in the Cataclysm's immediate aftermath. This boy is a soldier here by necessity alone, and he's lived his entire life underground, sheltered from weather and his opposing nation alike. There was no possible way for him to be prepared for this. For *any of them* to be prepared for this.

But thanks to Isek's reinforcements, they won't face the rest of this fight alone.

"Dayfolk! Stay behind me!" I shout, struggling to be heard over freezeshot and heatshot, the rapid beating of wings, the unceasing exchange of mighty blows. "Let us lead the fight against our own!"

Hearing my orders, the remaining armored fighters regather themselves, disengaging from their individual skirmishes, forming a tight pack of secondary defense. A spark of stubborn hope lights in my chest. With a nightfolk army to take point . . . Thaane's can still be stopped. Kori's people can still be saved.

Belowground, Chloe represents another equally imminent threat, but if I think too hard about that—if I let myself imagine Kori down there, without me, forced to fight her own mother to save her entire society from obliteration—I'll collapse in on myself, as surely as the sobbing dayfolk boy I just protected.

So I set my focus securely aboveground. I fight with everything in me, with every ounce of strength the Diakópsei bestowed. Energy blasts from my hands, my feet, the sharp edges of my wings. It's blue fire in my throat, my wild scream manifesting as power that blasts enemy fighters out of the sky. I'm lost to time. I'm lost to Pagomènos. Were I presented with a mirror, I would hardly recognize myself. In the name of the most human love I've ever felt, I surrender to my most animal instincts. I become a weapon of war, and nothing more.

Sand sticks to blood in patches along my arms, embeds itself underneath my claws. I ache like an exposed nerve, in body and in soul. I'm panting, every muscle screaming, my half-healed left wing aching more fiercely than ever, when I feel an unexpectedly gentle hand on my forearm.

I whirl to lock eyes with a face equally familiar and unexpected.

"My queen," says Eridian, no longer cowering before torturous Thaane, nor bearing blood from my teeth along her throat. I haven't seen her since I ordered her released from our custody, berating Thaane for tormenting her with fear of herself. Not so long ago, Thaane messaged my comms tablet that this very woman was rallying Azarii's forces against me. But that doesn't square at all with what my eyes are seeing.

I balk, words nearly failing me altogether. "When did you . . . ? *Why* are you here?"

"You showed me mercy once, where your brother-in-arms held only hatred." The spikes along her spine, no longer deliberately hidden, shimmer in the sunlight. "I want no part of a planet he rules. None of us do."

"Us?"

With an extended claw, Eridian points to the skyline, and hope floods my body like a wave of pure day.

Wings and claws and bared teeth. Freezeblades and rifles and blazing spheres of energy. More nightfolk soldiers. *Reinforcements*. And no longer cowering behind makeshift armor, nor trying to tear their gifted augments from their flesh.

My own reinforcements were not the last wave. I sputter, overcome. "Did you splinter off from Azarii's forces?"

"We *are* Azarii's forces," Eridian counters, even as my mind spins. "When General Isek warned of the betrayal—many of Azarii's own rebels having been in Thaane's ranks—myself and others approached Azarii with a plea."

"Others?" I echo, even as I feel a telekinetic tug on my shoulder.

"My lord," says Neo, somehow free of the cell where I left him to rot. Presumably, he escaped confinement when Kori did, during the serpent attack.

In rapid succession, someone says, "My queen." Disbelieving, I behold his sister, Lail, whose single gray eye steadily holds my own.

"Azarii said his rebellion was in the name of peace," Neo says, gaze alight with barely controlled fury, overgrown ginger hair blowing wildly into his face from the desert winds.

Eridian inclines her head in agreement. "You may be a monster queen, Adria," she says, "but you are not the one who called for war on the innocent."

Standing upon two of her arms, Lail crosses the other four defiantly across her chest, her tail coiled close to her body, ending in a tightly clenched seventh hand. "Once, Adria, I pocketed a memory of my greatest hope, rooted in resisting your rule. But now," she says, voice rising above the ongoing tumult of battle around us, "it is your life, not your death, that gives us hope. That there may yet be peace. That Thaane can be stopped."

I stare at the horizon without believing my eyes. Perhaps the heat has addled my brain; perhaps the whirling sands and haphazard freeze-shot and heatshot have caused my vision to deceive me. But no, those really are a second wave of reinforcements, rapidly approaching to fight back Thaane's assault. And at the head of the descending battalion, far older than my memories of him, face deeply lined by hundreds more sleep cycles: Azarii himself.

Despite our civil war, I haven't seen him with my own eyes since my childhood, when my father condemned him to an Elysian cell.

If Azarii truly hates nightfolk evolution as much as the reports indicated, he has very much to hate about himself. Among the nightfolk, he is a singular creature, exceptionally built for battle, his mutations among some of the most overt our people have to offer. Two sets of arms. Two pairs of wings, smaller than my own, more akin to Thaane's—spread in a more insectoid formation, built for speed above power. Four horns, one pair angled up and the other down, framing a devilish face. Strong square jaw. Amber eyes like hot coals.

This is the man who called me the ultimate monster, the usurper. My last living family, dedicating his entire existence to overthrowing my rule. Yet now he flies to my side, fresh soldiers assembled at his back—to take up arms not against me, but alongside me.

In the final hour, the enemy of my enemy becomes my friend. I showed a comparatively small mercy to Eridian, sparing her life in interrogation, but now she offers me far greater grace in return: a real shot at stalling the apocalypse.

Jaw set, Eridian pumps the barrel of her shotgun. "Lest Thaane destroy us all," she says, resolved, "Azarii's army stands with you."

Fresh energy surging through me, I spread my wings wide. Blue energy blazes into being around my fists. "Then let's make sure we win," I say, even as we split apart, diving headlong back into the tumult.

My whole world again becomes the battle haze of discharged weapons, beating wings, and frantically firing dayfolk. In my peripheral vision, I catch snatches of my new allies, formerly my foes, fighting with all they're worth to stop Thaane's invaders.

Eridian, blasting slugs of freezeshot clean through rib cages.

Lail, simultaneously holding three opponents aloft, her many arms crushing enemy windpipes—alongside the seventh hand at the apex of her tail.

Neo, unleashing waves of overcharged telekinesis that reach as far as thought. Soldiers collapse in heaps before him, lay down their weapons, and even wail as their own will to fight is exorcised by someone else's mind. He may not be a soldier proper, but he's quite possibly the best we have.

And Azarii, darting deftly through the skies, launching blasts of gifted energy at the scrambling soldiers below. Amidst the fighting, our gazes lock. There is no exchange of words, not even of signals, but I feel an understanding pass between us.

After all that's happened, we may never truly be family again—but for now, we are far from foes. Thaane's warriors fall in droves before his power. I'm more thankful than any sentences could possibly express. With his reinforcements' arrival, my uncle brought me a fresh injection of hope. And our locked gazes say more than enough.

Then his eyes suddenly go distant, cloudy. His rapidly flapping wings pull suddenly taut.

My stomach lurches.

No.

No, no, no, no, no.

"If you truly resent your strength, Azarii," Thaane says, claws piercing deep into the rebel leader's chest, "then you don't deserve to have it."

Azarii's mouth works, but no sound is coming out, only bright blood bubbling on the quivering lips. His eyes roll back into the empty skull. His body goes rigid, twitching, seizing, and then utterly slack around his killer's claws. I hear a scream, so loud that it echoes in my eardrums, and barely register that the voice is my own.

"So I will free of you of the burden," Thaane says, as Azarii's body thuds with heavy finality into the sand.

I am truly the last of my bloodline now.

From the sky, Thaane turns his attention back to me. "Hello, little princess," he hisses through his teeth. It does not escape my notice that he no longer calls me a queen. And as for *princess* . . . there is no reverence in it.

Thaane flies headlong into me. My oldest friend, my little brother, the best soldier I ever knew—his triple-clawed feet drive my wings into the sand, his own four wings slicing viciously through the air.

Despite myself, I make up for his monotone with an answer that bleeds emotion, each syllable a stabbing pain. "Hello, old friend."

With all the strength I can muster, both wings already hurting worse than after the sun serpent attack, I fling him off me, then meet him in the sky, both of us grappling for the advantage, my lower lip dripping blood from the force of my gritted teeth.

We trade blows amidst the searing sunlight, every sound amplified by the immense emptiness of the Daylands' seared surface.

"There's still time, you know," Thaane snarls between punches. "You could lead our army into the Daylands, not make these sands your grave." Every strike hurts worse than the last, but I'm bigger than my body now, adrenaline embodied, moving faster than thought. "You could bring our people into a golden age."

My forearm stings from blocking his blows, the impact reverberating down the bone and into my tightly clenched fists. "They're not so different from us, Thaane."

"Maybe not." This time it's Thaane's teeth that sink into my arm. I howl, my blood coating his tongue and teeth and lips as he presses in farther, through muscle, down to bone. "But they're weaker. You could crush them into dust. Reclaim Pagonian history for the nightfolk. Why fight for them, when you're the strongest of us all?"

Eyes stinging with involuntary tears, I tear my arm free of his fangs. "Because that's what strength is for." I drive both fists forward in a rapid flurry, arm hot with blood, my pulse roaring through me like a battle drum. "Do you think I wanted this?" Every blow glances off his lean, honed muscle, but I don't stop. "Both parents buried? My body mutated beyond recognition? My waking and sleeping both haunted by what I've become?"

My knuckles are bleeding now, too, scarlet speckles scattered about the sky. "But this planet needs its monsters, Thaane. It shouldn't, but it does. Only a monster can hold back the dark. Only a monster can keep the last of the light burning."

I taste rust and salt. I spit on the sand far below. Thaane's gaze is lightless, loveless, desperately hungry, not the eyes I've known since my youth.

"So I'll be a monster," I say. "But not *your* monster." With all my strength, in a whole-body blast of planetary energy, I hurl Thaane back down toward the ground. "The worst one—so I can be the last one."

He falls, limbs sprawled, mouth open with no sound coming out. I hear his spine crack against the swirling sand.

The cycle ends here.

I hope to the stars, to sun and shadow alike, perhaps even to the dayfolk's Dreamgiver, that Thaane will be dead when I land. I hope I won't have to look him in the eyes when I sever his poisonous presence from the planet. But hope is a fickle, flickering thing. When I land, his spine is indeed twisted, wrecked.

But his eyes still know me.

"I could've been . . . good to you, you know." His chest rises and falls with great effort, shivering, some ribs likely cracked, too. "All . . . our lives . . . I've craved it . . . dreamed of it."

I shake my head, unable to process. I want to curse him, to silence him forever with a final blow, but instead I choke out, "You don't know what you're saying," knowing in the pit of my stomach that he absolutely does.

Thaane's broken voice becomes a demonic snarl. If he retained control of his limbs, I have no doubt that his claws would flay the flesh from my bones everywhere he could reach. "But you had . . . to have . . . that *girl*." His gaze is wild, afire, but heinously lucid. "When you . . . could've had . . . *me*."

And suddenly it doesn't matter that I can see his eyes, that I'll probably see them in the darkness every time I close my own. I don't see the person I thought was my brother, my brethren, familiar as my own bones.

I see a boy who disguised his selfish need as familial loyalty for a lifetime. I see a predator who stalked my steps with silent thirst, with selfish hunger, despite knowing full well my heart was fundamentally inclined away from any man's.

Every comforting hand on my shoulder, every reassurance he would remain by my side, every lingering glance that I thought spoke of loyalty—a bid for something I could never give. How long would he have kept up the ruse? And had the tables of war turned in his favor, would he have done worse than kill me? Asked me to smother myself and take a throne beside his, the ultimate feminine trophy of his victory?

My own tear-streaked face gleams in his pupils, so I close my eyes.

I seize Thaane's neck with both hands and twist, and *twist*, till the head pops free of the shoulders.

Silence surrounds me despite the battlefield's clamor. I'm utterly alone in the chaos of warfare. I kneel in the puddle of blood, crimson soaking through my robes, painting me as a family killer thrice over—twice of birth, once of family found.

Thaane's windpipe snapped, but I still hear him howling inside my head. His unseeing eyes still pierce like twin freezeblades. Hardly knowing why, I ease the lids closed with the pads of my fingers. And I'm not sorry, but I'm not a monster. Not really.

I grip both my horns with my hands, fingers buried in my overlong hair, and sob.

A gentle gloved hand on one shoulder brings me back to the battlefield. Weeping, choking, I lift my head to discover the same soldier I attempted a pep talk with not long ago. Folina, her yellow wrist bandana already ragged and torn, its edges smeared with scarlet.

"They'll scatter without him," she says, gesturing to Thaane's corpse. "Look."

I scan the combat, and indeed, Thaane's rebels are wide-eyed and thrown off-balance. Their strikes are broader, less controlled, more fear than fury, even the six-limbed giants mostly punching the air.

"We can hold the line out here," Folina insists. "You have to win the war down there." She tips her head toward the elevator that leads down into the settlement. "Go to Kori."

I swallow hard against another sob. "But how will I find her?"

At that, Folina stares at the sand, unable or unwilling to meet my eyes. "Follow the gunfire."

CHAPTER 31

KORI

Guided by Jelza, fueled by pure terror, I find reserves of strength in this body that I never knew I had. My feet and ankles crackle electric blue, every step like a miniature rocket, propelling me forward to intercept my mother before one press of a button ends the world as I knew it.

As we gain on Chloe, Jelza nods in the direction of my pistol. "At least give that thing to someone who can use it."

Throat dry, I toss her the weapon. I know full well that it needs to be fired. I simply don't know how.

We all collide again at the control room. Realizing she can't outrun us, Chloe whirls at the closed door and launches a blast of electric energy from one palm into my chest. I collapse in on myself, teeth rattling in my jaw, a curse caught halfway between my lungs and my tongue.

Jelza darts past me, firing heatshot once again, this time with twin pistols. Chloe claps both hands together with a *crack*, causing more energy to erupt in a clean circle of protective shielding, conjured by her fingertips. Jelza's heatshot dissolves into the barrier like it was nothing.

Distantly, in some small part of my brain that hasn't yet joined the rest in screaming into the void, I'm not sure what was worse: my mother not telling me I'm a synthetic life-form, or my mother not filling me in on all her improvements.

"How many enhancements can you seriously *have*?" I half shout, half laugh as I haul myself up from the floor. If I don't laugh at this point, I will sob until I split myself in two. "What was next on the features? Laser eyes? Chest that doubles as a microwave?"

"Insolent girl." Chloe sighs, launching an utterly terrifying stream of energy from both narrowed eyes.

Jelza cleanly slides under the assault, breathing hard, and lands so that we're back-to-back again. "Damn it, Kori, now you're just giving her ideas." She lifts both pistols, short of breath. "She's going for the door!"

Frantically, Chloe taps out an access code on the entry panel.

This time some of Jelza's heatshot barrage actually connects with my mother, and it's all I can do to keep my footing. I want to tackle Jelza to the floor. I want to pummel Chloe with my own bare hands. I want to be anywhere else, *anyone* else, than I am in this moment. I've suffered from flashbacks turned nightmares as long as I can remember, but this is by far the worst one. I can already feel that this moment—taking up arms against my own mother, with our entire world on the line—will haunt my sleep for the rest of my life.

When the firing stops, Jelza's twin pistols reloading a fresh charge, all the breath goes out of my lungs.

Burns gleam brightly on Chloe's back and shoulders, a few even on the nape of her neck, unprotected by her tightly bound hair. But they clearly didn't pierce through to anything vital. Beneath her synthetic flesh, wires tangle like alien limbs, smoke hisses a foul black, and unnatural blue light flickers and simmers. Shots like that would've gone straight through a mortal limb. For the immortal, they simply reveal the sick science beneath.

I can only imagine how I would've reacted if I'd somehow been reckless enough to get a third-degree burn and discovered robot parts inside my limbs. Probably would've been convinced I imagined it. Probably would've been told that by everyone I trusted. Probably would've believed them.

Chloe wheels to face us, sneering, and Jelza desperately opens fire again. This time she aims for the face. I scream, reduced from language to noise. Chloe doesn't even flinch, batting away all she can with freshly conjured shields.

It isn't quite enough, though. When the guns fade out, a whole side of Chloe's visage, from eyebrow to chin, is freed of synthetic flesh—just a quivering mass of sensors, wires, panels, programming. I expect to smell burnt hair, but it's more like a scrap pile, like a malfunctioning forge. A rusty, smelting, mechanized rot of a stench.

It's all somehow worse than gore. I struggle to time my breathing. How long has my mother been this . . . this *thing*, so unlike herself? Or is this who she always was, before the body transfer, before Evolution—ever calculating, cold and unfeeling as metal, every system driven by a need for control?

Chloe brings one hand up to scrape the remaining synthetic flesh away, bits of face coming away like damp paper on her fingertips. She moans in obvious pain, and distantly I wonder why an Evolved would have pain receptors at all. Perhaps she thought it would keep her human. But her own pain is the only kind that really matters to her. Not anyone else's.

A shrill *beep*. Horrified, I watch the control room's doors slide open.

The last barrier to Chloe's genocidal plan is gone.

Click. Click-click. Heatshot cartridges need to be charged on the surface. Jelza raises both pistols, jaw slack. "I'm out."

"Tell me you have spares," I breathe.

"I'm *out*."

Seizing the opportunity, Chloe breaks headlong for the farthest control panel.

My mouth tastes like rust and salt, my nostrils full of thick, choking mechanical smoke. My vision shimmers at the edges, absolute panic threatening to lock me in place, but I shove it down as far as I can, from my stomach to my legs to my feet, which rocket me forward in a blast of energy.

"*Enough*!" I scream as I tackle Chloe headlong from behind.

We roll across the metal flooring, a tangle of limbs and curses. Jelza must be close behind, but I can't see her, the room spinning and flipping like a dreamscape around me.

The only things that stay in focus are Chloe's eyes, one an elegant brown like my own, the other all machine—like an overly large pupil, buried in the wiring viscera of her face, blinking rapidly across the color spectrum, on and off, black and white and blue and red. Always unable to process that it's her own daughter who finally pins her to the floor, chest heaving, heart in her throat.

I press my knees into Chloe's ribs, holding her fast. "I said, *enough*."

Chloe sighs. "You're wasting your time," she says, visible electric currents racing along her limbs.

But Jelza slides in behind me, beating her down with both spent pistols like blunt weapons. If they had any ammo, they'd probably explode from the energy overload. But empty, they absorb the charge as well as any protective Pagonian gear.

"You lose, Chloe," I say, panting. Loose hair and sweat stings my eyes. My legs feel like rubber, my arms like empty weaponry. "Stand down."

"You think that's how this ends?" Chloe spits synthetic blood on the floor, then throws her whole body weight against me, flipping our positions. "You think I surrender to my own *daughter*?"

I cry out, wrestling, but even stung with heatshot and with half her face torn apart, Chloe is terrifyingly strong. Her hands go for my throat.

Everything blurs. I think I see Jelza trying to pry Chloe's hands off me, then Chloe hitting a heavy backhand into Jelza's skull, and then I can hardly see anything at all. There's a fleshy thud that I think must be Jelza's unconscious body hitting the floor. Weak wheezing noises that I think are me. The hands at my neck tighten, squeeze, then deliberately ease up just long enough for the half mother, half robot face to swim back into my vision. The exposed sight sensor is bloodred; the human eye is streaked with tears.

"I only wanted what was best for you, Kori," my mother says, voice quivering, hands still squeezing the life from me. "Best for everyone."

My voice barely slips through her tightening fingers. I have to choose these words—quite possibly my *last* words—with perfect precision. My world shimmering, my limbs going numb, I take a last desperate gamble and cough, "I . . . know."

The stranglehold hesitates, loosens.

At once, Chloe drops me entirely.

"Kori, Kori . . ." Her palms cup my face, pull it close to her mangled mess of wires. "My darling, my daughter, I knew deep down you had to understand." She strokes my hair with burn-pricked fingers, smothering me with the stench of rising smoke. I'm limp and raw and shuddering in her embrace. "When it's all over, when the new world is born, it'll be everything you wanted," she says, almost singing in her reverie, almost laughing in her depraved hope. "I only want what's best."

"I . . . know," I breathe into her neck. "I know." I force one hand's fingers to curl into a fist, squeezing every ounce of my pain and fear and rage and hope into energy that shimmers along the knuckles. "But you don't get . . . to decide that . . . for everyone else."

I launch the punch with everything I am. It drives directly into Chloe's damaged skull, leaving a visible indent, scattering loose gears and wires and sparks. She screams like starships colliding, metal on metal, grating. She collapses at my feet, some critical sensor damaged, trying and failing to stand again.

My entire right arm glows blue, imbued with the same radioactive power that once terrified me in the nightfolk. All along, the planet

Pagomènos was fueling me, too. All along, who we were was never about whether we'd been raised in light or darkness, birthed frail or strong, deemed royal or rebel. The choice was always ours.

I look down at my mother—broken, sputtering—and rage fills me from head to toe. My shining arm slowly transfers the light entirely to my fist, synthetic muscle and bone and tendon all craving justice for everything that's been done here. For all the lies and control Chloe imposed on me. For all that she tried to inflict upon her own citizens, her own neighbors.

I could finish it here.

"Kori!"

The shout came from the doorway.

I spin on my heels to meet Adria's terrified gaze as she barrels through the entryway, both wings clearly straining, tearing both the doors clean off their hinges in her haste. Her robes are dipped in blood, her muscles soaked in sweat, but all she seems to see is me.

"I'm all right," I breathe, before turning back to where Chloe lies defeated. "She's lost."

I don't know when I raised my fist, but sparks leap between the knuckles now, my hand like a cluster of brilliant starlight. I could drive it through Chloe's already-wrecked face. I could end the life that aging ought to take from her anyway.

Chloe glowers at both of us, lip curled in disgust. "So finish it."

Adria's bulk at my back casts me into shadow again. Slowly, she drops to one knee, her breaths tickling the shell of my ear. Gently, hardly putting any pressure at all on my exhausted bones, she lays one hand on each of my shoulders. "I can't be the one to stop you." She sighs against me. "But if you do this, Kori . . . Take it from someone who knows—you will never be the same."

I swallow. Set my jaw, square my shoulders, push a stray hair out of a tearful eye. I look from Chloe's fury, demanding I gratify her with a death, to Adria's deliberate softness—touching me just enough to promise her presence, loosely enough to let me decide for myself what's right.

We are not our mothers. My final insult to Chloe, my greatest victory since I first dared to leave home, is that I'll turn every knife she plunged into my chest into a chisel. From this sun-scorched, shadow-cursed planet, torn apart by its own people, I'll carve out something new. I'll mold a place for possibilities.

Heart steady, stomach settled, I lower my fist.

My radioactive energy blinks out. The red glare of Chloe's exposed eye doesn't—and on my watch, it never will.

"We'll lock her in the Shadowlands," I whisper, stepping away, "where you're equipped to contain an Evolved. When the time is right, she'll stand trial here—before the very people she tried to kill. And they'll decide what righteous law demands."

Chloe's lower lip (or what's left of it) quivers violently. "Pathetic child. You will never have the strength to lead."

"Not like you," I say.

"You ally yourself with *monsters*."

"I see only one monster here."

"Kori, that's enough," Adria says. It's almost a snarl, but she holds it back, tethers her rage, anything but the monster I once believed the nightfolk to be. "You're better than her. The best of all of us." I feel her smiling mouth against my ear when she adds wistfully, "And the Daylands are going to need you."

"And what then?" I ask.

Adria presses her lips to the nape of my neck, a promise without words. She smiles and says, "Then we build something new."

Once upon a time,

sunlight and shadow

called a truce for their children.

CHAPTER 32: AFTER

KORI

"And *then*," Dawn proclaims, waving her glitter-studded magic wand with a flourish, "the fairy godmommy turned the robot . . . into a princess!"

Aspect plants one hand squarely on their hip, the many, many ruffles of their sparkly blue dress shifting with the motion. "A princess?" they ask, their ruby-red optical processors slowly blinking, on and off, on and off.

Dawn claps and enthusiastically agrees, "A princess!"

"A PRINCESS!" Aspect shrieks at a keening pitch that makes me cover my ears. They spin in the fastest circles they can muster. Now that their peg leg has been replaced with a properly matching knee joint, they're alarmingly fast—royal costume poofing, sparkles sparkling, and arms akimbo, knocking a vase of flowers down from a nearby shelf in their wake.

The flowers were artificial, and the vase as plastic as Dawn's wand, so the actual destruction is minimal. Jelza can afford to replace a child's vase, and the second-grader's raucous laughter is more than enough to justify what led to the damage.

In these easy moments, it's all too easy to forget the pressure that yet looms, even with Chloe's plan thwarted. Sub-settlements A through Z are presently selecting their representatives for the tribunals. The voice of the people will determine what's to become of Chloe, the Evolution Project, and the remaining Evolved altogether. When Chloe made announcements as monarch, she disseminated them digitally—it wasn't as if anyone else had a say in her proclamations, after all. But this will be different. This will take everyone.

For justice to be properly dealt, the entire community harmed must come to a shared conclusion.

Right now, the traitorous Evolved are being held in nightfolk prisons. Those who stood up for freedom face an uncertain future, still undeniably set apart from the rest of the human race. Nearly a hundred of us remain alive after Chloe's defeat. Some fell in a hail of nightfolk freezeshot. Others, who stood with Chloe to the end, fell by the hands of their selfsame kind. Despite their heroism in the final hour, now even the bravest Evolved have huddled in their homes, cut themselves off, until the verdict falls.

As the closest thing the Daylands have left to a leader, I can't afford to hide. I have to organize the tribunals. And while that falls into place, I'm determined to undo what little damage I can—as is, to my own surprise, Ednit.

I didn't have to threaten, coerce, or even suggest a course of action for Ednit to offer Jelza a return to her original body, which remained untouched in cold storage. His science may have veered into perversion, but beyond the shadow of a doubt, his sincere goal all along was collective progress, not slaughter.

The kind, gentle doctor who could put younger me at ease with a simple smile or a wry joke wasn't merely an illusion. Despite his sins, despite how Chloe sought to use his discoveries to advance a tyrannical dynasty, the Ednit I knew is still in there. I can only hope the tribunals will see that, too. I can only hope that my words—and

Jelza's, for that matter—will nudge the populace toward redemption, not vengeance. The future of every Evolved, including myself, hangs in the balance.

Jelza. Where is she? How long can the procedure possibly take?

A lingering fear worms its way into my gut, that perhaps even with Chloe stopped and the Evolution Project put to a halt, transferring anyone back to their original body will prove an impossible task, after all. Then I hear a sharp *beep* from the home's entry door, and my terror blessedly dissipates, as surely as if by royal magic.

"Dawn," I say, taking the child by her hand, "come with me."

Aspect toddles after us, their heeled shoes clacking with every step.

The Jelza standing by the kitchen table looks, at first glance, no different from the Jelza who helped me stop the apocalypse. The same deep-brown skin and perceptive brown eyes, the same carefully braided black hair frizzing at the edges, the same soft but serious face. But when this Jelza enters, the air in the room immediately lightens. My shoulders lift. It feels as if I've only ever seen this woman behind a pane of glass, like when I tried to communicate with her through the window, but now she stands before me truly present, truly *here*.

"Dawn?" Jelza says, kneeling to reach her child's eye level.

The little girl looks from Jelza to me, then back to Jelza. She squeezes my hand tighter.

"Dawn, baby," Jelza says, her voice trembling. "I'm home."

In an instant, I see what's truly happened process behind Dawn's wide, suddenly watering eyes. She drops my hand and runs—no, *sprints* forward, weeping, collapsing headlong into her mother's arms, face buried in her shirt, little fists clinging to the fabric. Her unbound cries nearly cut off her voice. "Mommy, you came back!"

With her own hands—born of flesh, not forged of Pagonian plate—Jelza rubs her daughter's back in gentle circles. "I'm here, baby," she breathes, her own voice hitching on a sob. Her gaze lifts to hold mine, brimming with joy that transcends any language. She presses a kiss to

Dawn's forehead, brow tensed against open weeping of her own. "I'm not going anywhere."

Behind me, a mechanical voice says, "Aspect—has no eye water—to let Aspect's—feelings out. But Aspect's feelings . . ." They throw their arms wide, heedless of the nearby kitchen counter, a silverware stand nearly falling victim to this round of poorly planned body language. "ARE VERY BIG!"

Jelza clings to her daughter, her daughter clinging back, the artificial barrier between them finally rent asunder. My eyes sting, my own tears threatening to overtake me.

I screamed at Ednit until my throat burned raw. I pored over the Lexicon until I fell asleep leaning on a records shelf. But he was telling the truth. My body—my real one, the one my mother carried in her own—was destroyed once my Evolution was deemed a success. Deep in the magma pits beneath Pagomènos's surface, my DNA was incinerated, irretrievable.

My comms tablet buzzes in my belt pocket, as if Adria could sense my pain from halfway across the planet. Stars above, I miss her so fiercely that it aches, but there's nothing she could say right now to alleviate my anguish.

This grief is a solitary thing, a conversation I need to have face-to-face with only myself until all words are utterly exhausted. No one else can understand this burden; no one else can carry it for me. Not Aspect, not Jelza, and certainly not Adria.

My body is gone. Forever.

I will never age, only mechanically wear and tear. I will never kiss Adria with my own lips. I will never carry biological children of my own. I don't even know that I would've wanted to be pregnant, but the decision being made by someone else, permanent ink blotting out so many possibilities, makes the room clamp down on me as surely as my mother's hands around my throat once did.

"Not just you, Aspect," I say, salt water tracing down my cheeks. "My feelings are big, too."

The upper half of the hourglass is full when the tribunals begin, but I have no doubt it will run utterly empty by their conclusion.

The settlement's dining hall is quite possibly the only room large enough to accommodate all dayfolk citizens: a domed, centralized chamber with multiple levels of concentric floors, all connected by stairways. Aspect organized the other mechs to clear the hall—pushing tables and benches to the sides, mopping the food-stained floors, and finally, assembling a makeshift wooden stage in the center of the room, with a simple ramp allowing access.

All around the elevated circle's rim, twenty-six chairs for twenty-six sub-settlement representatives sit at attention. Massive screens surround the stage, ensuring that the speakers' words can be seen and heard from anywhere in the room—and will be recorded for posterity.

And in the center, a simple box, a lectern, and a mic. My last chance to present my case to the dayfolk. That I am not my mother's daughter. That the Evolved are not fundamentally evil. That there's still a way forward, for all of us. Maybe even for Ednit.

Nevertheless, the settlement's inhabitants are squished together like ration packs, barely fitting into the hall. But it's better than requiring everyone to don full-body armor and meet amidst the desert winds. Everyone who isn't Evolved, that is.

My stomach threatens to empty its contents directly onto the stage. I would give anything for Adria's reassurance at my side right now, but nightfolk can never tread inside the settlement without infecting the controlled atmosphere with radiation. *I have to do this alone*, I messaged Adria via comms. *But I don't know if I can.*

You can, she sent back, no hesitation. *You risked the Shadowlands to awaken Aspect. You loved me at my lowest, even when I pushed you away. You stood up to your own mother's apocalypse, then still found the courage to spare her life.*

I shook my head, staring numbly at the comms tablet, typing, deleting, and typing again, before finally landing on a response: *Will any of the dayfolk see it that way?*

A painful stretch of silence, then the buzz of another reply. *One meeting will not be the thing to fell you, love. When the dust settles, you'll still be standing.*

And then you'll come back to me.

It's the promise of safety beneath Adria's wings that puts strength back into my legs, bravery back into my blood, and carries me up the ramp and to the lectern. Heart in my throat, I step forward, cross my arms over my chest, and speak into the hastily wired mic: "The tribunals are called to order."

They start with a simple question: What is to become of the Evolved?

"My fellow dayfolk." I look out over the crowd, varied in ethnicity, in gender, in age, in physical ability . . . but united as a human race. One I will never physically be part of again. "You may very well not consider me one of you anymore," I say. "But I do."

I expect an interruption, perhaps a thrown shoe at my head. But the crowd only looks at me, a hush falling heavily over the room.

"My mother took my body away from me. She never gave me a choice. Even for those Evolved who *were* given a choice, the result was often nothing like what they expected . . . and they were never allowed to go back," I say. "When Chloe revealed her true intent to raise an immortal army, eradicate anyone they deemed unworthy, and invade the Shadowlands, many of the Evolved stood with you. *I* stood with you. Because even if not by blood anymore, I am still dayfolk. I am still the heiress in Chloe's absence, if you'll have me."

Still no shoe throwing. Breaths shuddering, I steel myself and press on. "So all I can ask is that, as you debate what ought to become of us, remember that we are still your neighbors," I say. "Remember that I would rather have laid down a deathless life than watch the dayfolk fall to my mother's machinations."

The assembled representatives deliberate. At first, I fear the people will demand death for Evolved altogether, after what my mother has done (and tried to do). But I'm far from the only one who wants Chloe's violence to end here. The Evolved who did participate in Chloe's plan are condemned to remain in the Shadowlands, until the passage of time does eventually take its toll on all-but-immortal bodies. My mother is the only one whose endless imprisonment will be in a solitary cell. Surely, as her daughter, I should visit her. I don't know if I can find the will to do so anytime soon, or ever.

As for the Evolved who fought back? While she may no longer be Evolved herself, Jelza's unflinching presence on the stage, Dawn clinging tightly to her hand, is enough to sway the settlement toward unification. Evolved will no longer have the privilege of anonymity, our government IDs labeled to identify us as more than human. But we are still part of this society, as surely as when we still bore our original bodies.

Even so, yet another question looms: What is to become of the Evolution Project altogether?

My gut instinct was to publicize the Lexicon's records and decommission the research entirely, ensuring that no one will ever create an Evolved body again. But Aspect's protests in the Lexicon branded themselves into my mind.

Becoming Evolved without my consent was utterly traumatic. Jelza's Evolution nearly destroyed her relationship with Dawn beyond repair. But not all the Evolved hate what they've become.

With the project revealed, some dayfolk want access to Evolution tech themselves. Some disabled citizens see those experiences as part of their identity, while others want bodies that transcend their current struggles. Some have experiences of gender that are discordant with their current bodies, even after affirming procedures and hormone therapy. Others face terminal illness in the absence of a drastic solution.

It's also possible to construct Evolved bodies that decay similarly to original ones as sleep cycles pass. Transition to an artificial body doesn't have to mean cheating death, if one would rather live a standard stretch but simply in a preferred form.

Despite my horror upon discovering my own identity, Evolution has applications beyond warfare and deception.

While nightfolk can't enter our settlement, the tribunals also include recorded footage from the Shadowlands. Many of Azarii's rebels, despite siding with Adria in the final hour, still sincerely believe his rhetoric that their gifts from the Diakópsei are abominable. Some would welcome the opportunity to transfer their memories into new bodies, more akin to those of dayfolk. No more wings, claws, and fangs. No more supernatural abilities. Nothing but synthetic flesh and a chance to begin anew. That would require a whole new line of research before it would become possible, but that research can only continue if Evolution altogether is allowed to continue.

Chloe wanted to impose her choices on everyone. Moving forward, the fate of the Evolution Project must allow everyone to choose for themselves.

So choose they will, the people decree. And it is Ednit—weeping, contrite Ednit, who drops to his knees on the stage, pleading for a chance to still do good with his life's work—who is subsequently tasked with heading the redeemed Evolution Project. Now the Evolution *Program*, to which anyone can apply.

The only remaining question is who will lead the Daylands at large into this bold new future. It's put to a vote: Does my role as heiress still hold any weight, after my mother's crimes and my own artificial bloodline? Can I, an Evolved myself, be trusted to lead us through the aftermath of a near apocalypse? The answer, as my heart threatens to beat clean out of my chest, is *yes*.

Yes, the people can't imagine a better leader than one who would fight her own mother in service of the greater good.

I feel that mantle's weight descend on me like the heaviest of crowns. No matter what, I will dedicate the rest of my potentially very long life to protecting this settlement. To ensuring that every single dayfolk gets to choose their own future in peace and security.

When the tribunals are finally dismissed, and I descend from the swiftly constructed stage, the most desperate desire on my mind is for *sleep*. But first, I have one more loose end to tie with Evolution.

"Aspect wanted—to talk to—triple dog." The mech's annoyance is the furthest thing from subtle. Their optical processors seem to blaze extra brightly, a hellish shade of crimson. As they lean back in their chair, they cross their arms over their chest. They stomp one foot as a final flourish, just in case I still wasn't getting the point. "But Kori said—this talk—is very important—for Aspect."

I nod. "Yes, this is very important," I say. "Very, *very* important. Can you listen to me for a moment, please?" I lean forward in my own chair, taking Aspect's hands in my own, my gaze steady on theirs. "And then I'll let you talk to Russ on the comms tablet as long as you want."

Aspect makes a peculiar *beep*, something akin to a human snort of breath through the nostrils. "Okay," they say. "So what—is so important—to tell Aspect?"

I inhale heavily and hold it, counting to ten before I let it go. For so long, Aspect's sentience was an utterly wild dream, existing only vaguely on the edges of possibility. I never allowed myself to consider what would happen *after*.

A *child*—artificially built, but a child all the same. With their own feelings, their own wants and hopes and fears. With their own choices.

"Aspect, you listened during the tribunals, didn't you? On that wonderful stage you helped us build?"

Aspect nods. Their joints creak with the motion; I really need to oil them again.

"You heard when we talked about Evolution, about new bodies. That anyone can apply to the program now. Anyone can decide how they want to look to the world, who they want to be." My pulse roars in my ears. "Aspect, that includes you."

The mech cocks their head, processing. "Aspect—does not understand."

"You're a *person*, Aspect," I say in a rush. "Not just a machine, not just something to be programmed however someone else likes, but a *person*. And . . . there are no people who look like you, Aspect. You're the first mech to be . . . awake . . . like this."

There remains the possibility that the Coalition, the enforcers of the Morpheus Market, will take issue with how I've repurposed human memories. But thanks to the Evolution Program, new dayfolk law clearly outlines that even a completely artificial body can qualify as a person, a citizen. The Coalition can threaten consequences for the creation of *another* Aspect. But Aspect as they already are—in all their wacky, wonderful ways—has legal rights.

Especially since Aspect didn't consciously *choose* to become a sentient being (that was all me and my experiments), they can't be punished for being here now. At most, *I* could be punished for creating them. But the Coalition exists to ensure both law and secrecy on the Morpheus Market. Entering open conflict with the dayfolk's most visible leader might mesh with the former, but it's a massive threat to the latter.

It's in the Coalition's best interest to let this one go. And that's exactly what I'll tell them, in no uncertain terms, if they try to threaten Aspect in any way.

Aspect looks down at the floor. "Only Aspect—is an Aspect."

"Yes," I say. "But if you want to look like the dayfolk do, Aspect . . . if you want a body like mine, any type of body you like . . . you can apply to the program." My hands are shaking, and I don't know why. "You can look just like everyone else. You could even change your name. Nobody would have to know. You could start your life all over again."

I expect Aspect to take a moment to consider. Maybe longer than a moment—a recharge cycle, two, seven. But I've hardly finished my sentence before Aspect yanks their hands from mine and shouts, full force, into my face: "NO."

A chill shoots straight down my spine. This is a first. A milestone. An accomplishment beyond what science could've ever predicted. After I spent so long fighting to awaken Aspect, they're actually capable of saying *no*.

But I'm utterly dumbfounded that their first *no* is to *this*.

Balking, overwhelmed, I trip over my words. "I . . . You . . . What do you mean, *no*?"

"Aspect—says—no."

"I got that part. But I mean, no to an Evolved body?" I say, my mind racing at starship speed. "Lots of people want an Evolved body, Aspect. There's nothing wrong with it, if that's what they choose. You can have that, too."

"Aspect said—NO."

I shake my head, disbelieving, struggling to find the right words. "Aspect, people are going to treat you differently. They've never met anybody like you. They may be cruel. They may even want to hurt you. I will *never* let that happen, I promise, but Aspect, please listen to me . . . If you really say no to this, you're going to be set apart. One of a kind. The only Aspect. Forever." My eyes sting. The shaking in my hands is traveling up my arms, too. "Is that really what you want?"

Aspect rises from their chair. Their optical processors never leaving my gaze, they nod furiously. "Aspect—likes being—Aspect," they say, without an ounce of hesitation. "Aspect—does not want—to look like—anything else."

I stand from my own chair. Without thinking, I pull them into a hug. "I love you," I breathe, squishing as tightly as I can. "I love you being Aspect. I would never, ever want you to be someone else."

"And Aspect—loves Kori back." I very nearly start crying into their mechanical shoulder, but they quickly add, "Now Aspect—wants to talk—to *triple dog*. Or there will be CONSEQUENCES!"

CHAPTER 33: AFTER

ADRIA

The Shadow Court holds their assembly in a cylindrical meeting tower, on the sixth of seven fortress floors, overseen only by the ever-present torch that marks sleep cycles for our people. There is only one entrance, at the very bottom—then a long, winding, spiraling staircase, unless one elects to use wings or telekinesis to ascend. So I carry Kori in my arms. Kori, the greatest blessing to ever enter my lonely life. Kori, the greatest threat to my continued royal standing.

She leans into me, trusting me to hold her fast against my chest as we rise higher and higher. Her breaths stay steady, little puffs of warmth against the exposed skin of my neck.

It's hard to believe she was ever completely hidden from me, locked away in that accursed suit of armor. It's hard to believe I was ever able to stand the distance, now that I know the heat of her skin against my skin, the gorgeous green-flecked brown of her eyes on mine, the untamed cascade of her brown hair flowing past her shoulders, nearly tangling with my wings as they rise and fall.

All I want is to hold her. To let the world pass us by and find someone else, anyone else, to fight its battles.

But I place her gently on her feet, fold my wings against my back, and face the arbiters of my fate.

All around this tower's rim, a dozen little boxes jut out from the wall, each lit by twin azure braziers. Each contains one of twelve court members. Some elect to hover above their boxes, aloft on wings or telekinetic power; others lean forward on their elbows, so far that they look like they might simply tumble over and fall into the smoky dark; others stand as tall as they can, spines pulled taut, shoulders rolled back, regal. Varied in gender, varied in the composition of their horns and wings and claws, but all of considerable age as compared to my youth—these are the dozen nightfolk who will judge me worthy of a continued crown or declare me sorely lacking.

A little squeeze of my hand. I think it's supposed to be a tight grip, but Kori will never have physical strength that competes with mine. "Trust yourself, Adria," she whispers. A little louder than a whisper, really, so she can be heard despite her head not even reaching my shoulder. "Just be who you are."

Placing Kori gently on her feet, I pointedly clear my throat. I close my eyes for the briefest instant, finding my center. Then I stare straight ahead at the closest court member—a six-horned woman, twice my late mother's age, wrinkled face already curled in a rictus of disgust—and say, "I am under no illusions about what I've done."

"And what is that?" says one of what could be a dozen voices. It all echoes around the chamber, a ricochet of damning judgment.

"In the wake of my parents' murder," I say, forcing myself to speak slowly, to enunciate each syllable, to select every word with care befitting a queen, "we were thrust into civil war. Then, more than that, we were beset by desert monsters, deadly serpents, that put all our lives at further risk. Never has there been a greater need in the Shadowlands for competent leadership, dedicated above all to the well-being of our people."

I pause, expecting an interruption, but the court sits in thrall, simply listening. Somehow the silence is worse than an immediate decree. I choke back a fresh wave of terror and continue.

"But I allowed myself to be swayed by matters of the heart." I look to Kori, then, hoping to the Beyond that she can still sense the depths of my affection, even as I bring forth the ugly weight of what I chose to do in response. "I said I was holding the sun princess for ransom, to end the civil war, to bring peace back to our people. But it quickly became more than that, as I'm sure is more than evident by now. I became distracted, overwhelmed. Vulnerable."

My eyes shift down to the floor despite myself. "In my longing, I nearly allowed the destruction of the nightfolk altogether. I failed to see my own brother, beneath my own nose, plotting war with our own armory." I let loose a long, razor-sharp sigh. "I failed," I say. "I failed as your queen. And if the court so wills it, I will accept my role as a mere figurehead, to be directed by your generational wisdom, for the sake of the Shadowlands and everyone in it."

I can feel my pulse behind my eyes and in my wrists and in the deepest pit of my stomach. I think I may collapse. I think I may explode. Kori squeezes my hand between both of hers, her skin blazing hot against me. I can't stop shivering.

A nightfolk fist crashes down on stone. "It is a blessing to us all," someone booms a hundred times over, "that you approach this with contrition, with humility. It will make the transfer of power far easier than if—"

"WAIT."

An uneven clatter of feet sounds behind me. I turn, confused, to see none other than General Isek, standing tall and uncowed. On his left side, a leg of nightfolk flesh; on his right, an early mechanical prototype, clearly constructed from spare parts. Thankfully, since Azarii's rebellion elected to ally with me against Thaane, Isek never had to fend off a secondary assault back in the Shadowlands. But he suffered this wound before I ever discovered Thaane's betrayal, during the sun serpent attack.

In the past, a nightfolk soldier who was wounded so severely would inevitably have died on that selfsame battlefield. But General Isek's men carried his battered, bleeding body to the infirmary, despite the severity of his wounds. Risking their own lives. Risking, perhaps, the entire outcome of the battle against the sun serpents.

Such a thing would never have happened under my parents' rule. Despite my catastrophic failures, despite my best attempts to behave as the fiercest creature of us all, I've ushered in a new age. One where more than monsters can survive war. One where, when the blood dries, there can still be softness. There can still be humanity. Isek the elder needn't be buried alongside his son.

"General." I choke on my own voice. "What are you . . . ?"

He steps forward, unsteady on his new leg, but not the least bit slowed or shamed by it. "I am here to address the court," he says, "on behalf of a woman I am still proud to call my queen."

I don't deserve this. I could *never* deserve this. I close my eyes, squeeze them as tightly as I can, spots dancing across my empty vision, but I see Isek the younger's severed head anyway—bouncing, unmoored, along the stones.

"My son . . ." Isek starts, before his voice staggers on a sob. He recovers his composure more than I do. A strangled, sickly sound slips out from between my teeth. "My son was the first to fall in the name of overcharge. In the name of relentless, reckless pursuit of power. I was never told the details. I never saw the body. But I saw the way my son's ghost haunted my queen. I know . . . I *know*, in the marrow of my bones, that his death could have been prevented. But with every passing sleep cycle, I have watched our queen toil to atone for that death. To build a world where no one's son is buried in an unmarked grave, never to come home."

"No," I burst out, not even thinking, every cell of me throbbing. "No, I failed. I *failed*, General. For all my good intentions, for all my guilt and grief, I allowed myself to be overcome by matters of the heart. I neglected the war. I neglected the never-ending quest to honor the loss of your son."

"And in the final hour?" Another voice, a woman's. I look to my left, and Lail hovers, slowly descending, her long white hair waving and gleaming half blue in the braziers' bestial light. Then I look to my right, and I see her brother, Neo, his overcharged telekinesis bringing both himself and his sister to a gentle landing on either side of me.

"You flew across the desert expanse," Neo says, "no hesitation in sight. Not just to snatch up your lover and fly home, mind you. But to defend the innocent, wherever they might be, however they might live."

Language has abandoned me. I open my mouth, but words fail to form altogether.

Neo lifts his chin high, a wordless entreaty to the gathered court. I imagine he would throw his arms wide if he had any. "By now, you all know full well the depths of the gifts the Diakópsei bestowed upon me. No one, not even our queen, could hold me against my will. Yet I sat in this fortress's prison. I waited for the queen to come to me. I did all I could to alleviate her agony, because it was never only for herself."

"Even her reckless affection for the dayfolk heiress was born not of a power grab, not of any ransom demand, but out of stubborn, inescapable empathy," says Lail. "They felt each other's pain. At times, it may have prompted foolish decisions. But in the end, it was that stubborn love they held for each other that caused them to fight to save our planet, to protect our disparate people. Together."

My mouth tastes, absurdly, like salt.

Another footfall behind me—this time, Zalel. Small in stature, younger even than I in age, he nevertheless stands impossibly tall to face the court and declare, "I am Adria's personal attendant, and a lead healer. I have been since her coronation in blood. Perhaps more than anyone else, I have seen firsthand that even amidst bloodshed and burials, her war has always been for peace. No one's longing for healing is greater."

"You don't have to do this," I say. "My sins are mine to carry. My crown is to be earned, not merely insisted upon. I can step down. I can bear a probationary period. It would be the least I could do, to atone for my negligence."

General Isek stamps his metal foot on the stone. "I am among the greatest of your soldiers, am I not?"

"The greatest of them all."

"Then heed me when I say—I will never fight for any elder council, set in their old ways, clinging to cobwebs and memories of what once was or ought to be. Not the way I will fight for my queen." Crossing his arms, Isek lifts his chin high. "If the court asks Adria to step down, to serve as a mere figurehead until some future time that they deem her fit, they will need a new army."

"And a new healer," says Zalel, for good measure, despite us having many healers who could replace him in a heartbeat.

Lail's tail whacks heavily against the ground, the hand on its end curled into a tight fist. "So, too," she says, "the army of the late General Azarii." Whom we still need to bury, whom his disbanded rebellion still needs to properly mourn, but here Lail stands, risen in my defense anyway. "For all the preceding bloody conflict . . . Azarii sacrificed himself in Adria's defense, in the name of *her* vision for the nightfolk's future." Her single gray eye stares each court member down in rapid succession.

"Not the vision of a court that hung back in their tower," says Neo, "watching the proceedings from their safe boxes, taking notes on their dusty old scrolls."

"Not *one* of you," says General Isek, his voice rising to a tremulous shout, "was seen on the battlefield, when the apocalypse came for Pagomènos proper. It was Adria who fought for us." He steps forward, laying one hand firmly on Kori's shoulder. "And so, too, the dayfolk heiress."

Again, the court's voices meld and echo all throughout the room. "Kori of the Daylands is an aberration. Nay, an abomination."

"Who has the planet not corrupted?" Isek bursts out. "Who among us is untouched by what Pagomènos has become? We gather here with wings, with claws, with gifts beyond flesh, some even to the point of manipulating minds," he says, looking briefly to redheaded, red-faced Neo, "to call someone else an abomination?"

Kori has gone nearly as pale as a nightfolk. On shaky legs, she takes her own step forward to address the Shadow Court.

"Let it be known," she says, her own voice ricocheting all around the chamber, "that I speak for the Daylands when I say our alliance is with Adria, queen of the Shadowlands. Not an enigmatic court, noting sins from their tower. If we are to truly pursue a greater peace, a further alliance than our peoples have known for generations, it will be with Adria. Or not at all."

She lets the words hang for a moment before concluding, "We will go back underground. We will end communication. Our records, we'll keep to ourselves. Our resources, we'll hoard. Our ever-evolving technology, we'll continue to escalate without your knowledge." Her eyes blaze brighter than the blue braziers. "The choice is yours, so-called Shadow Court. But if you depose Adria as queen, the nightfolk will face their future alone."

Oh, this impossibly obstinate girl—lighting my way forward like a comet through infinite night, even now. I could hug her, but it would probably be hard enough to crush her bones. I could kiss her, but it would rapidly escalate into something entirely inappropriate for a political gathering.

"The Shadowlands have spoken," the court echoes, and echoes, and echoes. "It is decided, even if against our better judgment. You shall leave this chamber, Adria, as queen of the Shadowlands." My heart leaps into my throat, pounding out a battle rhythm. The assembly hangs their dozen heads in solemn defeat. "Do not waste the trust that your people, and the people of the light, have seen to fit to bestow."

I do kiss her.

Outside my chambers, Aspect and Russ can be distantly overheard—chasing each other in circles, one giggling and the other yipping, fur no doubt flying alongside glitter that keeps shaking loose from Aspect's joints when they move.

But inside my chambers, nothing else exists but Kori's lips on mine—up against the wall, our breaths tangle hopelessly together, her legs wrapped around my waist to keep her at my height, her fingers knotted in my overlong curls, my own hands holding her securely aloft.

Briefly, she tries to stop me. She tries to ask if I really know what I want—if I wouldn't rather have any other girl, perhaps closer to home, perhaps born of flesh instead of metal.

I stop her words with my own mouth. I kiss her until language is obliterated.

I kiss her like she's oxygen, and I've been drowning in dark water for a lifetime. I kiss her like she's a shooting star, and I have one chance to wish for a brighter tomorrow. I kiss her like I'd do so in a thousand lifetimes, on a thousand planets, as a thousand different versions of ourselves.

I kiss her like a promise that it won't be the last time—a pact that she will always descend back into the shadows, back to my domain, to recharge her gifted gemfruit as surely as her presence recharges my will to lead.

Eventually, we need to break apart for air. She trembles against me, fragile as a feather, not only from the exertion of balancing between my body and the wall.

"If I could freeze this memory . . ." She leans her forehead against mine, panting, breathless. "If it were worth a whole treasury, worth a kingdom . . ."

Her fingers find the curve of my cheek, the arc of my lower lip. Eyes drifting shut, I lean into her touch. Every point of contact is electric between us, an infinite power source, greater than any of this planet's gifts, greater than I could ever have imagined deserving.

"I wouldn't trade it for anything," she says.

I taste salt on my tongue. "Kori, Kori, my sunlight, my fallen star . . ."

I cradle her beautiful face between my hands. I press my lips to her forehead, lingering there, wishing she would never have to withdraw back into the sun. But we are both queens now. Between sun and shadow, between infinite day and ceaseless night, we are tasked with building something new. Something better.

I can hardly wait to see the memories we make.

"Neither would I," I say, and bring her lips back to mine.

EPILOGUE

Once upon a time, on a planet beyond its grasp, night and day laid down their weapons.

Pagomènos housed a people wrecked by conflict, as people are wont to be. Peace gave way to wars, and wars became apocalypse.

Once upon a time, the heiress of sunlight built a council like a constellation, chosen by everyone they would lead. The queen of shadow condemned her greatest enemy not to death, but to life—to an eternity of knowing that she had failed, and her own offspring would only continue to grow beyond her.

Once upon a time, the machine named Aspect became the first citizen of one planet's two worlds, with all the rights of any person.

Once upon a time, the doctor called Ednit oversaw the deconstruction of the Evolution Project. All records were declassified, exhumed, and he dedicated himself to caring for human bodies instead of decommissioning them.

Once upon a time, the deathless Evolved who revoked their loyalty became emissaries between the light and the dark instead, overseeing the construction of peaceful exchange. They were led by a woman once their own, but since returned to her body—the one they called Jelza. Like a north star, she guided them toward a peaceful future for her daughter and the generations to come.

Once upon a time, at intervals throughout the age, the sunlight heiress herself was said to plunge into the dark. Officially, she visited to maintain political peace and to recharge a well of power—a fruit granted as a gift by the shadow queen. Unofficially, everyone knew she slept in the queen's bed, covered only by the shadow of her wing.

Once, far from our planet, galaxies beyond the world we know, light and dark kissed outside of time, their collision iridescent against the starry sky.

THE END

ACKNOWLEDGMENTS

Telling a story starts with only an idea and a blank page, but in the end, publishing a novel takes a planet's worth of people.

First and foremost, Mindy: Every day, you teach me more about what it is for love to always protect, always trust, always hope, always persevere. You are the greatest gift God has ever given me. This book is about a girl falling for a girl because I fell for you so hard that drafting about a boy became impossible. I hope I get to tell stories for the rest of my life, but ours will always be my favorite. I would love you in every single unhinged fanfic AU.

Our three cats, Ribbit, Joel, and Ellie: I'm sorry that the only beloved animal featured in this book is a dog. If you were each one head on a shared feline body, you would make an awesome mutant outer space pet, too. But you're pretty great writing buddies exactly the way you are.

My family: Mom, you dedicated over a decade of your life to personally educating me, instilling in me a love for stories that has brought me to this moment. No, Kori's mother was *not* inspired by you . . . except the algebra homework. I am haunted by letters in my numbers. I never want to see an exponent ever again.

Dad, thank you for teaching me how to make slideshow presentations and publicly present my wildest ideas without being afraid. Hannah, thank you for the innumerable times that you listened to my latest "I just took a forty-minute shower and FINALLY HAVE THE BEST BOOK IDEA EVER!" spiel when we were kids.

My agent: Jen, from the moment I saw *How to Train Your Dragon* as a comp on your manuscript wish list, I knew you were my dream agent. You are a powerhouse in every sense of the word, and I'm beyond grateful that you represent my work. This is the highest praise I can offer anyone—Aspect would adore you.

My editor: Jonah, the first time I heard you talk about my characters, I knew you understood and loved them just as much as I did. Rather than overriding my imagination, your revisions always guided me toward a clearer concept of my own vision. Your passion for sharing queer stories for queer kids made me feel seen and supported at every turn. You are exactly the home Kori, Adria, and Aspect deserved.

My longest-running critique partner, Zena Zellers: Some people are lucky enough to have a friend who walks alongside them during a messy, fearful queer awakening. Others are lucky enough to have a friend who shares their passion for stories and encourages them every step of the way. You, my friend, are both. I almost forgive your wife for being a Cowboys fan. (GO BIRDS, MANDY!)

Among my earliest inspirations, and still one of my greatest: Leigh Bardugo, I fell for *Shadow and Bone* the way only a neurodivergent teenager could, fully and utterly obsessed. When I told you I also dreamed of publication, you could've offered some trite positivity and left it at that. But instead, you treated me like I was fully capable of achieving that dream. You took the time out of your own rapidly rising career to offer sincere, constructive advice, insight, and encouragement. You, my hero, believed in me so much that I started to believe in myself. So I say now, over a decade later: I've earned my steel, Leigh. Thank you.

My cover artist, cherriielle: I am a words person, not a visuals person. I can describe my characters in exhaustive detail, but when someone asks me to close my eyes and "picture them," all I see is a dark, formless void. You brought Kori, Adria, and Aspect to life in brilliant detail and vivid color. For the first time ever, my characters looked right back at me. I can't thank you enough for your beautiful work.

Thank you to my fantastic copy editor, Manu Shadow Velasco, who polished every rough edge of this book until it gleamed as brightly as the Daylands. Thank you to my excellent proofreader, who gets bonus points for being an Oxford comma enjoyer. Thank you to everyone else on the Peachtree Teen team, whether or not I know your name. Bringing this book into the world would have been impossible without every single one of you.

My *Street Fighter* community: The name on this cover is *Laura*, but you probably know me as Fem!Shep. In our shared competition, you made me believe I was always capable of improving just a little bit more, on an endless quest to achieve increasingly impossible things. That bullheaded determination to reach my goals is no small part of what brought this novel to its final fruition. So, while most of you don't know it, I have you to thank, too. GGs. In particular, thank you to Paragon, Powersurge, Iron Grid, Go for Broke, King of Shadows, Limit Break, and Hops & Stocks. I could fill an entire separate acknowledgments section with particular FGC people who have impacted me, but you know who you are. Take my love! Take all of it!

Music has always been my greatest muse. Beginning a tradition that I hope to carry forward into future novels, I'd also like to thank the top five songs that inspired this one, in no particular order: "Artificial Nocturne" by Metric, "Cosmic Love" by Florence + the Machine, "Jericho" by Iniko, "Pluto" by Sleeping at Last, and "St. Patrick" by PVRIS.

To my LGBTQIA+ community: Coming out as bisexual in my twenties was the hardest thing I'd ever done. To everyone who chose to see me in all my colors, who held me through the seemingly impossible walk out of a closet so deep, I very nearly met Aslan in there . . . you know who you are. You make me so wildly proud to be queer.

To the LGBTQIA+ kids: Whether you're shouting your pride from the rooftops or unable to say it out loud yet (even to yourself), you are exactly who you're supposed to be. Try as anyone might, you will not be erased. Thank you for reading and supporting this story. Above all else, *Between Sun and Shadow* is for you to escape into when everything else is too much. There is room for you beneath Adria's wings.

ABOUT THE **AUTHOR**

LAURA GENN writes about queer teens confronting fantastical challenges. She graduated with a BS in strategic communication and enjoys building with LEGO® bricks, having TV marathons, and playing competitive *Street Fighter*. She lives with her girlfriend and three goofy rescue cats somewhere in New Jersey, surrounded by an ever-growing collection of dragon tchotchkes.

Follow her on Instagram and Threads @LauraGennAuthor.